I0715453

"One of the best descriptive books I have had the pleasure to read. It's a great story about the time in Vermont when booze was illegal...but there were all the ways to get it anyway!"

"Growing up during the Great Depression in Vermont's hardscrabble Northeast Kingdom, young Joey Ross innocently becomes intertwined in a web of bootleggers and murder. The author deftly weaves historical facts of the era into the fictitious storyline that eclipses the last days of Prohibition in the early '30s, when some Vermonters turned to the illegal alcohol trade to supplement their meager pay. Follow this rum trail as it leads you, by hook or by crook through the story. You'll bump shoulders with bootleggers, gangsters, killers and the law, and will be challenged to find out who pulled a string of murders in the Kingdom, including that of a pretty young lady who's a recent arrival."

BOOTLEGGERS, BULLETS & BROTHERS IN THE KINGDOM

Bootleggers, Bullets & Brothers in the Kingdom

Moonshine, mystery and murder in Prohibition-era Vermont

PHILIP R. JORDAN

Burlington, Vermont

This book is a work of fiction. Names, characters and incidents are products of the author's imagination and are used fictitiously. Any resemblance to actual events or persons, living or dead, is coincidental.

Onion River Press
Burlington, VT 05401
info@onionriverpress.com
www.onionriverpress.com

ISBN: 978-1-957184-72-2
Library of Congress Control Number: 2024913141

Contents

To my wife, Edie

Foreword

Ever since the first pulp detective magazines and gangster films appeared, the exploits of cops versus robbers captured the hearts and minds of the American people. It was no different when, later on in the throes of the Great Depression, both the news cycle and Hollywood closely followed the gangbusting heroics of J. Edgar Hoover's G-men as the likes of Machine Gun Kelly, Baby Face Nelson and others were taken down, to the relief and applause of a grateful nation.

But a ripple of ambivalence ran through the minds of a thirsty public when it came to one kind of law enforcement between 1920 and late 1933, that of the Volstead Act, otherwise known as Prohibition. The sale, possession and transportation of alcohol—beer, wine and liquor—was illegal within the boundaries of the United States. And when Prohibition became the law of the land, suddenly a whole new kind of smuggling—known as rumrunning, or bootlegging—became a way for those willing to take the risk of capture and imprisonment to make good money, sneaking booze south across the international boundary line into the states from Canada, where booze was legal. Almost anyone with motivation, nerve and a fast car could—and did—try it. And, not surprisingly, criminals and gangs elbowed in on the rackets of the minor players, out-of-work young men playing a cat-and-mouse, cross-border game with the law. Some went to jail if they were caught; some paid stiff fines and got off lightly. Some paid with their lives.

The idea for this book occurred not long after friend Will Davis told me of a story related to him by his mother: the discovery in Lyndonville, Vermont of a bullet-riddled early 1930s car, possibly an abandoned rumrunner's vehicle that apparently had been stashed in a stable, its role in history lost to time. While New York State's Route 9 leading south to Gotham from Canada was a major rum traffic route in the '20s and early '30s, so too were the highways on Vermont's fabled Northeast Kingdom, south of Newport and Derby Line, where they led toward downstate towns and even Boston destinations. One of the most notorious bootleggers was a daring young woman, Marie Bushway, known in the press as the "Bobbed-Hair Bootlegger." Driving a twelve-cylinder Packard, she was apprehended more than once hauling beer toward Boston.

As the story set in Vermont's Northeast Kingdom in this book unfolds, it is 1932. An embattled and increasingly unpopular Herbert Hoover is President. Unemployment will surpass 23% by year's end. A good, steady job—where there is one—pays 50 cents per hour. Social Security and Railroad Retirement do not as yet exist, nor does the F.B.I.; Bonnie and Clyde will not team up and make interstate crime a buzzword in the tabloids until 1933. Vermont will not have a state police force for another 15 years. Night time on the highways along the Canadian border belongs to whoever dares to venture out. On patrol are local police, county sheriffs, U.S. Customs men and agents of the U.S. Border Patrol. There is gunfire; there are high-speed pursuits. Dodging the lawmen and their bullets are the rumrunners, some of them deceived into their role, others earning a living by it, others dying in it. This is the story of one of them, Joey Ross.

"Why don't they pass a constitutional amendment prohibiting anyone from learning anything? If it works as well as Prohibition did, in five years Americans would be the smartest race of people on earth."
-Will Rogers

"You can go a long way with a smile. You can go a lot farther with a smile and a gun."
-Al Capone

"It is permitted, in time of grave danger, to walk with the devil until you have crossed the bridge."
-President Franklin D. Roosevelt

Chapter 1

Prologue: Lyndonville, October 14, 1985

He'd been shot at. He'd been pursued by a criminal gang whose members wanted to kill him. He had witnessed a gun battle that had left many people dead. His testimony in a murder case had sent a beautiful woman to prison for the rest of her life. The memories pursued him, even as he slept and dreamed. And now, the shot came. The shot that startled him where he lay in his bed. It made him jump and quickly haul himself upright, where he felt cold sweat and fear creep over him in the dark, the same way it had, long years ago.

They were coming. Coming in growing numbers, it seemed. This time, their raucous sound was the roar of big, 18-wheel log trucks, heavily-laden with timber as they came thundering into Lyndonville, Vermont from the little village of East Burke and the forests beyond. One of the trucks had backfired, awakening him. Their loud exhaust brakes blatted away as they slowed and approached the intersection outside. The gray-haired man lying in his motel room close by the road relaxed as he opened his eyes, recognizing the sounds for what they were, and fumbled for his glasses. He put them on and tossed back the covers. As he groggily arose, he cast a glance at the bedside alarm clock; it was 6:15 a.m. He trudged through the dark room, went over to the window, parted the curtains, and peered out at the intersection.

Through a scrim of murky, pre-dawn fog he could see by the glow of a streetlight that the travel lanes were slick with rain that October morning. And that no one was standing outside with a smoking gun, intent on killing him. As he watched, an old pickup truck pulled up to the intersection's stop sign, then roared off into the darkness, its owner likely headed to work and running late. The room's windowpanes, dripping with moisture, rattled briefly from the bellowing of the truck's exhaust. Then, there was a lull in traffic, and all fell silent. The man chuckled, remembering something a friend and mentor had said to him long ago that apparently still held true: "Hell, son; there isn't a truck in this town that's got a muffler on it!"

He felt his way, Magoo-like over to the television set, his bare feet shuffling through the shag carpet. He stumbled over his shoes in the process, then turned the set on. Presently, the black-and-white image of the news anchor of a Burlington TV station flickered into life on a screen snow-flecked by poor reception, and the latest and greatest stories of this day of 1985 were revealed as the blank-faced man droned on: Tropical Storm Isabel was 125 miles off the coast of Florida and closing in fast to wreak havoc; the U.S. Treasury Department had raised the debt ceiling to two trillion dollars; the Senate was voting on whether or not to borrow fifteen billion dollars to keep government checks from bouncing; President Reagan was gadding about in Illinois like a smooth-talking huckster, peddling his massive tax cut package. The *Achille Lauro* hijacking and impending doom of its eleven American passengers at the hands of terrorists was also in the news: the Navy was about to intervene and dispatch fighter jets armed with bombs and rockets to the scene. The man sighed, sat down heavily on the sagging motel room bed, put his socks on and shook his head. The country was on the edge of disaster, as usual. But he had seen worse.

Con men, crooks, swindlers, car thieves, bootleggers and murderers. He'd joined their ranks once, just for a brief time, many years ago. Not by choice, but by necessity. It had been the most difficult time, but the most exciting time of his life, which had otherwise been spent afterward as a family man with a well-paying corporate job. What had he done? He'd run booze from Canada into Vermont during Prohibition, hob-nobbed with gangsters, driven a prostitute across the interna-tional border line and even shared a bed with her. He'd dodged bullets; he'd lied to people. He'd left town—and his girlfriend, too—without notice. He'd buried his father and then his mother, and not visited their graves. He'd never told his family about his exploits as a young man, and his son and daughter would likely dismiss anything he said to them about this now as blarney; a collection of an old man's yarns, a prelude to senility. He had left Vermont more than half a century ago and told himself he'd put it all behind him, as some people blithely say, but knew it was always right there, any time he looked in the rearview mirror. Now, he was about to come face-to-face with remnants of the darkest time of his past.

The man stood, stretched, yawned, and slowly got dressed. Not one of them—not his poker pals, people at the country club bar or even the checkout gal at the supermarket believed him when he started to talk about those bad old days. So, he—a 70-year-old retiree, a widower living in a gated commu-nity—had given up and stopped trying to tell them. Until he saw the news in the hometown paper he still subscribed to as an expatriate Vermonter. The news about a bullet-riddled rum-runner's car of the early 1930s being found where it had been left—hidden, actually—in a shed in northern Vermont's fabled Northeast Kingdom. His car. Well—not actually his, but one he had driven. He would explain—if anyone cared to listen. Outside the motel room's front door, rainwater dripped off the man's beige-colored Olds with Florida license plates.

The local Northeast Kingdom Historical Society, he had learned via the newspaper's pages, had worked diligently to put together a display of photographs, newspaper clippings, artifacts and also the shot-up car, a big Packard; all of that was to be on view this very morning in a quest to document the north country's Prohibition days. Reporters from newspapers, *Vermont Life* and even Burlington TV station WCAX had been invited to interview townsfolk and any visitors who, it was hoped, could tell what they knew about the days of the rum-runners, speakeasies and gin joints. He hadn't been invited, but maybe, just maybe, thought the man, they might listen to him and believe him.

When he had checked in the day before, it was late in the afternoon as he stood in the wood-paneled lobby, enjoying the warmth from low-level sunlight lazing through the big plate-glass windows. When the clerk at last ran the imprinter back and forth over his credit card—*chunk, chunk*—and asked him to sign the slip, he had looked up and spotted the old Boston newspaper from 1932 on display. It had been nicely framed and was hanging on the wall beside the desk, next to the water cooler and a table littered with tattered, month-old magazines. The paper's headlines and the captions underneath several grainy-looking photos spoke of gangsters and bootleggers hanging out and acting tough on the town's main thorough-fare, Depot Street. "See anyone you know there, Mr. Ross?" the clerk had asked, smiling naively at him.

"Can't say as I do," he'd replied, lying artfully as the sight of two men in one of the front-page photographs stirred memo-ries, ones that had gone on to haunt his dreams that night. And now, today, it was finally time to tell the world what he knew, and who he was. He would confront the ghosts in his dreams, the specters in his rearview mirror who'd been tailgating him for long years and do his best to make peace with all of them. All of them except one: his brother.

Chapter 2

St. Johnsbury, July 4, 1932

"Pull the damned car over!" shouted the policeman as he clung to the driver's side door of the massive 1932 Cadillac sedan he'd jumped onto, trying to stop it. "You're a wanted man!" Now, as the car rocketed forward, he wished he hadn't done that. But it was too late.

"I know *that*, pal!" said the driver as he poked his .38 through the open window and shot the rookie cop, point-blank in the chest. He watched in the rearview mirror as the body tumbled onto the pavement. It rolled to a stop in the gutter like a rag doll tossed out a window. And Mike McCone, otherwise known as "Cadillac Mac", smiling in satisfaction, put his foot down, driving even faster now, his load of illegal alcohol smuggled across the line from Canada secure in the back. After all, there were no witnesses to worry about this time.

Mike was a cool-tempered guy in a hot hurry. He'd been on the run from the law before sun-up. Nothing, not even the flat tire that had delayed him, would keep him from tonight's big cash payoff when he delivered his load of elicit beer. Like a pit bull off its leash that tasted blood and wanted more, Mike belonged to a well-organized mob of rumrunners who preyed on independent smugglers when they could, the little guys in the game of running booze across the U.S./Canadian border. But there was, after all, a code of conduct he subscribed to: you did unto others, before they did unto you.

Mike had his start as a booze runner for old Jake Mangano, who had moved up to the Northeast Kingdom from Brooklyn, New York back in 1918. Mangano, handsome and self-assured, bought a large estate with a big vineyard and winery. Incensed by Prohibition enacted in 1920, Jake set about replacing his lost income from closure of the winery by getting into the import-export trade. He imported Canadian beer, ale and whiskey, hiring on husky young men who needed work. Using autos from various sources, they ran the roads at night across the border, evading the attention of customs. They exported the booze, expertly evading the law, to thirsty people down country who could pay for it. And pay, they did.

Mangano adopted young Mike, a down-on-his-luck orphan who liked to tinker with cars. Mangano gave him one, even taught him how to dress to impress the ladies. And then Mangano, who was known as a person of means and as a crazy man behind the wheel, taught Mike not only how to drive, but how to drive just like him. Soon, Mike had himself a car. A Cadillac. And then, suddenly, the whole county was in jeopardy. Mangano paid his rumrunners well; by their accounts, Mangano had a heart made of pure gold. That alchemy changed when it got pumped full of lead, ending employment of Mike and his fellow wheelmen.

Mike knew it would be too risky as a loner, making the harrowing run down to a speakeasy and payoff in White River Junction. So, he accepted an offer from one Bernard LeClaire, a shadowy figure known as "The Beer King" who had come into the cross-border picture as a financier and Canadian mob boss. Bernie's cut, like a hungry shark's bite, was 15 percent.

But, LeClaire provided a fast car, contacts, and guaranteed protection, once Mike joined his 'outfit', setting him up as an independent contractor. One who might, on occasion, be given a contract to take out the competition.

Today, Mike had a chaser; not the kind that follows a beer, but a U.S. Customs agent pursuing him in a powerful Lincoln. The chase had started early on in up in Derby Line, Vermont where the northern boundary of the United States—dry since the Volstead Act of 1920 made possession of booze illegal—rubbed up against that of Canada, where it wasn't. Despite doubling back and dodging the agent, all of which added time and miles, Mike couldn't seem to lose his pursuer.

On the straightaway by Crystal Lake below Barton, Mike spotted the agent's car again, the red light on its bumper winking at him. Mike poured on the gas and lost his pursuer. But then, he made the mistake of rolling past a stop sign—directly opposite a pull-off where Highway Patrol Officer Ben Harrison was sitting on his parked motorcycle. Cursing his luck, Mike mashed the gas pedal down as he peeked in the mirror—just in time to see the cop kick-start his machine and pull out behind him. Any chance of dodging a speed cop was out of the question; Mike knew he'd have to high-tail it to St. Johnsbury and get across the river into New Hampshire, where the Vermont officer had no authority. But Mike wasn't counting on Railroad Street—the main drag in town—being blocked off for the Independence Day parade.

* * *

It had been a roasting-hot summer, but few people complained; winter remained in recent memory as one of hard times and empty wallets, a season of cruel cold, low woodpiles and high snowbanks in Vermont. Those times had not been forgotten, but overlooked on this fair day, the Fourth of July.

All along tree-lined Main Street, up on the hill above downtown St. Johnsbury—on what the old-timers called "The Plain", American flags and red white and blue buntings flapped and fluttered in the soft breeze, displayed on doorways and verandas of fine old homes. Graying veterans who had sucked in their bellies and stuffed themselves into musty service uniforms to march in the grand parade now rested their weary bones in rocking chairs, clustered in the shade on cool front porches. The men spoke of old battles; their memories of Amiens, or of San Juan Hill, sparked into flames of remembrance by sporadic explosions of firecrackers being set off downtown, the bursts sounding like distant gunfire. Young boys, the men's grandsons, sat huddled on the porch steps, enthralled as they listened in awe to the war stories that told of blood, guts, bayonets and battle. The women sat nearby in their own wicker rocking chairs, ignoring the old men, or else rested on porch gliders that seated three, sipping iced tea and lemonade, swinging gently to and fro while little children too young for war yarns ran around their legs and played hide and seek among the chairs, potted plants and tables. Time ticked on by unnoticed as the sun leaned into the west and the conversation among the women drifted onward from the stuffy weather to the outrageous price of beef. And then, how things had been much better, all things considered, back when Calvin Coolidge, not Herbert Hoover, was in the White House.

Downtown, the smell of popcorn and roasted peanuts wafting from a bright red huckster's wagon mingled with the acrid smoke from firecrackers going off in alleyways. The occasional *boom!* of an especially large, loud one would make everyone jump and shout. Children still whooped and hollered with excitement, even as the last of the marching bands packed up their instruments and parents began to lead children home—some of the more reluctant ones, by their ears—howling and kicking. The parade was over, but not the festive holiday.

Joey Ross, a teenager who'd been tooling around town on his hand-me-down bike, given to him by his brother Billy, looked on from the sidewalk along Railroad Street where he'd been standing to watch the parade. He was about to head home when Mike's Cadillac, diverted by the detour, came hurtling down the steep slope of Eastern Avenue, creating an exciting diversion and a halt to the homeward exodus of the crowds. Right behind the car came the cop on his motorcycle, a bright red light showing on its front fender and its siren screaming. Ben, in his gray uniform and cap, was hunched over the handlebars and gripping them for all he was worth, a look of grim determination on his face.

A little girl had been toddling across the street toward her mother and the rest of her family just as the speeding Cadillac approached and had frozen in fear and indecision—right in the middle of the travel lane. Her mother, standing on the opposite side of Railroad Street with two other small children in hand, hollered at her daughter to hurry up. At the last possible moment, the girl jumped and ran toward her, screaming "Mommeee!" and narrowly missed being mowed down by the speeding car as Mike flinched and swerved. The corner of the Cadillac's massive bumper neatly clipped and tore the hem of her pink dress.

Startled, Mike cut the wheel hard right to turn onto the concrete highway and go south—but lost control; he was going far too fast. Its tires screeching, the big car jumped the curb and overturned, coming to a hard stop against a lamp post with a sickening sound of crumpling metal and shattering glass. Ben braked the motorcycle to a halt behind the car, shut off the motor, put down the kickstand and dismounted. Then, except for the crying of the little girl and the sobbing of her mother as she tried to comfort her, there was silence on Railroad Street. With the indifference of the kind of man who deals with dangerous situations like this every day, the cop swaggered toward the car, his right hand resting on the butt of his holstered gun. In the awed hush of the aftermath of the crash, the *clicks* of his bootsteps were the loudest sounds in town.

A knot of bystanders—mostly just young children and a few old-timers loafing around after watching the grand July 4th parade—had gathered near the car, eyeing it cautiously. "Dunno what might happen," grumbled one white-whiskered gent to another, wagging his head. Across the way and farther up the street, a crew of out-of-town firemen from Hazen's Corners stood idly around their fire engine. They had been smoking and talking, preparing to go home after parade duty, but now, their focus was on the accident. The old-timer shot a glance up the street, where the firemen were now staring at the crashed car, apparently with great interest, then returned his attention to the wrecked auto. "Could blow up. I'd stay back if I were you," he cautioned another senior in the group.

"Crazy man at the wheel, I'd venture," observed another elderly downtown idler. "You know what they say about speed and where it'll land you: 'Jesus jumps out after 40'." He spat a wad of brown tobacco in the direction of the wrecked car that was resting against the cockeyed lamp post. "Wonder who it could be?"

None of them made a move toward the crumpled vehicle—nor to help its driver, who was still inside. A whisp of steam rose heavenward from the car's radiator like a spirit departing a mangled corpse, and from beneath the wreck, a trickle of amber liquid flowed across the sidewalk and into the street. A muffled groan of agony came from within the overturned car.

Galvanized into action, Joey jumped on his bike. Pedaling madly, he launched his bike off the sidewalk and headed straight down the middle of Railroad Street, looking neither left nor right until he pulled up, breathless from the effort, next to the parked motorcycle. More liquid was flowing from the car now, and it was forming foamy-looking suds in the street.

"Look!" yelled one of the old men loitering a judicious distance away from the car, pointing at it with his cane. "It's a booze car! Beer!" Joey ran over to the car, which the officer had now climbed up on in order to fling open one of its doors. Joey stooped, then kneeled in order to peer through the car's shattered windshield and came face-to-face with that of a young man peering back out at him. The man, Mike, was lying on his side and his head and shoulders were trapped between the steering wheel and the windshield. And while he had crashed a car and was lucky to have survived, he looked afraid. He was very likely afraid of what might happen next that could make things even worse.

"Get me out! Now! I think this heap's going to blow!" implored Mike. His pale, bloodied face, looking like that of a terrified man who is trapped and has seen a Frankenstein monster coming for him, was plastered against the glass, but the man's lips moved freely enough for him to speak.

"Hey son!" The words shouted from atop the car by Ben, the motorcycle cop snapped Joey out of his reverie. "I need your help! Come up here," the officer commanded. He beckoned to Joey to climb up onto the overturned car. So, Joey clawed his way up the chassis of the car, scaling it carefully, hand over hand. The officer grabbed one of Joey's hands and pulled him up over the running board.

"I have to get this fellow out of here," said the officer. "I'll grab him and boost him up; you nab him and pull him out, as best you can, while I push. Okay?" Joey, too excited to speak, nodded. The officer opened the passenger side door as far as it would go, then dropped down into the depths of the car, a large (and what had been up until now, a very fast and stylish Cadillac sedan) and disappeared. Shortly, after more sounds of moans and groans from within the car, the hands of the driver appeared, clutching the open doorway. "Grab him, kid!" hollered the officer from below.

"That's not it!" yelled some wag from the group of spectators nearby. "That's not the way. Kick out the windshield! Drag him out!"

And then, someone else in the group yelled: "Fire! Fire! Fire!" A wisp of smoke was coming out from under the hood of the car.

Joey kneeled on the side of the Caddy, grasped the driver's hands and pulled mightily while the cop within the car pushed the driver upward. In the process, he noticed the man had a large, oddly-shaped pink scar on the back on his right hand. "Put your feet on my shoulder, mister," the cop ordered the man, "and for Pete's sake, push and get yourself out!" Still pulling mightily, Joey rose to his feet; the young man got one foot free, somehow found a foothold on something in the car with it and propelled himself upward and out of the car. He then flopped onto his side, where he stared in dazed, glassy-eyed bewilderment at the onlookers nearby as if he were a fish that had been pulled from the deep with a hook still in its mouth. He was wearing a dark, pinstriped suit, white shirt and silk necktie, all covered in dust and spots of dampness. There was a nasty gash on his forehead, and blood elsewhere, too, on his lips and on the back of his right hand. He smelled of alcohol, no doubt due to the fact that the beer he'd been hauling had soiled his clothes.

"I had a hat, you know," he said, almost absent-mindedly, staring down into the car where the cop stood, dirty footprints on the shoulders of his uniform, glaring up at him. Then, he looked around at the lamp post, down at the car's crumpled fenders and mangled running boards, and at the hood, where black smoke was now wafting from its louvers and the paint on them was blistering from the heat. "Oh my God, the car!" he wailed. "The car! And the load! LeClaire's going to kill me!"

And then, like a wounded storybook character who suddenly and inexplicably makes light of his gory injuries and heads off, somehow invigorated, to reappear in another bizarre chapter unscathed, he jumped off the car and started running like a jackrabbit toward the railroad yards.

The driver had gotten no more than a few yards before the elderly, white-whiskered gent who'd been chatting with other bystanders flipped his cane around with the dexterity of a wild west gunfighter twirling a lever-action rifle. He deftly extended the crook, held the cane tightly, and caught one of the driver's ankles with it as the man came charging past him. The collapse of the jackrabbit-fast young man in the dark suit was swift and sudden, and the motorcycle officer, who had emerged from the wreck just in time, took full advantage of the situation. The cop now grappled with the driver while bringing forth a pair of handcuffs. The words, "You are under arrest," were almost lost to the bystanders, a group now grown to crowd-size, due to the loud sound of the siren sounding from the approaching fire engine, the one that had been parked just up the street.

Joey realized that people—a lot of them—were staring at him now. Feeling nervous—oddly enough, for the first time that day—he scrambled down from atop the car, just as the fire engine from Hazen's Corners pulled up and a dozen firemen jumped off it. They pried open the hood of the car and squirted streams of liquid from two upturned copper fire extinguishers on the flames. The motorcycle officer, with his prisoner in tow, walked over to Joey. "Young fellow," began the cop, "I'm grateful for your help. What's your name, son?"

"Joe Ross," replied the youth, "but everyone calls me Joey."

"Get water on it, boys!" bellowed one of the firemen through a megaphone. "You know what to do!" Joey thought the fellow looked to be the perfect image of a hero fireman, perhaps, even that of a fire chief. He was tall, swarthy, broad-shouldered and—oddly enough under the circumstances—he had a smile on his face. Gears crunched within the fire engine. Two brawny young firemen wrestled a hose and nozzle from within the truck, and soon a stream of water played onto the wreck, washing the foam and spilled beer into the gutter while four other men from the crew righted the smashed Cadillac. The two firemen with the hose now aimed water at the car's hot engine, and a huge cloud of steam immediately enveloped the car, making it nearly invisible while the others pried open a back door of the car and made themselves busy.

"Get in there! Pull that stuff out now!" hollered the fire chief, while great white clouds of steam and dark gray smoke swirled about, obscuring the car from view of the crowd, to which he ordered through a bullhorn: "Get back everybody! Get back!" And while the onlookers fell back and focused on the cop making his arrest, like a magician's mesmerized audience, the busy firemen removed many large, bulky-appearing objects from the back seat of the car and spirited them away into the back of the fire engine.

Another, different siren sounded and its source soon appeared: a large black Lincoln came charging down Eastern Avenue and skittered to a stop near the overturned Cadillac. A portly man in a blue serge uniform, all brass buttons and bluster, popped out of the driver's side door and strutted over to the group of idlers.

"Who's in charge here?" he demanded, scowling and looking about like a boxer whose adversary is late getting into the ring.

"Pretty obvious, ain't it?" grumbled one of the old loafers, leering at him and gesturing with his right thumb toward the speed cop, who was putting a bandage on the forehead of Mike, the handcuffed motorist. Mike's snub-nose revolver, its cylinder removed and emptied, was displayed for all to see nearby on the lawn.

The man in the blue uniform made his way through the crowd, shouldering bystanders aside. By the time he got to

Harrison, his face had turned beet red with agitation. "Harrison!" he bellowed. "That's my man. I've been chasing him since he came over the border this morning. He gave me the slip up around Orleans."

"That so?" responded the cop calmly, without looking up from his work. "Well, he's my problem now." Joey's attention strayed toward the crashed car. The firemen were packing up the hoses and fire extinguishers, securing them on their shiny red truck. Whatever they had taken from the car had completely disappeared.

"You're going to have a problem, Harrison, if you don't turn him over to me," growled the official in the blue suit. "Customs wants him. I want him, on federal charges." His fists were clenched. Sensing impending conflict, the crowd came closer and its members listened with rapt attention. Fireworks are always part of any Fourth of July celebration in the Northeast Kingdom, but fireworks of the human kind in which someone makes a spectacle of himself are much more intriguing any day of the week. It was no wonder, therefore, that the possibility of an entertaining dust-up between a U.S. Customs agent and a Motor Vehicles Department officer on that hot, late July afternoon had the crowd's eyes and ears.

"This man is under arrest for speeding, careless and negligent operation, destruction of public property and attempting to elude a law officer," said Ben Harrison, standing up, brushing off his gray uniform and facing the customs agent. The man behind the wheel in the fire engine cranked the motor. The firemen, other than those already in the cab, piled onto the truck's bustle on the back, where they held onto a steel handrail, preparing to leave. The crowd of old-timers, kids and other spectators cheered; the firemen waved, and the red fire engine with its now-heavy load salvaged from the crashed car grumbled its way up Eastern Avenue on its way home to Hazen's Corners and the sanctity of its one-bay firehouse.

"Now, you listen to me!" hollered the blue-suited customs man. "He crossed the border illegally! I've trailed him all the way from Derby Line! Hell of a day! He's probably driving one of LeClaire's booze cars and if you're withholding evidence, and the man, too, you're going to the jam along with him!"

"The only one going to the jam is this fellow," said Ben, pulling Mike to his feet. "He'll be hosted courtesy of the local P.D. The empty-handed booze cruise loss is your problem."

"This," roared the customs agent, striding toward the mashed Cadillac and opening one of its doors, pointing to its interior, "is evidence!" There was a long, pregnant pause while the man rummaged through the water-logged interior of the once-luxurious sedan. Seconds ticked by.

"Well?" asked one of the old gents nearby as he leaned on his cane and peered into the car. "What did you find? Got any booze in there? I could use a snort or two!"

"Beer? Whiskey?" asked another expectantly, shuffling his feet around.

"Maybe gin," proffered the first fellow. "I hear they make it clean, up there in Quebec, not in bathtubs, like they do down in White River Junction or Rutland. A shame, what happened to that fancy new Cadillac."

"Fancy? You old fool! A Cadillac ain't nothin' but a Chevrolet with two coats of paint on it," scoffed the other man, taking a moment to spit on the ground in disgust. "Hell, the car's probably stolen anyway, so who cares?" The customs agent rifled through the car. He removed the rear seat cushion and tossed it out the door. Emptied out the glove box. Tore the front seat off its tracks and heaved it outside. The size of the crowd that now surrounded the car had grown considerably and pressed closer. The agent tossed his hat aside, and it rolled down the sidewalk and came to a stop, where two little kids stared at it while their mother cautioned them not to take it. Beads of perspiration stood out on his forehead as he grimly went about his search for contraband. There was no beer, no booze to be found, anywhere within the smoldering wreck.

Walt Ames, a dimwit who worked over at the creamery cleaning milk cans sauntered by.

"What's he all lookin' for, that there customs guy?" he asked.

"Booze!" chorused the crowd.

"Ain't gonna find it in that heap," Walt offered. "Bet it's gone already. Mine's gone, too and it's a long time 'till payday." He wandered off, and the crowd snickered upon his departure.

"I've got it!" exclaimed the agent. He emerged from the wrecked car, holding a nip bottle bearing a brandy label. "Illegal alcohol!" He presented it triumphantly to Ben, who held it up to the light.

"It's empty," he said.

The customs man in the blue suit retrieved his cap, what was left of his dignity, and retired to the sanctity of his sedan, slamming the door shut. "You haven't heard the last of this, Harrison," he grumbled before he took off, the big Lincoln leaving two black trails of burnt rubber on the concrete.

"What's going to happen to that guy?" asked Joey, looking at Ben and pointing toward the driver of the smashed car. "Is he going to go to jail?'

"Oh, yes, he will be," answered Ben, as he greeted a local policeman who had just arrived. The cop promptly took custody of the prisoner—and his .38—and took him away. One by one, members of the crowd that had gathered now went wandering off.

"What about that man, the man from the customs office?" asked Joey, trying to figure out how the game was going to end. "Will he win the case?"

"Oh, him?" Ben smiled as he returned to his motorcycle, He mounted it, gripped the handlebars, turned, and looked at Joey. He smiled like the star of a Hollywood western who had jumped on his horse and was about to ride off into the sunset.

"He has no case, but he did get an empty bottle to show for it. Looks like any genie it ever had left a while ago, before he ever rubbed his hands over it. Like the old-timers say: 'Even a blind hog gets a little acorn now and then'."

The officer started the motorcycle and then roared off, headed back up Eastern Avenue. Joey watched the powerful machine and its rider disappear, then hopped onto his bike. Suddenly, that bike didn't seem large enough for him. It also made no noise. And its wheels were too small. The little world of Saint Johnsbury had expanded far beyond the noisome, brass-horn tootings of the local school's band concerts Friday afternoon, the Ross family's humble dinners of franks and beans on Saturday nights, with *Amos 'n' Andy* on the parlor radio afterward and the neighborhood softball games that followed on Sunday afternoons. Joey's world had just inexplicably become somewhat bigger, somewhat bolder and much more interesting than all of those things just a few short minutes ago. There had to be something that would let him continue moving on into this new picture, something on the order of a movie making its debut, with him in a starring role—but he didn't know what it might be. He didn't have to wait too long for it all to happen; it was like a story that seemed to unfold day by day, all by itself.

Chapter 3

Honor Among Thieves

It was almost time for the rendezvous. Long after the last fire-cracker had been set off late on the hot, muggy July fourth, Steve "Spike" Snyder—the nickname coming from his propensity to carry a deadly switchblade knife and his lack of hesitation to use it on anyone displeasing him—sped along Gilman Road in the countryside up above Lyndonville, his car's headlight beams probing the darkness of late evening. He did not want to be late for the meeting. A rush of cool, damp midnight air poured into the old car's open windows and this sweet-smelling breeze off the hayfields and dark, silent meadows along the empty road swept away memories of the heat of the day. Steve had his foot in the tank now and was pushing the ancient four-door sedan along for all it was worth—which, because it had already been several years old by the time Steve had been expelled from high school—probably wasn't much.

Steve was, however, a recent graduate—of the class of 1932 at the state prison, down in Windsor. Over the course of several years before becoming a freshman, so to speak, he'd racked up talents in the arts of breaking and entering, assault, and grand larceny. The theft of several expensive cars, a series of high-speed pursuits and the automobiles' subsequent unlawful sale in neighboring New Hampshire quickly gained him a reputation that went far and wide. While gentlemen may have preferred fast blondes, Steve preferred fast, V-8 powered cars—whenever he could get one of them.

With a sieve of bright stars up above and no one about on the dark road watching him, Steve pulled the dowdy-looking car he was driving and detested, a battered, dust-covered Essex coach, off the road and into a small park. It was, quite thankfully, deserted. There, a tiny bandstand, a Civil War monument and a white frame town hall building stood, just across the road from a cemetery in the sleepy little town of Wheelock. Steve killed the engine and doused the headlights, as he'd been instructed to. And checked his watch. Now, assured that he was right on time, he sighed. He knew it was going to be a waiting game, after all. He'd made his move; now it was time for the other guy to make his. The big guy.

From the dark, distant woods out behind the town hall came the yipping and howling of a hungry coyote on the prowl. The eerie, keening sound of the predator made shivers run up and down Steve's spine. It only served to make the murky, desolate setting seem more like that of a noir horror film in which the innocent victim is waiting to be savagely set upon. In a way, it was.

Steve was used to waiting; he did that a lot in prison. Unlike men "outside" during the Great Depression, he'd had no problem finding work during that time; after all, in that hell hole, hard labor was not encouraged, it was expected. Back on the outside now, he quickly discovered there was no employment to be found, other than pulling the kinds of jobs that had put him behind bars in the first place. Steve, a real hustler, had made a lot of business contacts in a short amount of time after getting out, one of which panned out. The offer he'd received, one to go to work at a job utilizing his driving skills while receiving good pay and a choice of any speedy car he would like to drive had intrigued him. But mostly, for Steve—when he got right down to it—it was the money.

Steve was nervous: he had lost his driver's license for life, and the boxy-looking Essex wasn't his. His brother Bob had loaned it to him with the admonition to get it back to his garage undamaged before daylight, after which time Steve and Bob's doting mother would come looking for it. His brother's good reputation would be ruined if the car's absence couldn't be explained. Steve's criminal record was about as long as the state line, something he crossed frequently during capers he'd pulled the past several years in avoiding the law. True, he'd beaten a murder rap years ago, but the stigma of that, as well as a new petty larceny charge and a paternity lawsuit hung ominously over his head. All things considered, a noose might have been more appropriate. But Steve, ever optimistic, was looking toward pastures where the greenbacks waved and beckoned to him.

Now, from off in the distance came the sound of a car approaching at a high rate of speed. It soon appeared, slowed, and then stopped just short of the park. Steve turned the headlights of the Essex on and off twice, the agreed-upon meeting signal that the coast was clear. The other car slowly drove around Steve's as if its occupants were inspecting it and—to his surprise—quickly motored off. "I'll be damned," he muttered. "What's wrong with those boys?" He fought the impulse to scoot off. Maybe the other party had gotten cold feet—or maybe they were setting him up for something. He decided to wait a bit longer.

The other party was LeClaire and his men. Steve had long thought about getting into the booze-running racket, but other men in "the pen" had warned him off, saying that LeClaire, a Canadian, "owned" the rumrunning routes that ran into

Vermont from Canada. If you were an independent booze-runner, they warned him, you'd damned well better watch your back. So, Steve had reasoned, maybe it made sense to set up a meeting with him, and get into his fold.

Soon, the car returned, with another following closely behind it. The first pulled into the parking lot and came to an abrupt halt in front of the Essex; the second pulled up closely behind it, blocking it from any possible exit. Two men jumped out of the lead car and strode over to Steve, one on either side of his vehicle. "Welcome to the club's application process, junior," said one of them. He stuck his head inside the old sedan, looked at Steve, and then peered around to make certain that Steve was alone. "Just making sure you're clean and didn't bring any uninvited guests to the party."

"He's a local, isn't he?" asked the other man, turning on a flashlight and playing its beam over Steve's face and then the car's interior.

"Yeah. I checked him out," replied the first. "Born right in town. Whole family lives there, too."

"You think he's good enough for the outfit?" queried the second man.

"Only one way to find out," he replied dryly. He turned to Steve and asked: "Ready to meet the boss and cut your deal?"

"Absolutely," Steve answered.

"Good. Let's go back and see the boss, LeClaire. And make it snappy; we've got some things to pull tonight elsewhere." Steve hopped out of the Essex and the shadowy figures of the men from the lead car accompanied him back to the second car, a big limousine. There were no lights to be seen inside it, except the orange pinpoint of a cigar someone in the back seat was puffing on; smoke rolled out the open window like a fog bank coming in off the ocean. It was too dark to see the person's face, or that of the car's driver.

"I'm glad you showed up," came a low, gravelly-sounding voice from inside the big car. "Nobody who skunks me gets a second chance. My outfit, it has rules. You follow them, it's easy. The other way, nobody wants to try that. 'Cause rule breakers don't work in my outfit. You break rules, you have no chance. You are no cat; you got no nine lives. And you are no rat, either. You want to live, right?"

"Right." Steve nodded. He propped his right foot up on the running board of the limo, which he recognized as a luxurious, expensive Pierce Arrow, the kind of car few, if any folks in this remote corner of Vermont could afford in these hard times. He leaned forward eagerly in order to listen closely.

"Get off that—now," came the calm voice from behind the cigar. "My car, my rules." Steve judiciously removed his right foot and put it back on the ground. "Good. So, now you know my rules. And here's my deal. First, you pay your loan payments on time. Second, you get good pay, $50 per trip you make for me, cash. I front the money for the buys you make, and I give you five percent commission on the sales. Weekly. And you have my protection; no hijacker will touch you or steal your load. It's as good as any franchise with territory rights."

"And the car?" asked Steve, almost breathless. He was too excited and eager now to even negotiate for more. He already imagined himself blowing the money on a fine suit, new shoes, top-brand gin, weekend nights out on the town and also getting himself a girlfriend who behaved like a wild animal, and would be a perfect match for him.

"You're not using that crate," came the reply. "I have whatever you will need for the job. Cadillac, Lincoln, Hudson—all fast, whatever you want." There was a brief pause as the shadowy figure in the back seat of the big car puffed on a small cigar. "But you will have to do as I say, without question. I hear you killed a man—stabbed him to death over in New

Hampshire some years ago and you beat that rap, before you got caught running booze in Vermont. You just did some time down in Windsor. Is that right?"

"That's what they say about the rap," replied Steve coyly, shifting his weight on his feet. "I got set up. But I didn't rat on anyone. And yeah, I got pinched making a run. I did my time on that one."

"So, you can keep your mouth shut, eh? And you are tough enough for the job, eh?"

"Yes."

"Now I know you are lying," came the reply from the person behind the cigar. "Because I know certain people you don't know of, who have checked you out. I know who you killed. And how. And why you say you were set up. You are clever, at least, when you have a blade in your hand. But you don't have one on you now, do you? So, shut up."

"But," Steve began.

"I said, shut up. You told me you can keep your mouth closed. So don't lie to me about that ability again. Now, I will ask you a question and you can answer this time: Are you in?"

"I'm in," answered Steve.

"Good. Keep one thing in mind: if you steal from me, God help you, because I won't. Now, another thing: a condition of employment is that you can keep your mouth zipped about my outfit. No matter what anyone asks you or does to you. And you will have to prove it. Now."

The two men from the lead car grabbed Steve's arms and shoved him up against the side of the limousine. The one on Steve's right then grasped his hand and forced it up onto the car's windowsill. LeClaire ground the lit cigar onto the back of Steve's hand—and left it there for a long time as Steve writhed in pain, but clamped his teeth together and endured it in silence.

"Excellent," murmured LeClaire from the depths of the dark Pierce Arrow, and at last lifted up the cigar and tossed it away; its orange glow made an arc into the bushes like that of a falling meteorite as the two men finally released their grip on Steve, who nearly collapsed when they let go of him. LeClaire then handed Steve a piece of paper with instructions written on it. "Be at this garage in Barton at 10:00 p.m. tomorrow night to pick up your first car, like this note says. You got a piece stashed at home?" Steve shook his head. "Get him one tomorrow, boys," ordered the mysterious LeClaire, who then rolled up the window and kicked the back of the front seat to signal that it was time to leave. The car's driver promptly cranked up the engine and the limousine drove off rapidly into the night, its twin taillights fading away into two tiny red dots in the distance.

"Any second thoughts, kid? Gonna back out of the deal now that the boss is gone?" asked one of the two toughs, chuckling as he did so, as they prepared to enter their car and leave.

"No, no second thoughts. I'm in. I'm solid. I won't back out," declared Steve, although thoroughly shaken, and nursing the burn on the back of his right hand with the palm of his left. He stifled the urge to curse and scream out in pain.

"Hope not," said the man casually, opening his door of the car. By the dim illumination of the car's dome light, he had just written something down on a notepad, which he stuffed into the breast pocket of his jacket. He then looked up at Steve, and stared at him, stone-faced. "Keep this one important thing in mind, kid; Vermont 3-320. People should drive carefully. The roads are a dangerous place to be on, both night and day. Accidents happen." He grinned at him, got in and slammed the door. Steve, momentarily dumbfounded, suddenly realized as the car sped away that the number 3-320 was the license plate number of his sweet, innocent old mother's car. Steve was in, alright. But in much deeper than he'd ever planned on.

Chapter 4

Mother's Worry

The rest of the long days following the fourth were scorchers, and when at last the dog days of August came, they, like this one, seemed even hotter—and lasted longer. If today was truly for the dogs, many would miss it; most of them had spent it thus far like Joey's pooch, lying in the cool shade underneath the rear porch of the back-street, two-story house where Joey's family lived on the east side of St. Johnsbury. Up above Joey's sleeping dog, the battered screen door opened with a creak of its rusty hinges and slammed shut as Joey's mother, Beth stepped out of the house holding a basket heavy with freshly-washed laundry, and prepared to hang it, piece-by-piece on the clothesline. One by one, damp red work shirts, white boxer shorts, denim blue jeans and other garments recently wrung through the wringer of the washing machine (one of the few luxuries in the austere Ross household) dangled from the line as Beth clipped them on. They appeared in full view of the neighborhood almost like colorful signal flags being hoisted aloft on a navy ship's mast as Beth tugged on the line, the pulleys turned and squeaked, and they jerked in fits and starts toward the distant pole in the back yard.

With the men of the family out of the house, the old scruffy-looking building, sagging slightly with age after bearing generation after generation of working-class tenants on its weary floorboards, was silent this afternoon. Beth sighed with relief as she hung up the last of the clothes, picked up the empty laundry basket and returned to the porch. She set down the basket and then dropped into a wicker chair, savoring the quiet. It was briefly interrupted by the rumble of a train coming into town, then the thunderous clash of couplers as another was being made up in the freight yard where Bud, Beth's husband, worked as a brakeman.

Beth picked yesterday's newspaper up from a side table and fanned herself with it. *Goodness, it's hot*, she thought. She stopped, unfolded it, looked at the headlines and her eyebrows shot up. *Good Lord; another police raid of a speakeasy in the county. Booze confiscated by a sheriff stolen right out from under his nose from his evidence stronghold. Young gangsters, out-of-state drivers who brought rum and whiskey in from Canada at night and peddled it down country; they were hanging out during the day on the streets up in Lyndonville, harassing women passers-by. Lord, that was worrisome.* Beth put the paper down and scowled. Beth was an avowed teetotaler, not of the hatchet-carrying Carry Nation variety, but close. Enough of a staunch advocate to worry Billy, who sneaked a pint of whiskey home from time to time on his commute. Beth worried about her two boys, especially Billy, who seemed to spend a lot of time hanging out with his pals in Lyndonville after work. And Joey, too. Joey worked hard, too hard. And Bud, too. A proud union man, a good man, a professional, a lifetime railroader. Beth worried about him, working that dangerous job, night and day. Whenever Beth was not cooking, cleaning or doing dishes or laundry, Beth was busy—being a professional worrier.

* * *

Over at the railroad yard, Bud Ross clung with one gloved hand to a grab iron on the side of a grimy Canadian Pacific boxcar. He had just uncoupled it from a string of seven others just in from Newport on the daily freight. He, too had a newspaper, one that was rolled up and clutched in the other hand, using the white paper as a signal aid. Once his fellow brakeman Andy had lined up the switch for the siding into the maple candy factory and waved to Bud, Bud looked back at Chuck, the engineer of the locomotive eight cars back. Chuck was waiting for the signal to shove the car into the siding, and up to the loading dock. "Okay!" hollered Bud, waving the newspaper in a circle to signal him. "Kick it!" The steam locomotive snorted and blasted black smoke into the air as it surged forward, shunting the boxcars along. Then, Chuck hit the brakes and Bud's boxcar, free of the rest rolled briskly along onto the siding. Bud clambered up the car's ladder, hugged the brake wheel and gauged the distance the car had to travel before being stopped. As the end of the track and a large, ugly-looking bumping post appeared, he spun the wheel—harder and harder; then, the car's brake shoes finally took hold and the boxcar of maple syrup—all 30 tons of it—slowed to a crawl and finally came to a halt, its door precisely aligned with that of the factory.

With years of practice at his job, Bud had made perfect in his role as a railroad man who knew how to get a dangerous job done well and without damage to the goods or to himself, or to his fellow workers. On the railroad, there were schedules to be maintained, orders to be followed and rules to be obeyed. His union brothers obeyed the rules, followed the orders and kept the schedules. Trains ran on time, pay was regular and it was an honest life, a simple life and a good life, one where a man kept his word and looked out for his co-workers because they looked out for him. Bud considered himself to be a professional who worked with his equals and was a happy man.

So, Bud had never worried. Not even about Billy. But—perhaps he should have.

* * *

The girl in the white bathing suit stretched and yawned, looked at the boy sitting next to her, and then wriggled her damp bottom onto the dry canvas seat of her lounger. The swim had been refreshing, and now the baking heat of the late afternoon sun was convincing her to make a choice between plunging into the cool water again, or having another whiskey on the rocks. She wiggled her toes, and turned and looked at the boy, Billy Ross, who was sitting beside her. He hadn't been in the water yet, but had thus far taken off his shirt and his shoes in anticipation of taking the plunge. Her gaze was almost as much in admiration as it was a sort of critical assess-ment—the way a bettor sizes up a race horse in the paddock before laying money down at the window. He was tall, tanned and muscular, with an unruly shock of dark brown hair. And he was obviously enjoying the drink she'd poured for him. To her, he was like a powerful genie she had summoned forth and released into her custody, one who could fulfill her wishes, and hers only. After all, it was she—Catherine—who had rubbed and then opened the bottle that the two of them were drinking from. And then it had slowly become clear to her in a hazy way as she drank, and swam, and the afternoon went on in slow motion—that was becoming slower as the minutes ticked by and the sun sank lower in the west—that Billy would indeed be her magic man. At least for tonight.

She spoke to her genie, now, softly: "Billy! Aren't you going to go in? You'll catch on fire if you keep on lying out here." She rolled over and smacked his right arm. "If you don't—I'm going to peel those grubby clothes off you. I'll peel you like an onion!" She smiled and stretched her legs out where she was sure that he could see them, but his eyes were closed.

Billy laughed now; Catherine knew how to make him laugh and make him happy. And Billy liked that. He liked Catherine, liked her just as much as Doris. At this moment Catherine, blonde angel haunting the dreams of every young, single man within 20 miles of St. Johnsbury, was the greatest, because Billy, of course, liked to live in the moment. And he was savoring every moment he spent with her, just as much as he was savoring the whiskey in his glass. Yes, Catherine was great by a long shot, but after all, Billy thought, he should hedge his bets; he never really dumped a girlfriend when he latched onto a new one, one like Catherine. It was always good to keep another babe or two in reserve, just in case, Billy mused as he opened his eyes, drained his glass and the ice cubes sliding toward him from the glass's bottom abruptly bumped into his lips the way Catherine's did when she and Billy were making love. The whiskey made him feel almost weightless and giddily carefree. He let his thoughts float away from that thought toward memories of Jane and Doris, wondering what they were doing right now. And whose lips theirs were bumping into. "Hey—are you listening to me?" Catherine asked peevishly.

She reared upward in her lounger, giggled and tugged on his right earlobe, and tried to tug him over backward into her lap. Billy turned and smiled at her, putting thoughts of Doris aside for the moment. He and Catherine Hollingsworth were sitting on chaise lounges at pool side at her folks' place. *A swimming pool—that was really something in these troubled times, wasn't it*, he thought? Catherine's folks were different from the parents of Billy's other girlfriends; they had money and weren't afraid to spend it. That was a quality Billy admired in people. And here he was at Catherine's fancy home, romping around the grounds and delving into the pantry and the well-stocked liquor cabinet like an adventurous bear. Neither Catherine's daddy or momma was home, and they wouldn't be for a while.

Let Goldilocks play, thought Billy to himself. *So what if it isn't my house?*

"I'm worried about you," Catherine grumped. She pouted. Turned her pretty nose up. Just for show.

"Why?" Billy wrinkled up his forehead until it resembled a washboard's symmetrical ripples and put on a huge, innocent-looking smile. "What's there to worry about?" There truly wasn't much. Billy had knocked off work early at Coughlin's funeral home and thumbed a ride over to Catherine's after she'd stopped by and invited him over; her parents were away at a convention in Burlington and would be for the next two days. This was encouraging. Enticing, also. Billy accepted.

"You work too hard. And you've got that awful job, driving that hearse for Junior Coughlin."

"So?"

"I mean, Billy; do you—do you handle bodies?"

"No." Billy sat up, rolled off his socks and tossed them onto the lawn. He paused and appeared to be deep in thought for a moment before turning to face her. He now looked very serious. "Well, actually, yes." Catherine looked at him in wide-eyed horror. "Now I'll come clean with you, Catherine. It *is* true, but—the only body I've ever handled is—yours!" Billy pounced on her, grabbed her, tickled her ribs and then pulled her, screaming, from the lounger. And the two of them plunged into the pool.

"You are so bad!" Catherine yelled, once she'd popped to the surface.

"Yes, I am. Like it?'

She hugged him, and they started to sink beneath the water. Bubbles escaped from her lips as she said: "I do." And they slowly went to the bottom. They kicked their way apart, fought their way to the surface and paddled toward the sides of the pool, and then held onto them, looking at each other, getting their breath back. Billy, ever like a coyote on the hunt, smelled the chlorine on her body and it intoxicated him more than the whiskey he'd been drinking. She smiled at him. Beads of water sparkled like little pearls on her arms and legs and white swimsuit in the hot sunlight. "Not a chance you're getting your hands on me tonight," she said, grinning at him, and coyly swam away.

"Wanna bet?" leered Billy, letting go of the concrete and dashing after her, churning water into foam like a paddlewheel steamboat as he went. Billy, ever confident, wasn't worried about losing any game; Billy always hedged his bets.

* * *

Joey, meanwhile, was working his afternoon job at Sam's Cash Market, stocking shelves, sweeping floors, and now and then helping the owner, Sam Rivard with some chores in the meat department. Sam, quite the raconteur, had been a Navy man long ago, and often told tall tales at the store about his service aboard Admiral Dewey's flagship, the *Olympia*. Today, standing at the butcher block, "Sailor Sam", as the local wags called him, was spinning a yarn about the Battle of Manilla Bay. "There I was, standing on the bridge with Captain Gridley that morning, the first of May. I offered to take the ship's wheel, but he told me to stand by for action on deck where I was needed. Oh, it was hot, hotter'n blazes up in that steel tower. Just like today. And then the admiral came in." Sam stopped to clear his throat, hoping the pause in the story would evoke greater curiosity in his audience: two old-timers from out of town, who stared at him with glazed-over eyes.

"This gonna take much longer?" grumped one of them.

"Okay, Sam," said the other, fidgeting a bit and sneaking his pocket watch out where he could take a peek at it. "Then what happened?"

"That's when Dewey gave the order to attack. I looked out and I could see all those Spanish ships. And then, all hell broke loose." Sam had been grinding hamburger before he started, and now he absent-mindedly wiped bits of fat and blood off his hands onto the white apron wrapped around his ample girth. "He said…"

"You may fire when you are ready, Gridley," Joey whispered to himself, just as Sam spoke the same words. Joey was sweeping up a mess nearby where a carton of oatmeal had fallen off a shelf and burst open on the floor. Joey had heard the story many times.

"Oh, I'll tell you, right after that, I saw action on the deck and then some! We fired everything we had at those Spanish ships. That was a turkey shoot, that battle! Well, fellows, anything else today?" They shook their heads. Sam went back to the hamburger, scooped up the pound of meat the men had ordered a full 15 minutes ago, ripped a hunk of butcher's paper off a roll and plopped the meat onto it. He deftly wrapped it up in the paper, finally tying it with a bit of string. He yanked his pencil from where it was tucked behind his right ear and with it, wrote the price on the packet of meat. "Thank you, boys. Always good to see you!" The two men sauntered away toward the cash register, and Sam went back to work, perhaps thinking of whatever tale he might tell the next patron.

Had the truth been told (and it seldom was at the meat counter, a place where magnificent lies and tall tales were told from both sides of it) the men would have learned that Sam had actually been a galley cook on the ship, and had simply brought coffee to the wheelhouse for the captain. He actually *had* offered to take the wheel, stating his opinion that the helmsman didn't quite know what he was doing, and furthermore, that the captain didn't either by letting him steer the ship into the bay. The captain, with no time for nonsense and with Admiral Dewey breathing down his neck, had ordered Sam off the bridge and below to the galley. The only action on deck Sam actually saw in Manilla Bay was his own, as prescribed by the captain for insubordination: swabbing it with a mop for a week after the battle was over.

Sam had built a good business over the years, even though he had a bit of a reputation for skimping on portions of packaged goods, no doubt a skill he learned in the *Olympia's* galley when provisions ran short on a long voyage. "A pint's a pound the world around, except when Sam Rivard's downtown" went a little ditty the neighborhood wives often repeated among themselves. Sam knew the value of a dollar, and Sam knew how to barter. Like a plucky sea duck, Sam rode the wave of the Depression up and over it when it hit. He could make money on the way up, and he could make it on the way down.

When deer season was open, Sam would cut any hunter's deer brought to the back door and put up the meat any way desired, all for less than a dollar. He'd then salt the deer hides that were left over, roll them up and sell them to an old Frenchman for a quarter or so apiece, after considerable dickering, which Sam thoroughly relished. A sign at the cash register of Sam's emporium stated: "Of all the cheap, low-down, no-good propositions, I like yours the best!"

"All customers bring happiness," Sam observed to Joey one day, with a wink. "Some by coming in, others by leaving." In the latter case, Sam was without doubt referring for the most part to the notorious Mrs. McBride. The elderly, quarrelsome lady was a regular, a lady of some means who came in once a week to do her shopping. All things considered, she was a regular pain, a vociferous fussbudget and a cheapskate of epic proportions, although she stood barely five feet tall. "Lady McBee," as store staff called her, could pinch a penny, Joey thought, until Lincoln's stamped profile bled copper. And, on this particular day, into the store she waddled in her unfashionable 1890s Oxfords. After a brief tussle to free one of the store's wire shopping baskets from a stack of them, she tossed her bulky black purse into it. Sam saw her coming, and decided to go out behind the store and have a smoke. Jennifer, the cashier, cringed.

"Why, oh why, do you people have to jam all the shopping baskets together?" the old lady groused to no one in particular, as she hobbled down the aisle. "I should take my business someplace else." Jennifer looked at Joey, rolled her eyes, and put her hands together as if in prayer.

Joey chuckled and looked out the front window of the store. Sure enough, there was Mrs. McBride's large and somewhat outdated Franklin sedan, one of its front wheels up on the curb, right where she had parked it, being a tad too short to see over the car's big steering wheel. Mr. McBride, who was a real peach, sat in the back, wise fellow that he was, in order to distance himself from the missus. Sullen and resigned to his fate, he could have passed for an elderly dog awaiting the return of his master—which, in effect—he was, poor fellow.

"Oh, my; not again," came Mrs. McBride's frustrated voice from the condiment aisle. "Why, oh why do you have to put the ketchup way up here, where nobody can reach it?"

"Hang on, Mrs. McBride, I'll help you!" volunteered Joey, swiftly coming to her rescue. "Which one of those would you like?"

"That one there—no, that one has something on it. Take that one." Joey grabbed the bottle and lowered it to her shopping basket for her.

"Oh, please do be careful; don't crush my loaf of bread!"

"Yes, Mrs. McBride. Anything else I can help you with?"

"Yes, young man. I need a quarter pound of salt pork. No more, no less."

"Yes, Ma'am," replied Joey. He headed over to the meat counter, lame old Mrs. McBride following him closely, her shopping basket in hand, swinging it back and forth as she pitched along, bumping into things along the way and knocking canned goods off shelves.

"These shopping baskets, these awful, awful baskets and these tiny narrow aisles of yours," she groused. Joey stepped behind the counter, bent and removed the cover from the storage crock. The pieces of fatty salt pork, key ingredient for homemakers who still made baked beans the old-fashioned way, floated serenely in brine like vile-looking medical specimens. Not without a small amount of distaste for the task, Joey grabbed a pair of tongs, fished one of the slippery, slimy pieces from the crock and set it down on butcher's paper on the block. He sliced off a piece and put it on the scale. Ever-watchful, Lady McBride moved closer to the counter, and stood on tiptoe to look and make sure Joey didn't have his thumb on the scale. "It's just a little over, ma'am; four and a quarter ounces. Is that okay?" asked Joey. He braced himself for the reply.

"I said no more than a quarter pound, young man. I'm not paying for any extra." Joey removed the salt pork, trimmed it, and put it back on the scale's platter.

"There we go. One quarter pound, on the mark," announced Joey. Mrs. McBride nodded sternly. He quickly wrapped the blubbery purchase up, penciled a price on it and handed it to her. Just then the back door opened and Sam let himself in. He had rolled up his sleeves in the heat outside, and it was now apparent his arms were covered with tattoos. They provided mute testimony to his tales of years spent in the Navy and the many ports he'd visited on shore leave, although in many cases, Sam, who had liked his booze as well as the next sailor did, could not remember when—or where—he'd gotten those many mementos.

"And now I need a little slice of cheddar," announced the old lady. "Just a very thin slice."

Joey stepped over to the big wheel of cheese, removed the cover and set it aside. He carved off a wafer-thin slice. "Too big," she grumbled disagreeably. Joey tried again. "Still too big."

"Let me help you, Mrs. McBride," offered Sam, who had come to Joey's rescue. He sidled over next to Joey, saying, "I'll get you the smallest piece possible." Sam picked up the long, sharp knife, waved it over the wheel of cheddar like a magician about to saw a volunteer lying in a box in two—and then slowly passed its tip directly underneath the old woman's bony nose. Frozen with fear, she stared at the blade—and then at a tattoo on one of Sam's arms, one of a bare-breasted mermaid—in terror. "Here" said Sam generously to her, smiling devilishly. "I'll let you sniff the knife."

"*Mister* Rivard! Have you lost your senses?" shrieked Mrs. McBride. She turned to Joey, who was struggling not to laugh. "You see, young man, what I go through to shop here? Honestly! I have been complaining about things in this store since before you were born!" Off she went in a huff toward the cash register, mowing down a four-foot-high display of canned soup as she went reeling along.

Sam chuckled as he set down the knife on the butcher block. He pointed at the two slices of cheese. "How about it, kid?" he asked Joey, turning toward him. "Let's have some cheddar and celebrate."

"Aren't you worried about losing a customer?" asked Joey.

"Don't worry about her; she'll be back." Sam and Joey munched on the cheddar for a bit. Then Sam spoke up. "You know what they say: A bad penny always returns." He chuckled a bit. "I don't know how her poor old husband stands her." Then, he snapped his fingers as something else swiftly came to mind. "Say, Joey, I almost forgot: I have to slab a whole crate of chickens this afternoon, and there are some deliveries to make today. I can't do both. How about if you take the truck and make the rounds for me?"

"Sure, Sam! That would be great," answered Joey. He had been learning how to drive the last several months. Between a few sessions piloting Sam's Chevrolet panel truck around the back parking lot under the grocer's tutelage, and several others closer to home (with his dad Bud as instructor, driving the old Pontiac of his around back streets) he'd gotten the hang of steering, braking, and shifting vehicles with non-synchromesh transmissions. A driver's license? That could come later, as so many believed in the tough but uncomplicated 1930s. Sam reached into his pockets for the key to the store's delivery truck and handed it to Joey. "Just be careful. Keep her under 50, so the fenders don't fall off," he added, with a wink.

"Will do, Sam," answered Joey, taking the key. Within the next ten minutes, he loaded up the truck with sacks and boxes full of groceries to be dropped off. Sam's old black Chevy, hand-lettered for his market, was something of a relic. It had started out life as a paddy wagon for the Montpelier Police Department; later on, it found its way to a capital city cracker company that used it for deliveries until it proved to be cantankerous and a notorious oil-burner. Sam bought it at an auction and put up with its mechanical eccentricities and its occasional conniption fits, much as he did with those of Mrs. McBride, together with its propensity to lay down a smoke screen wherever it went. But it would do until times got better. "Make it last, wear it out; make it do or do without" was the credo of many business people in the Depression, and ever-frugal Sam, an unpaid subscriber of sorts, wholly endorsed it.

Joey slammed the twin doors on the back of the old truck shut, and a trickle of brown rust filtered down onto the ground beneath the latches. He opened the driver's side door, hopped onto the battered seat that sagged even under his light weight, and pumped the gas pedal twice. He put the gearshift into neutral, pulled out the choke a bit, turned the key in the ignition and pushed one foot down hard on the floor-mounted starter pedal. The engine turned over reluctantly a few times until the ignition finally caught, sputtered in protest, and the truck came into life; it apparently wasn't too happy at having its afternoon siesta disturbed. It backfired and belched black smoke out the tailpipe at first, and then the engine settled down into a grumpy-sounding idle once Joey pushed the choke in.

The delivery route was pretty much the same every week, Sam told him. There were two stops way out on Higgins Hill Road to the east, several on the west side along Cliff Street, Winter Street and Spring Street, and then three up along Pleasant Street and another on Breezy Hill Road, to the north. With his delivery list stuffed into a pocket, Joey nursed the old truck along Portland Street until it got up to temperature and, once it did and the Chevy was running smoothly, he drove south more confidently and then turned right, heading up Eastern Avenue. An afternoon matinee had been playing at Tegus' Palace Theater and now that the movies were over and the curtains had closed in the dark theater, a crowd of young people streamed out of its doors, almost as blind as bats in the strong sunlight.

Lila Larsen, 16 years old, going on 17, and burdened with no cares in the world at the moment, other than what to do after watching the matinee and who to do it with, was essentially happy-go-lucky and fancy free—other than having taken a fancy to Joey just before the school's summer vacation. Like everyone else emerging from the dark theater, she blinked. And then she saw the object of her affection at the wheel of Sam's delivery truck. Long, tall and skinny as a rail, she sprinted after the ugly black truck like a long-distance runner. She caught up with it at the corner by the Union Bank when it slowed to make a stop, and jumped onto its running board with the verve of a grasshopper popping up out of a field onto a moving hay wagon. She quickly stuck her head inside, squarely in front of a startled Joey Ross, grabbed his left arm and hollered, "Hi Joey boy! Where are you goin'?"

"Holy cow, Lila!" I can't see where I'm going! Let go of my arm!" Joey blustered in momentary panic. Lila just giggled and made eyes at him. Joey stood on the brakes and the truck screeched to a stop. Passersby on the sidewalks stared and car horns blared as Lila, all the while holding up traffic, quickly let go of Joey's arm, hopped off the running board, ran around to the other side of the Chevy and let herself in before Joey could say a word. For Lila, it had been a successful ambush on the order of a wild west stagecoach holdup. For Joey, 17 going on 18, he felt it probably had all the appearances—to the gawking kids in the theater crowd just down the street—that he was robbing the cradle.

Joey let out the clutch and the truck lumbered forward again. "Where the heck did you come from, Lila?" Joey gasped. "You're lucky I didn't hit you! What were you thinking?"

"I was at the Palace," answered Lila. She tossed her dark hair, now in a tangle, over her shoulders and then stuck her bony right arm out the window to catch the breeze. "No one took me to the movies. So, I took myself." She turned, rolled her eyes at him and gave him a wan smile. "Don't suppose you could give me a ride back home to Lyndonville, could you?"

"Look," said Joey, trying to concentrate. He pulled the delivery list from his pocket. "I've got a whole bunch of drop-offs to make. He shook the piece of paper, trying to straighten it out. Lila snatched it and started to read it. Joey frowned; the truck was a trifle hard to steer and kept wandering toward the side of the street. His mind was wandering, too. He actually liked Lila, but he had a job to do. "I'll be lucky to get back home before supper time."

"Oh, well then, you could drop me off too, couldn't you? I can help you! I really can!" Lila said, looking over the list in her hand. "Look, I know these people up on Cliff Street and Winter Street. The Smiths? I used to babysit for them. The Johnsons, too. Oh, c'mon, Joey, let me help!" Joey stayed silent, kept on driving, and stuck his jaw out. Lila pouted.

Lila was a tomboy who could have out-Sawyered Tom Sawyer, Joey reckoned. And she looked the part, seldom seen in anything other than her own, raggedy-Lila outfit of a scruffy-looking skirt or patched blue jean overalls and a checkered, hand-me-down blouse. Shoes were optional on most days come summertime when school was out. And Lila wore a straw hat when she went haying with her neighbors on their farm, or fishing with her father, a large man who had a temper to match his size.

"Old Sam wouldn't want anyone who doesn't work for him riding in his truck," groused Joey. Lila crossed her arms, pushed herself backward in the seat and then stuck her feet up on the dashboard, as if to imply she wasn't going to get out of the truck any time soon, even if Joey tried to pry her out of it. Then, Joey relented: "But—I guess if we can make it a quick trip, it should be okay."

"Oh, that is so nice of you!" Lila blurted, uncrossing her arms and reaching over to slap the back of his right hand playfully. She giggled, took her feet off the dashboard, sat up and then, before Joey could ask what she was doing, Lila turned in her seat and rummaged through the groceries in the box behind her. "Okay," she announced, "these are Smith's groceries. When you stop at their house, I'll run right up to the door and have them sign the grocery slip." When she returned to her seat, Joey looked at her and saw that she had a peach in one hand, and was starting to eat it.

"Lila! What are you doing? You can't eat their food!" Joey exclaimed. But it was too late; Lila by now had taken a couple of bites.

"Look," she said, still munching a mouthful of the juicy peach, while holding up what was left of the fruit for him to see that it was bruised. "It's got a bad spot on it. You wouldn't want us to deliver that to Mrs. Smith and have her turn her nose up at that basket of peaches, would you?" After this righteous question went unanswered, she again propped up her feet on the dash, and looked out her window. She became very animated by catching sight of something—or, someone. "Oh, my God!" Her feet crashed to the floorboards.

"What is it, Lila?" queried Joey, turning quickly to look at her. The truck was motoring down a quiet side street now and approaching a big white house where an elderly man, his back toward the street, was mowing the lawn, in a spot where it ran closely along the sidewalk.

"It's Mr. Eriksen, my substitute teacher from last year. That old goat!" She hauled back one arm and pegged the peach at him; it missed its mark, and thankfully sailed clear over his head. Startled, the white-haired teacher looked up, completely absorbed in observing the trajectory of the peach that had suddenly materialized, as if he were watching a comet that had mysteriously appeared overhead. While watching it, Eriksen absent-mindedly wandered off course and pushed the lawnmower into his flower garden, shredding several petunias into confetti in the process, while the half-eaten peach neatly disappeared into a clump of bushes. By the time he turned around in bewilderment, the truck had reached the end of the street and was gone.

Lila laughed so hard that she bent over double in the seat; Joey suppressed a chuckle and kept on driving until the truck reached the Smith house. Lila grabbed the sack of groceries with its little basket of peaches and ran with it toward the front door. Mrs. Smith's housekeeper, Florence Bickerson had seen the delivery truck coming, and stepped out to greet her and sign the grocery slip. She took the grocery sack and handed something to Lila, who came charging back to the idling truck. "Look, Joey! I got tip! From old Ms. Bickerson!" She held two quarters in her hand. "Did you ever get a tip?"

"No," Joey replied, quite surprised. "Can't say as I've ever gotten one."

"Joey," cooed Lila, "I think we're on to something here." They drove on.

Florence watched the two of them leave and shook her head. "That man, Mr. Rivard, making a poor bitty-little girl do a boy's work, trying to earn a tip or two, while that boy of Rivard's just sits in the truck, loafing," she said to herself. "Shameful. What is this world coming to?" She looked down into the sack of groceries. It looked to her as though Sam Rivard had shorted her on the number of peaches she'd ordered. Like most fuss-budgets, she had a keen eye and didn't miss much. She'd have to have a talk with that man.

* * *

All deliveries accomplished, Joey and Lila rolled into Lyn-donville with an empty truck and a tidy little collection of small change from tips Lila had collected along the way. They stopped briefly at a small store to buy two bottles of cold soda. "My treat," said Lila. "And then, I'll split the change with you." Joey cranked the Chevy and they drove on.

"Where to?" he asked. He had no idea where Lila lived, only that her father worked at the local funeral parlor, where Billy did, too.

"Let's just go up Hill Street a bit," she directed. Joey steered the truck off the highway; it bumped clumsily over the railroad tracks where Hill Street crossed them and then ground along in low gear up the steep hill the street was named for. "Now make a left," Lila instructed. Then, "Pull over here."

"What?" asked Joey. "In the church parking lot?" Lila nodded. "Are you going in for confession or something?" She shook her head. Joey shook his head. He shut off the engine. "You don't want me to drop you off at your house?" Lila shook her head.

"You don't know my father," she said, frowning. "If I came home with a boy, he'd go insane. He's so old-fashioned. He worries about things he shouldn't. My ma, when she was alive? She was even worse. C'mon," she said. "Let's go sit." She got out, took her soda with her, and Joey followed. They climbed up a steep set of concrete stairs and—momentarily winded from the effort—sat down on a park bench in front of the stately brick edifice of St. Catherine's Church. They drank their cold sodas in silence.

Almost the whole of downtown was spread out before them like a mural as they looked down on its rooftops that bristled with chimneys, pipes and smokestacks, and heat waves shimmered from them in the late afternoon heat. There was a hum and buzz of machinery at a mill somewhere, the muted rumble of traffic coursing lazily through town and the occasional honk of a car horn, but it seemed filtered and far off, as if it were coming from a distant land below them instead of the center of a town just several hundred feet away.

"That's my whole world there, Joey," exclaimed Lila, swigging down the last of her drink. "My whole little world."

"But you know so many people, Lila," stated Joey. "This can't be your whole world. You know Mrs. Smith, old Miss Bickerson, Sam Rivard, Mr. Ericksen. I know you know just about everybody—not just here, but down in Saint Jay, too. And my mom and dad, and my brother Billy, too."

"Oh, I know Billy. And that scruffy crew he hangs out with," affirmed Lila. "Yup. I know just about everybody. But there's one person around here that I don't know yet." She set the empty soda bottle down on the grass and nudged his shoulder. Before Joey could move, she leaned over, craned her neck and drew very close to him, until the two of them were almost nose-to-nose. He could smell her sweet breath, smelling of cherry soda pop, and then she smiled and blinked her eyes. She gazed into his, drew a long breath, let it out and hugged him, feeling the warmth of the first boy she'd ever fallen in love with. And then, she whispered something into his ear. "You."

Chapter 5

The Daily Double

Steve Snyder, his trademark switchblade knife prudently concealed, had certainly made his rounds with due diligence during his first day on the job, buying alcohol bottle-by-bottle, store by store and getting along with it, at no extra charge, the knowing looks, winks and nods of various clerks and barkeepers along the way. While he could only speak a few words in the French language, and not that well, the money, for the most part, did the talking. He had spent nearly all of the American dollars LeClaire had fronted him with in the course of visiting a variety of markets, bars, back-room clubs, diners and small restaurants in Coaticook, Compton and even little Dixville in rural Quebec, buying up fifths of choice brands of whiskey, gin and brandy all afternoon. Each establishment had dutifully sold him, under Canadian law, the prescribed limit of liquor per person per day, and at a tidy exchange rate, too. Now, with the car LeClaire had provided him with, a late model Marmon pulled over well off the highway and behind the cover of a grove of trees, Steve was busily concealing the various bottles within its doors, secret compartments beneath the seats and containers underneath the floorboards. The big black sedan was indeed powerful, and Steve looked forward to pushing it to its limits tonight on the highways. Sure, this was probably going to be a just test run before LeClaire gave him real, productive territory, but he was going to do his best. Darkness was coming and with its cover, the time to make his first bootleg run down to White River Junction.

Once these preparations were over, Steve sat down on the running board of the impressive-looking automobile, close by the driver's side door. He shuffled his feet, lit a cigarette, tipped his hat back, and smoked slowly after he watched the match he'd tossed away burn out on the ground between his shiny, brand-new shoes. He had bought them, together with a new suit, with the money LeClaire had advanced him; things were indeed looking up. He then glanced at the back of his right hand and the burn mark on it, something that was gradually turning into a circular scar, then looked away, trying to ignore the mark and the pain it still caused him now and then. He tried not to give in to a feeling of uncertainty as he looked up and watched the setting sun, like some now-elusive symbol of life and goodness, slink behind a row of pine trees. It slowly dipped into the west and began to disappear. Like a stealthy fugitive on the run, it seemed to dodge his gaze behind the screen of treetops as he tried to watch its departure during the late afternoon, flickering in and out of sight. At long last, while he watched, it finally sank into the darkness it created with its departure from the land.

He wanted to believe that this deal with LeClaire would work out. And belief in something solid—something like steel—like the car—or fancy shoes and a new suit—was important for a person like Steve, who had no solid lifestyle. Yes, the car—and the booze the boss's money had bought—those things were convincing. So far, so good. But to further assure himself that he was on the right track and in control of his destiny, Steve pulled his newly-acquired .38 revolver from his belt, drew back the hammer and spun the cylinder. Clickety-click. Yup. Six bullets were in there. All present and accounted for, ready to go. He put the gun back. *All for one—and one for all; me and all mine,* he thought. Out of habit born of stealth in his profession as a thief, he turned and looked over his shoulder to make sure he was not being watched. Stars were twinkling in the darkening eastern sky like a showgirl's earrings in a stage show, one in which the curtain had just been pulled back. And he realized, as he turned back around that there was no denying it now; the show was on, and Steve was the star of the action tonight. People were waiting for him; he hoped to hell they were the right ones.

"Time to shove off," he mumbled, after taking a look at his wristwatch, squinting to make out the numbers in the fast-fading twilight. He took a long, last drag on the cigarette, tossed it away and rose to his feet. Tonight's run would be about 120 miles and it wouldn't be easy; that, he knew. Along the route were several chokepoints where Steve would have to bypass the law, among them, downtown Lyndonville. The first obstacle to circumvent would, of course, be the customs office on the U.S./Canada border, just a few miles south of where Steve was. A truck with a noisy muffler rumbled by on the highway, heading south; then all fell silent. Steve walked cautiously to the edge of the grove of trees that screened him and the car from view to a point where he could see the old pickup disappearing from view, and then looked about if any other traffic was approaching; there was none to be seen. He returned to the car, got in, drew a breath and started the engine.

The first few miles of travel south toward Vermont on the highway were uneventful; there still was no traffic, and to avoid any suspicion among the locals—even though the area was sparsely settled and the houses few and far between—Steve drove slowly. He slyly reasoned that any vehicle speeding through the area at night might well be reported to authorities. Even though few homes in this remote part of

Quebec had telephones, he had been told, there was no sense in taking any chances. Steve judiciously checked the rearview mirror frequently to make sure that he was not being tailed. When he came to a junction with a certain side road, *Chemin de Stanhope*, he turned onto it, driving even more slowly now until he came to what he had been told to look for: a single-lane farm road on his right, its entrance marked by a battered rural mailbox that stood atop a post jammed into rusty old milk can amidst a patch of weeds and sumac on the road's shoulder. He followed the road, little more than two tire tracks, remembering well his instructions, and briefly took one hand off the wheel to wipe away beads of perspiration that were trickling down his forehead. *God, it's getting dark*, he thought.

Off in the distance, Steve could just make out dim, yellowish rectangles of light, the windows of a farmhouse whose shape he could barely discern in the dark; beside the house loomed the forms of several outbuildings and a large barn. And there they were: two specks of light near the peak of the structure's roof coming from kerosene lanterns hoisted high aloft outside the haymow. It was the signal that the hidden border crossing ahead, just beyond the cornfield, was the route to take. "Yeah, I get it," Steve had said, remembering the words about Paul Revere's ride he had learned as a schoolboy, when LeClaire's men had told him about the system and how it worked. "Two if by sea." That signal meant the way to 'invade' with the contraband tonight was to ford the river just south of the cornfield and bypass customs. One lantern meant: Take the highway crossing, the customs office is closed. No lanterns meant: Too dangerous, go back; the customs agents were out and about.

Steve breathed a sigh of relief, and cautiously steered the big car down a rutty, mud-puddled lane behind the barn past an old wagon, the heavily-laden Marmon's fenders brushing aside cornstalks as it heaved and lurched through potholes, and its wheels slung manure-scented mud up underneath the fenders. Soon, he came to the river and eased the Marmon into it, following the tire tracks on the river bank and steering toward those he could just make out on the opposite side. The water churned about the car, trying to push it downstream, and the tires stumbled over what might have been a few large, smooth rocks on the river bottom. Then, the moon broke free of small clouds that had shrouded it and now Steve could see that the car was in deep water—water so deep he panicked for a moment, fearing it would soon be coming in the doors. He punched the gas pedal; stones rattled underneath the Marmon as it responded heroically to his commands born of urgency and the car, after a brief and rather unsettling struggle, gained the other bank. Steve was grateful now for the weight of the load of liquor that had no doubt given him some extra traction. And grateful to have gained dry land, in the state of Vermont. "Paul Revere!" he triumphantly called out to no one in particular, as he braked the car to a halt, once he'd gained higher ground.

The car's big eight-cylinder engine ticked over idly as if bored, marking time as the Marmon sat there, now south of the international boundary line in a grassy field in Norton, Vermont, moths fluttering excitedly about its big, brightly-burning headlights while Steve rummaged in his pockets for something and caught his breath. He finally found and brought forth a half-finished nip bottle of whiskey he'd brought along for just this occasion, opened it, and tossed the contents down his throat like a man pouring a quart of motor oil into car's engine during a service station stop. There; all better now. He was back in familiar territory. But he had miles to go tonight; that, he knew. He wiped his lips dry with the back of one hand and with the other, tossed the empty nip bottle out the Marmon's window and watched it sail off into the night. Something was bothering him: what was it? What was the rest of that saying? There was something more to it, wasn't there?

It was so familiar to him. Ah, that was it! It was in a poem he had heard, had recited back in school. He had miles to go, Steve did. And then he remembered the rest of it, now that he recalling briefly looking at the figure of the man he had killed, three years ago, lying dead in an alleyway. The man had looked very peaceful, as if he were asleep. Yes, that was it. "Before I sleep," he said to himself, as the whiskey warmed his belly and steadied his nerves. He smiled, put the Marmon into gear, and drove up out of the field and onto the highway with a renewed sense of confidence, heading south toward his destination.

* * *

Miles and hours later, after taking the cut-off around Lyndonville and then motoring sedately through downtown St. Johnsbury in order not to attract attention, Steve picked up the pace again, pushing the car along at 60 or better wherever Route 5, with its curves and narrow shoulders, would allow it. Once beyond the city limits and in the open countryside, the highway opened up; the roadway was flat and level, and Steve mashed the gas pedal to the floor; soon, the heavy car was rolling along nicely with the needle of the speedometer flickering at the 70 mile-per-hour mark as if having a nervous fit. Now and then the car's headlights would catch the reddish eyes of an animal lurking in the underbrush that would quickly dart away at the car's rushing approach, and once, a large deer leapt out from behind a grove of trees and bounded in a series of graceful arcs across the road, causing Steve to stomp on the brakes, swerve and curse.

For several long, lonely miles below St. Johnsbury, the railroad closely paralleled the concrete highway just to its east side. Presently, a passenger train came rushing along the two ribbons of silvery steel rails, heading north, the faint yellow lights in its coaches trailing along behind the panting, hurrying steam locomotive giving it the appearance of a long, glowing electric eel. The oily-black waters of the Connecticut River flowing alongside the railway, its ripples glistening with moonlight, only added to this momentary illusion. Then, the train with its dark locomotive hammering along the tracks was gone, leaving behind a dragon's-breath smudge of pungent-smelling coal smoke that momentarily cloaked the moon like a black shroud. Any further view of the river and the tracks was briefly censored by the silhouette of a large, round barn and a farmhouse that flashed by the Marmon's windows as the car sped along; then, too, those were gone. A delirium of moths and insects splattered against the windshield, clouding Steve's view of the road ahead, and now Steve cursed them, too, as he had the deer. Soon, very soon, he realized, he would have to pull over and clear the windshield.

Just up ahead, Steve could make out the lights of what appeared to be a small general store. As he drew closer and slowed the car, he could see two spindly gasoline pumps out-side, silhouetted against the light from the store's windows. He also saw that there were two vehicles, a sedan and an old truck—perhaps the one that had passed by his hidden spot behind the grove of trees in Canada earlier on—parked outside the store. A stop here might be risky, reasoned Steve, but he knew he just had to wash the windshield. He steered off the highway, pulled up in front of the gas pumps and carefully looked about, finally shutting off the car's motor once he saw that there were no signs of activity. There was no sound to be heard coming from within the store, nor the parked car or the truck, only the faint squeak of rusty metal as the round Tydol gas sign over the pumps stirred and gently swung to and fro in a gentle breeze. Then, all was quiet. Too quiet. He never heard it coming. Steve felt a cold, round piece of steel he instantly recognized as the barrel of a gun being shoved against the left side of his neck, and heard the command: "Show me your hands!"

How could he have been so stupid? The question played over in Steve's mind several times in the next few seconds as he raised his hands, and the man holding the gun beamed a flashlight around the inside of the Marmon. *Smart fellow*, reasoned Steve; the man must have been hiding behind the gas pumps all the while, watching the road, and had gotten the drop on him as soon as he pulled in.

"Nice car, fellah," said the gunman, and a moment later, his flashlight caught the round burn mark on Steve's right hand. "Well, I'll be damned!" came the exclamation; Steve felt relief as the gun being held against him was withdrawn. "I know you! You're with our outfit! Come join the party!"

"What party?" asked Steve, lowering his hands. He felt a longing for another nip of whiskey. He turned and looked into the face of the gunman; it was one of the two men he had met the night he'd committed to go to work for LeClaire. "And who are you?"

"We hit the daily double here, kid," answered the man. "Hey, relax; sorry, I didn't recognize the car. You're that new guy, Snyder. My name's Nick." Now minus the gun, his right extended in anticipation of a handshake, he apologized. "Sorry about that little kerfuffle there. No hard feelings, right?"

"Yeah, right" said Steve, pushing his hat back on his forehead and relaxing somewhat. He shook the man's hand. "That's me, alright. What do you mean, daily double?"

"We stopped that truck you see over there, and now we've got the load that was on it. Pretty classy merchandise. Name-brand booze; the best. The driver's a lone wolf, but he lucked out; he rolled right through customs; they must have been asleep up there—or maybe they were paid off. We ran across him, tailed him all the way down here 'til we finally got out in the open, then he tried to give us the slip and lose us, but he's not smart enough and that truck's not fast enough. We finally put the red light on in our car and it must be he thought we were customs, or the cops, and so he stopped, 'cause he found out he couldn't outrun us! What a chump! And our boys just cleaned out the cash register and got some goods in the store. The owner won't mess with us and won't report us—if he knows what's good for him. So—that's our daily double."

"Smooth," said Steve, smiling a thin smile as he opened the door of the Marmon and stepped out. "But I've got to get going." He went over to the gas pumps, stooped and picked up a bucket that had soapy water and a rag in in. "Got to get the damned bugs off the windshield," he said.

The gunman nodded. "You ought to fill 'er up while you're at it," he advised, grinning as he did so, pointing a thumb over his shoulder at the two gas pumps. "Get yourself a tank full of ethyl, while it's still on the house. Hey, want to see the catch of the day? Come over here." He walked over to the dust-covered truck and lifted a flap of the canvas cover draped over the tailgate. Steve, who'd just begun to scrub the bugs off the Marmon's windshield, nodded. He set the rag down on the car's hood, walked over to the truck and peered inside, as the gunman held up the canvas. There, beside several wooden crates of Canadian whiskey, was the figure of a man, struggling mightily; he had been bound, gagged and blindfolded. "That's the not-so-bright driver."

"What are you guys going to do with him?"

"Well, we're going to find out who his connections are, who he sells to. We'll take him some place where he can talk."

"And, if he doesn't come across?" asked Steve.

The gunman shrugged. "That's his choice. He's not one of our guys. So, we don't care how, or where, he winds up if he doesn't want to co-operate and spill the beans. The outfit is the winner in this game; the independent runner, he doesn't stand a chance. You know that; you made your choice. It was the right one." He smiled, then frowned, and turned and yelled in the direction of the store: "Hurry up! We don't have all night!" He strode over to the car that was parked beside the truck, opened the driver's side door, hopped in, and started the engine.

"You know what, Steve," said Nick, turning toward him. "Me and the guys—we're out here for you. This is what we do, out here running the roads. Every night. We're the cops, the judge, the jury and the executioner. And also," he paused to toss away his smoke, "as you must realize, by joining the outfit, we're talent scouts."

Two other men came hustling out of the store and thundered down the rough wooden steps, carrying burlap bags that were heavily-laden with whatever they'd plundered from the shelves. One of them heaved his bag into the back of the truck, then jumped into the cab and started it; the other got into the passenger side of the car beside it and slammed the door. The hapless man lying in the back of the truck groaned and kicked his feet against the back of the cab in a vain attempt to free himself.

The gunman turned back to face Steve, and chuckled evilly as he pointed toward the truck. "That wise guy in the back, there? Even if he thinks he's as good an escape artist as Houdini," he said casually, "he's no magician. If he doesn't come across, well—he could wind up just like Houdini did, running out of time— breathing in water. Just his luck running out, right? Steve nodded. "You know how it goes, Steve." He winked at him for emphasis as he slammed his door shut. "Somedays you're the bug—some days, you're the windshield."

Chapter 6

Coughlin's Coffins

Getting paid for being laid, and getting paid to lay someone to rest, are, of course, two quite different things, but it could be said the tradespeople involved in performing both of these services perhaps have something in common. Besides prostitution, one of the oldest professions in the world may be that of the mortuary trade.

And when it comes to the mortuary trade, consider if you will that just as several generations of skilled Vermont marble and granite workers—many of them descended from immigrant craftsmen from Italy, Poland, Sweden and other countries who came to America in the 1800s—earned wages carving memorial stones, so have many generations of family funeral directors plied their trade among the Green Mountains. A good many of them who passed down to their offspring the practices of tending to those who have passed away started out in the furniture business.

Coughlin's Furniture and Funeral Service was well-known in Lyndonville and had its beginnings in a humble carpenter's workshop, Harry Coughlin's, that turned out tables and chairs in the horse and buggy days. It built its reputation as it went, transitioning from pounding together crude, inexpensive pine furniture favored for its low price and durability by tavern owners (after all, it often found use either as bludgeoning weapons or else as defensive armor during spirited brawls) on to crafting fine furniture from oak, maple and cherry. And as the population of the town grew in the rough-and-tumble days of building railroads, logging, and doing side-hill farming, so inevitably did that of the local cemeteries. It suddenly dawned on Harry Coughlin Junior one day that he was missing out on an amazing opportunity to benefit himself. It was the day his father died, a happy man, in the bed of a woman other than his wife.

Young Harry was thus presented with two rather pressing problems early on that otherwise-splendid day in 1907 in a town small enough—and quiet enough—that some said a rumor whispered among the stacks inside the Cobleigh Public Library could be heard clearly all the way down at the end of Depot Street. First, how to discretely spirit his father's corpse away to a place where a timely and appropriate demise could be staged. And, second, how, and where he could possibly buy a coffin on short notice (and at a reasonable price). After all, Harry Junior by now controlled the company's checkbook; his father's send-off would of course be written off as a business expense, but Junior hated expenses as much as his father had hated him (and his quarrelsome mother, too).

So, Harry Junior, who considered himself sly and smart as a whip, having survived years of drudgery working for his father, sat himself down and thought, and a plan began to take shape in his mind. He knew, from what his father had told him, that the best combination to have in growing business is a partnership. One where your partner has the qualities that you yourself do not possess. Harry Junior wanted to make some decisions. So, rather than continuing to toil in the workshop and emerge at the end of each workday covered in perspiration, wood chips and sawdust, craving a snort of alcohol, he now sought out a lumberjack, a river rat. A man that he knew *knew* wood and how to cut it and bend it to his will. This man was a big, powerful fellow who had just sobered up after returning, penniless after blowing a year's pay during a weekend of drinking, whoring and carousing down in Holyoke, Massachusetts. That was after spending a winter logging and then driving logs down river to the mills come springtime, using not much else except a peavey pole, spiked boots, bravado and a steady stream of profanity and spent tobacco juice. Harry Junior hired him on the spot to make coffins. His name was Sven Larsen.

But that was only one part of the business equation and the solution to the problem at hand; Harry Junior needed a hearse. Badly. After having Sven knock together a pine coffin for the elder Coughlin, he quickly purchased a used wagon, had Sven cobble together a boxy-looking canopy for it and then painted the contraption black. The "removal" (as it is called in the funeral trade) of the deceased's body went off smoothly and discretely. The grieving widow was told Harry Sr. had died of heart palpitations while being told of the idea for expanding the family business, and then trying out the very first coffin the store had manufactured. "He died happy, Ma; that's all I can really tell you," attested the junior Coughlin with complete honesty.

The enterprising young Harry then engaged the services of a funeral director from Barton, and pumped him for information while the funeral director pumped the elder Coughlin full of embalming fluid, down in the basement of the furniture store while young Harry jotted down notes for future reference. The young Coughlin was on his way to becoming not only a funeral professional, but the sort of social gadfly who makes connections and knows how to use them. And soon after Harry Sr. made his own connection (with the earth) a large granite marker was plopped atop the old man's grave to ensure that the old man couldn't arise early, before the angels' trumpets sounded on Judgement Day. Old Harry's young son then hired (after dickering over the cost) an Italian master carver down in Barre to craft the stone; the words on it read:

Harry Coughlin Sr.
1851-1907
Here lies old man Coughlin
Asleep in a very fine coffin
His son made the grade
And now used the spade
To cover up what he kicked off in

As the funeral business began to increase, Harry Junior, who the locals by now referred to as "Junior" had Sven cut an opening for a small door in the back wall of the furniture store. This new door, located some three feet above the ground, allowed helpers on wagons, or else the makeshift hearse, to slide coffins or bodies discretely into the store without alarming customers by the sight of such deliveries being made "out front". As the years passed by, the junior Coughlin bought and annexed a house next door and converted it to full-time use as a funeral parlor. Sven married and started a family. And as the auto made its inroads into the Northeast Kingdom, so did Junior purchase a motorized funeral car, a Ford. Then came a more upscale Hudson, which gave way in 1931 to an elegant Packard hearse. Despite the ill effects of the Wall Street crash of October, 1929 in which disenchanted stock brokers dove out of high-rise Manhattan windows en masse in order to bring their troubles to an end, and during the resulting fallout in which millions lost their jobs, business in the funeral trade was consistently good. Bad things, such as the inevitable demise that befalls all people, no matter whether they are good or just plain rotten at heart, never come to an end, it seems.

Soon afterward, the hearse was augmented by the purchase of a second Packard, a stately-looking, all-black limousine to accommodate mourners. The staff of the combined businesses grew also, chiefly because Harry Junior learned early on that Sven, who had a one-track mind wasn't capable of running a two-car funeral. That's when he hired tough, young Billy Ross as a driver and helper.

But other business opportunities had earlier on gained the attention of Junior. Prohibition had been the law of the land since 1920, and the parched-dry citizens in the Northeast Kingdom had quickly devised new schemes to satisfy their thirst for booze. After all, citizens in the Northeast Kingdom who were willing to fork over hard-earned cash for moonshine, or rum sneaked across the border from neighboring Quebec, were to Orleans County what tulips were to Holland.

One method was for the more enterprising locals in remote areas to set up stills out in the woods, where the odds of being raided by a revenuer were low. Another was for the locals who owned fast cars to surreptitiously drive under cover of darkness across the border into Canada, where the making, sale and possession of beer, whiskey and other such libations were legal, and then drive the clinking bottles back into Vermont where they were worth a greater amount, all the while risking arrest, imprisonment and confiscation of their vehicles.

Junior's funerary business had established a territory extending well across the international border into Canada by the mid-1920s; it included the Canadian towns of Stanstead and Highwater, and so now and then, Junior would be called to bring the body of a Quebecer who'd been born in Lyndonville or some other town in Caledonia County across the line for burial in Vermont soil. Suddenly, this cross-border traffic increased exponentially, but the busy men in blue suits with brass buttons who staffed the U.S. Customs Offices did not seem to recognize something: that Canadians in the Memphrémagog

Regional County Municipality of Quebec born south of the border in Orleans County were apparently, if anyone cared to do the math, popping off in numbers not seen in decades.

Up in Canada, by government standards a pint is not a measly 16 ounces but an Imperial pint, and as such it weighs one and a quarter pounds, exclusive of the glass bottle it's in. Billy would be sent north by Junior to an appointed spot in Canada, driving an empty coffin across Derby Line and dutifully registering with the authorities. But the contents on the return trip would be carefully calculated, bottle by bottle, to not exceed 200 pounds, and the coffin would be tagged with a falsified certificate of death. A dummy dressed in a suit and wrapped in gauze, with a smidgin of roadkill stuffed inside it would be placed atop the load of contraband before the coffin's lid would be secured. On one occasion while traveling south into Vermont with a load, Billy was questioned closely about the coffin's contents by an overly-inquisitive U.S. Customs Officer, one who perhaps had too much time on his hands. "He's in there, alright," Billy brazenly attested, gesturing toward the rear of the vehicle with his right thumb, "and he's pretty ripe. Laid dead in his house for a week before anyone found him. Take a look, if you like, but hold your nose." The agent, upon opening the hearse's rear door and sniffing around the coffin quickly covered his mouth, slammed the door shut, and told Billy to get his hearse, his smart ass and his damned cargo down the road.

Just down the highway from Junior's establishment on U.S. Route 5 was that of Theodore "T.R." Donovan, a man who'd opened a gas station and repair shop shortly after returning from the Great War in France. Business boomed when Ford's Model T found acceptance in the area and people were crazy to get rid of Old Dobbin, the feed bag and the buggy and get themselves a motor car. T.R. soon tired of pumping gas and turning wrenches, and branched out into another lucrative business, but one that was—as some people jealous of tycoons and dismissive of their genius say—mostly water.

T.R. built himself a vast ice house on the banks of Pierce Pond so his men could harvest ice in the winter, put it up in storage and then sell and deliver it year-round to homeowners' kitchen ice boxes that, years hence—little did they know—would be replaced by refrigerators as more and more homes got electric power lines strung to them. Junior's Packards were well cared for by T.R.'s staff at the gas station, and it soon came to pass that an arrangement was made that T.R., with his distribution network, would retail what arrived in Junior Coughlin's coffins. Burly-looking ice men driving chain-drive Mack trucks drove regular routes, and with the delivery of a block or two of ice and acceptance of cash upon receipt came the delivery of a pint or two of bonded, four-year-old Canadian whiskey.

Everyone from the cross-border rumrunners and backyard still operators eventually learned that far south of Vermont, in the city speakeasies, even in upstate Saratoga, New York, there were those who would pay much, much more than the local going price for illegal alcohol. Junior was one of those men who finally figured that out. But it took new connections with some down-country wheelmen—young men who drove back and forth between the big city lights and the Kingdom—to take advantage of that. Thus, Junior's collaboration with T.R., and his little scheme of illicit cross-border commerce worked rather well. He was smart and he was careful. Of necessity, Junior did bury some empty coffins, but never any mistakes; he was, after all a mortician, not a doctor.

One day during summer vacation, Joey decided to ride his hand-me-down bicycle—the one he used to get to work, clerking at the cash market after school, earning 20 cents an hour—the nine miles up to Lyndonville to see his brother Billy. He remembered that, on a whim, his brother had bet him a dollar he wasn't tough enough do it, especially on a kid's bike.

When he rode into the back lot of the furniture store and braked to a dusty stop, he saw through the open door that Sven was hammering a coffin together in the workshop.

"Hi Mister Larsen," Joey called out. "Is my brother around?" At this, Sven put down his hammer, and spat out several nails he had been holding onto—in between his lips. He came sauntering out of the workshop like a large, powerful bull that is in no particular hurry to gore a toreador once the gate has been opened.

"Ah, so then, that's you, then? Billy's little brother, eh?" he inquired, wiping his nose on the sleeve of his red flannel shirt. There was sawdust on his arms and shoulders.

"Yes, that's me, Mister Larsen."

"In that same school as my daughter Lila, ya?"

"Yes, sir," replied Joey. The big man moved closer—very close. Joey could see brown stains of tobacco juice on one side of his mouth and could smell the man's sour sweat. Then, Sven Larsen planted one of his big feet against the front tire of Joey's bike.

"Ya tell me now, young feller," inquired Sven, tapping Joey's chest with a dirty forefinger the size of jumbo cigar, "You been sexin' my daughter?" His eyes were bloodshot, and looked wild with pent-up anger. Joey's mouth ran dry, and he swallowed hard before answering.

"No, Mister Larsen. I've heard a lot of bad things being said about me and about her. It's not true, if that's what you're asking about." Joey remembered the time both he and Lila had been sent to the principal's office in school. Someone had lied about him starting a fight with another boy, but Lila hadn't lied about fighting with a girl who'd told a lie about her. So there Lila had sat, next to Joey, with a big black eye, a skinned elbow and a cut knee that had a big bandage on it. Joey looked unhappy; Lila, pigtails in disarray, and with a rip in her skirt, had a big smile on her face; she'd won the fight. Like her dad,

Lila was a scrapper. And then the wild stories created by the loser began circulating about two supposed love birds smooching outside the principal's office and carrying on a romance afterward, highlighted by an after-school tryst in the janitor's closet.

The wags who started schoolyard rumors knew, of course, that Sven had a short fuse and if provoked, could quickly rearrange a foe's front teeth to a new spot in the back of his throat.

Joey, nervous as could be, quickly explained all this and Sven listened. Joey left out one part; Lila had a crush on him. She had ever since he volunteered to go into the principal's office first so she could think up a good story to tell him about what had happened. The rumor mill had made much of the report of seeing Joey and Lila sitting together on the bench for what seemed half a school day afternoon. "So then, that's it. So, okee dokee. I think you tell the truth, young fellah. I don't think you're like your big brother," said the big man. He shook his massive head and pouted. "The boys around town here, and those fellas over at the garage, they say a lot things they hear. Say things they don't know about. I should not have said what I said to you just now, but I am a father, and I try to be a good father and take care of my child. Sometimes I, too, say things I do not truly know about. I am sorry. Shake hands?" He stuck out a calloused, baseball-catcher's mitt of a hand that nearly enveloped Joeys, and pumped it vigorously, nearly crushing it. "But I do think my daughter, she likes you, ya?" He nodded as if in approval.

"Yes, I think she does, but we're just friends, Mister Larsen. Do you know where my brother is?" asked Joey, glancing at his wristwatch.

"Ya, sure; you betcha!" exclaimed the big man. "Down street a bit in that there garage of Mister Donovan's, or else out in that big ice house. He hangs out with those boys of T.R.'s when he's got no business to do here or out on the road. But they do some business there, with that crew from down country that comes up every few days, I tell ya." Sven turned and looked away down the road toward the south. "I don't know what they do, but they must do an awful lot of it down there."

"Thanks, Mister Larsen," said Joey, pedaling off and waving goodbye to the big man. Joey was soon to find out an awful lot about the types of people who'd hang out after work at T.R. Donovan's ice house—including his brother—and how awful they could be.

Chapter 7

Brother! Can You Spare a Dime?

Some days it just doesn't pay to get out of bed, it seems. And the main part of the problem with those gnarly, awful days is that by the time it dawns on you that everything is going to go dead wrong, you are nowhere near your bed, where you could crawl back under the covers, pull them up over your head and make the world go away. The lesser part of the problem is that when you think things could only get worse with what's left of the day, you find that you are dead wrong again. Especially when it is an otherwise beautiful, sunny day, smack dab in the middle of the hot, humid month of August in Vermont (and for everyone else, it seems, life is just plain peachy).

There was a lot on Joey's mind as he left Coughlin's and pedaled his bicycle along, heading south toward the ice house, and then St. Johnsbury. As a teenager about to begin his senior year in high school, he tried not to think about the stigma of being seen riding a dowdy-looking kid's bike. But the immediate concern was of being hit by cars whizzing by too closely, and then joining the ranks of dead animals lying belly-up along the guardrails. The speed limit was strictly imposed—whenever there was a speed cop or a sheriff out on patrol, which was seldom in these parts. Most motorists had little tolerance for sharing the narrow highway—without shoulders in many places—with anyone riding a bicycle. Another concern Joey had was finding his brother so that he could collect the dollar bet from him. A dollar, for example, would buy 10 pounds of potatoes, a pound of butter and a king-size loaf of bread. This Joey knew from working afternoons at the grocery store, a place where he needed to be, stocking shelves and sweeping floors, in just a few short hours.

Joey stood up on the pedals to add leverage to his efforts as he huffed and puffed his way up over a small hill and then around a sharp bend in the road that crooked around the huddle of houses near the tiny post office in Lyndon. He ground on, slowly conquering another incline that was more gradual but much longer, and then coasted briefly downhill, enjoying the short-lived breeze that chilled the beads of sweat trickling down inside his T-shirt before pedaling furiously again. Several miles below Lyndon, the road paralleled the ruler-straight railroad tracks. The steel rails shimmered in the waves of late afternoon August heat, and Joey smelled the acrid scent of creosote bubbling up from the brown crossties beneath them. Where dairy cows appeared in distant corners of pastures far beyond the railroad, they were gathered in small clusters, switching their tails back and forth, sharing what shade from the roasting sun there was to be found beneath small stands of trees.

At last, Joey spotted T.R. Donovan's garage on the west side of the highway. It was a small, white-frame building that had begun life as a farm stand and had been converted into a filling station afterward. It had been added onto over the past several years as traffic on Route 5 boomed with the proliferation of automobiles; a large shed had been erected close to its back wall to serve as a garage, and an even larger, newer one now sat behind the first. There was a heap of junk tires, old batteries, burst radiator hoses and a pile of rusty, dented oil drums next to the building. Several large signs clung to its side. "Auto Wrecking/General Repair" read one, and, "Ford Parts, Repairs, Tires" read another. Farther out in the woods behind the shed loomed T.R. Donovan's massive wooden ice house. Beyond it, through a tall stand of pine trees, Joey caught a glimpse of the waters of Pierce Pond, where ice was harvested in the winter. He could feel sweat trickling down his back between his shoulder blades, and the damp palms of his hands stuck to the bike's gummy rubber handlebar grips.

Heaving a sigh of relief at arriving safely, he caught his breath and coasted into the parking lot where an old one-armed man, likely the attendant, sat, sound asleep in a rickety-looking chair propped back against the building's wall near the gas pumps. The man's sole arm and its greasy hand were stuffed into a strap of his suspenders, which looked as if they and the hand were straining to keep his ample belly from bursting. His mouth was wide open, and Joey could hear the old fellow snoring like a buzz saw. A beagle lying at the man's feet arose, padded over to Joey and barked; this awoke the attendant, who blinked himself out of whatever he'd been dreaming about, and glared menacingly at Joey.

"Whaddya want? Use the air to blow up your tires? We ain't got no free air here," he groused. He pulled his arm free of the suspenders and brought the chair back on all four of its legs with a *thunk* that startled the beagle. The man pointed toward the air hose, coiled up and hanging from a hook on the wall where a small sign was displayed, indicating, "Air is free for gas customers. All others, five cents per tire." He looked cross, probably embarrassed that he'd been caught sleeping on the job, and swore softly after spitting on the ground. At this, the beagle cringed and put back its ears. It scuttled away to another spot, where it whined and sighed loudly, then laid down beside a stack of discarded brake drums and broken wheels.

"No, I'm looking for Billy Ross." Joey hopped off his bike and ambled over to the attendant. "Is he here somewhere?" The man at first ignored him, looking instead at a late-model Chrysler roadster that had pulled in and sidled up to the gas pumps. The driver didn't wait long for service; after peering through the windshield a scant second or two at the attendant, still seated in the chair, he honked the car's twin, chrome-plated horns and waved at him to come over to the gas pumps.

"Don't know," mumbled the still-sleepy attendant as he got to his feet and shuffled off toward the Chrysler; the dog dutifully got up and followed. "Don't know who that is. I don't know any of those guys who come and go at all hours. Go out back and see whoever's out there. They can probably tell you. I mind my own business here." He looked over his shoulder at Joey. "You should, too."

"Fill 'er up, and make it snappy!" commanded the well-dressed fellow in his car, a man who, glancing at his wristwatch with a look of concern, was obviously in a hurry. Joey returned to his bike and headed out back, looking over his shoulder to see if the bedraggled little dog would change its mind and follow him. It did not. It circled the Chrysler once, then lifted one of its rear legs and peed on one of the car's fancy whitewall tires. As he pushed his bike along, Joey heard the old man snap at the driver after being asked something while he pumped the gas: "No, mister, like I told you: we ain't got no restrooms!"

Joey walked past the larger of the two sheds behind the filling station and then leaned his bike against the wall. There didn't seem to be anyone about. The doors to the shed bearing "Keep Out!" signs were closed, but—undeterred—he tugged one of them open and peered inside. It was dark, but despite the gloom he could see one of T.R.'s big, bull-nosed Mack trucks awaiting repair and also three large, new, expensive cars parked beside it. Cars that no one in Lyndonville or St. Johnsbury could even dream of owning. One was a big Lincoln touring car; another was a late-model Cadillac sedan that had had its hood and radiator removed. The third was a large, eight-cylinder Hudson; all three had New York license plates. Joey's attention was drawn to the dust-covered Hudson, which was headed into the garage and had been jacked up off the floor for some sort of repair. There were several round puncture holes in the car beneath the rear window. Curiosity overcoming him, he stepped into the garage to look closely at them. He stuck out a forefinger and plunged it into one of the holes that was shiny around the edges with bare metal. The holes were bullet holes. Caught by a warm breeze, the large door slammed shut behind him, but just as soon as it did, someone yanked it wide open and it smacked against the side of the shed with a sound that made Joey jump. Somewhere outside the shed, alerted, the beagle barked again.

"Hey! Mr. Nosy! Are you lookin' for trouble? Or are you just lookin'?" Joey spun around to see who the voice belonged to. He hadn't noticed this bare-chested young man in jeans and a stylish-looking fedora who had been walking quietly along behind him up before he stepped inside. He was holding a switchblade knife in one hand and a bologna sandwich in the other. Nor had Joey spotted the man's two companions, who had been throwing their own knives at a target nailed to a wooden post farther out in the woods among the pines beyond the yard. He could see them now through the doorway, ambling over toward him in the casual way in which lions approach an animal they are in no particular hurry to kill—because they intend to play with it a bit beforehand for amusement.

"I'm just looking for my brother," answered Joey nervously, glancing back and forth, first at the man in the fedora, then at the other two men. "Billy Ross."

"You won't find him in here, chump," said the man. "Now, beat it, before I wrap your bike's handlebars around your neck. Or maybe you'd like me to let some daylight into your tires with this shiv while you stand there making up your mind?" He grinned and twirled the knife menacingly.

"What does he want?" yelled one of the other men as they approached.

"I think he wants to get carved up like a jack o'lantern," said the first. "You know what? I'll bet a pumpkin's got more guts than he does. You won't have to wait until October, boys. Want to see?" He grinned wickedly as he flourished the knife briefly, like a skilled barber about to shave a customer. Despite making this ominous threat, he closed and pocketed the knife, grabbed Joey's shirt collar and pulled him closer. "Who sent you here?" he demanded. He put his face up within inches of Joey's, brought up his bologna sandwich and snapped at it like a shark hitting a bait fish. He bit off a huge chunk of the sandwich and chewed it slowly, savoring it as much as Joey's apparent distress. "Who?" Bread crumbs from the crumbling sandwich tumbled down the front of Joey's T-shirt and onto the ground. Joey looked at the man's shoes: they were brand new and looked as though they'd been spit-polished. Joey reasoned the man couldn't possibly be from anyplace nearby in the Kingdom; his jeans had no patches on them.

"Nobody sent me. I came here on my own."

"Well, now, is that a fact?" retorted the man thoughtfully as he continued to chew.

"Yes, I did. Is Billy here?" Joey felt sweat trickling down the back of his neck as he asked the question.

"Maybe his is, and maybe he ain't," sneered the man as the two others entered the shed.

"And maybe you're his brother, and maybe you ain't. Guess what? We're gonna take you over to see old man Donovan, and when he gets ahold of you, we'll find out who you are and why you came here. C'mon." Rough hands grabbed Joey from behind and dragged him out of the shed and off toward the ice house. Joey's shoes left furrows in the dirt like a plow being dragged through a field by a pair of strong draft horses as he tried in vain to wriggle free.

"I'll take care of the bike," grumbled the man in the fedora as he finished eating his sandwich, closed the shed doors and walked around the corner. "If that young fellow wants to squeal about something, he'll do his squealing here. Like a stuck pig."

* * *

It was dark, and, not surprisingly, damp and cool inside the huge ice house. The walls, fully two feet thick and filled with sawdust to serve as insulation, kept T.R. Donovan's vast quantities of ice—in blocks, chunks and crushed form—ready to truck to any customer within a 20-mile radius no matter how warm the weather might be. And in order to quench the thirst of those customers, ample quantities of beer, wine, whiskey, gin and brandy were also kept on ice, well hidden under straw and sawdust within the walls. So were the dead now and then, in such times in which the capacities of Junior Coughlin's establishment were taxed beyond their limits. Times when Junior sought short-term storage, handing off a fresh corpse or two for T.R. to stash temporarily near the bourbon barrels until Junior caught up with business at hand over at the mortuary. After all, as the old saying goes, one hand washes the other.

There were other hands at work inside the ice house office the day Joey Ross got dragged into it by the young, out-of-town toughs. Or, more exactly, those hands were working only at playing poker with Billy Ross, dealing cards under the glare of a lone lightbulb dangling from a wire over a table. One of them was Dudley "Dud" Pierce, who had lost the family farm and Pierce Pond to T.R. Donovan in a similar but high-stakes card game some years ago, thus enabling T.R. to build up his empire. Another was Buck McCabe, a well-known townie and a poacher whose venison steaks were popular all over Lyndonville. The third was Denny "Dodo" Quill, a bachelor whose morals, honesty and personal hygiene were all questionable at best. He was the heir apparent to his father's legacy, a shack just up the road and not much else; Denny was the last in a long line of ne'er do wells in his family, and it was obvious to townsfolk that his nickname implied inevitable extinction of his swarthy species. The memory of his father William, an alcoholic of some repute, would nonetheless be kept alive by repetition of a little ditty repeated by generations of local school children: "William Quill from Lyndonville, never worked and never will." Denny helped out at T.R.'s every now and then, whenever his pockets became empty and he sobered up, dry as a bone in the desert and at odds with himself. The apple never falls far from the tree, it seems.

A stairway near the table led up to a private room where T.R. spent his days (and nights, too whenever his wife had thrown him out of the Donovan household, a fairly regular occurrence in recent years before she divorced him). A motheaten trophy, a large buck deer head hanging on one wall seemed to stare over Billy's shoulders at the cards in his right hand. Its glassy eyes seemed to be bulging in disbelief at what he was holding, for Billy was, despite his calm outward appearance, losing. The deer's apparent expression, frozen in time, may, in fact, have been the one on the deer's furry face when Buck McCabe shot it out of season in the back woods up near Wheelock. On the opposite wall was a framed photograph of President Theodore Roosevelt (who T.R. ardently admired) a mounted bull moose head, and a movie poster filched from the billboard of the theater in St. Johnsbury. The colorful broadside advertised the new gangster movie starring James Cagney and Jean Harlow, *The Public Enemy*. The boys in the ice house had been using it as a dart board, and someone had scored a direct hit with a green-feathered dart; it protruded from a spot right between Cagney's piercing eyes. A nascent cartoonist among the rowdy boys had drawn a word bubble above Jean's pretty face and inscribed the words: "Who says crime doesn't pay, honey? You just slipped me a twenty for what I did last night!"

"Lookee what we got here!" hollered one of the men who'd hauled Joey into the office and now stood behind him, looming six feet tall, broad-shouldered and intimidating. "A trespasser. Nosing around our cars. Catch of the day." Joey coughed and cleared his throat, which had run dry. Dudley, Buck and Denny briefly stirred at this interruption, glanced at Joey, shrugged, and then turned their attention back to the game. But Billy stared intently at his cards all the while, trying hard to conjure up a spectacular act of magic that would change his bum hand into a flush so he could win back his money.

"Yeah," said Joey's other manhandler, who was dressed in gray slacks, a white dress shirt and gray vest. He dusted off his fingers as though he'd been handling refuse. There was a diamond ring on one of his pinkies. "A spy. Sneaking around the garage. I guess the coppers are sending around teenagers to do their dirty work now. How do you like that?" Still standing behind Joey, he kicked one of his legs out from under him, making him collapse of the floor. "This fellow," the man said, pointing at Joey but now looking at Billy, "says he knows you." Billy, intent on playing his hand, kept his eyes on the cards.

"Don't know him. Never seen him," grumbled Billy dismissively, without glancing up. "Pass." Denny made his move, grunted something Joey couldn't hear and tossed a quarter into the middle of the table.

"Okay, then; we'll throw our catch of the day back. Into the pond, that is," commented the other man, who wore a slouch hat and a blue suit, "when we're done with him. No one will think to look for him in there. C'mon, you." He reached down to grab Joey, but Joey was too quick for him; he sprang up and scooted over toward the table where Billy sat.

"Billy! What are you thinking? Tell them who I am!" he implored. But before Joey could reach the table, one of the ruffians tackled him and took him to the floor again. Still, Billy did not look up; the curse of bad luck was upon him and he couldn't shake it. But he played on, holding his cards, praying for a break. Denny lit a cigarette as he stared at the spectacle of Joey, now being pinned to the floor, then he waved the flaming match until it was extinguished and tossed it into an ashtray. Buck, the bulk of his posterior overhanging the small chair he sat on, giggled behind his cards, reached for his glass and drained the last drops of whiskey from it.

It was then that T.R. Donovan made his appearance, opening the door at the top of the staircase, roaring, "Bully! *Bully!*" before emerging. Stout but tall, severe of countenance and blessed with a walrus mustache tailored to resemble that of his role model, Teddy Roosevelt, he staggered out onto the landing, beet red in the face, reeling along like a sailor on the heaving deck of a ship in high seas. He grabbed the railing and held on like a man about to give a speech. A man who suddenly realizes he's forgotten his notes and hopes he can conjure up something knowledgeable to say before his audience packs up and leaves.

Joey had seen T.R. before on trips the businessman made into St. Johnsbury, but Joey had never seen T.R. drunk. And T.R. was spectacularly soused today. It took several seconds for T.R. to regain his composure. He let go of the railing. He patted each of his vest pockets until he at last found his glasses, put them on and peered down curiously at the goings-on around the card table. "A teenager!" he hollered finally, as the cobwebs in his head cleared and he spotted Joey. "A damn teenager. What's he doing in here in my joint?"

"I caught this kid snoopin' around, T.R.," answered the man in the gray vest. "Caught him foolin' around with our cars, out in the garage. Stickin' his fingers where they don't belong."

Billy slapped his cards face-down on the table and looked at Joey in astonishment. "Joey! What the hell? I never told you to come here. Beat it! We got stuff to do here. We're busy."

"We had a deal, a bet, Billy. Remember?" Joey, regaining his composure somewhat, got up and put his hands on his hips. Now, despite the threats from the three men he'd encountered, he felt anger welling up in him, not fear. What was a dollar? Joey knew the value of a buck. That was what men at the foundry in St. Jay earned for two hours of hard labor. It was what he, in fact, earned for five hours of work on Saturdays at the cash market. He stooped to brush the dirt off the knees of his pants, looked up and continued. "Look—you bet a dollar, a whole buck, I couldn't make it to town on your old bike, all the way up to Coughlin's, but you weren't there. Mr. Larsen figured you might be here. That's why I'm here. To collect."

There were howls of laughter from Billy's fellow players and the men who'd dragged Joey into the building. "Good luck collecting, young man!" said the thug in the blue suit. "He's losin' bad! He's apt to be a bit short today. He's quite the wheel-man, but he ain't much of a card shark. So, you really are his brother, huh?"

"Look, Dutch, he's my little brother. What's it to you?" groused Billy. The man shrugged, shook his head and stuck his hands into his pockets. Joey feared that one of those hands might reappear at any moment—with a gun in it.

T.R. had been watching silently the whole while. No doubt in order to keep the room from spinning, he sat down on the stairs in order to clear his head a bit, and now he spoke. "Billy Ross? You set a fine example." He removed his glasses from their perch on his nose, pulled a white hanky from a pocket and polished the spectacles' lenses as if they were gem stones.

He put the glasses back on and shook his head to clear his vision, which was playing tricks on him, and he admitted it: "Both of you! I thought there was perhaps *some* honor among thieves!" He roared with laughter at this, and then said, "Pay your brother. Now, Dutch: you and Ace; get him out of here fast and get his ass back on the highway."

There were three quarters and a dime on the table next to Billy's cards. Billy pitched the dime to Joey, who caught it and glared at his brother. "It's all I can do; these stiffs are killing me here," Billy complained. "I'll make it right with you later."

"Yeah, don't take the loss of a dime so bad, Ross," said Dutch, lighting up a cigarette and snickering at Billy. "You got to pay your kid brother. Look at it like a kind of tax. You don't pay your taxes, you get into trouble, just like what happens if you don't pay your loans on time. Hey, look what they just did to Capone for not paying his taxes, right?"

Billy glared at him. "C'mon, Dutch. You and Ace take a hike, and put my brother back where you found him. And he'd better make it home tonight—in one piece."

"Okey kid," growled Dutch to Joey. "Let's take a little walk."

* * *

Dutch and Ace strongarmed Joey back outside. He wriggled free of them and stuck his elbows into their sides. "I can walk by myself just fine!" he snapped.

"Look, pal," said Dutch. "I'm sorry. No hard feelings, kid, okay? We didn't know you were really Billy's brother. He's a good egg, and he can keep his yap shut; we trust him, and he's one of the best wheelmen up this way we know of."

"Wheelmen?"

"Wheelman. Like us, Ace and me, see? We're drivers. Delivery boys. We pick up and deliver packages, goods, only we don't drive around no stiffs like he does now and then."

Joey halted to turn and look at Dutch, as Dutch tossed away his cigarette butt into some bushes. "Now and then? But that's all he does."

"Oh, I see; got it," remarked Dutch. He rolled his eyes as he glanced over at Ace as they walked along toward the garage, where Joey's bike was leaned up against the wall. Ace shook his head. "He just does some stuff on the side, that's all." The man in the gray fedora was leaning against the wall also, watching them approach. "Like us."

"Where are you guys from?" asked Joey inquisitively, his brow furrowed.

"Me, I'm from Saratoga," answered Dutch. "Ace, here, he's from Albany. We're independent contractors. You could say we moonlight off our regular jobs. We come up here every couple of weeks or so. It's a nice, quiet, healthy little place to visit." He stopped and pointed to the bike. "There you are." He pulled aside his gray vest and patted the wooden grips of a snub-nose revolver tucked into his waistband. "Be nice. You be quiet, too. Nice and quiet." He paused and put a thumb and forefinger up to his lips as if to zip them shut. Then he smiled, a thin, cruel smile and added, "And believe me, if you do, you'll stay healthy. And so will your brother. You know what they say; you got your health? Your health is everything." Then Dutch, Ace and the third man were gone, stalking off into the pine forest, joking and laughing as they went.

The more he thought about his brother, the more Joey realized how little he really *knew* about his brother. And perhaps how little Billy really thought of Joey. Billy, it seemed, was for Billy—all in. Joey was out.

Joey turned to look at his bike in time to see the beagle slinking away from it, and now there was a puddle under the rear tire—and both the rear and the front tires were flat. He looked closely and was relieved to see that the tires hadn't been slashed; the third man must have let the air out of them.

Still shaken by Dutch's thinly-veiled threat, Joey wheeled his bike around to the front of the filling station; the wooden chair was empty and the old, one-armed man was nowhere to be seen. Joey grabbed the air hose and pumped up the front tire. He had just started to fill the rear one when he felt a heavy hand fall on his right shoulder and squeeze so hard that he thought his collarbone would break. He quickly turned his head and came face-to-face with the grizzly, grumpy old man. "I told you, dammit all, air ain't free, not for nobody!" the old man fumed. "This'll cost you one thin dime. Pay up. Now. Or you ain't goin' nowhere."

Chapter 8

The Bucket of Blood

After supper, as soon as he was able to, Billy quietly let himself out of the house. Catherine had called him right after he'd gotten home, and asked him what time he'd be ready to meet her to go out on the town. He was unaware that Joey had arrived from work just in time to overhear every detail of the brief conversation from where he stood, around the corner from the hallway telephone. The windows were open, as they had been all afternoon, and now, as Billy walked away from the front porch toward town, he suddenly heard the rumble of laughter. It was coming from the big, floor model radio in the parlor, where Bud had tuned in to the Saturday night radio broadcast of Jack Benny's comedy show and was sitting comfortably in an armchair.

Beth, who had looked upset at supper, had excused herself early on and retreated to the bathroom. Later on, after the meal was finished and as he and the boys cleared the table, Bud had mumbled something to them about his understanding that Beth was undergoing "the change in life" and that she might need some privacy. And that was all he had said, although it was obvious to them that she'd been crying. Indeed, no one—including Bud, blissfully unaware as usual of any such occurrence evolving into a crisis—heard her now over the sound of the radio as she locked the bathroom door, sagged against the sink, sobbed and began to draw a hot bath for herself in the clawfoot tub.

While Billy didn't expect to be asked where he was going or what time he'd come home, he nonetheless didn't want to risk having any such conversations taking up his time while he was on the move and the night was young. Time, after all, was one of Billy's most valuable commodities. Like money, he wanted to spend it where and when he chose, not having it usurped and wasted by anyone—including his parents and his brother.

Stepping along briskly in his dress shoes usually reserved for funeral duty, he walked three blocks over to Portland Street. He spotted Catherine at last, sitting in a square, dowdy-looking Oldsmobile coupe parked along the sidewalk near a street light. That she had driven the Olds here tonight was a good omen; it was her mothers' car and when Catherine used it instead of her father's new, smart-looking Buick, it was a sure sign that both parents were away on extended travel. Billy ran his mind over several possible scenarios that involved staying out late—very late, tonight—before he approached the car and tapped on the passenger side window. Catherine leaned over from the driver's seat, smiled at him and unlocked the door; Billy opened it, heaved himself onto the seat, scooted over and availed himself of an armload of sufficiently-coiffed and nicely-perfumed Catherine.

"I was worried that you weren't going to come," she said softly. She reached over and straightened the collar of his white shirt. "It was starting to get late."

"Family business," said Billy dismissively. "You know how it is. They're hanging all over you all the time whenever you're in the house. You don't have five minutes to yourself." Catherine nodded in sympathy. Billy nudged her playfully and leered at her. "Hey—aren't we going to dance tonight? Or are you gonna hang out here on the street by yourself, soliciting?"

"Oh, William Ross! You are awful!" screamed Catherine. Then she laughed and kissed Billy.

"There. Now, that little deed will cost you five whole dollars, mister. And if you want the works, well, you'd better be able to pay tonight. Hmmm?"

"Let me see," mumbled Billy. He made a show of rummaging through his pockets. Out of one of them came a few crisp bills and a handful of quarters. Out of another came even more quarters. "That good enough for us to have a good time with?"

"Where did you get all that?" she asked. While Catherine came from money, she seldom saw it; someone else paid all the bills.

"I robbed a bank, Catherine," Bill chuckled. "A small one." He pointed a thumb back over his shoulder at the opposite side of Portland Street. "Let's go have some fun and spend it." From across the street, the sounds of fun—loud music and raucous laughter—beckoned; they flowed from several open second-floor windows of what Billy knew to be a dance hall, situated in a large, rough-looking wood-frame building; in its ground floor, the rolling thunder of bowling balls knocking down ten pins could be heard. Next door to it was a dimly-lit restaurant; smells of greasy food wafted from its screen door. Billy jumped out of the car, quickly walked around it and grabbed Catherine's arm just as she got out, urging, "Let's go, doll."

"A bowling alley?" asked Catherine. "You took me roller skating across the street the last time we were down here, and then to the diner downtown. I thought maybe we were having dinner somewhere—someplace nice tonight. So, now, we're going bowling?" She looked confused. And a little a disappointed.

"No, we're going upstairs. Dancing. There's a hot band up there tonight, the Catamount Mountain Ramblers. We can get some eats up there and have a few drinks. Eh?" He looked about to make sure no one was watching him, and tugged open one side of his suit coat. With the other hand, he slyly pulled a small silver flask just high enough out of a pocket so that Catherine could see it, and then put it back. He gave her a smile of smug satisfaction at having taken care of providing an important part of the evening's entertainment. Most of which would probably be his.

"What is that place?" she asked, peering at it. "I don't even see a sign on the building."

"That," answered Billy, "is The Bucket of Blood."

* * *

One of the better-known credos of old-time Vermonters, handed down through generations of families like well-worn pairs of pants that are patched up and a bit ragged around the edges, but are still too good to discard, is this one: "If something was good enough for grandpa, then it's still good enough for you."

True, that may have been the reason why not only Grandpa Will's baggy old shirts and moth-eaten sweaters, but also his red union suits (the so-called "long johns" that nearly all men wore during winter in the chill environs of the Kingdom) were handed down—first, to Bud—later on, to Billy—and finally to Joey, long after Will's passing and shortly before Joey entered school. But that credo might also have been the reason why so many households in the North Country—as was the case with the Ross family's—were reluctant to demolish the family outhouse, even after indoor plumbing had been installed.

Thus, the little structure remained, a nod to 19th century architecture, a humble little privy in the back yard that remained idle, for the most part. It was visited on occasion, however, by the male members of the Ross family during times when Beth's friends came by to play bridge late into the evening on

Friday nights, tying up the bathroom for interminable periods of time, or otherwise during the afternoons when Aunt Josie and Aunt Sue came by to visit.

Like the fanciful jug of moonshine with a cork stuck in its neck at a jaunty angle, the lone wooden sap bucket hung hopefully on a maple tree come March, or the once-familiar sight of a hardy side hill farmer coaxing his straining team to drag a plow through the rocky soil of a forbidding landscape, a few outhouses remained as icons of Vermont's bygone days, partly due to their owners' sentimentality—also because an outhouse can be a place of near monastic solitude—where one may go to sit and think. Thus, the outhouse in the Ross family's backyard survived, despite its lack of amenities and the fact that its seat was no more than a rough board with a hole cut into it. But—be that as it may, just one splinter—and the owner's well-felt affinity for the classic outhouse might well have been over.

The small structure had little in the way of accoutrements—a roll of toilet tissue and an ancient Sears catalogue; its tattered pages as much for possible use as toiletry as they were for reading enjoyment. A wooden peg on the wall served as a hook for the kerosene lantern one would have to bring along for illumination after sunset. And it was inside this outhouse, later on that night, that Joey sat after answering the call of nature, engrossed in thought; Beth was still occupying the bathroom.

Joey thought about his brother. And then, the realization came to him: Billy was for Billy. Joey had had only one quarrel with him. It had gone on almost all of his 17 years.

Billy, the charmer and teller of tall tales. Billy, the smooth-talker, who could talk you into playing his game like a carny pitch man. Like the young, slick fellow commanding a tent at the big fair over in Tunbridge Joey had seen last fall, a huckster who was egging on people to hurry up and put their hard-earned nickels and dimes down on big numbers painted on a counter and play a game of chance to win a fortune—one described as so large they'd need two strong men and a boy to help carry it home. Then, smiling broadly and cranking his arm, the pitch man wearing a straw boater hat at a jaunty angle had spun the big wheel that went clacking around and around—then slowing down, down, down, while every person who had bet money held his breath, eyes pinned on the whirling wheel for the final countdown.

All the while, the rank smoke from a hundred frying hamburgers and hot dogs, a thousand lit cigarettes and millions of sparks from fireworks exploding overhead wafted through the tent like an acrid, blue-gray cloud, while little children ran wild and screamed with delight outside as they dodged each other and swung around on the ropes that grounded the tent, as if they were hordes of mischievous circus monkeys. Bellied-up to the counter inside were wide-eyed farm boys in sweat-stained flannel shirts and patched-up overalls with manure on their boots—rubes fresh off the farm, sucking on straws; unshaven men in battered gray fedoras smoking evil-smelling cigars, thumbs tucked into their suspenders, talking in low voices confidently and smelling of beer; dandies from down country in white dress shirts, slacks and shiny spats, all excited about betting their money, their wives tapping them on their shoulders, tugging at their belts and pestering them to quit while they were still ahead and to go home with them.

Billy's deceptive practices started late one night many years ago—so many that it was back when old Grandpa Will, long of beard and well along in years, was still alive and had the bedroom Joey now occupied. That was in the days when Joey and Billy shared a bedroom whose only window looked out onto the back yard. It was Christmas Eve, and Joey, excited as he was about the prospects of Santa visiting, had nonetheless fallen asleep after urging Billy to wake him up if he saw any sign of Saint Nick's arrival. "Of course I will, brother!" he promised.

And it was only a few short hours later, in the dead of night, when Joey was awakened by Billy's voice, as urgent as it could be while being kept to a whisper. "Joey! Joey! Get up! I heard a noise and looked out the window. There's an old man with a white beard out back, and he's wearing a red suit! He's heading for the house! I think it's him!" Billy stretched out one leg, kicked Joey's bed for emphasis and thereby shook him completely out of his dreams.

Joey had flung the covers back off his bed, hopped out and lunged over to the window, where a tiny circle of frost had been scraped away, presumably by his brother in making this startling discovery. The floor was so cold it made the soles of his bare feet sting, but he nonetheless stayed, pressing his face to the ice-encrusted window as he stared in wonder at the figure shambling along a pathway between snowbanks in the yard. Caught in the feeble yellow glow of the back porch light and seen through the peephole, there, indeed, was Santa. The figure was portly, clad in red and topped with a red cap, and the man had a long white beard. Joey emitted a whoop of delight, sped toward the bedroom door, tumbled down the stairway, ran across the living room and into the kitchen where, just as the back door opened, he came face-to-face with grumpy old Grandpa Will. Will, having just visited the outhouse, was wearing his red union suit. A page torn from a Sears catalogue was stuck to the sole of one of his boots. "Go back to bed, young man," he grumbled, "or Santa ain't stoppin' here tonight."

Fool me once, shame on you. Fool me twice, shame on me.

Joey's reverie was interrupted by the sound of footsteps coming down the walkway from the house, and then the sound of someone knocking on the rough-hewn boards of the outhouse door. "Billy!" came a young woman's voice from the other side. "Billy! Is that you in there?"

Joey coughed, cleared his throat, and tried to think. Fast. "Who is it?" he asked in a low voice, checking to make sure the door was locked. It was.

"It's me, Doris. Doris Martin. C'mon, I know you're in there. Your dad said you'd gone out. And we were going to go out tonight—Saturday, you said—remember? You promised last week. So, hurry up—whatever it is you're doing in there." She giggled, and waited, but there was no response. Now, Doris drummed her fingers on the door impatiently.

"Oh, I can't," mumbled Joey at last, doing his best to imitate the sound of his brother's voice. "I'm sick—really sick." He groaned and moaned, then went silent, trying hard not to laugh.

"Let me in, Billy. Come on, I need to see you. It won't be the first time I've seen you with your pants down." She laughed, and pounded on the door. "You can't be that bad off."

"I am. You've got to believe me," grunted Joey. "I am sorry, darling," he added.

"Darling? You've never called me that!"

"You're the best, kid," whispered Joey. "It's just that—oh, I've never gotten this sick. I'm so sorry, but I can't go out with you tonight. I'll make it up to you somehow."

"But," she began.

"No," grunted Joey. You can't see me like this."

"Billy Ross, did you drink too much? Did you already get soused today?" Doris queried, starting to become very annoyed. Whatever his problem, she realized Billy was obviously not himself tonight, and that was putting a damper on their dalliance—and Doris's social life, insofar as what other things she had planned for the evening.

"No. Couldn't hold a drink if I wanted to." Joey moaned as if in distress. "You'd better get out of here."

"Okay, Billy, I think I will," replied Doris, pouting and crossing her arms. She took a step back and for a moment considered kicking the door down, but thought better of it. She wasn't sure whether to believe Billy or not. "But if you're skunking me, well, I'll never forgive you. You just think about that." Then, there came the sounds of footsteps as she strode off down the back yard pathway in a huff. Joey breathed a sigh of relief as he put one eye to a crack between two boards just in time to see her turn the corner and stalk off down the street.

From the living room of the house came a ripple of laughter and then a round of applause booming from Bud's radio as *The Jack Benny Show* continued. Then, Joey started to laugh. He laughed all the way through the commercial for Canada Dry nature water by the glass, which Benny said he didn't need to tell the audience about because they knew about it already.

This time, the joke would be on Billy, Joey thought. And while Billy was just about through with Doris, which Billy knew deep down already, Doris didn't. But she would know—soon enough.

* * *

The polished hardwood floor of The Bucket of Blood fairly heaved with all the couples swaying, weaving and spinning to the smooth, two-four rhythm of the latest western swing music as the Catamount Mountain Ramblers played on into the night. Even after the band took its second break, the lights were dimmed and a few slow numbers were played, still more young couples packed themselves into the hallway outside and soon appeared at the door, paid the 25 cent per person admission fee and entered a fog of cigarette smoke and a funk that was a steamy melting pot of cheap perfume, pungent after-shave and alcohol; it reeked of gaiety and good times— while they lasted.

On one side of the cavernous old dance hall, a few orange dots glowed sporadically in a dark corner where young men who'd come to the hall "stag" smoked cigarettes and silently passed around a bottle of whiskey, taking a sip here and there in order to get their courage up. Those who succeeded would now and then walk onto the floor to tap the shoulder of a fellow dancing with a particularly pretty girl and cut in. Over on the other side were the powdered-up dance hall girls, the taxi dancers who'd oblige other, more bashful fellows who'd arrived single for a dime a dance, and no funny stuff. They'd take cash or they'd accept tickets (which the dance hall sold) and the cut with the house was 50/50 on the proceeds. The band played on.

As Billy swung Catherine around, he briefly lifted a hand to wave to two men he knew, standing in the corner with another he didn't recognize. Catherine felt the brief absence of his fingers, and not without a tinge of suspicion, asked: "Who'd you wave to?"

"Oh, just two guys over there I know, Tom and Seth," said Billy dismissively. "They do odd jobs for Junior; the other guy in the suit with them, I don't."

Over in the dark recesses of the stag corner, the man in the suit nudged Tom while pointing to Billy and Catherine. "Think I stand a chance of cutting in and taking a whirl with that dame?"

"Dunno," Tom answered diplomatically. "You know what they say in baseball: 'You can't hit if you don't swing.'"

Billy felt a hand come down—not very gently—on his left shoulder. With Catherine in his arms, he swung around and came face to face with a high school classmate he'd not seen in several years: Steve Snyder. He'd been big trouble—not for Billy, but for a lot of other kids—before he'd been expelled in his senior year. He wondered where Steve had been all this time—and why he was back in town, of all places, right now. "Mind if I cut in?" asked Steve, slightly slurring the words as he looked over at Catherine—and looked her over.

"She's my date, but okay, pal," answered Billy. "Just for old times' sake." There was no sense in refusing him; the well-dressed Steve, Billy realized, was probably drunk. It wouldn't do to make a scene and get thrown out of the hall. After all, a barrel-chested man who worked at a local factory as a guard, Austin, six foot one and tough as nails, moonlighted here as a bouncer. He stood over in another corner looking like a watchful grizzly bear sniffing the air, eyeing the goings on for any trouble, sporadically cracking his knuckles. Billy didn't want to provoke him into using them. Catherine shot a quizzical look at Billy as Steve spun unsteadily away with her into the crowd on the dance floor, then looked at Steve and managed to produce a wan smile while keeping her new partner at a judicious arm's length. When she looked into his eyes, dark and pitiless, it was like looking into the eyes of a shark.

Billy noticed that one of the taxi dancers was waving to him, so he walked over to her. A chat with another woman would break things up and ease the tension he felt, now that Steve had waltzed off with his prized possession. He also wanted to breathe in some of the cool evening air blowing in through the open window, and rest his aching feet; Junior's funeral-best shoes apparently weren't meant for dancing. "Remember me?" asked the woman. Her black hair was bobbed, her green eyes heavily outlined. She was chewing gum, and she tapped one foot to the beat of the music as she tugged her skirt up a bit.

"Yeah, sure I do," answered Billy, although he was struggling to remember. Then, it came to him. Something about meeting her several years ago—on hot summer night, the first time he'd gotten drunk, and a fumbling tryst in the back seat of a DeSoto. Maybe. Unlike the way it was with new cars, which were distinctive and classy-looking, the older women all seemed drab and looked alike to him. He glanced out the open window behind her in time to see an attractive-looking young woman walking down the sidewalk below. Something about her was familiar, much more so than the face and figure of the dance hall maven. And then he realized who it was. It was Doris. How true; he could always recognize the newer models.

"Who are you looking at now?" asked the dancer, peeved. Billy shook his head.

"Just someone I thought I knew, that's all," he said, lying promptly and easily. In fact, he had known Doris for a couple of years, and now, things were pretty much over between Billy and her. One of his stand-by girlfriends he kept on reserve, once Catherine came onto the scene, Doris hadn't been discarded, but she'd certainly been circling the drain lately. Then another thing occurred to him; she'd asked him about going out a week or so ago. He'd said, "Sure, maybe Saturday." But of course, he didn't say which one, or at what time. She probably wouldn't understand if he stood her up, but he didn't much care right now, either. So, it all worked out for him.

The band stopped playing, and Catherine came hightailing over to Billy. "Billy, he mopped the floor with me!" she exclaimed breathlessly. "Let's get out of here." A man in a red jacket got up on the small stage where the Catamount Mountain Ramblers were, and announced that the last dance number was next. He then began the ritual of passing his hat around, collecting tips for the band.

"Pony up, ladies and gents, for the best darned dance band in the Kingdom!" he bellowed. "Let's hear it for the Ramblers!" Cheers and applause erupted as loose change and the occasional half-dollar or dollar bill got stuffed into the man's fedora as it made its way around the hall.

"Oh, Catherine, don't let him spoil our night out. It's the last dance, our last dance. I'll warn him off if comes back and bugs us." He grabbed her hand and steered her out onto the dance floor as the band began to play again. And then Steve wandered over to them, and began to reach out to Billy to cut in.

"Nothing doing, Steve," Billy barked at him. "She's my date; shove off." He and Catherine spun around and tried to dance away from him. He followed.

"You don't run this joint, and you two aren't married. What's the big deal, chump?" he groused. "You've been hogging the floor with her all night. Give me another turn."

"You'll get a turn all right," Billy warned. "You'll get turned upside down if you don't shove off like I said. Now, beat it!" Steve reached out, this time shoving Billy away from Catherine. Other dancers moved away, sensing a fracas was about to take place; they were right. Catherine made her escape and none too soon. Billy staggered backward, but after recovering he lunged at Steve, fists clenched. And then the grizzly bear, Austin, jumped in between the two men.

"You two knock it off, right now," he growled, pushing them apart. Steve lost his balance momentarily, then regained it and grappled with Austin. The big man grabbed one of Steve's arms and started to twist it to force him into submission. But, with his free hand, Steve deftly pulled a knife from one of his pockets, and a long, lethal-looking blade quickly shot out of it; he took a swipe at Austin's arm, ripping the sleeve of his shirt. A deep, red stain quickly appeared as Austin dropped Steve's arm and bellowed in pain.

"I'll get you for that, kid!" he roared, clutching his wound. But Steve had already gotten away, running toward one of the back windows. The band played on, despite the rumpus, and two men sitting out the last dance on the sidelines speculated about what would happen next.

"I'll bet Austin thumps that kid pretty good," posited one, "and throws him out by his ears."

"He looks pretty handy with that knife. Maybe he'll cut off Austin's big old ears," said the other. "I wondered when a fight was finally going to break out. Hell, I've never seen a Saturday night here when there wasn't one."

Just then, Steve brushed past them, on his way quickly grasping the hat with the band's tip money from an astonished woman who had been placing a dollar into it. He quickly crushed the old fedora into some semblance of a parcel to contain the cash, and jumped out the closest open window onto the fire escape. Then, he was gone.

"Who is that kid, anyway?" pondered the first man, still sitting in his chair.

"I hear he's from out of town, up Lyndonville way," said the second fellow as the band stopped playing. "They say he's a crazy man behind the wheel. Runs the roads with those other punks at night. Got danger written all over him." Looking back over his shoulder as he got up and shuffled off toward the door, he added a few more words of wisdom: "In fact, I think that kid's just plain crazy. One of these days, he's going to kill someone...if he hasn't already."

Chapter 9

Beaten to the Punch

"My dad would go absolutely insane if he knew we were here together right now." Lila dabbled her feet in the river after she peevishly said this, then looked up at Joey. She pouted, and with good reason: summer was coming to an end and with it, fewer opportunities such as this one to see him. It was difficult enough right now as it was. Today, they had once more shared the sagging front seat of Sam Rivard's wheezing old delivery truck, while Joey made his rounds near Lyndonville.

Now they were sharing another seat, a large rock that jutted out into the slow-flowing waters of a popular swimming hole. Long rays of late afternoon sunshine filtered at a steep angle through tall trees that shielded the spot from view of the road. It was a scant hundred or so feet from where the rough timbers of a covered bridge carried Lyndonville's Center Street across the snakelike course of the Passumpsic River. The passage of the occasional car over the rickety-looking whitewashed structure made its ancient floorboards rumble and thump, but otherwise, there was little noise other than bird song from above, or the sounds of water burbling peacefully along.

As popular as this little spot was with the locals on sunny August days like this when the temperatures soared and young people came to plummet into the cool water, Lila and Joey were the only two people there, and today they enjoyed this little bit of heaven as if it were their own private beach. Joey scrunched his toes deeper into the cool river mud, feeling the water flow around his ankles, and smiled. He picked up a small stone, and skipped it across the water.

"Yeah, well, maybe a little," he replied. He turned and looked at her as she pulled her feet out of the river and brushed droplets of moisture off one ankle.

"Oh, a little? Maybe *just* a little? Are you kidding me?" she blustered. She stuck her face into his until they were nose-to-nose. She popped her green eyes wide-open, as if for extra emphasis. "The only person I've heard of who's just a *little* insane around town is old man T.R. Donovan. And maybe your brother is, too, for hanging out at his place!" She giggled, and poked him in the ribs. Joey had taken his shirt off, and Lila took advantage of this display of Joey's anatomy to quickly tickle a few of his ribs. "Look at those ribs! I swear; someone should iron those out!" she squawked, before convulsing in laughter.

"Stop! Oh my God, your hands are cold!" he hollered in protest.

"I'll stop if you stop hollering," Lila replied. She stuck her chin out and held her head up, posing as if she were a bratty small child. "If you keep yelling, someone'll call the cops. Then they'll call my dad. He'll find out where we are and he'll come down and thump you. Deal?"

"Okay, deal!" Joey said at last, laughing out loud. Once he had settled down, he frowned and asked, "But what *do you* know about T.R. and his place? I dropped in there not too long ago to see Billy on the same day I met your dad. A couple of the guys there—I don't know who they were—were going to rough me up just because I walked into the place, and he called them off. Billy doesn't tell me much about anything he does, either there or anyplace else. And, by the way," Joey added, "I think your dad was going to rough me up, too, but I talked him out of it."

"Joey, you don't know much about this town, do you?" Lila asked. Joey shrugged.

"Like what?"

"Like, if you got into real trouble with guys like the ones who hang out at T.R.'s, you might not be able to talk your way out of it."

"Why?" queried Joey. He reached around for his shirt; it was getting late, and he knew that he should get back on the job.

"I can't tell you." Lila blinked, turned away from him.

"So, you know, but..." asked Joey, puzzled.

"Like I said, I can't. Just be careful. You can see others just like them hanging around any late afternoon, raising hell and bothering people on Depot Street in town. Before they get in their big fancy cars after dark and drive like hell all night."

"You mean, then, they're gangsters? Booze runners?"

Lila bobbed her head slightly. "There," she said. "I didn't tell you."

Joey stared at her, letting this revelation sink in before finally saying: "Okay. I understand. I'm glad I'm not in over my head." He sighed, momentarily scratched his chin, as if in deep thought, and then asked, "Say, want to go in one last time?"

She nodded and scrambled to her feet, looking as tall and skinny as an axe handle in her baggy shorts and scruffy, hand-me-down blouse. She flipped her long brown hair back over one shoulder and put on her battered old straw hat as Joey, broad-shouldered and sturdy for a boy of 17 going on 18 also got to his feet, rolled the legs of his pants up a bit farther than they were, and then took Lila's hand. They waded casually into the water, almost out to its middle and then stood facing each other, closer together than they ever had been. There were no gangsters, jealous fathers, troublesome brothers or worrisome mothers for them out here. The water swirled and gurgled pleasantly around them, carrying away whatever worries they had brought with them to some place downstream, where they no longer mattered to anyone, anyone at all.

* * *

After Joey dropped Lila off at the corner market and went his way, heading back to St. Johnsbury, she entered the store and gathered the items on the shopping list she had brought along: frankfurters, a half-dozen eggs, a loaf of bread, a head of lettuce, and a small glass bottle of milk. At the front counter, she briefly removed her old, broad-brimmed straw hat, gathered her hair up into a pony tail, and put it back on before signing a slip for the purchases on her father's account. "I like your hat, miss!" commented the white-aproned clerk as he placed the groceries in the cloth sack Lila had brought along; he smiled and thanked her. Lila, as happy and lighthearted as an angel tap-dancing on a cloud, waltzed out the door, turned the corner and headed home east along Depot Street, thinking only about Joey—after all, was there anyone else for her to think about? She ambled along, almost in a trance and didn't notice them—the slick, well-dressed hoodlums she had warned Joey about—lounging on the running boards, bumpers and fenders of several big out-of-state cars parked on her side of the street. Townsfolk going about their downtown business were avoiding them, wisely using the sidewalk on the opposite side of the street.

The first of the hoods, a rakish-looking, well-dressed fellow, perhaps in his mid-20s, launched himself off the fender of a dark blue Lincoln he'd been sitting on and came strutting over to her. "Hey, Tomboy Sawyer!" he yelled. "Nice straw hat you've got there. You must be a country gal. I've been looking all over to find me a real country gal in this town." He started walking along close beside her. "Wanna dance?"

Lila stuck her nose up and ignored him. "Oh, giving me the cold shoulder, huh?" groused the man. Lila walked a little bit faster. So did he. He turned and waved to four or five others of his kind who were standing around their cars, smoking. "Lookee here, boys! She's being standoffish!"

"What's Little Red Riding Hood there got in the bag?" hollered one of them. He headed toward Lila and the others followed him. Soon, they were stepping along close behind her. "I could use a snack before I head down-country."

"Whose girlfriend is she?" asked another one.

"Who cares?" asked another. "She ain't mine. Look at those legs of hers. I've seen legs like that before—on a Steinway." There were guffaws of laughter from the whole pack of men.

The first man stuck one arm out and lifted Lila's pony-tail. "Well, I'll be darned, fellows; look at this!" he exclaimed in mock surprise. "There *is* a horse under there after all!" The others howled with laughter, and now people passing by along the opposite side of the street stopped and stared in curiosity. Then, he dropped her hair and stuck his hand into the cloth bag; Lila tussled briefly with him before he yanked out the head of lettuce. He threw it to one of his pals, and then the men scattered around Lila, tossing it back and forth among themselves like a basketball in a team's practice session.

"Nah, guess she doesn't want to play ball with us," the man groused. "Tisk, tisk!" Lila walked on a bit faster. Then, despite Lila's efforts, he pulled the half-dozen eggs from the bag. But Lila was able to intercede, grasp the flimsy cardboard package, and crush it against the man's head. A mass of egg yolks and goo ran down his face and onto his dress shirt, silk tie and dress trousers. And that was when Lila saw her chance and kicked him.

"You little bitch!" swore the man, as his pals roared with laughter. And then, he slapped her. Lila dropped the sack, turned and ran like a deer—ran several blocks to Coughlin's establishment to shed a volume of tears and tell her father, Sven, what had happened.

* * *

About 15 minutes later, the editor of the local weekly newspaper, the *Passumpsic Chronicle* was working at his roll-top desk in the paper's second-story office on Depot Street. Frustrated by finding himself at loose ends while trying to compose his editorial for the next edition, he was distracted by a commotion he heard going on in the street below. He asked his wife, who was sitting next to the nearest open window what was going on. She set aside the glue pot and scissors on the layout table, wiped her hands on her apron and peered out the window at what appeared to be a fight taking place on the sidewalk. "I think you'd better come here and see for yourself, Ed," she said in a distressed voice.

The editor, a seasoned sports reporter before he had bought the newspaper, knew a free-for-all brawl when he saw one. He looked out the window just in time to see Sven Larsen deliver a knockout blow to a well-dressed young man, and then toss his limp body into the back of an open Buick touring car as if he were a rag doll. On the sidewalk lay another man, arms and legs splayed out as if he had been run over by a steamroller. Three more lay motionless, draped in various positions like corpses over the fenders of as many cars parked along the curb. Their hats, crushed and dented, lay on the sidewalk among a scattering of groceries and shards of glass from a broken milk bottle. A small knot of spectators had gathered around the scene a respectable distance away from it. "Should I call the sheriff?" asked the editor's wife.

"No need to," he replied, as he grabbed a reporter's notepad and prepared to hustle downstairs, his editorial now quickly taking shape in his mind. "Looks like Sven Larsen's beaten him to the punch, and cleaned up all the down-country, hooligan riffraff in this town."

Chapter 10

Things Get Complicated

"It's beautiful. Just beautiful. It's a wonderful stretch of land. I wish I owned some. Maybe all of that spread down there." Billy gazed off into the distance after saying this. His eyes feasted on the panoramic view of the rolling hillsides and the lush, green valley far below the large, lavishly-appointed house where Catherine's parents lived in relative splendor. It was where he, Billy, was sitting together with Catherine, drinking ice-cold gin beside the pool. Catherine's parents were away in Canada on this sweltering hot August weekend, and no one—not even the worst gossip in town—was the wiser for Billy spending some recreational time here, hanging his hat on Catherine's northwest corner bedpost and raiding the family's well-stocked liquor cabinet for good measure while he was staying over, indulging himself in the same kind of discrete pastimes Catherine enjoyed, too.

Closer to him, about a mile away and downhill from the Hollingsworth estate, the twin red silos of old man Silas's farm could be seen, poking up from behind a dense forest of tall pine trees. Just beyond the broad spread of the spiky green woodland that clutched the rocky hillside, the landscape opened up and Billy could see the tiny specks of dairy cows meandering about it on an open stretch of verdant pastureland. He had emerged from the pool and toweled off just a few minutes ago, but errant drops of water still trickled down his calm, unwrinkled forehead, much like the beads of moisture that dripped down the smooth sides of the glass he was drinking from; as usual, there were no worries or cares for him to deal with here today. He gently shook the cool tumbler and swirled the ice around in it tentatively, watching the chunks swish around in the bottom, then raised it to his lips and drank until the ice gently nudged his teeth. By God, it had been quite a summer. It really had. And it was hot today. And, the gin was good. Billy finished draining his glass, placed it on the arm of his Adirondack chair and looked over at Catherine. The shards of leftover ice fizzed and popped as they quickly warmed to the late afternoon sunlight and began to melt.

"You know," she said, "we still have to talk."

"About—what?" responded Billy casually, although he was instantly on his guard. He picked up his glass and waved it gently, rocking what was left of the ice gently about inside it, as if asking for another drink, which would uncomplicate matters. Catherine, seated in a lounger less a foot or two away, shook her head at him.

"About me going back to college next week. And about us, and what I hope you do— 'til I get back for Christmas break in December."

"What about Thanksgiving?" Billy asked, waving one arm and bumping into the glass on his chair a bit clumsily. "You're not on break then?" He was feeling splendidly intoxicated and, until now, had been in a wonderful, relaxed mood. Now, he thought, things were going to get complicated. "Where did that go?"

"Billy, I told you before," explained Catherine, now beaming her brightest if somewhat condescending smile at him, "I'm going up to Quebec with my friends from the Ladies' Ski Club that week. We're going to take skiing lessons at a hotel near Saint-Sauveur. It's a whole bunch of us girls, and skiing's a new, sort of Norwegian sport we've been learning, going cross-country. Remember?" She had been swimming in the pool too, and now she wiggled in her lounger, settling further into it before she, too, finished her drink. The wet canvas seat squeaked its protests under her bottom until she was still.

"Oh, yeah, that's right," muttered Billy. He stared down into his glass, now empty, save for the ice that seemed to be disappearing as quickly as his vision of the future. "I guess you did tell me."

Christmas was a long way off. As far away as the moon, as far as Billy was concerned. And now, even the moonlight was getting dimmer.

"There's some man—a sportsman, I think—who wants to cut trails on the mountain and put in some kind of uphill tow line, so everyone who wants to can ski," Catherine added. "It's a new idea!" Then, she changed gears. "So, now—will you please sign my yearbook like I asked you to? You just don't know how much it means to me!" She picked up her copy of the yearbook from a glass-top table and thumbed through it. The yearbook was black, pebble-grained, and had a broad gold stripe running down one side of its cover. Over the faint aroma of juniper wafting from his glass, Billy could smell printer's ink, still fresh, on the pages of the college yearbook as Catherine flipped from one page to another before finding her junior-year class photograph.

"Here," she announced, handing the book to him. "Please tell me you'll be my true love until the moon and the stars don't shine! I want to see those words! I don't want it to be a secret any more!" Somehow, she had managed to quickly clip an ornate fountain pen, probably one of her father's expensive ones to the page. *Clever girl*, thought Billy. He smiled at her, nodded, took the yearbook, and placed it in his lap. For a moment, a picture flashed before him: Moses having the Ten Commandments handed down to him. He grasped the pen, opened it, and prepared to write. The book felt heavy. Very heavy.

When he had finished writing, he put the yearbook aside to let the ink dry. Catherine, meantime, had taken his glass inside to refill it. He gazed out at Silas's distant pastureland, where he could see the figure of a man, no doubt one of the farm hands, riding along in a farm wagon pulled by two sturdy-looking oxen that were yoked together. It was a marriage of kinds, a pairing borne of hard labor. The beasts strained and tugged as they pulled the heavily-laden wagon through the fields. Billy capped and replaced the pen, finding there was now a tight feeling all around his throat. Suddenly, for him, the future wasn't what he thought it would be just a few minutes before. But—another glass of gin would be sure to help.

* * *

"Whoa!" Joey seldom hollered at anyone and, in fact, seldom spoke when driving, but this time, it was necessary. Lila had scooted over to him on the seat of Sam's old truck and flung her left arm around his neck, clinging to him like an octopus trying to open up a clam. Joey flinched, and the truck wandered across the center line of the highway before he tugged at the wheel and brought the old Chevy under control. Lila let go, and tickled his right knee. Off the Chevy went again, this time skittering off to the right-hand side of the road. "Stop it!" he yelled, suppressing a giggle, "Before you get us both killed!"

"Oh, Joey, we'd make fine corpses then, wouldn't we?" she joked, pulling back and sitting up straight. She retreated to her side of the cab, gathered up her long hair, leaned up against the door and let her hair blow back outside the truck where it flailed like the tail of a speeding race horse. She pulled up her legs and sat cross-legged on the seat. Then, she stuck her head all the way out the window to enjoy the breeze for a moment, then popped her head back into the cab. "Your brother could set us up, side-by-side, the nicest dead couple you've ever seen!"

"Lila, if your father finds out we've been riding around together again, I'll be the only one Billy's laying out on a slab," Joey shot back. "C'mon. Now, what's our next stop? I can't remember."

"It's my uncle Hansen's farm," said Lila, looking at the list Sam had made out back in St. Johnsbury. "Way out on Kingdom Road." She looked up and suddenly realized where they were, exclaiming, "Oh, I'm sorry; turn! Turn right here!" Joey jabbed the brakes, yanked at the steering wheel and barely made the corner; the Chevy leaned far over as it heeled to the command and plowed through the curve, kicking up clouds of dust.

"Lila, you've got to give me a little more warning!" groused Joey. Then, after recovering his composure, he asked: "So, what does your uncle grow—if he's ordering lettuce, tomatoes and onions and other things from Sam?"

"He grows stuff," replied Lila. "He sugars, sells a little cordwood and he hays some, too, even though the cows are all gone, but he still grows some crops." Joey glanced at her, giving her an unsettled look that wavered between an indication of annoyance and one of intrigue. "I can show you—if he's not around." Joey's eyebrows shot up a tad; intrigue won out in the end. And then, she added this proviso: "But don't tell anything to anyone. You know what they say—curiosity killed the cat." A faint smile flickered on her lips, and then vanished.

The old truck ground up a short hill and slowed when Lila called out at spotting a rusty, battered mailbox surrounded by clusters of weeds and orange day lilies, so buried in the underbrush it was almost invisible. She told Joey to turn into the dirt driveway beside it that was flanked by two gnarled, badly-neglected apple trees. He did not fail to notice the boldly-lettered "No Trespassing" sign that was nailed to the post supporting the mailbox, nor these added, hand-lettered words: "Trespassers will be shot on sight. Survivors will be shot again." Joey could hear what sounded like a large and very aggravated dog barking from somewhere within the barnyard ahead.

He pulled the truck up beside a swaybacked old house that appeared as though it likely hadn't felt the touch of a paint brush since Joey's father had been born. Piled on the front porch beside what had once been a fine, overstuffed easy chair —now in tattered, mildewed ruins—stood a stack of egg cartons and an overturned wooden washtub. Almost immediately, a huge black dog lunged at the truck from a spot underneath the house's front porch and stopped just short of the truck's front fender. The chain tethering the animal went taut with an audible *snap* and the animal stood its ground after recovering from the jolt of the restraint, snarling at Joey. "That does it!" exclaimed Joey. "I'm not getting out; you shouldn't either!"

"Oh, don't be ridiculous!" laughed Lila. "He won't hurt you —that's Laurel. My uncle wouldn't hurt you either."

"How in the world do you know? For one thing, your uncle hasn't even met me yet."

"Because he's not even here," answered Lila.

"How do you know that?"

"Because, Laurel's only chained out here when Uncle Hansen's gone, and he takes Hardy, the other dog, with him. And," she added, "Hardy's the really mean one. The one that bites." Lila hopped out of the truck, ran around it and yelled at the big black dog. "Laurel! Laurel! Go lie down—now!" She clapped her hands together for emphasis and Laurel cringed, then quickly retreated to a spot underneath the porch, where the big animal laid down on the damp earth, yawned and sighed. "See?" asked Lila, turning toward Joey. "Look: he's all bark and no bite."

Eyeing the dog warily, Joey opened his door, climbed out and went around to the back of the truck, opened the twin rear doors and brought out the cardboard box containing Hansen Larsen's grocery order. "He left the money under the washtub on the porch," Lila called out, beckoning to him. "I'll get it if you'll just put the box inside the front door.

Still leery of Laurel, Joey walked gingerly up the steps to the porch. "Just look at you!" giggled Lila. "Still worried about old Laurel, aren't you!" Looking ridiculous, she flapped her arms up and down and clucked like a chicken to get his attention. Joey stuck his tongue out at her and turned away to hide his smile. Holding the repurposed banana box with his right arm, he grasped the handle of the dreary-looking home's baggy-looking screen door and pulled; the door's rusty hinges groaned in protest, and when he let go of the door and stepped into the dark front hallway—redolent of a house of horrors at a carnival, with its peeling wallpaper, cobwebbed lights and creaking floorboards—the door abruptly slammed shut behind him, sounding like a gunshot.

Joey set the box down on a rough wooden table. Beside it was an old rain slicker, perched on something propped against the wall—perhaps a broom. He bent over and looked to see what it had been draped over; it was a double-barreled shotgun. Lila's uncle, he reasoned, was either distinctly anti-social or else anticipated having to fend off the wrong kind of visitors. He turned, pushed aside the screen door and stepped onto the porch, letting the door hammer shut once more, and Lila handed him the money her uncle had left. Joey counted it, scribbled the word "paid" on the grocery invoice and handed it to Lila. "Here—better tuck that under the washtub where the money was. I guess your uncle has some systems here. I don't think I'd want to cross him."

Lila just smiled at him, snatched the piece of paper, knelt and stuck it under the washtub.

"There," she said, after standing up and dusting off her hands. "That'll make him happy."

"I don't think I'd want to see him when he's *unhappy*," ventured Joey, managing a wry smile.

"Now, are you ready to go?" he asked.

"No, Joey; you haven't seen the farm yet!" She tugged at his sleeve. "C'mon; I want to show you around this place. I used to play here when I was a little girl, back when Aunt Agony was alive. Knee-high to a grasshopper! We'd go out to the garden and pick peas and then we'd sit on the front porch—right over there—and shell them. And she'd talk to me in Swedish. And we picked tomatoes, too, and squash. And Uncle Hansen would come in from the fields for dinner and there'd be venison stew cooking on the stove. We'd have it with boiled peas from the garden and potatoes from the root cellar. It was so good!"

"Aunt Agony? That was her name?"

"No, it wasn't," explained Lila. "Her real name was Agnes. She always moaned and complained to everyone so much about her bad back, her rheumatism and bursitis and all that, so, well—someone just nicknamed her Agony. And it stuck."

"What did you uncle Hansen think about that?"

"Oh," replied Lila, giggling, "He liked that! He started calling her Agony, too!"

"I'll venture *she* didn't," observed Joey. Together, they walked beyond the old farmhouse and past a barn with a hogbacked roof of moss-covered cedar shingles. Its door gaped wide open like a huge animal's mouth, frozen in the midst of a yawn borne of long years lying idle, revealing empty stalls inside that might have held draft horses long ago. A rusty hayrack, its useful days well over, was propped up against the sagging barn like a lamed retiree in need of crutches, seeking support from a sympathetic old companion. All the farm's other outbuildings, too, seemed to share this symbiosis in a stage of tumbledown ruin.

Lila and Joey padded quietly along an overgrown pathway behind the barn, weaving their way through a jungle of weeds and improbably tall sunflowers where in the cool, shaded places, beneath where ash and maple trees had sprouted, sprung up and flourished, ferns brushed against their legs and ankles. Grape vines had overtaken some of the smaller trees and now a web of their slender runners and leaves had them in their over-running clutches, and in the dark places beneath them where their roots dwelled and prospered, ever branching out, there was a graveyard smell of damp earth and decay.

"I still don't see a garden," ventured Joey.

"Oh, you will." Lila turned to smile at him.

"So, is this some kind of secret?"

"It *is* a secret. *En hemlighet!*" Joey stopped in his tracks.

"What was that?"

"Swedish, for: a secret. Can you keep one?" The pair began walking along the pathway again, and came to a clearing.

"Yes, but..." Joey halted again at the sight of what he saw. A patch of land a few acres wide and long, studded with tall poles that had been driven into the ground. Stretched among them from their top-most reaches, reaching from pole-to-pole, was a network of barbed wire connecting them all. A multitude of lengths of heavy twine descended from the wires, and growing up each and every piece of twine was a heavy growth of green vines spiraling upward, bristling with things that looked like tiny pine cones. "What is all this?"

"Hops, Joey," explained Lila. "Uncle Hansen grows them, and people buy them. Brewers." Joey stared at her, dumbfounded. "Oh, c'mon! Hops. What they use to make beer. You know? He harvests them and puts a big crop up in the barn every fall. And then, my uncle sells them. The guys who brew beer buy them, and that's how he paid his mortgage; that's how he finally was able to keep the farm after the bank told him it was going to take it." Joey looked at Lila in amazement; all of a sudden, it made perfect sense as to why Lila's uncle would keep a shotgun by his front door, and why he would own two ferocious-looking dogs. And perfect sense why Lila's uncle could keep his hardscrabble farm going without raising any vegetables or doing any plowing or harvesting, and still afford to buy groceries from Sam Rivard, paying cash on the barrelhead. And perfect sense as to why Joey should keep his mouth shut about what he was looking at. All totally illegal, as everyone well knew, ever since Prohibition became law.

"En hemlighet?" asked Lila. Joey nodded. At that, they turned, joined hands and headed back to the barn. "I want to do one thing, one thing I do whenever I come here," she said. "It won't take long."

"What is it?" asked joey.

"Just a little something. You'll see. I'll bet you'll like to do it, too."

* * *

The massive beams in the wide-open space of the barn's loft were easily 14 or more inches square. Laid together end-to end, supported by posts below, they went the length of Hansen's barn. They served as the dividing line of the barn's two sides, and stretched across the space from the north wall to the south wall. Far below them and on one side were rows of empty stalls that smelled of dried, age-old manure and feed. Long-disused horse collars and bridles hung from rusty nails on their walls. On the opposite side was an enclosure filled with hay. It had been mowed, tedded and put up here before it went to seed, and the smell of that, too, wafted up to where Joey and Lila had ventured out onto the beam, one after another, tip-toeing along, arms held out, balancing themselves carefully. They occasionally wavered and corrected their course as they proceeded to the barn's midsection, like two amateur acrobats out on a circus wire for the first time. Then, they stopped to look down.

"So, this is where you want to jump?" Joey was a trifle nervous.

"Yes; I always did, right here. I never got hurt. The hay's deep enough."

"It's not the same hay, Lila; that was years ago. And, there could be a pitchfork down there."

He squirmed in anticipation of colliding with one—one that would be judiciously have been left aimed, however-inexplicably—upward.

"Oh, don't be such a silly goop, Joey! Nobody leaves a pitch-fork sticking upside-down in a hay mow." She pouted at him. "And, the hay's just as deep now as it was years ago," she replied. She crossed her arms and stood up on one leg. Then, she tried to copy a few moves that she had seen a ballerina do once, in a theatrical production. The sight began to make Joey dizzy. In a few seconds, he rationalized that the only way to do away with the impending sense of vertigo that was making his head spin was—to jump. "Look—the hay's way up to the top of that window down there," added Lila. "Ready?"

"Yes."

"Friends forever?" she asked.

"Forever, Lila!" affirmed Joey, smiling. They looked at each other briefly, then sprang off the beam, sailing silently down into the hay. The drop was quick, the landing soft, and they sank deeply into the hay. In up to his head, Joey clawed his way up to the surface where he found Lila just emerging. He stretched out his hand in an effort to claw his way toward her and it encountered something hard and metallic. He brushed a bit of the hay aside and saw something round, smooth and shiny beneath it. He cleared away more of it, and, digging deeper encountering a headlight.

"What is it?" Lila asked. "What did you find?"

"It's a car, of all things," answered Joey. "I'm lucky I didn't fall on it!" Joey brushed away more of the hay while Lila churned her way over to him. Soon, he had uncovered a chrome-plated hood ornament: a miniature leaping greyhound. Beneath it was the blue oval of a Ford emblem. "It's a brand-new car, Lila; a Ford V-8." He was spellbound; it was the first brand-new automobile he'd seen in his life. It even smelled new; he could distinguish the mingled scents of fresh lacquer, new rubber tires and car wax despite the aroma of the dry, dusty hay that nearly provoked him to sneeze.

Lila reached out and grabbed him by the hand, and the two finally made their way to the car's running board, where they clambered up onto it and cleared away more of the hay in order to gaze inside the car through its closed, driver's-side window while they held onto the door handles to steady themselves. The keys were in the ignition, and there was a black, murderous-looking Thompson submachine gun lying on the front seat. "Uncle Hansen," whispered Lila, "Oh my God; who have you been hiding this car for? And why are you hiding it?"

They hopped off the running board, turned and then pawed their way through billows of hay as they made their way over toward the open barn door. Just as Joey stepped into the square of sunlight beaming through it onto the earthen floor, something in one of the horse stalls caught his eye, and he halted and turned to look at it. It was the glint of light reflected off bare steel on the the blade of a shovel leaning against the wall. The center of the stall's floor was mounded slightly with dirt —not old, dried manure, but something freshly-turned. Joey stared at it, transfixed in horror; he'd been to some ill-kept cemeteries with his hearse-driving brother Billy enough times to know what a poorly-dug grave looked like. Lila covered her mouth with one hand in surprise momentarily. And then whispered, "Oh my God, Joey, don't say a word, please, about any of this. I'm really scared. It could get complicated. I think we'd better leave, right now." She was shaking noticeably and before she turned toward Joey and kissed him for the first time ever since she had known him, eyes wide open, she asked, simply: *"En hemlighet!* Right?"

Chapter 11

The Target

"He'll send a car for you when you get there," the caller had said. Then, there'd been a *click!* as the man hung up. Steve Snyder had just been instructed that his presence was required by LeClaire, the big boss, at a meeting up in Canada. Steve was to get on a train the next day that would drop him off at a remote country town in Quebec, someplace south of Sherbrooke and—as far as he was concerned—civilization. The tiny railroad station where he stepped down from the coach onto the concrete platform late the next afternoon was far north of Vermont, flat out in the middle of nowhere. Here, there was birdsong, a clear view of open fields that gave way to the blue expanse of the distant northern reaches of Lake Memphremagog, a dirt road that wound out of view beyond a stand of scrubby trees to the north and—not much else.

The elderly station agent shuffled out of the tiny depot as soon as the train left; it chuffed away northward rapidly now as if eager to turn its back on the lone passenger and the uniformed little man who had just emerged from this lonely outpost. With his official blue cap bearing its brass Canadian Pacific badge perched jauntily on his head, as if in parody of a Gendarme, he prepared to padlock the door to the waiting room, his duties done for the day. "Say now, is someone coming for you?" he inquired of Steve. "Sure do hope so, eh? There is now no taxicab in this town, sorry." He stood there, looking down momentarily and pawing absent-mindedly through a jumble of brass keys that dangled together on a hoop as he searched for the right key.

"Yeah, I've got a ride coming, thanks," replied Steve. At this, the old man snapped shut the padlock, tried it, then promptly turned his back to Steve and ambled off down the dirt road, presumably to a welcoming home, supper and a pleasant evening. Bluebirds swooped about in the sky chasing insects, and oblivious to this, large orange dragonflies skittered busily about the tawny fields as the sun sank lower into the west and Steve's shadow on the platform grew longer. The departed train's melodic chime whistle sounded in the distance as it hastened its pace and hurried away farther off to the north, as if taunting him for getting off in this god-forsaken spot. Then, finally, the car came.

It was the long, stylish Pierce-Arrow limousine Steve remembered from the night he decided to join LeClaire's outfit. It rolled to a stop close by the platform in a cloud of dust and one of its back doors popped open; one of the men inside beckoned to Steve to get in. He clambered into the car and had barely dropped into the back seat before the car jerked into motion and one of the two big men facing him, sitting on jump seats, pulled the door shut. Much to his surprise, Steve found himself sitting next to Nick, the person who'd recruited him and was also the gunman he'd met at the little general store being "cleaned out" as Nick called it, during Steve's first run.

"You, too?" asked Steve, as he looked at Nick. Nick nodded soberly. "Where are we headed?"

"Chateau du Roi," he answered, warily eyeing the two men in pin-striped suits and slouch hats sitting ahead of him. "LeClaire's place. You know how he calls himself the beer king, right? So, that's the chateau of the king, in French. King of the booze rackets, too, just like yours and mine." He pulled a pack of cigarettes from his pocket and offered it to Steve, who shook his head and instead began to reach for his own smokes.

Without so much as a word of warning, the large man sitting opposite Steve lunged forward and yanked at the lapels of Steve's coat. "What the hell!" hollered Steve, as the man frisked him, discovered his treasured switchblade and swiftly pocketed it.

"Just relax, and you'll be okay," said Nick as he withdrew a cigarette and lit it with a match. "I've been through this before." He moved to roll down the window and toss out the match; the man sitting opposite him reacted as if reaching for a gun. Nick froze, blew the match out and dropped it into an ashtray in the car's armrest. "Christ! Come on, now!" Nick complained to the man. "He and I are both clean! What is it with you guys getting so jumpy, anyway?" he groused. The big fellow glowered at him, crossed his arms and settled back into his jump seat. He sat immobile now, like some monstrous, forbidding gray stone idol blocking a jungle pathway, placed there to frighten any explorers from going farther.

"Got any idea what all this is about?" queried Steve.

"Maybe," answered Nick. "My guess is he's gonna make us partners. I've been working with Mugs, down your way, you know. Steve nodded thoughtfully, remembering the late-night encounter on U.S. Route 5. "So anyway, as you know, we busted up some small-time rackets and runners down there and pulled in new business—good business. And all of a sudden, Mugs told me he got onto something big, really big." Nick paused to take a long drag, then spewed smoke in the general direction of the pair sitting across the way to see if that would annoy them. It didn't.

"So—then what happened?"

"He told the boss he could find a way to help him open up a brewery operation south of here, just over the line in Vermont, and put all the indies in the Kingdom out of business. That would save the outfit a hell of a lot of transportation time. He was going to either work the guy over or put a button on him. The boss got Mugs a new Ford car nobody had seen before, some cash and a nice new piece, and Mugs and I split up. Mugs would do the legwork, figure out all the angles and put it together any way he saw fit. I wasn't in on all of it; my deal was to run interference, create some diversions and keep the cops busy. And I eyed the cops like a hawk to make sure they didn't get in on this and burn it down before Mugs made his move. It had something to do with beer business; backdoor two and three-barrel brewers. Once Mugs gave me the high sign, we were going meet up and pull the job. And then—well, Mugs just plain disappeared before he and I hardly ever got started on it." Steve bobbed his head sympathetically.

"What the hell happened?" asked Steve. "Did somebody take him down?"

"It wasn't the cops, and from what word was on the street, none of the small-timers iced him,"

Nick continued. "And, I doubt Mugs would have gone renegade. The money here's too good. He'd never go to work for some small-time hick rumrunner in the woods, with no protection out on the highway. I just don't know what the hell happened to him." He glanced out the window and said, "Oh, look; we're here already."

Steve stared as a complex of buildings resembling some sort of castle hove into view. Presently, the limousine turned into the gravel driveway of a well-manicured courtyard, slowed to a discreet pace and then came to a stop beneath a portico of the grand Chateau du Roi. "Don't get too impressed just yet, pal," ventured Nick. "This is the service entrance; the dames, the

Johns, LeClaire's pals and the high-rollers use the front gate and the big main door."

"The Johns? You mean he's got hookers here?"

Nick laughed. "He's got anything anyone could want here. All kinds of people come up from the states to stay and play here, where booze is legal. And this place has all the toys." Steve stared in wonderment at a parking lot that was jammed full of expensive cars that bore New York, Vermont and Massachusetts license plates.

Now, as the limousine stood idling away quietly, its chauffeur as stiff and silent as a mannequin behind the big steering wheel, LeClaire's two well-dressed leg-breakers got up from their jump seats. They strong-armed Steve and Nick out of the car and hustled them up a set of stone steps, down a long hallway and then into a dark-paneled antechamber furnished with oriental rugs and several large leather-covered easy chairs. There were no windows and only one other door, which was closed. "*Asseyez-vous, vous deux*," growled one of the two strong men.

"What's he saying, Nick?" asked Steve, beginning to get nervous.

"He's ordering us to sit down. 'Sit down, you two'. Probably doesn't know a word of English, the big dumb lug. Pure French. Pretty rude treatment for two of the boss's loyal guys, don't you think?"

"Oh!" grumbled the strongman. "*Asseyez-vous deux, sil vous plait.* That means, in case you're interested," the man said, "you two, sit down, *please*." At that, grinning with pleasure at having revealed his expertise in English, he shoved an astonished Nick down into one of the chairs. Exercising discretion in the face of newfound adversity, Steve quickly found a seat without any such assistance. The two big gray-suited men continued to stand, looming over the chairs occupied by Steve and Nick like belligerent bull elephants.

Presently, the door on the opposite side of the room opened and a large, tough-looking man dressed as a butler emerged. He made a show of peering about as if he had poor vision, finally asking: "Nick?" Nick stood, buttoned his jacket and tugged at the cuffs of his shirt. "Monsieur LeClaire will see you now."

Trying his best to look dapper under the present circumstances, Nick turned and flashed a smile at Steve as he rose from his chair. "I'll buy you a drink when we get done here and get our marching orders, Steve. It's gonna be great working with you." Nick turned, walked through the doorway and the butler followed, closing the door gently behind him. There was silence for the next few minutes, then Steve could hear the muffled sounds of a heated conversation. Nothing again for a moment and then—the dull *thud!* of what sounded like a gunshot.

Steve could feel perspiration trickling down his neck during the next few minutes that slowly ticked by. And at last, the door to LeClaire's inner sanctum opened once more. Almost in parody of the bumbling innocence of a new staffer, the man peered about again before asking: "Steve Snyder?" Steve arose, and shakily made his way toward the door. "Monsieur LeClaire will see you now."

LeClaire's office–if indeed it was one, or else a study, was dark—so dark it was impossible to see little more than a table upon which stood a bottle of scotch, a glass and a handgun. It seemed to be illuminated by a spotlight high up above. Steve could just barely discern the figure of a large person seated far behind the table, lurking in the shadows. The person—without a doubt, LeClaire—was smoking. Steve could see the large, orange dot of a lit cigar through a haze of acrid smoke. Instantly, Steve recalled the night of his initiation into LeClaire's outfit and imagined feeling a stab of pain where the burn from that bizarre ritual had left a permanent scar.

"What's it going to be?" came the familiar, gravelly-sounding voice from the shadows. "Take a shot at me, or have a shot, and drink to my health? Step up to the table." Steve did as he was told. "They're both loaded, that bottle and that gun," said LeClaire. "But all you get is one shot. You're either loyal to me, or to someone who's double-crossed me and disappeared." Steve stared down at the bottle, the glass and the gun. The gun was an automatic; the slide had either been pulled back and cocked, or blown back when the gun had been fired. Nick was nowhere to be seen.

"What do you need me to do?" asked Steve, fishing and angling for time. "Find Mugs?"

"Find him. Track him down and find out what he was on to —then, make him, and anyone else he let in on it pay the price for running out on me. He promised, but he did not deliver. He stabbed me in the back, so you can stab him, but—do it any way you see fit."

"Anything else?"

"Get back that new Ford car I trusted him with, and the new weapon he had with him. What he stole from me can be yours to use as your reward. But I want it done." Steve looked down at the floor. It was dark and dusty as far as he could see, except for a large rectangle of bright, polished wood where he was standing, the spot where a rug might have lain—for a long time, perhaps just until several minutes ago. Despite the gloom, he could see where something had been dragged from where he stood, all the way through the dust, over to a side door. "Look, this is sink or swim!" rumbled LeClaire. "This is your call!"

Trying to remain calm, Steve leaned far over the table and reached out for the bottle. As he did so, he tried in vain to see if the automatic's safety was on. Steve liked to hedge his bets but so, probably, did LeClaire, he reasoned. Steve grasped the bottle of scotch, and rather shakily poured himself a drink, wondering if LeClaire had a gun, other than the one on the table. "Good," grated the raspy voice coming from the shadows.

"What else?" asked Steve.

"So, you will go and find out what this fabulous find of Mugs was—which lying Nick swore to me he knew nothing about—and you can send him straight to hell. And any more of those penny-ante rumrunners down there, and back-door brewers; I want them iced, too, if you can't get them into our outfit. You know how I put old man Mangano and his winery out of business long ago. Now I have all the vineyards, all the big rackets running booze over the line, and now all the beer business—that I know of. But of all things, I want whatever operation Mugs took over. I want you to deliver what he didn't." The orange dot of the cigar grew larger as LeClaire leaned forward expectantly. "Can you do that for me?"

"Yes," croaked Steve, raising the glass to his parched-dry mouth. "I always worry about getting a job done right, especially if I'm in it all on my own." He poured the whiskey down in one, swift gulp. "This is risky business. So now, I'm the Johnny-come-lately, and it looks like I'm on the spot." He set the empty glass down on the table, and waited to see how what he had said would play. And then, emboldened by the booze, he played a card—as it turned out, a bad one. "What's in it for me, besides the car and the weapon?"

"You know what I say in my business?" LeClaire replied matter-of-factly. "This is my advice. And you'd better learn to heed it, too." Steve could hear LeClaire chuckle briefly before speaking again. "If you heard the shot, then that means you weren't my target."

Chapter 12

Just the Ticket:
August 24, 1932

On the same afternoon that Steve Snyder found himself standing alone on the platform of the rural railroad station in Canada, with the train that had brought him to that remote spot fading from view, Billy Ross found himself standing on the platform of the expansive brick railroad station in downtown St. Johnsbury. He was going to say goodbye to Catherine, who was headed back to college in Burlington, but any semblance of a family-involved sendoff would be relegated to Catherine and her parents. Billy, the boyfriend Catherine seldom mentioned to her parents, might as well have been a figment of Catherine's imagination, as far as her mother and father were concerned.

Billy was sitting on a baggage cart, smoking, a good distance from where the three, drab-looking passenger cars of the train that headed for the northwest quadrant of Vermont sat, the boiler of the grimy locomotive in charge of them seething with steam as if in anticipation of tackling the steep grade up out of town. Unperturbed, its fireman methodically shoveled scoops of coal into the locomotive and stoked the fire, provoking it to a roaring frenzy until the smoke wafting from the stack was interrupted by a plume of white steam hissing out of the safety valve. The train's old engineer, hunched over a long-necked oilcan, puttered about the locomotive, dribbling oil on pistons, side rods and valve gear while a brakeman fussed with baggage checks on luggage. He then passed suitcases along to a handler loading one of the cars. The conductor periodically consulted his gold pocket watch as he stood there like a ser-geant major in a field drill, commanding passengers as they arrived on the platform to form lines and then climb aboard one car or another.

An expensive-looking auto's twin trumpet horns sounded, heads turned on the platform, and Catherine's parents' car, a fancy new Buick sedan swept to a stop nearby; the well-dressed man in the driver's seat stuck one hand outside and waved a dollar bill imperiously at the baggage handler. The driver, Catherine's father, motioned toward two suitcases strapped to the car's luggage rack on the rear bumper, and pressed the bill into the young man's hand when he stepped up close to the car. Billy watched as the handler took the dollar, hefted the suitcases and took them to the brakeman while Catherine and her mother alighted from the Buick with the aplomb of debutantes arriving at a celebrity ball. "What a show," Billy grumbled to himself. "I should have brought a movie camera." He stubbed out his cigarette on the wagon and tossed the butt out onto the nearby railroad tracks in disgust.

Billy watched, almost bored to tears as Catherine kissed her father goodbye, then hugged and kissed her mother—although their farewell was apparently not a tearful one. Unmoved by the low-key drama of this moment of what had become a familiar goodbye ritual, the father already had his paper—no doubt the *Wall Street Journal*—out and was reading it by the time Catherine—assisted by the conductor—stepped aboard the second car of the train, found a seat, and waved out the open window to her mother. The conductor swiveled his head, scanning the platform in both directions, and once he determined there were no late arrivals scampering toward the train, hollered: "Board! All aboard!" and waved a signal to the engineer. After two short whistle blasts from the locomotive in acknowledgement, there came the sigh of air escaping as brakes released their grip on the wheels of the cars and the train began to move. Just as Mr. Hollingsworth's big yellow Buick backed out of its parking spot and departed in a huff, the conductor picked up his step-stool from the platform, tossed it aboard the vestibule and swung onto the train. Billy, who already had his sights set on the open steps of the last car on the train, followed suit. His goodbye with Catherine would last a bit longer while they shared a seat together aboard the train, and be a bit more intimate than the one he had just witnessed; he'd drop off the train when it made its stop at Danville, then hitchhike home. True, he had no ticket to ride, but he did have a coveted railroad pass, a little card guaranteeing unlimited free passage. He'd lifted it from his father's wallet the night before. Clever boy, Billy. Billy loved free rides.

* * *

"That'll be twenty cents," said the swarthy, unkempt-looking man in charge of the admission gate to the Ferris wheel, a cigarette dangling from one corner of his mouth. Joey fished in his pocket, found two dimes and handed them over in exchange for two tickets; Joey handed one to Lila, and then he and Lila passed through the gateway and stood, first in line, waiting for the ride to stop. The motor driving the wheel towering above them sputtered and coughed now and then and tossed sparks out of its muffler into the early evening air, but the man in grease-stained coveralls holding the lever that controlled it seemed as unconcerned as the kids and few adults aboard the ride, whooping and hollering as the wheel went around and around. It was late August, and the annual county fair had come to Lila's home town. For a few all-too-short days and nights of fun, the cares of the Depression could be forgotten when this annual event brought joy and festivity to town.

"Look," said Lila, "the wheel's slowing down." The lights strung along the girders of the Ferris wheel were on now, but they blinked off and back on as the worker tending the motor pulled on the lever and the giant, spidery contraption slowed to a somewhat jerky halt. He reached out and lifted the bar across the first of the cars that came to a stop at a little wooden platform, and the first of the pairs of riders aboard to land hopped out as the car swayed to and fro. The process was repeated until all the cars had been emptied, and the worker in grubby-looking coveralls waved to Joey and Lila to step aboard.

They had no sooner settled down onto the hard, narrow seat than the man in coveralls slammed down the bar, and pulled a lever that jerked the wheel into motion again. He stopped it seconds later to load more riders; the car swung back and forth violently as if somehow determined to pitch Joey and Lila out. Lila giggled, and when she did, Joey looked at her and laughed out loud. "What," she demanded, clutching the bar, is so funny, Joey?"

"You."

"I'm funny? I think it's funny *you're* not scared. Scared you might fall down onto a pitchfork, like you were at my uncle's farm." She looked at Joey, crossed her eyes momentarily to make fun of him, and then she, too, laughed. The Ferris wheel jerked again, then stopped; the whole structure wriggled momentarily, making the lights blink, and the car rocked once more, as if some unseen force within the wheel's spindly girders was trying to frighten them.

"Lila, the only thing that scares me now is your dad. I think he'd kill me if he found us here."

"Oh, honestly, don't be so ridiculous!" she scoffed, and then, added, just to add a little twist: "If he wanted you dead, he probably would have killed you by now!"

Joey laughed out loud. "I'm glad I survived this summer! But I sure wish it wasn't over."

"It isn't, Joey. And even if it was, there'll be another one coming around." The wheel ground into motion but kept on going this time. Joey and Lila's car swooped up backwards, carrying them aloft into the darkening sky; then it pitched them over the highest point of the wheel's orbit as if it would hurl them up into the early evening stars. It plummeted back down until it seemed it would collide with the ground, the man in coveralls leaning against the lever and the blurred faces of onlookers standing in line...and then, the process began anew.

"But it'll be a long time before we can meet up and do anything like this again," Joey observed ruefully. "Classes start next week, and I won't be doing much of any deliveries for Sam after that. And you've got classes too, but not at my school." Their car rose again to its highest point, affording them a fleeting glimpse of some of the lights just beginning to come on in in town, and as it plunged back down, it brought them into a world of brighter lights and the mingled smells of popcorn, roast peanuts, cigar smoke, candied apples, frying food and the exhaust of the motor driving the Ferris wheel. Once more up into the clean, crisp air that hinted at the arrival of autumn, and then the wheel slowed as if to say the ride—and, summer, too— was all over; Joey and Lila's car swooped to a stop at the bottom, and gently rocked back and forth.

The hairy hand of the man at the controls of the motor reached out, yanked up the restraint bar up on their car and Joey and Lila tumbled out, unsteady on their feet, not sure really of which way they would go now. "Let's go if you're goin', folks," the operator grumbled to the next carload as he brought their car to down and stopped it. He released them, too, to make space for the next couple who'd take their place on this wheel of fortune that would spin around through the dark, pitching them heavenward up against the stars where they could catch their dreams for a pair of quick heartbeats, and then swoop back down to earth. "Time's a'wasting!"

Chapter 13

The Plot Thickens

Much like other women housekeepers whose husbands have retired, pretty young Daisy Wood was always looking for a good reason to get her better half out of the house. Daisy found just such a reason one bright, clear morning when she awakened and discovered that Silas Scrivvins, 38 years her senior and her husband of slightly less than two years, had passed away during the night while hogging the bedsheets, and was now as stiff as one of the kiln-dried boards in his downtown lumberyard.

The marriage of Silas and Daisy had come about as the result of an incident that had occurred when Daisy's previous suitor, on his way from Massachusetts to Montreal to have some fun with her, had put her out of his car following a spat. This happened just down the road from Silas's farm. The fellow had then gone on his merry way to find someone more amicable and possibly less expensive to keep around for company. Silas, a widower and a sturdy side-hill farmer of strong disposition (except when it came to resisting the charms of attractive women at the time) had made quite a reputation for himself as a prosperous farmer up Wheelock way. Quite the opposite of the fellow who's "all hat and no cattle", his dairy herd grew to number well more than 200 milkers. Always on the lookout for business opportunities Silas, shrewd fellow, never invested in stocks prior to the Wall Street Crash but in land, harvesting timber and establishing a lumberyard that was both a money-maker and major source of employment. His wife of many years, Hetty, was known for both her irascible temper and her penurious penny-pinching during her lifetime, most of which was spent nagging poor old Silas before her demise.

Thus, when Daisy wandered up onto Silas's front porch one day like a stray cat that had been dumped out of a passing car, offering up her big blue eyes, a sorrowful face and a hanky full of crocodile tears, old Silas took in both her and her battered suitcase full of exotic, overly-perfumed clothing in one big, geriatric heartbeat. It was a quick ride through the proverbial tunnel of love after that for the two (despite their difference in ages) during which Silas observed that Miss Daisy was like no other woman he'd ever met. Billy had taken quite a few rides through that tunnel of love, too, emerging with a young man's sly observation that, in the dark, all cats are essentially alike. For those who knew old Silas, though, their assessment of this parody of an amusement park diversion involving love boats going downstream was that Daisy had been taking her aged husband for a ride all along; only Silas was in the dark.

No one knew where he kept it, but Silas had money, and he knew how to stretch a dollar until it squeaked—until he got crazy about Daisy. Then, there was no limit to what he would spend—on her. When Daisy said she'd like to have a car, Silas drove her up to Natole Motor Sales in Newport City and bought her a jazzy-looking little Plymouth Deluxe road-ster. And when she asked for a horse, Silas bought her a fine-looking Morgan. Out in the barn and in the fields, Silas's hired hands wagged their heads and whispered that perhaps the old man had gotten soft and gone off his rocker; after all, a woman who likes animals needs only two of them in her lifetime to keep her happy, they claimed: the world's most perfect horse, and a jackass to pay for it.

Billy had made the first call and the removal of Silas's body using the Packard hearse on Wednesday morning, and by Thursday Daisy, no slouch, had worked with Junior to plan an elaborate Saturday send-off. A grand reception was planned at the Scrivvins' farmstead following committal, with a liberal amount of provisions (including a barrel of beer smuggled in from Canada) being prepared for the occasion. Silas was going to go out in style, if Daisy had anything to do with it, and so was she; she quickly arranged to leave Vermont before the winter snows came, abruptly announcing plans to close up the house for the season and take up residence in Florida until next spring. Shortly before his demise Silas, perhaps having come briefly to his senses, had confided to the manager of his sawmill that for all the good his money seemed to be doing when it came to making Daisy happy, she might just have well have been throwing it into a hole in the ground. That had apparently now come to pass, simply because Daisy—not wanting to play the part of a cheapskate—had spent enough cash on the burial and rushed creation of Silas's ornate coffin to feed a family of four for a month. Sven, his artistic abilities taxed to the maximum, had worked overtime in Junior's basement workshop doing the fancy woodwork and finishing.

In the midst of all the goings-on associated with Silas's whiz-bang sendoff, Daisy's younger sister Mary Lou Lamar came up from Atlanta on the train. The porter of the Pullman car she arrived in—and every man loitering on the platform of the Lyndonville railroad station that afternoon—paid close attention to her legs and high heels. No doubt they were preparing to rush in and scoop her up if she missed one of the steps as she stuck her pretty nose up, wiggled a bit and then daintily descended from the train like a gazelle wandering down a jungle pathway to an inviting watering hole amongst a company of indolent hippos. An especially-gifted grifter-in-training who had taken her cues from Daisy all along, the summons to Vermont to attend the funeral and afterward oversee upkeep of the homestead over the course of the winter were a blessing to Mary Lou. This blessing was a welcome, free ticket to ride—also one to flee the incoming flurry of mail consisting of envelopes containing past-due bills and demands for back rent, things that had now taken up a more or less permanent residence in her apartment's mailbox back in Georgia. Some divorced women went from paycheck to paycheck. Much like her sister Daisy, Mary Lou went from man to man.

Billy, oblivious to all this, motored slowly southward following the car leading the funeral procession after departing the church where Silas's services were held that Saturday morning. Junior had let him take the hearse home beforehand—empty, of course—last night so he wouldn't have to hitch a ride in. Easy-peasy. Nice of Junior. Now, it was back to work, with Silas firmly ensconced in the mahogany coffin in the back, surrounded by lavish displays of flowers. The funeral entourage drove along Route 5 at a sedate pace, the concrete road more or less following the winding path of the Passumpsic River. Junior, at the wheel of the limousine up ahead, was obviously in no hurry and perhaps neither was the pastor seated in the limo's back seat. They might well have been casually passing a flask back and forth across the rolled-down division window, talking about fishing and telling incredible lies as their big black limo rolled along.

Billy lit a cigarette to relieve the monotony. Smoking in company cars was prohibited by Junior. *So, screw him, anyway*, Billy thought. He'd dump the ashtray after the committal and wipe it down; Junior wouldn't be any the wiser.

Although it was late summer, it was uncommonly warm for this time of year in the Kingdom; Billy had his window rolled down and was enjoying the rush of air pouring into the Packard's cavernous interior. While trees on the upper reaches of the hills were beginning to be dappled with a hash of red, orange and brown leaves, a sure harbinger of autumn, the lower parts were still holding out in magnificent shades of green. The Passumpsic reflected the splendid deep, cerulean blue of the cloudless sky and the colors of the leafy trees along its banks in perfect order. All things considered it was a great day in Vermont—to have a funeral.

As the procession ground on and neared St. Johnsbury, the hilltop cemetery and its little white hearse shed—which once housed the long-disused horse-drawn predecessor of Junior's hearse and its like—finally appeared on the left; Billy stuck his arm out the window to signal the turn onto the curvy, narrow drive that wound its way up the hillside. Billy's job was made easy by the stalwart fellows who'd worked for Silas on the farm and in the lumberyard; there was no want for help to slide the shiny coffin out of the Packard and into its assigned space. A hundred or more sorrowful folk gathered 'round to hear the pastor's words as the committal service began; there were so many that Junior had run out of chairs for them all. After the pastor had droned on and said his last, close friends of the family stepped forth and added their words of praise for Silas. Billy retreated to the shade of some nearby trees, where Tom and Seth, the gravediggers, were lurking, smoking quietly, leaning on their shovels and ogling the well-dressed women among the mourners.

"That there is an import, I'll tell ya," offered Tom, giving a nod in the general direction of Daisy, who stood primly on the edge of the drop-off that led six feet down to Silas's final resting place. He flicked his burned-out cigarette butt off into the woods and rummaged in his shirt pocket for another smoke.

"No it ain't, you dummy," retorted Seth, looking slightly annoyed at Tom's seeming incompetence and lack of local lore. "That's the widow, Daisy. Old enough to be your momma, if she got lucky at 16. Sure as hell unlucky if she had you. But that there gal beside her is a new arrival, though; she just got off the train from down country the other day."

"So, mister know-it-all, who's that babe in the black candy-wrapper?" asked Billy, looking at the girl who was wiping her eyes and standing beside Daisy, putting on a pretty good show of distress herself.

"Daisy's sister. Southern cookin'. A tasty-lookin' little bag of groceries, if you ask me," said Seth proudly.

"Hey, shut your pie hole!" whispered Tom "She's lookin' this way." And so she was. Always prepared to put on a good show for any new lady deemed eligible to take a trip through his tunnel of love, Billy, clad in his fine black suit, nodded and flashed the most scintillating, pearly-white smile in his repertoire. Tom and Seth, clad in dirty jeans and ragged, well-worn flannel, leaning on their shovels, stared at her, agape, almost as if they'd just seen a bear walk out of the woods. The game was on, and it was clearly starting to go in ever-charming Billy's favor.

"So, who is that guy in the suit?" whispered Mary Lou to her big sister. "The guy in the suit, the hearse driver. He's kind of cute. Know anything about him?"

Daisy hugged her sister, appearing to comfort her and whispered in her ear: "Local guy. Works for Junior. Hey—he's single. What the hell; he's got a full-time job. You should meet him." Daisy, who had put quite a few notches in her lipstick tube over the past few years before meeting Silas, knew how these things worked. And Mary Lou respected her and her wisdom, even though Mary Lou had already, in her short lifetime, slept in more places that George Washington was said to have had, and never told the truth about any of them, or who she'd shared the bedsheets with.

"Lord have mercy!" muttered Tom, chuckling and then emitting a sigh as he ogled the ladies one more time. "Just look at those gals! Right now, boys, I can't even remember if I had breakfast this morning." He set the shovel down, hitched his suspenders up and smiled an innocent smile.

Billy broke the silence. His words and evil smile invoked a quick, visual inspection on the part of Tom. "Check your shirt."

The last words of the service sounded, and Silas was lowered to take his place as a new arrival on the ground floor of the family plot, thick like a forest as it was up top with the granite headstones of the family members who had passed before him. The crowd slowly dispersed, some walking by the gravesite slowly, heads down; others hustling along, heads up, bright-eyed and bushy-tailed, stepping smartly along to their cars so they could leave quickly and arrive early at the farm for the reception so they could be the first at the punch bowl, the cold-cut platter or the beer tap. Daisy and Mary Lou lingered, and then—only then—Mary Lou whispered to her sister, "I'm going to faint right about now." She looked at her, rolled her eyes toward Billy, then back to Daisy and winked. "Whatever you do, don't try to catch me." And with that, down she went, emitting an appropriately-loud moan of distress. Billy, ever the man of action when there was an apparently unescorted damsel in distress, rushed over to at first fan her face with his hat, then to help her to her feet, and finally to walk her carefully over to a nearby bench, where she sat and then invited him, all out of breath, to stay with her and talk a bit to put her mind at ease.

Mary Lou explained how sad she was. First of all, how sad it would be for her to carry on all alone over the course of the coming winter in that big house, overseeing the farmstead while Daisy was in Florida. Secondly, she was so sad that Silas had passed away; after all, he had been such a kind and generous man. Mary Lou was hedging her bets that Billy could be kind and generous too. Billy offered that he was kind and could be most generous when the occasion presented itself.

He humbly admitted he couldn't exactly afford to paint the town, but he knew where there were places to go where you could jump, shout and dance 'till your shoe leather gave out. He knew a pretty girl when he saw one, which wasn't often in his neck of the woods, and he knew how to treat one right. He knew how to show one from out of town a real good time. Honest, he did. And so, Mary Lou flashed her most honest-appearing, dazzling smile. She clasped his hands, looked him straight in the eyes and softly said: "Show me."

And that, as Tom and Seth later remarked over illicit beers in a tavern, weeks afterward, was where Mary Lou, after falling and getting a few grass stains on her skirt, got Billy to fall for her. She'd soon find out if he had money and if he did, she'd be going through the greenbacks like a rabbit working its way through a lettuce patch. So, this, in fact, was where Billy and Mary Lou's ride through the deep, dark tunnel of love began.

Chapter 14

Even Steven

To the disappointment of many in St. Johnsbury, the much-awaited Labor Day weekend dawned cold and misty-white as a ghost. Streets were slick with rainwater, and eaves of houses everywhere dripped moisture. A veil of fog blanketed the valley like the bed sheets drowsy residents pulled up over their heads as they decided to sleep in. Like a raspy swan song, the sporadic chirping of the solitary cricket in the Ross family's garden delivered a solemn warning that summer was over, and that colder days lay ahead.

Beth's voice could clearly be heard from where she stood at the foot of the stairs, brandishing a frying pan like a weapon: "Bill-*yyyy*! You come downstairs this instant and help Joey and your father, or I'll have him haul you out to the wood shed and give you a licking!" Beth had the patience of a saint, but once that patience was exhausted, the devil would be in her apron strings, and she could play the part of an ill-tempered Marine drill sergeant.

Billy came clumping downstairs, offering trite apologies to his mother as he sauntered through the kitchen. Head-down in a well-practiced posture of shame, he was still buttoning up his shirt as he kicked open the porch door and strode out into the yard, letting the door slam shut behind him. His hair was disheveled, and he rubbed his eyes red as stop lights as he halted and stood before Bud and Joey. He'd been out late, drinking and playing cards last night. Sneaking into the house well past midnight, he'd crawled, crab-like up the stairs and dropped into bed, crash-landing with the aplomb of an empty beer bottle landing in a gutter. "Mornin'," he muttered. "Sorry to keep you waiting. I'm ready to help Dad and Joey. Got here as soon as I could." Billy had actually gotten there as soon as he wanted to.

He put on his most engaging smile, then stretched and yawned like a brawny lumberjack who's finally ready to get down to work. Like the rumbling of a lion awakened from slumber, the sound shocked the cricket into silence.

"Morning, Billy! Now, daylight's burning, boys! Let's get at it!" said Bud, exhorting his two sons to step up to the cause: preparing the family car for an outing. Today would be one of those rare ones each year when Bud could afford to take time off and treat the family to a ride, and what entertainment his meager budget would allow. The car, an obsolete but proudly-maintained 1926 Pontiac, was about to be tuned-up, washed, waxed, and made ready for the trip to a fishing and picnic spot at Joe's Pond, over in West Danville.

Billy, still bleary-eyed, trudged off to the tool shed to fetch a bucket, soap, and the wax and cleaning rags. Birds chirped excitedly high up in the maple trees surrounding the weather-beaten house, as if jostling for perches where they could watch the rare spectacle of the Ross brothers co-operating. "Let me see you check the oil, now, son," Bud asked Joey, who opened the hood, grabbed a rag from a back pocket, and pulled the dipstick. After wiping the stick clean, he plunged it back in and then pulled it out once more.

"The oil's right on the mark, Dad," Joey announced.

"Good. Put it back now and let's see you check the ignition points." Joey stepped to the driver's door, opened it, set the parking brake, then placed the gearshift in neutral. He walked back to the front of the car, removed the distributor cap, and wrestled briefly with the fan, turning the engine over slowly by hand until he got to the proper point. "Here; you can check the gap with this," Bud said as he handed Joey a gauge, one he had borrowed from the railroad's shop mechanic. "You know, you could check it with a matchbook to set the gap and get it to run, but let's do it right. This car has to last. Got to outlast this rotten Depression. I've always said: If you take care of your car, it will take care of you."

"And now, like we say on the railroad, you and your brother can 'wash the hog' and then you can wax it," Bud ordered. He turned, walked back into the house, and the screen door bumped shut behind him. Then Billy, brawny and muscular from his job at Junior's (and now apparently fully-awakened) emerged from the tool shed with a bucket. He glowered at Joey as he came, as if he were some dark, lanky locomotive leaving a roundhouse, its boiler steaming with malice, ready to explode.

"Great day for a ride, ain't it?" he grumbled. "And now we've gotta polish the old man's Jazz-Age jalopy. This'll be as pointless as giving a hobo a shoeshine." He strode over to the outdoor faucet and ran water into the bucket, after adding some soap. "It's a hog, alright. So now, we get to put lipstick on a pig. An ugly old sow."

"It's supposed to be swell today, out on the pond," replied Joey. "But you don't want to go, do you?"

"Oh, of course, I'd love to," groused Billy facetiously as he finished filling the bucket. "It's just that I have a lot of other things I'd like to do that I love a lot better, besides riding around in an old heap, picnicking with geezers and Sunday school kids, and trying to catch a few dumb fish."

"Like what?" Joey shrugged and held out both hands, palms up.

"Like some things I'll tell you about some day when you man up and can catch yourself a girl," Billy snickered. He hooked a garden hose to the spout and sprayed water over the dusty Pontiac, then grasped the bucket and motioned Joey to come and get it. He waved the nozzle at Joey like a robber threatening a bank teller with a gun. "Oh, come on. What—don't trust me?"

"Oh," said Joey matter-of-factly, ignoring the threat, "like seeing Catherine and cutting bait on Doris? How's that going? You caught yourself a big one this time, didn't you?"

Billy dropped the bucket, scattering soap bubbles into the air and gave Joey a dirty look. "Hey, you go mind your own damn business. My girlfriend's my business. I was chasing tail back when you needed Dad to read you the Buster Brown Sunday comics and tie your shoes. Now get busy with the suds and wash this stupid car."

"It's not stupid, just old. Dad knows how to make things work."

"Well, so do I. That's why you're going to 'wash the hog' and I'm going to watch you do it to make sure you do a good job. Now, get busy. I know how to make things work, too. And, I know he can afford a new car. After all, a new V-8 Ford sedan's only five hundred dollars."

"Five hundred? *Only* five hundred?" Joey's jaw almost dropped. He whistled. "C'mon; that's a lot of money. Good pay right now where there's full-time work is 50 cents an hour."

"Sure it is, but the old man's got it."

"What makes you say that?" Joey's brow furrowed in disbelief.

"I know, Joey. I just know," answered Billy, a sly smile on his face. It disappeared as swiftly as a wallet in the hands of a pickpocket. "I know how to make money, too. Easy. My way.

It's just that Dad doesn't. That's why he's a slave to the railroad. So, wash the car."

"Oh, so—you know how to *make* it, too. So then—you know how to *take* it? Is that what you're saying?"

"I never said that. Smarten up and shut up, before that Kaiser in the kitchen hears you and gets us both on the march. So, scrub."

"No, I won't." Joey crossed his arms. "But I'll split it—and the waxing—with you, 50/50. All for the cost of a quarter."

"Like hell," Billy groused. He picked up the rags and the can of polishing wax, and threw them at Joey. "I'm not playing your game."

"Then I won't play yours," said Joey. Seasoned from playing high school softball, he deftly caught the can of wax. "Unless you pay. And unless you do, I'll tell Dad you know he's got money stashed away. And then he'll ask you how you know about it—and then, I'll bet he counts it to see if you're stealing. You say you know how to make money. And that means *you've* got it. So, pay." Billy's face flushed the color of a stoplight.

"Everything okay, boys?" asked Bud blithely upon opening the screen door and emerging onto the porch. He hooked his hands around his suspenders and sniffed, savoring the morning breeze. "I'm going to walk down to the store and buy a newspaper. Better have the hog prettied-up by the time I come back; she's a mighty sorry-looking mess!"

"We will, Dad" answer Joey cheerfully, knowing that at last, he'd one-upped Billy. "We decided to split things up, to make it go easier." Bud nodded, pulled his blue denim cap down tighter on his head and ambled off down the driveway, a happy family man content in the belief that his sons were of one accord. He hadn't noticed Billy's face had the unsettling appearance of someone stifling a mighty curse.

The ritual of the washing of Bud's vintage Pontiac began at its front, where a copper-faced and chromed warbonnet image of the great Indian chief graced the top of the car's grille, in the form of the car's radiator cap. Below it were two copper medallions set into the radiator shell, one of them stamped with a profile of Chief Pontiac (which, like the radiator cap, looked nothing like him) and the words: "Chief of the sixes."

The ritual of getting the two boys to set aside their gripes and co-operate sometimes caused trouble for Beth, although Bud more than often seemed blissfully unaware of any strife under the Ross family's roof. Much like the routine of washing the car and the agitation of the otherwise placid, ripple-free contents of the bucket to make suds—the agitation often began in Beth's front—her forehead—as a headache. Billy and Joey had both worked for whatever copper medallions—pennies—they could earn as schoolboys. They were both self-reliant, toughened by being stamped by their peers with the stigma of growing up poor in Vermont, and living on the wrong side of the tracks. But there, they differed, those two. If there were any laurel leaves to be bestowed upon the brothers, they would chiefly go to Joey. Any laurel leaves for Billy would be a product of his own imagination.

Billy, giving in at last to his sensibilities, reached into his pocket and finally tossed Joey a quarter. There were plenty more of them left over, deep within that pocket.

* * *

The sun had finally burned through the overcast and was warming the day by the time the Ross family's elderly Pontiac labored up the hill east of Danville. Cresting the steep grade, the old car bounced and tossed its four occupants around as it bumped across the hilltop tracks of the St. Johnsbury & Lamoille County Railroad, then slowed as it passed Hasting's Store, where two men in faded work shirts, overalls and manure-splattered barn boots sat on its front steps, smoking their pipes and watching cars—and time—pass by.

At the fork in the road beyond the store, Bud steered to the left; the car lurched as it made the turn and crossed the railroad tracks again where they led off past a derelict-looking train station, hugging the northern shoreline of Joe's Pond. Far from being encircled by a necklace of tidy white cottages owned by summer people, the pond did, however, have a few humble cabins on a point of land sticking out into the water. "Here we are," announced Bud, breaking the silence that had ensued since leaving home. "Point Comfort. Beautiful spot, isn't it?" he turned to look at Beth and saw that her jaw was jutting out like a rock outcropping, a sure sign she still wasn't quite over chastising Billy for lingering in bed. He noticed also that she had her pocket-size Bible in her lap.

The car turned off the highway and passed through a parking lot near a small filling station and restaurant, loping along in low gear. Joey looked out the window, studying another building, a rustic-looking dance pavilion. As Bud drove the car cautiously down a rutted driveway, chipmunks and squirrels scampered about. Carpeted with pine needles, the way was lined with cabins nestled under tall, dark trees. It led off down to land's end where sunshine sparkled out on the water. Bud pulled up beside one cabin where a small blue boat sat upside down on a pair of sawhorses. Swallows swooped around the trees, the cabin, and rickety-looking stairs that led from the cabin's backyard down to a dock. There, water lapped softly at its pilings, and ducks could be seen paddling around them. Hanging over the cabin's front door was a hand-lettered sign bearing the place's name: Harmony.

* * *

Joey rowed hard, put his back into it, and the blue boat moved swiftly away from the dock. The oars made a pleasant gurgling sound, and water swirled around them as the craft surged into open water. It was nice to see the image of Billy, standing on the dock, growing smaller and smaller by the minute, Joey thought. It was a newfound and very satisfying way to put him in his place: far away. "It was awful nice of Dave to let us use his camp and boat today, son," commented Bud. He stopped fiddling with lures and looked up at the sky, judging what the weather might be like later on. Joey nodded his assent, and kept on rowing. It felt good to stretch his muscles—to show his father that he, too, besides Billy, was strong. The figure of his brother was now pint-size, and the cabin had now assumed the minute appearance of a toy building. Beth was sweeping the porch, and Billy was gesturing to her as he walked away—probably because he needed to go somewhere to make good his escape.

* * *

"To hell with this," muttered Billy as he tossed his fishing rod down on the sawhorses where the boat had sat. He dumped his bait bucket and gear onto the ground in disgust. The boat with his brother and father on board was now just a speck far out on the water. *Good for them*, he thought. Then, music—sounding like relief from what he anticipated would be a boring holiday—sounded in the distance. Billy decided to investigate. After all, Beth—with the cabin's little kitchen now under her control, would probably be settling down to reading the scriptures. There would be no sense in hanging around; after all, there was no telling when she might suddenly go all Presbyterian on him.

Following the tantalizing sounds of a dance band playing, he padded down the pine-needled drive and soon found himself nearing the dance pavilion. He saw that other young people were heading toward it, too. "Who's the band?" he asked another young man sauntering along, hand-in-hand with a pretty young girl.

"Dunno," the fellow replied, grinning and tugging at his girlfriend's hand. She made big eyes at him and giggled. "Guess we'll find out when we get there. They sound good 'nuff for me!" The girl nudged her date playfully, indicating it was high time to go. Billy's eyes kept track of her as she left, sizing her up as a possible dance partner. She stepped along with an enchanting wiggle to her walk he couldn't take his eyes away from. A crowd had gathered at the dance pavilion, and up on its deck, a fiddler, a drummer, two guitar players and a vocalist stood. Guitar strings twanged, there were a few random drumbeats, and then all went silent. There was a collective sigh of disappointment from the crowd that had gathered.

"Folks, we're just tunin' up," announced a band member. "We ain't playing yet, and we ain't drinkin' yet. But if just two of you want to come up and dance around to make us look good—when we play a few bars—well, maybe we can get some inspiration and get down to business a whole lot quicker!"

Billy fairly jumped up the steps to the pavilion's dance hall floor to stake his claim and in an instant, a lady bounded up the steps right behind him. To Billy, her footsteps sounded like opportunity knocking. Sight unseen, he'd naturally take a chance, as a gambler, on starting a romance with whoever the girl following him might turn out to be. Then, the music began to play. Billy turned expectantly to face his partner, a dazzling smile on his handsome face. It vanished when Doris Martin hit him—hard, and square on the jaw. "You two-timing bastard," she yelled as Billy—momentarily stunned—lost his balance, staggered backward and fell to the floor. "You lied to me that you were sick—the same night I found you went out big time with Catherine. I'll get even with you—if it's the last thing I ever do!"

The band members turned away from the dust-up, stifling their amusement, and went back to tuning up their instruments as the crowd of onlookers hooted, hollered and guffawed. Billy sat up and rubbed his sore jaw, aware that he had no chance of regaining his poise before the rowdy spectators. The young man who'd said the band was "good 'nuff for him" roared with laughter and squeezed his girlfriend's hand as Doris skittered down the stairway and stalked away. "If I'd known there was going to be a fight today," he chuckled to the girlfriend, "I would have brought bettin' money! I would've bet on the lady in this bout!"

* * *

"Boy, he hit hard," commented Joey as he rose, tugged a bit to make sure the hook was set, and then decided to play the fish. He let the line run out; it went whizzing away and then he hauled back on it cautiously. He repeated the process until—without warning—the line jumped as though it had been hit by lightning. Then—it went limp. "Heck," muttered Joey. "I lost him." He reeled in the line dispiritedly, and expressed surprise at what finally came aboard. It was half a trout; the fish had fallen victim to something larger, savage, and apparently very hungry. Joey grasped what was left of the fish and started to work the bait hook free. "What would do that, Dad?" Joey asked incredulously.

"Northern pike," answered Bud. "I've heard rumors there are some in here now. They're wild; they'll eat anything, including game fish. It's a dog-eat-dog world down there below. Seems there's always a big fish eating up little fish." Just then, Bud felt something hit his line. He yanked, tugged and tussled. "I think I'm snagged on something," he grumbled. Just then, as he gave one final, mighty tug, the line came free and Bud reeled it in.

The shiner was still on the hook, but so was something gray and soggy. Bud grasped it and looked at it closely. It was a piece of pinstriped fabric torn from someone's clothing; a button was hanging onto it by a few strands of thread. Bud and Joey exchanged worried glances, wondering to themselves: *What— or who, in God's name—is down there? And why?*

Chapter 15

All Rise: September 10, 1932

Once Labor Day had come and gone, with the dance pavilion still open but most of the little cottages at Joe's Pond now boarded-up for the season, and the holiday weekend receding into memories of the past, the attention of the locals in the Northeast Kingdom turned to preparations for winter.

T.R. Donovan's preparations, however, were of a different sort. The weekend following Labor Day, the old man was preparing to send out feelers among certain men he trusted to find out what the hell had happened to Dutch, who had not returned with payment from a run down to Albany, New York on Labor Day eve with a particularly-valuable load of T.R.'s top-shelf Canadian whiskey.

It was on the beautiful, sunny, Sunday afternoon following his untimely disappearance that Dutch finally surfaced. As usual Dutch—famous among his friends for his sharp wit—as well as his penchant for carrying a sharp knife—was the hit of the party. In this case, it was a birthday party picnic being held by a Bible study group on the shores of Joe's Pond. Despite the lack of an invitation, Dutch made a dramatic appearance anyway and once this had been done, he stuck around for a while, bouncing gently, his feet barely touching the earth almost as if in time to the soft music playing on someone's radio on a nearby cabin's porch, but all the while staying out of reach of the women folk who were eager to pick a dance partner. The sight of the humped back of his soggy, once-magnificent suit poking through the water, looking like a large fish, possibly a sturgeon, was just enough to make the more curious young boys attending the party commandeer a boat, and row out onto the pond to make his acquaintance.

The boys quickly determined, upon attempting to drag this whopper into the rowboat, that their fishing rods and hooks weren't up to the task at hand. They beckoned to the minister standing ashore who had been watching these odd proceedings to assist them. He gamely paddled out awkwardly in a wobbly old canoe to meet them, whereupon the righteous man of the cloth reached out a bit too far, fell out of the canoe, and in the process of trying to stay afloat came face to face with poor old Dutch. It was immediately apparent that mouth-to-mouth resuscitation would be a gruesome and rather obvious waste of time—also that Dutch, his suit and body bearing holes that would do credit to a king-size chunk of Swiss cheese, was obviously the victim of a certain form of lead poisoning known to be fatal.

Once the boys, the by-now drenched minister who had regained his senses, the capsized canoe and the body of Dutch had made it to shore, one of the party-goers was dispatched to hustle over to Hasting's Store and telephone both the constable and the county sheriff regarding the discovery of a dead body. Knowing that both of St. Johnsbury's morticians were out of town, the sheriff ordered the body to be taken to Junior's, pending contact with the state's chief medical examiner. Of course, the party line had a thousand ears and soon the news spread far and wide.

The coverage of Dutch's demise and recovery began, so to speak, with a blanket being placed over his lifeless form and would continue otherwise in print in the local papers for days afterward. The flashbulbs of news photographers had *popped* and then dropped like spent champagne corks that evening outside Coughlin's funeral parlor in Lyndonville as the corpse was carried inside; excited reporters peppered the weary county sheriff standing outside the front door with their many questions. The lawman could only state the obvious: organized crime had likely come to the Kingdom, and that the body had been found bound and tied to several window sash weights, plus the frame of a wrecked (and highly-illegal) slot machine to make it sink; concrete for appropriate weight had presumably not been available. This deduction made perfect sense: gangsters live for the day, die by the gun and spend money just as quickly as they steal it. They do not contribute to sinking funds.

All over the area, in Danville and West Danville and clear out to Greensboro Bend as lights went out that evening in homes, the uncommon sound of doors being locked was heard for the first time in recent memory. In the households that were fortunate (and well-off enough) to be linked by telephones, the party lines buzzed anew with worried homeowners' speculations about who might have killed the well-dressed stranger and dumped his body—and who might be the next person to wind up in a watery grave with a makeshift tombstone trussed to his ankles. Wives of henpecked husbands clucked warnings to them to avoid traveling the roads at night. Like birds of a feather the papers, knowing how a murder headline can cause a newsstand sell-out, all rushed to get pictures of Dutch's final public appearance on their front pages without bothering to postulate a motive for his demise. Money does talk, after all.

For those who quietly dabbled in the illicit liquor trade and evaded the startling headlines, the cause for this rub-out needed no speculation; an outsider was cutting into someone's booze racket, and this was a concern. The wages of sin were death, to be sure, but when it came to the oft-overlooked sin of hauling moonshine or Canadian booze into and through Vermont it could be said the money earned, on the other hand, could help pay bills and put food for a hungry family on the table.

For those who derived the major portion of their income from this sort of trade (and successfully hid it from the public, the law and competitors) Dutch's demise was not just a concern, but a call to action. No one who is a cheap, wily crook like T.R. Donovan, reaping obscene profits from a winning game, resents anyone else as much as another cheap, wily crook who muscles into his territory and interferes with his operation, especially by taking down a trusted runner who is a key part of the game. Dutch did not have a cash value; *So, to hell with Dutch*, thought T.R. but the load—which had disappeared along with Dutch's car—had been of considerable value. T.R., upon learning of Dutch becoming the catch of the day and taking up temporary residence on the basement cutting board of Coughlin's Furniture and Funeral Service like a cloudy-eyed flounder, immediately called a conference with his boys. First, the enemy had to be found. And once he had, the enemy would pay the price. T.R. Donovan's.

Thereafter, once he had spread the sobering news, cautioned his boys to keep quiet and had abstained from imbibing gin for what he considered an appropriate amount of time, T.R. eased his bulk, of a size not considered fashionable since President Taft occupied the White House, out of his office and down the stairway, eyes watery, hands gripping the bannisters in stages as he went. He waddled out to his LaSalle sedan, a car of commodious proportions, and—after fumbling with the keys and the ignition for a short time—set off for Coughlin's funeral establishment, driving somewhat shakily northward along Route 5 at a prudent rate of speed.

Oblivious to the presence of the crowd milling around outside the front door of Coughlin's establishment once he arrived in Lyndonville, because he chose to park at the rear entrance on a back street, T.R. squeezed out of the car and—pushing a discreetly-hidden doorbell button—announced his arrival. He hadn't counted on seeing a variety of lawmen walking into the mortuary's work room via the office entrance just as Junior opened the door and let him in. Junior frowned at him, then raised his right hand to his lips, put his thumb and forefinger together, and drew them across his lips quickly like someone pulling a zipper shut in one hell of a hurry.

"Fellows, this is T.R. Donovan, a businessman from down the road a piece, a fellow who's a friend of mine," announced Junior to the group that had just formed a ring around the body of Dutch as it lay supine under a white sheet on a stainless-steel table in the middle of the room. Heads turned toward T.R., including those of Motor Vehicles Department Officer Ben Harrison, which was topped with a gray, peaked, military-style hat fronted by a silver badge. Dutch's head remained still, eyes seemingly focused on the ceiling. The room smelled of disinfectant, isopropyl alcohol and rubbery-smelling chemicals, much like the odors that waft out of the open bag of a country doctor making a house call. "He owns Donovan's Ice and the Donovan's Roadside Service down toward Saint Jay."

T.R. removed his glasses, pulled out a hanky and wiped them clean, but in this action was unsuccessful in clearing the slight haze that still impeded his vision. Introductions were made and, with exception of Dutch, all the men present shook hands and chatted with each other briefly. "What's your interest in this case, Mr. Donovan?" asked Ben, noting T.R.'s flushed face and somewhat bemused appearance.

"He thought," began Junior, but T.R. interrupted him.

"I thought that since John Doe here might take a while to be identified, it would be good to consider putting him on ice, a service I provide for Junior here, from time to time," T.R. replied.

The county sheriff, his deputy and the constable from Danville nodded thoughtfully in approval. Their three heads bobbed in unison.

"Right," affirmed Junior. "We don't know who the deceased is, so I don't know who will pay for embalming. I'm not sticking my neck out for the stiff, if you'll pardon my saying so. He's not going into so much as a pine box, until I know who's going to foot the bill. Are you going to chase down some I.D. on this guy?"

"You took the words right out of my mouth," answered Ben. "If you'll help me, I'm going to get prints off him right here and now and get them down to Montpelier tonight for analysis. There are risks with everything; the big one to take right now is to assume that whoever popped this guy off won't come after someone else in this area, especially if we sit around and wait, and wonder who's at fault." He pulled a small packet from the pocket of his uniform, from which he produced a small stamp pad and several pieces of specially-marked paper. "How about it, Junior?Want to help me roll some prints?"

Junior nodded his assent, grasped Dutch's right arm and brought it up to chest height. Although Ben was at the ready and soon pressed the first of Dutch's cold, clammy fingers onto the inky surface of the pad, and then transferred the images to paper, he didn't miss the nervous glance that was exchanged between Junior and T.R.

"I've never seen that done, as long as I've been in my office," volunteered the wide-eyed constable from Danville. "How soon will you get results?" He scratched his head in wonderment and then hitched up his gun belt. Ben looked away from his work briefly at the constable's weapon and recognized it as a long-barreled Colt M1878, an obsolete, double-action revolver, one that had likely been carried by the man's father in the Spanish-American War.

And that was the problem the law had fighting crime when going up against the gangsters and other criminals starting to make their appearance on Vermont highways and in its small towns, Ben well knew. What chance did a lawman with a beat-up Model T Ford, a badge pinned on his chest, and a six-shooter first made in 1878 on his hip have against a ruthless criminal on the run with, say, a tommy gun and a fast car? What would the constable's wife and family think if it was the young constable lying dead on Junior's slab, and not a man who very likely may have deserved a gruesome death at the hands of ruthless peers?

"I can tell you fellows one thing," announced Ben as he calmly worked prints off onto ten different segments of the paper he was holding. "I scouted around the pond this afternoon and found a car. A big Cadillac, New York plates, abandoned. Pushed off a highway pull-off. It was down over a bank and jammed up against a tree."

"Anything of interest in it?" asked the county sheriff, John Johnson, first tipping back his big hat and then hitching up his gun belt, one that was generously studded with extra bullets. "Liquor? Guns?" And then, after a pause and a glance all around to gauge his audience: "Pair of a lady's silk stockings?" There were guffaws from his deputy and the young constable.

"No," replied Ben. "It was interesting that with a car that expensive, there was really nothing in it. Nothing at all. No personal effects, that is. The car's registered to someone in Saratoga Springs, New York and it was stolen several weeks ago; the plates are stolen, too. But I did find something outside the car. Probably where it was tossed." Finished with the inking and rolling of the deceased's left-hand fingers now, he nodded to Junior, who dropped Dutch's left arm. It slowly wagged back and forth until it stopped like the pendulum on a grandfather clock that has run out of time. There was a diamond ring on the left hand's pinkie finger, and it had caught the light from the overhead lamps, reflecting it onto the wall in a pattern that had swung, too—almost hypnotically, the sheriff later thought —until all motion had ceased.

Ben lifted the sheet completely off Dutch and looked at his naked body. "Just like I thought," he murmured thoughtfully. He scratched his chin, leaving a small, black streak of stamp pad ink on it.

"Where is it? And what is it?" asked the sheriff. "By the way, Ben, you were supposed to ink the stiff, not your chin!" The men laughed all the way 'round.

"Over there, on the side bench, right where I left it when I came in. It's wrapped in a white cloth; look, but don't anyone touch it."

"What is it?" asked the sheriff, heading over to the table.

"An ice pick," answered Ben, intent on examining the body. "More than likely used to torture our house guest here. That's what the mob guys do, in order to get information, before they decide to kill someone. When you're done looking at the dried blood stains on it, come take a look at Mr. Nobody's many small stab wounds here. To be sure, this guy got shot also, but he was stabbed many, many times, probably beforehand. He looks like a voodoo doll with all the pins pulled out. I'll take samples too, and find out if it's a match."

The sheriff unwrapped the bundle of cloth and emitted a low whistle. "Yup, I see it. Looks like dried blood, alright. Got prints off this already, do you, Ben?"

"I sure do. Look at the handle on that pick, too. Donovan's Ice and Auto Repair, it says on the handle."

"Your's, T.R.?" asked the sheriff. He turned and winked at the big man and laughed. "I can't take you in tonight, though;

no room in the jam. Too many vagrants!" He and the deputy, and the constable, roared with laughter.

"Not mine. I mean, but yes, these were all mine; I had hundreds, maybe a thousand of these made. I gave 'em away by boatloads. I don't think there's a household in 20 miles that doesn't have one of these handy, sheriff," blustered T.R. There was crimson color working its way up into his puffy cheeks now. He fidgeted in his pockets for his handkerchief.

"A boatload? That was pretty good, T.R.!" remarked the deputy, Sam. "This old boy here was a boatload today for the preacher man. You sure you didn't off him?" He chuckled, and rapped his knuckles against the table the corpse was lying on. "You know what? We should all be gettin' home now." He yawned, as if to emphasize this point. "No sense tryin' to figure all this out tonight. Mister nobody here, he can sleep tight, over on T.R.'s ice, 'till Ben gets an answer on those prints."

"Okay by me," said Ben. "But there's one more thing." He stepped over to the ice pick, pulled a pencil from his jacket pocket and used it to pick the ice pick up by the end that had a metal bottle-opener on it, opposite that of the prong. "Can you guys see it?" The men all gathered 'round and peered at the ice pick's wooden handle. "There's a name carved into it: Dutch."

Ben stared at the five men facing him who were intently peering at the small, 12-inch-long object dangling from pencil's tip. He noticed as he did so that the Adam's apples of both T.R. and Junior moved up and down ever so slightly. It was his first subtle indication, like that realized by a preacher who hears an off-key note sung during services, that not everyone in the room was on the same page in the proverbial hymn book.

Chapter 16

Trick or Treat

There was nothing quite like the first few days after a Labor Day weekend to ruin a teenager's enjoyment of life, one of Joey's classmates and best friend—Paul—observed as classes began in the fall of '32. This had been discussed as he and Joey had trudged side-by-side down Eastern Avenue, books in hand, once classes had let out that afternoon. And now, here it was on a Monday, long weeks later—Halloween, to be exact—that Paul was grousing about his pet peeves as he and Joey walked along together, late on that cold gray afternoon. But it wasn't school Paul was complaining about. This time, it was—of all things—movies.

"You're sick of watching movies?" asked Joey, incredulously.

"You bet. Fed up with 'em all."

"But why? "You get to see them all for free, one every night and two on Saturdays!" Joey stared in amazement at Paul, who worked as an usher at the theater that lay just ahead, a hundred feet or so down the avenue. Although it wasn't dark yet, the glitzy marquee that jutted out over the sidewalk was already illuminated. Up above it, blinking chase lights ran circles around the name of the movie theater with the zany speed of a crazed dog in pursuit of its own tail.

"Because I've seen 'em all, that's why. I could see them in my sleep." With that, Joey and his companion halted in front of the theater's entrance way. *Scarface*, starring Paul Muni playing the role of gangster boss Tony Camonte—a character based on mobster Al Capone—was showing. "Look at that," Paul said, pointing at the gaudy poster advertising the film. "Just look at that. What a sappy-looking crew. That's what they call a gangster movie? And this is the second time this movie's been here, as if once wasn't enough." He crouched, slicked his hair back with his free hand and launched into a parody of Camonte's acting on-screen: "Whattsa-the-matter, honey? You know I'm-a the best!" Joey laughed so hard he almost dropped his books. "See, Joey? I've seen it so many times, I know all the lines. I'm bored to death with that movie."

"Yeah, now I see. So, I'm kind of bored, too. I've got the night off; things are slow at Sam's. I sure as heck could stand to see a movie." He stared at the glass-encased poster. "The only thing going on in town tonight's the Halloween parade— for peewees; little kids."

"Then I've got an idea. My treat, your trick. You fill in for me tonight. It'll be real easy for you. Because it's Monday and it's Halloween, there'll be a small audience, and no little brats to deal with or toss out; they'll all be out trick or treating. I'll square it with you so you get my pay, and you can keep any tips. I've got a pal who promised he'd get me into The Bucket of Blood to go drinking and dancing any time I slip him a buck or two. He says I'll pass for 21, easy."

"Tips?"

"Sure, tips. There's a few well-heeled guys who have pre- ferred seats, you know? They bring in a bottle on the QT and a fancy girl, too, and they like to have their privacy, so I put them where they can have some dark and quiet space. Where they can kick back and enjoy themselves without anybody bump- ing elbows with them and getting noses into their popcorn and candy—if you know what I mean—while the movies roll. And for this, I collect some change; ka-ching!"

"Okay," ventured Joey, "I'm all for it. Now what?"

"So, let's go in," said Paul, bringing a key out of his pocket and twisting it in the lock one of the front doors of the theater. "I'll show you around, and I'll give you my jacket and cap, so you can wear them tonight and play the part." Paul paused, and then inspiration struck. His face broke out in a broad smile. "Hey—look—you should wear a mask, too! That'll make it even easier—and a lot of fun, because it's Halloween." They stepped into the lobby, and then Paul turned and locked the door behind him.

"Before we leave, we'll go to the office upstairs so you can meet the lady who runs the ticket booth and I can tell her what's up, and then we can go see old guy who's the projectionist, before he starts drinking. Sometimes he falls asleep and I have to run up there and wake him up before he misses a reel change. *That* would be really bad."

"What time do I have to be back here?"

"Be here be 6:30 to be safe; the show starts at 7:30."

"What about your big tippers?"

"The only one you might have here tonight loves this dumb movie; he's seen it twice already. A new guy who just started showing up a few weeks ago. I'll show you what his seat number is. He's a sharp dresser; has a different dame with him every time he comes. He even *looks* like a real gangster, not like-a that Tony Camonte in that-a movie!"

"Oh, yeah? What's the guy's name?"?

"It's Steve."

* * *

Billy, a bouquet of fresh flowers in hand, rapped his knuckles hard on the door of the guest room at the farm of the late Silas Scrivvins. It was late, way late in the murky afternoon that was letting on to Halloween eve. The sun emerged briefly from the clouds, seeming to brood hesitantly over the western mountains. It finally melted away to a pinpoint of light— then disappeared. And the mood of the day turned from one of suffering the monotony of another drab day before winter's arrival to one of all things witchy, ghostly and mischievous that moved creepily about in the dark on Halloween.

Mary Lou, pert and pretty, pulled open the door and then pulled Billy in, too, by the lapels of his jacket. "Come in, mister," she cooed, flashing the kind of dazzling smile a debutant dishes out in a well-staged Hollywood newsreel appearance. "Oh, my goodness; I've been waiting up a long while for you!" Once inside, Billy yanked off his hat and tossed it at a coat rack, missing it by a wide margin, but his well-timed kiss landed squarely on Mary Lou's waiting lips. She pulled away, clutched the flowers, and winked at him. "Now, silly boy, you swear to me straight up, right here and now you didn't snitch these off some poor little girl's coffin, and I'll fix you a drink!"

"Mary Lou, I *do* swear! And there aren't any girls good enough except you to make me buy flowers like these, I'll have you know." Billy hugged her, lifted her off her feet, and then she was soaring to the blue heavens of her dreams, taking off for a flight that she figured would be good to at least get her through the rough patch of her first Vermont winter. And maybe, like a lot of those between other take offs and landings she'd made, it would be an enjoyable one while it lasted.

"Hey," questioned Billy, "little girl; have you got some candy? It's Halloween, and I want some!"

"Trick or treat!" shrieked Mary Lou, sounding like a mischievous prankster. "You want some candy, boy, you come and get it!" She scampered off into the bowels of the dark farmhouse with the bouquet in hand. Billy tossed off his coat and darted after her. The chase ended minutes later in the master bedroom of the main house, where Mary Lou had thoughtfully turned the lights on (but down low) hiked her skirt up and turned down the bed. Then, she sat on it and waited for him to pounce as he finally deduced where she was and came pounding up the stairs. By now, a rose from the bouquet was clenched in her teeth.

Billy paused after he stepped into the bedroom to loosen his necktie, and he glanced out one of the bedroom windows briefly. He could see the distant pinpoints of light from the big, fancy house belonging to Catherine's parents situated a mile or so away. He vaguely remembered sitting on that homestead's lawn with Catherine many weeks ago, longing for the paradise of the land old Silas once owned. But now, paradise was here, and it was revealed to him in excess a moment later when he turned back from the window and saw that Mary Lou, bothered slightly by his inattention, had dropped the rose and unbuttoned her blouse, revealing another, more intimate and tactile paradise.

"You know," she said, smiling coyly once she had Billy's undivided attention as she undressed further and he came closer, now breathing heavily, "I don't do this for just anybody."

* * *

Promptly at 6:30, Joey arrived at the theater and said hello to the gum-chewing lady in the ticket booth; she put down her dime novel long enough to look at him and wave him inside. He climbed up the stairs to the office, where he donned Paul's maroon-colored usher's jacket, with its many brass buttons, and his cap. In addition, Joey put on a black costume mask he'd bought down at J.J. Newberry's 5&10 to cover his eyes. "You look like a bank robber wearing a monkey suit," said the grizzled old timer preparing the movie projector for the show. "I sure hope you don't scare the hell outta them." He reached around underneath the movie projector after he finished tinkering with it, brought forth a flask and took a swig from it. "Want some?" he asked Joey, who shook his head in reply. "You sure? This'll be a long one; six reel changes."

Moviegoers sauntered into the lobby after buying their tickets and then wandered off to find seats. But once the lights had gone down and the projectionist, presumably still sober rolled a newsreel film, Joey guided movie goers through the darkness to seats, using Paul's flashlight to show the way. Few people were attending the showing tonight, and there were no kids among them who might cause trouble, so Paul had indeed been right. Finally, as the newsreel ended and the trailers of coming attractions rolled, Joey padded up the aisle and through the doors into the lobby, where corn was popping like rapid gunfire, white puffs of it ricocheting off the glass walls of the popper; the smell of hot butter, candy and perfume had overtaken the previous stale smell of the lobby. The door to Eastern Avenue swung open and a slim, well-dressed man with an impish-looking brunette in tow entered. "Two, please, hon," said the man to the ticket girl. He pushed money toward her under the glass window of the booth and turned to smile at his date.

"Got the seats saved for me, Paul?" he asked, turning toward Joey. The man had a razor-thin smile on his face. His eyes were dark, expressionless. The smile disappeared when the expected answer didn't come.

"Whichever ones you want," replied Joey. He turned, opened the door into the theater, and gestured for the couple to follow him. He had taken just two steps into the theater when he felt himself being spun around; the man yanked the flashlight out of his hands, turned it on, and held it up to Joey's face.

"Are you setting me up for something, kid? You're not Paul. If you were, you'd know my seat numbers and have them saved for me, and besides, Paul has a mole on his chin."

"Look, I didn't say I was," stammered Joey nervously. "I'm filling in for Paul tonight." Then, once he'd regained his composure, he said, "So, you're Steve, right?"

"Maybe I am and maybe I ain't. You'd better tell me right now what your game is."

The girl with him fidgeted nervously, sensing conflict. A few people had turned around in their seats to see what the tussle was about. "C'mon, honey, let's go," she whispered "People are looking."

"So what's your name, kid?" asked the man. He let go of Joey's shoulder and yanked his mask off to get a better look at him.

"My name's Joey Ross. And aren't you Steve? Paul said for me to take good care of you."

"Joey!" blurted the girl. I know you. I know your big brother, Billy; I'm Doris. Remember me? Oh, Steve, don't be so silly; Joey's all right; he's just helping his friend out tonight—can't you see? C'mon, let him go!"

"Okay, pal," said the man, handing the flashlight to him. "Yeah, I'm Steve. Sorry about the little kerfuffle there. No hard feelings, right?" He patted Joey on the shoulder he had been gripping. "I always like to know who I'm dealing with. Especially in the dark. Now, find me my nice quiet spot in the back near the exit, and keep everyone away from us. And, I don't want anyone sitting behind me." He stuffed a dollar bill and some loose change into the pocket of the uniform Joey was wearing.

Joey, feeling more than a bit uneasy, led the couple a short distance down the hushed aisle just as the feature was about to play. "Thanks, pal. Now I know I'm in good hands," whispered Steve, as Joey ushered the couple into two seats an unoccupied row, where there was no one seated within ten feet of them. "C'mon, Doris," Steve said in low tones, settling into his seat and removing his fedora. "You can tell me all about how you know Billy—and who he is and what he does—later. But right now, I'm up for a good show."

Chapter 17

An Uncle's Monkey

Once the October page of the calendar had been turned to reveal November's, it was what the locals call "stick season." The time that follows the splendor of foliage and tricks or treats of Halloween. It lasts well past the time the blizzards blow into the Kingdom, until spring. It's when the bare brown hills and purple mountains—except where spruce, evergeens and pines hold sway—are as prickly as an ornery hog's back, bristling with naked, spiky-looking trees.

Billy's acquaintances Tom and Seth, cemetery caretakers and gravediggers extraordinaire, were out in the woods late one cold night during this dreary time of year. This was hardly odd at all because, for one good reason, the ground in area cemeteries would soon be frozen solid and there would be no burial or caretaking work for them. The bodies of folks who inconsiderately kicked off during the frigid winter months were Junior's problems, solved either by storage of the deceased in T.R.'s ice house or else in a crypt down in St. Johnsbury. So, the two boys, Tom and Seth, longtime pals, hung up their spades well before Thanksgiving Day and worked odd jobs afterward, using their battered old three-ton truck. They cut timber for firewood, or so they said, out among the tall trees up in the high, sunny hills and down in the dark, quiet valleys and hollows clustered around Hazen's Corners.

Tom had come from a long line of military men. His father, Frank had died over in the trenches in France during the Great War, back when Tom was seven years old; his grandfather had perished in the Philippines during the war with Spain, back when McKinley was President. And Tom's great grandfather had paid the ultimate price on the battlefield at Gettysburg. Tom's mother decided the family had done its part for America and sent Tom, who had wanted to enlist, off to Bayley-Hazen Academy instead for a proper education. Tom's academic career began with a bang. Its trajectory was much like that of a man fired from a cannon who initially soars to great heights, then descends to earth in a gentle parabolic arc and lands. Tom landed on his head on the football field one day, without benefit of a helmet and once the game was over, Tom decided he had had enough of the private school, its complicated tests and its droning teachers; he grabbed the business end of a shovel and went to work digging graves after he joined forces with Seth and then, seasonally, worked with Seth out in the woods.

Seth, who had met Tom at the arcade in St. Johnsbury one night, came from a different background. Seth's great-grandfather had been the first man in Hazen's Corners to be hanged for the offense of horse thievery. His grandfather had gone AWOL while in the army in the Philippines and deserted, and his father had left town for parts unknown shortly after Seth made his appearance in the world. He grew up rough, tough, and full of bluff. Unlike Tom, he went on to graduate from an institute of higher learning, albeit one that was somewhat unconventional. But no one who knew Seth from his one-room schoolhouse days of breaking windows and kids' noses, stealing children's lunches, or else their bicycles, expected him to emerge any smarter from it; after all, he'd gone off to reform school for four years afterward, not Bayley-Hazen Academy.

Sometimes, to tell the truth (something Tom and Seth did infrequently at best) their activities in the woods involved the hastily-contrived acquisition and discreet removal of recently-felled hardwood logs lying unattended and stacked beside the road—logs actually awaiting pickup by their rightful owners. Occasionally, while cruising old back roads the pair would run across a particularly fine cherry tree that caught their fancy and would chop it down. No lies were told at the sawmill when dollar bills with George Washington's face on them were counted into Tom or Seth's calloused, grubby hands, simply because no questions were asked about who cut down the tree, or whose it was. Then, too, now and then a tempting stack of freshly-planed lumber drying outside some remote, idle saw-mill would catch the attention of the boys as they made their nocturnal rounds in a distant town, driving their old Graham Brothers log truck that had two mufflers attached to it in order to silence the sounds of its cantankerous, grumbling motor. And the "hot" load of boards they absconded with would find a buyer in a either a builder or else a lumberyard manager farther down the valley, someplace where honest folk were a little slow on the uptake and news didn't travel fast, but where the two boys could, in order to make their unscrupulous living.

Their late evening activities were referred to by the frustrated cops and the local press as the predations of a mysterious gang referred to as the "Midnight Logging Company". It wasn't odd at all, considering the opportunities at hand, that the jobs the two boys pulled and invariably got away with also concerned the disappearances of seasoned, cut-to-length cordwood that was sold later on in neighboring towns. As things go, what went on in the woods—far out of view of the boys' family members—and the law—stayed in the woods.

Tom's Uncle Eric and his forefathers before him had picked rocks and then tilled the soil on the hardscrabble side-hills of Hazen's Corners for years, almost beyond recollection of anyone in the village. It was a quiet place where stone walls kept good neighbors. Where the tall white steeple of the Congregational church stuck up primly among the forested hills like the upraised finger of a person holding it to his closely-pursed lips, a signal made to invoke silence and discourage idle chatter. Where gossip rolled freely off tongues, but secrets were kept stashed away like potatoes, dark and unturned, in the depths of spiderwebbed root cellars.

Eric had milk cows, and also grew and harvested corn, beans, squash and pumpkins. As well, there were acres of sugarbush on the farmstead to tend to. Each spring, Eric and his boys, including nephew Tom and his friend Seth, made the rounds and tapped the many maple trees that abounded on the family farm. Using hand drills, mighty curses and determination, they bored holes through the armor-like bark of the trees, hammered in taps, one by one, and then hung wooden sap buckets beneath them to catch the dripping nectar of the trees as sugaring season began in March.

Then came the gathering, making rounds on a horse-drawn sledge with a tank on it, collecting sap, bucket-by-bucket, tree by tree, stopping and starting, making the bells on the horses' harnesses jingle; the boys yelled to each other, and the horses snorted and stamped their feet in the mushy snow in impatience with the cold at every halt. And finally came the days of boiling in the sugarhouse, far down a single-lane road behind Eric's barn, a lane that turned into a pudding of brown mud as the days warmed, the sap fairly gushed into buckets, and the earth warmed to the spring season at hand. The still-chilly air made a fog of the sweet-smelling vapor that came billowing out from the rough-cut sugarhouse cupola, and the gray smoke that spiraled up into the bright blue sky from the rusty round stack sent a signal to townsfolk far down the valley that it was maple sugaring time in the Kingdom.

But tonight wasn't a night for making maple syrup. It was night for making something else, something far more in demand and more profitable than what folks liked to pour over their pancakes: moonshine, to pour down their gullets. Tom had recently, on the sly, decided to tap into his Uncle Eric's supply of firewood, set aside for the next season's boiling, and use it to fire up a still he'd made. Getting the corn, making the mash and setting it aside had been easy. Making the still hadn't.

First, Tom and Seth had dragged a rusty old maple syrup evaporator, one Eric had junked long years ago, out of the field and into the sugarhouse. The firebox would serve its original purpose; atop it, the two boys fashioned a boiler out of a discarded grain funnel they found outside a feed store over in Danville. Soldering joints with a blowtorch as they went, they added a long brass tube scrounged from a discarded bed's headboard, connected it to a barrel, and then joined that to a series of spirals made from copper tubing that would serve as the contraption's condenser. With this invention safe from prying eyes until it would have to be removed and hidden come early spring, Tom followed a sort of business plan that he had cooked up, much like the sludge of smelly corn mash that was about to be distilled into pure alcohol in the contraption he and Seth had assembled.

Most successful business partnerships involve the synergy that naturally evolves out of the combined forces of one person with a strong mind and those of one with a strong back. Weakness in both of these regards may have doomed the partnership of Tom and Seth from the very beginning, but with a sufficient supply of firewood, mash, and what had come to the surface of a crock of hard cider after it froze the night before —pure alcohol—Tom and Seth were in their element tonight, dipping into the crock for a bit of inspiration while they waited for their still to get up to temperature, and provide more of what they wanted.

"Nice!" proclaimed Seth, after taking a sip from the battered tin cup he had dipped into the clear, cold liquid above the crust of frozen hard cider in the brown crock resting by his feet. The bite of the naturally-distilled moonshine warmed his throat nicely as it trickled down into his innards. He looked at Tom, not sure which of the two images of him was the one he should be talking to, and then gave up on any further concerns. What the hell—it was Saturday night, there was a roaring hot fire going, despite the chilly weather outside, and he and Tom were going to make some awesome booze in their own still. All it took was corn, of which there was plenty, firewood, which was on hand, and some cold water from the little brook nearby. It should be easy—right?

"This is hard," proclaimed Tom, staring at his own battered little tin cup. He had just stoked the fire under the still, the conglomeration of tin work and pipes that had a large coil of copper tubing extending out of it. At its end, almost expectantly, another tin cup had been placed underneath it, awaiting the first few drops of pure alcohol. He eyed it the way a hungry fox watches a hen house. Tom licked his lips.

"You think?" asked Seth. "Of course, it's hard."

"I mean, it's hard *work*, Seth. We're drinkin' the last of this booze made the lazy man's way. Look at all this plumbing here. And the wood; I worked my butt off building this fire. Hope to hell we get somethin' for all this trouble." He tossed the contents of what was in the bottom of his cup down his throat; in a few moments, his toes and fingers tingled with the buzz of the booze. He set the tin cup down heavily on the rough table beside him as if it were made of cast iron, and tried to clear his head.

"Yeah, me too." Seth rubbed his forehead, trying to think straight and say exactly what he meant. But now, he didn't know quite what he meant to say. "I hammered all that tin and did the soldering. Hell of a job. Hey, poke that fire, would you?"

"I just *did*, Seth," groused Tom. "Look here, we have to watch this." He tapped the thermometer that was strapped to the improvised boiler with pieces of rusty wire. "Can't let it go over 78 degrees. Unless, of course, you want to drink something that's mostly water." The mash gurgled like someone's upset stomach. Smoke that belched from the firebox coursed through stovepipes that had been salvaged from a junk pile and been jury-rigged to the main smokestack of the sugarhouse.

Seth shook his head, and looked around the ramshackle building. It was redolent of Eric's family history in farming. Old license plates from vehicles long gone dangled from rusty nails on rafters overhead; cardboard signs advertising chewing tobacco, snuff, and show dates for circus tours had been tacked to the rough boards of the walls, where little signs had been posted concerning epic sap runs and maple syrup yields of long ago: "Twenty one gallons of fancy, 3/21/18" read one. And there was graffiti, too, carved into the boards: "To hell with the Kaiser; we're Americans" went one saying. As if to contradict that inscribed opinion, there was a faded, dogeared photo tacked up next to it of Tom's Uncle Eric in his doughboy uniform, young and handsome, hugging an even younger-looking Aunt Marie. The front porch of the family farmhouse, crowded to overflowing with smiling visitors holding small American flags was in the background. "Back over here at last!" had been written on the photograph in a lazy scrawl of blue ink.

Tom was engrossed in studying a page torn from a Canadian magazine. The page contained a diagram of a still, a list of materials and a recipe for distilling whiskey from corn mash, once such a contraption had been built. The writer, quite naturally, had gone on to say that manufacture of whiskey without a government license was an offense, in order to indemnify himself from prosecution. Banned in America, the magazine had no doubt been bootlegged, just like rum and other spirits, into Vermont. Tom had followed the directions as best he could, and now was double-checking everything. Not without some difficulty; they were in French, and Seth had translated them as best he could, with some help from a friend, and had made copious notes on the tattered pages.

"Hey, Seth, what's this word here?" he asked, passing the article over to his pal. Tom was pointing to one in the comments about the recipe.

Seth wrinkled up his forehead as he tried to concentrate on the word, but it was blurry. "Says here—ob, obyew, obfu. Hmmm. Oh, obfu—scation." He looked up and smiled, quite pleased with himself for pronouncing the word—even if he wasn't sure that was quite right—or what it meant.

"So what the hell does that mean?" asked Tom.

"Must mean you can't do something here," said Seth. "Oh, yeah, I think I get it: 'Do not obfuscate the process by letting the thermometer fog so an accurate reading can be determined.'

So you've got to make sure the glass ain't all foggy."

"Dammit, I knew that! Can't let the temp get over 78!" He turned his attention to the fire and the boiler, which looked somewhat like an enormous tin can with blobs of silver solder huddled around the joints where it had been crudely fastened together. He tossed another piece of wood into the firebox; red sparks flew out at him like angry hornets before he closed the door by kicking it with one of his muddy black barn boots. He consulted the thermometer strapped to the boiler; it read exactly 78 degrees. Not without a degree of smug satisfaction, he dipped his battered tin cup, made for sampling maple syrup, back into the earthenware crock and raised it to his lips. And he took a swig of hard apple cider 'shine. "This had better be good. This is one helluva lot of work," he grumbled. "More than just lettin' old Uncle Eric's cider turn hard and freeze so we can drink what floats off the top."

"Look!" exclaimed Seth, almost jumping off the old wooden crate he was sitting on. "Well, I'll be a monkey's uncle! Or maybe you will be! Here it comes!" He pointed to a tiny drop of liquid that had just appeared at the end of the coiled copper tube, and was poised over the tin cup that had been set there to receive the alcohol.

"I'll be damned!" hollered Tom. He leaned over and snatched it with his left forefinger before it fell, stuck out his tongue, and placed the droplet on it—and swallowed. Hard. The 'shine burned its way down to his stomach like molten lava.

But it was good. Wicked good, in fact.

"Hey, I was going to drink that!" bawled Seth. He watched attentively for more droplets to appear.

"Cool your pipes, boiler boy, and read those instructions," retorted Tom. The fusion of corn mash whiskey and apple cider moonshine was now beginning to take effect. Tom felt as though he was no longer seated on a crate, but floating over the dirt floor of the sugarhouse. He was warmed by the booze and also by the fire. He was also glad that he'd winterized the sugarhouse as best he could, tacking up tarpaper around the outside to keep out the cold, stuffing rags in any place there was a chink that let in a cold draft. He might spend some quality time here tonight, he thought, sampling the wares. Alcohol now trickled freely from the copper tubing into the receiving cup, and puffs of steam exited several places in the boiler where seams hadn't been completely sealed with solder.

Seth grabbed the cup after a scant few drops of alcohol had plunked into it, and poured the cup's contents down his throat. "Oh, yeah," he murmured, almost reverently as he swallowed. "This stuff's got a real kick to it." He exhaled, set the cup back down under the dripping condenser's spout and read again from the magazine article and the translated notes on the pages, thoroughly engrossed in it and its pictures, pondering over the strange words while Tom drowsed and the temperature of the boiler increased steadily: "The notion that stills blow up is pretty much a myth. However, it has been known to happen from time to time in instances where a still is in a closely-confined space without ad—adequate—vent— Tom: what's this darned word?"

He held the magazine article up and Tom, startled and momentarily dumbfounded, stared at it steadily for a couple of seconds until the explosion took place, blowing the windows out of the sugarhouse and promptly setting it—old circus posters, the boys' jackets and other things—on fire.

Tom's worrisome Aunt Marie knew trouble when she heard it, knew trouble when she saw it. And during times when she neither heard nor saw any trouble, that worried her, too. It was all too quiet that night, she thought to herself. It made her wonder what Tom and his friend Seth were up to at this late hour out in the woods. No doubt, monkey business. It had kept her up late, fretting, although they had told her not to be concerned: they'd be cutting firewood out by the sugarhouse. But that was long hours ago. Her first concern was the soft *thump* that came from outside the family farmhouse, off to the west. It wasn't a gunshot, nor the sound of a car backfiring; that, she knew. So, it must have been something even more sinister, she reasoned. She pulled apart the curtains in the parlor and looked to the point where she knew the sun had sunken into the depths of the mountains a few hours ago. There was a red glow out there in the woods. Then, orange flames flickered and cast long shadows among the tall maple trees. She hollered for Eric, his milking chores in the barn done a while ago, who was fast asleep in his bed upstairs; Eric snored on, oblivious. Marie cranked up the telephone, got on the party line and called out the local fire department. It just so happened that a wily

Treasury Department revenuer over in the next town who had been about to call in a report to his superiors was listening in.

* * *

"What happened?" asked Tom, dazed, of the fire chief, who had dragged him over to the fire truck and had sat him down on its running board. The chief plopped down beside him. It had begun to snow, and the truck's engine and water pump were running full tilt; the firemen had dropped a suction line and strainer into the brook near what was left of the sugar-house in order to supply water, and a stream of it was now being played on smoldering ruin by two brawny men in black helmets, rubber coats and boots. Others poked away gingerly at what was left of the collapsed roof, looking for hot spots, pulling smoldering pieces of tarpaper and chunks of wood out from under it with pike poles into a pile where they could be better extinguished.

"I was going to ask you, son," grumbled the chief. "Don't tell me you and your pal were makin' maple syrup out here." He looked over at Seth, standing nearby, who was swaying slightly and looked as though he might topple over at any moment. His eyebrows had been burned away, his hair singed, and his red, checkered Johnson jacket looked like it had been worn for a decade by a coal miner—even though he had rolled in the snow for quite some time after the explosion, as had Tom—to put out the flames consuming it. "You'd better sit down here, son, before you fall down," advised the fire chief. Seth stepped over, turned his back to the truck, and collapsed on its metal running board next to Tom.

"You're Eric's nephew, now, ain't ya?" the chief asked Tom, turning toward him. Tom nodded solemnly—but not soberly— and then stared down at his boots, wishing they could some-how walk him backward through time and far away from the sugarhouse. "I knew your dad. Army days," added the chief.

He twirled one end of his gray mustache as if in deep thought, took off his white helmet that had a brass badge on it, placed it between his knees and now stared into it, as if it was a well from which he could conjure up stories and secrets of days gone by. "He saved my life one time. He was a good man." The chief was silent for a moment, then added, upon further reflection: "When he was sober."

"Here's something!" hollered one of the firemen excitedly from the depths of what had been the sugarhouse. He and another fireman, not without some effort, dragged the dented steel boiler, the blackened brass tube and the coil of copper from the ashes with a pole that had a big hook on its end. "Look at that, chief! That's worth saving!"

The chief looked away from this discovery as he heard the loud, crackling crunch of footsteps approaching on the icy farm road to his side. He stood, grasped a spotlight on the truck and beamed it in the direction of the sound. Caught in the glare of the powerful light was what Tom, Seth and the fire chief instantly recognized as a uniformed Treasury Department officer. These officers—the revenuers— had been the stuff of legend and out-of-state newspaper articles—up until now. "I'll take it from here," said the man in a clipped, official-sounding tone. "This still and this crime scene are under my jurisdiction now."

"What's a jurisdiction?" mumbled Tom, blearily. The chief could see that his eyes were as glassy as those of a stuffed animal. Tom leered at the revenuer, adding, "Is that where a judge takes his you know what and he..."

"Shut up, son!" whispered the chief to Tom, poking an elbow into the boy's ribs to give him an added incentive to be silent. "I'll handle this." He waved his arms to the men holding the nozzle of the hose. "Shut it down and bring that hose back here," he hollered. "We're done; let's pack it up. The rest of this can burn itself out."

"Who are you two?" queried the officer as he stared at bedraggled boys sitting next to the fire chief and walked closer to them.

"They got here first, helped us knock it down," attested the chief. The revenuer nodded, then strode over to where the components of the ruined still sat. He poked them vigorously with the toe of one of his boots, as if he expected booze to flow forth from them. Then he turned back to look at the boys.

"Tom and Seth, sir," answered Tom. "We're woodsmen." The chief jammed his elbow into Tom's ribs again.

"No liars here tonight, right fellows?" asked the officer, a thin smile on his face.

"No sir," answered Tom, running his fingers through a mop of charcoaled hair. "We ain't lied yet."

The fire chief rolled his eyes toward the star-studded night heavens and put his helmet back on. It was getting late. The two firemen with the hose brought it over to the chief. He stood, and they handed him the big brass nozzle; the end of it was dripping wet. The temperature had, by now, dropped well below freezing, and as the men breathed, their exhalations appeared as billows of steam in the cold night air. They looked at the chief, perhaps wondering why the fire engine's pump was still pumping, the red lights on its roof still blinking.

The chief grasped the hose, casually turned toward the revenuer, and made pretense of fumbling briefly with the valve on the nozzle as he did so. He cursed. He spat. He wrestled mightily with the hose and the nozzle like Tarzan would have in a movie in a great show of force, struggling with a python. And just then, a jet of high-pressure, ice-cold water doused the officer, soaking him to the skin and making him stagger backward. The officer swore, turned and ran up the farm road toward his auto, which he soon drove away in, in order to drive home and change his clothes before he froze solid. "Accidents happen," mumbled the chief, reaching out to shut down the pump on the fire engine.

* * *

At dawn the next morning, the revenuer drove back to Eric's farm. Now, with tire chains fitted on the rear wheels of his car, confident that he could he drive farther than he had the night before, he motored down the bumpy, rutted farm road right to the spot where the sugarhouse had been. There was no sign of a still; the boiler, the barrel, the copper coils were all gone. The officer cursed his luck, and the people who'd bamboozled him.

There were only charred rafters, bits of tarpaper and the remains of two cast-iron maple sugar evaporators at the site, where the snow had melted from the fury of the blaze to reveal bare ground within a 10-foot radius of the building's footprint. He dutifully filled out his report to the effect that a suspected moonshine operation he'd investigated had turned out to be nothing more than a fire of unknown origin. It had destroyed an old sugarhouse, and that was all; there was no evidence of a still to be seen that morning. His conscience clear, he drove to Montpelier to file his report.

After all, he hadn't lied—yet.

Chapter 18

Conflict: December 3, 1932

It was the cold, snowy weekend after Thanksgiving. Mixed up in the flurry of chatty, homeward-bound passengers stepping off the train and settling onto the platform, Catherine's sensationally-fashionable appearance as she arrived in St. Johnsbury, and daintily descended from the coach for the most part went unnoticed, except for the attentions of Tom and Seth. Taking on an odd job as a favor for Billy, they had driven to the railroad station to pick up and then deliver several crates of furniture addressed to T.R. Donovan. They were sitting in their old truck, smoking and passing away the time, waiting for the express car and the crates to be unloaded, as they saw her mince down the steps of a passenger car in her high heels, aided by a doting conductor who held one of her kid-gloved hands until she landed on the platform. "That's her, I'd swear it," remarked Tom. "Catherine what's-her-name, Billy's better half, back before that Mary Lou got to be the lay of the land."

"You mean *that* Catherine?" asked Seth, craning his neck to get a look out the side window of the cab. "I thought Billy told me she said she wouldn't be back until Christmas."

"How many Catherines do you think there are in this county, Seth, that have the dough to buy a fancy fur coat like the one she's wearing?" grumbled Tom. "Cripes; I'll bet after they made that coat for her, there wasn't a mink left within 50 miles of here." Then, he leaned around Seth so he, too could gawk at well-coiffed and impressively-dressed Catherine, who was waiting on the platform while a porter brought her suitcases to her.

Seth wiped away the condensation from his foggy window to have a better look just as Catherine glanced in his direction and told the porter to take the suitcases to the taxicab—one that was idling right beside the battered old truck. "Yeah," Seth conceded. "You're right."

Seeing Seth's hand motion and mistaking it for a wave, Catherine waved, and started walking briskly toward the truck. "What the hell did you do?" blurted Tom. "Now, she's headed over here."

"Nothin'. Who knows? Maybe she's full of whiskey and feelin' frisky," chuckled Seth. "Lucky us!"

"She won't be frisky when she finds out where Billy's been spending his time after hours," Tom said in a low voice. "That'll be a bigger blow-up than that damn still you half-ass cobbled together with your blow torch. Keep your mouth shut. It's not our fight."

"Yeah," sighed Seth. "It'll get all marital-like. Or worse." Catherine approached now, smiling and stepping along smartly. She hopped up on the running board and rapped on the truck's driver-side door. Seth hesitantly rolled it down a bit.

"Oh, it really is you, Seth!" she chirped. "I thought so!" And, peering farther into the cab, "And you, too, Tom!" Tom waved feebly and then looked the other way.

Seth coughed, and then replied, "Yeah, that's the same old us. Still kickin' and not bitchin'."

"Are you working?"

"Oh Lordy, Catherine, I don't know when we ain't," Seth said, shaking his head and pulling a cigar from his shirt pocket. He fumbled in another pocket for matches. Perhaps some cigar smoke, he thought, would serve as a repellent and deter Catherine's anticipated inquiries. "We just can't keep up with it all." He finally found a kitchen match, struck it on the dashboard of the truck and lit the cigar. He puffed on it and gazed out the windshield reflectively. "Wicked busy. But not with Junior's stiffs; it's the off season."

"Yeah," observed Tom. "We aren't goin' in the hole anymore," he added with a chuckle. "Done diggin' till spring gets here, and we hit some more paydirt!"

"So, have you seen Billy around?" Catherine inquired. "I've written to him, but he doesn't write back." There was a dramatic pause, and then she added: "Ever." The smile was gone from her face now.

"Not in a while," answered Seth solemnly.

"How long?" The expression on Catherine's face had changed to one as icy and imperturbable as the appearance of a glacier in a dark mountain ravine.

"A *good* long while, I'd say," said Seth, nodding thoughtfully and also puffing mightily on the cigar. He had, as a matter of fact, seen Billy and Mary Lou less than half an hour ago, walking into the J.J. Newberry's 5&10 just up the street. But Seth held that card with the sagacity of a seasoned poker player.

"Well, if you fellows see him, please tell him to call me. Okay? I'm just in town for the weekend; then, I go back to Burlington on Monday morning. I really, really want to see him."

"Oh, we will, for sure, if we spot him," vouched Seth. "You can bet on it."

Catherine stepped back off the running board. "Everything okay, miss?" asked the porter, who had long ago finished piling the two large suitcases into the trunk of the waiting cab. How she'd managed to hang onto the grimy old truck, standing precariously on its rusty running board in her high heels was beyond his comprehension. He also was waiting for the customary tip. She pressed a few quarters into his hand and jumped into the back seat of the cab.

"Where to?" asked the driver.

"Lyndonville. But first, please stop up on Railroad Street at the 5&10. I need to get a couple of things."

* * *

Mary Lou wasn't quite through shopping, but Billy had by now become irritated by all the walking around and the waiting. It was getting late, and Billy detested being in a five and dime store, looking at nothing more than clothing, home goods, fabric and cookware. But at least Mary Lou's tastes didn't run quite as expensive as those of Catherine; for that, Billy was grateful. It was getting on toward the Christmas season, and displays of toys, gift ideas and notions crowded the narrow aisles and creaking floorboards. Only Sam Rivard's grubby little cash market could have displayed more obstacles that would stop shoppers in their tracks to ponder whether or not they had found a bucket-load of bargains, or marked-down items that might as well have been fool's gold.

"Mary Lou," asked Billy, stealing a look at his wrist watch, "I'm going to go steal a look at some magazines while you make up your mind." She was trying to decide which of two blouses she liked the best; both were on sale. He stifled the urge to start tapping one of his feet in impatience. "Maybe we should just get both of them and get going." She shook her pretty head.

"Oh, look at that, will you?" she commented cheerfully, ignoring him as she poked through more clothing in the display she'd been looking at, shuffling through negligees hanging on the rack. She yanked one of them off to examine it. It was a fluffy little garment in a rather outlandish color. "Here's a green one—in just my size! I do love that color," she cooed in her south-of-the-Mason Dixon Line accent. "Snake-belly green!" Billy turned, put his hands in his pockets and trudged off as Mary Lou proceeded to paw through other clothing on her protracted treasure-hunt. He wandered through the pet section, where colorful parakeets twittered in their cages, hamsters snoozed beside their idle wheels and fish swam lazily 'round in circles in bubbling tanks of water. At the end of the aisle, he turned the corner while still staring at the goldfish, and came face-to-face with his former flame, Doris Martin. It was more, however, than just a face-to-face meeting; it was a head-on collision, and Doris tumbled backward onto the floor. She grasped a nearby countertop and began to pull herself back up off the floor as Billy stood there, stunned and, for once, speechless. At last, he stooped and held out a hand to help her.

"I don't want your hand, Billy Ross; I don't want any part of you," she sputtered in disgust as she hauled herself upright and brushed herself off. "I guess this proves that all those other girls of yours are right; you sure as hell know how to sweep a lady off her feet."

"Doris, honestly, I'm sorry," began Billy. He glanced over his shoulder, praying that Mary Lou wouldn't suddenly appear on the scene. He took a breath and tried to speak, but Doris beat him to it.

"I'm sorry too. Sorry I ever got mixed up with you. But I think getting dodged when I came looking for you that night at the outhouse, and then finding out I'd been dumped was the best thing that ever happened to me. I've got a man now who knows how to take care of a lady. To treat her nice." She straightened up the starched white apron on the gray uniform she was wearing. She smelled of cheap perfume, and the scent blended nicely with the aroma of the assortments of penny candy and saltwater taffy on a nearby countertop.

"And you're—what? Working here now?" asked Billy.

"Yes, I am. I run the lunch counter. It pays my bills. I got hired right after Alma Anderson lost her job. She got fired for giving a sandwich to some poor bum who came in, begging for a free meal, back around Thanksgiving time." She glared at Billy. "She felt sorry for him. That was her mistake. I made one, too, when I felt sorry for you and took you in after you had that fall-out with Jane. And I guess I paid the price when you ditched me and took up with Catherine. I'll never, ever feel sorry for you again, Billy Ross." She turned on her heel and stalked off toward the lunch counter, where several old ladies hunched over their grilled cheese sandwiches and bowls of soup had by now looked up and turned to stare, after listening to the exchange that had been going on in the aisle. Their heads then turned in the other direction as he wood-framed glass door at the front of the store swung open, and Catherine walked in.

With the reflexes of a fox fleeing the hunt, Billy darted back into the aisle he'd come from, then peeked around the corner to survey the situation before going any farther. What he saw was distressing: Doris had gotten Catherine's attention and was waving her over to the lunch counter. And just then, Mary Lou wandered out from another aisle and sauntered along the entire length of the counter, a bundle of purchases in her hand and her pretty nose high up in the air, blissfully unaware of Catherine's arrival. The old biddies at the lunch counter, unabashed, swiveled on their stools now to gawk at her. Then Doris pointed at her—and Catherine followed suit—before Mary Lou disappeared down another aisle. *Crap*, thought Billy.

Conflict. He ran off as quickly as he could to intercept Mary Lou and get out of the store—perhaps through the back door check-out counter. Before all hell could break loose.

* * *

Several minutes later, a worried-looking Billy Ross hustled Mary Lou out the back door of the dime store, carrying a large shopping bag in one hand and dragging her along with the other. "I declare, Billy Ross, I don't understand just what the sudden all-fired hurry is all about!" she snapped. Billy steered her up a side alley toward Railroad Street. As they reached the corner, Billy spotted a taxi parked at the curb, its motor idling and the driver comfortably slouched behind the wheel, reading a newspaper.

Billy quick-stepped to the cab and opened one of its back doors; the driver dropped his newspaper and spun around to look him. "We need to go to Lyndonville, and step on it," Billy barked.

"Can't," replied the driver laconically. "Got a fare already and I'm waiting on her. She's in there shopping." He jabbed a finger in the direction of the 5&10. "Hey, close the door, Bud; you're lettin' all the cold air in." Billy stifled the urge to utter a curse, and slammed the door shut. He turned to face Mary Lou, then looked up and down the street, hoping to spot another cab, without success.

"Now what?" queried Mary Lou, pouting and putting her hands on her hips. "I am freezing out here. You said we'd take the bus back home." She peeked at her wristwatch and frowned. "It doesn't leave for half an hour."

"I'll think of something, Mary Lou." Just then, Billy spied a familiar vehicle making its way up the street: it was Tom and Seth's decrepit truck. In desperation, Billy jumped off the sidewalk as the grimy vehicle drew near, and flagged it down. It came rumbling to a stop, and Tom obligingly rolled down his window. Cigar smoke wafted out of its partly-open windows into the chilly air.

"Need a lift?" a bemused Tom inquired, looking Mary Lou over from head to toe.

"We need a ride up to Lyndonville, guys," answered Billy. "Can you swing it?"

"Sure," answered Tom. "As long as you don't mind us making a stop along the way. We've got some furniture to drop off at T.R.'s. Some stuff he ordered to feather his nest and pretty it up. The old boy's getting' married again soon. Buyin' himself an honest-to-gosh mail-order bride is what I heard." He leered at Mary Lou. "No offense, ma'am."

Mary Lou stiffened up as if she'd been slapped. She stood there agape as the door of the truck swung open, and then fussed mightily when Billy took her arm and boosted her up onto the running board. "Up you go," he ordered.

"Billy Ross, this is not my idea of a nice day off in town!" she complained. Once on the running board, she teetered momentarily, then flailed her arms as she suddenly lost her balance. Tom had the presence of mind to reach out, grab her by the hand and haul her into the cab. She landed next to him on the tattered seat cover like a sack of potatoes being tossed into a grocery store's bin. The truck's cab reeked of cigar smoke, sweat, sour old grease and motor oil. Sparing his new passenger from the sight of his act, Seth discretely rolled down his window, leaned far out and consigned his plug of chewing tobacco to the pavement of St. Johnsbury's main throughfare. "Oh, my goodness," Mary Lou blurted. "This does smell a bit in here." She wriggled like a fish out of water and managed a wan smile as Billy clambered into the cab, sat beside her and closed the door, and she found herself wedged tightly in between him and Tom.

"Me, I take a bath every Saturday," attested Tom, before going on to his apology of sorts. "But this old truck, here, well, she's probably due for one, one of these days." Gears clashed and howled as Seth got the old truck into motion. Billy stuck his head out the window and craned his neck to look back at the J.J. Newberry's 5&10. One of its front doors was open, and standing in the doorway were Doris and Catherine, staring at him.

It was Mary Lou who broke the silence, with her southern, bourbon barrel-aged drawl: "What all is it you two boys do?"

"We're not busy with it now, but when it's not winter, we're grave diggers," answered Tom.

"Yes, miss, that's what we do," added Seth. That's how Billy knows us, through Junior. "Fact is, I wrote me a little poem about us."

"My oh, my, poetry? You two boys *are* rustics, aren't you!" exclaimed Mary Lou with feigned interest. She looked at him, horrified at finding out she was sitting with two roughnecks whose livelihood was putting dead bodies six feet under. Tom looked back and smiled gamely at the pretty girl, wondering just what in hell a rustic was.

"Okay, here it is," said Seth. "Ashes to ashes, dust to dust. If it weren't for cadavers, our shovels would rust!" He and Tom roared with laughter.

Mary Lou turned her attention away from this bit grave-yard doggerel and looked disapprovingly at the palm of her hand, where Tom had grasped it. It was smeared with grease. Tom caught the look and offered an apology. "Sorry about the mess, miss."

"Oh, don't you worry one bit," she replied, turning to smile at him cheerfully while Billy stared out his window and pretended to be interested in the scenery. "I'll just wipe it all off on Mister Billy Ross here, first chance I get!"

Chapter 19

Setting the Trap

"Look, girl," said Doris after she had peeled Catherine's kid-gloved fingers off the door handle of the five-and-dime store, "I know you're in a world of hurt right now from what you saw when those two dodged you." Doris then half-steered, half-dragged her—as stunned as a wide-eyed doe that has just been hit by a car—into the 5&10. Tom and Seth's old truck, with Billy and Mary Lou crammed into its cramped, rank-smelling cab, was fast disappearing up Railroad Street in a blue haze of exhaust smoke. "Sit yourself down at the counter," Doris advised. "I'll pour you a cup of coffee."

"I still can't believe it, what he's done," spouted Catherine as she collapsed on one of the lunch counter's stools, "and what that evil little slut has done to me." Doris, just a short time into her new job but already the epitome of the gum-chewing, wise-cracking waitress, expertly plunked a cup and saucer down and waved a coffee pot over them. Then, she flooded the cup with the aplomb of a busy speakeasy's bartender pouring someone a double, without wasting a single drop in the process.

"I can believe it. You know it happened to me," vouched Doris. "You just didn't know it was happening to you—it all happened behind your back. Your man Billy's been trotting that little debutramp Mary Lou around all over town—Lyndonville, too—showing her off like a prize filly at a horse show."

"Damn her!" sputtered Catherine. "Now that I've heard that, it's even worse than I could ever have imagined." She regained her composure momentarily, then added icily: "I will *not* let someone make a fool out of me!"

"Cream and sugar, hon? They're right here if you want 'em." Doris pushed the containers over to Catherine, who had yanked a napkin free from a dispenser and now was wiping away tears.

"Don't ruin your mascara like that on account of her *or* on that boy, Catherine. Don't look back," Doris advised. "He's a two-timing cheat. He's burned me more than once. And I was a fool, because I let him get away with it." She turned away to return the coffee pot to the burner, put her hands on her hips and glared at the old ladies seated on faraway stools who'd been listening in. Duly chastened, they expressed sudden new interest in their bills, pulled their bulky purses to the ready and prepared to pay up and leave.

"What do I do now?" asked a still-tearful Catherine, in desperation. "Maybe I should call him. It might not be too late."

"I wouldn't call him, if I were you. Don't waste your time."

"But, shouldn't I at least try?" asked Catherine. "I need answers."

"Good luck on that, girl," said Doris. "Good luck catching up with him, for one thing. I've heard he runs booze for someone. He makes a lot of trips up to Canada. Amazing how many people supposedly die up in Canada and want to be buried here in Vermont, don't you think?" At this, Catherine stared at her, almost in shock. Now, stopping short of accepting that her charming boyfriend was actually the womanizing, two-timing skunk Doris claimed he was, she was beginning to put the dots together. Dots that tied Billy's booze, his money and frequent absences due to trips north all together, to form a web of lines that pointed to criminal activity.

"So, when did he take up with that girl?" asked Catherine. She sipped coffee, holding the cup with both of her hands, but the cup, despite all her best efforts, was shaking.

"She made a play for him at old Silas Scrivvins' committal service last fall, after you left for college. My sister was standing right next to her, and saw the whole thing. She, Mary Lou, pretended to faint to get his attention, and Billy came over and swooped her up. He was all over her like white on rice after that. Fell for her like a blind roofer, he did."

"Damn her!" spat Catherine. "Where does trash like that come from, anyway?"

"Down south where she'd been living large until she had to skip town when the rent was due and the bill collectors came knocking. She came back to Vermont to take care of Scrivvins' house over the winter while her big sister Daisy took off for greener pastures, and another old man with more money than brains. She's one of five girls in her family, all originally from right here in the Kingdom. They lived large and never paid their bills, not one person in that whole family. Gold diggers, every one of 'em. Mary Lou's the youngest. You do know what they say about the last kitten in a big litter, don't you?"

"No, I don't, honestly," replied Catherine, eyebrows arched in anticipation of the answer.

"The last one in the litter's always the bitch kitty, hon."

"And Billy Ross is the pawn in her hands that I came home to try and say hello to today, because I missed him so much, and wanted to invite him to the university's winter carnival. I already told everyone he'd be coming with me," fumed Catherine. "I am so mad with myself right now for wasting my time on him, I can't stand it. He was so stupid to fall for that rotten tramp. And I was stupid to fall for him."

"Listen, hon," advised Doris, pulling herself closer and whispering. "There's no use getting all worked up, blaming yourself for what happened. Look at it this way: you're getting your education in the school of hard knocks; you just paid the price of admission. Billy's the kind of mistake you'll never make again."

"Oh, I know that now!" answered Catherine softly. Her fists were clenched, and her kid gloves were off. "But I am worked up over that rotten, trashy whore, Mary Lou, getting her hands on my man. He was mine, after all, damnit!" She slapped the countertop with her right hand, hard enough to make her cup and saucer rattle. "And I'll tell you right now, if there's one thing I've learned from my dear old daddy and his business, it's that you don't get mad; you get even."

"I think I know *just* what you mean," replied Doris, a sly-looking smile working its way across her face. "I have my score to settle, too, but it's with that slick Billy Ross, who stood me up. More than once, like I said."

"I should go now, Doris, I really should," Catherine said, gulping down the last of the coffee. Her empty cup clattered down on the saucer hard enough to be heard clear across the store. "Above all, listen: no hard feelings. We'll talk again, I'm sure," she added.

"I'm sure we will, Catherine; we will," Doris added. "I've got some ideas already!"

"Thank you," said Catherine, gathering herself up to make a graceful exit. "I have to figure out exactly what to do from here, but I'll be glad for your help. I'll call you when I get back to Burlington. You know, I can't even remember what I came in here for—but what I've learned from you is much more important than anything money can buy."

"And it's *my* buy today," declared Doris as she slapped a dime down on the counter, loudly enough to be heard and attested to by the old ladies nearby as Catherine walked out of the store and strode over to the taxicab waiting for her at the curb.

The cab driver, spotting Catherine at long last, put down the sports section of the local paper. His son, Paul, played basketball with Joey Ross on the high school academy's team. That team, hotter than a hornets' nest this fall, had been getting its share of ink in the press. The papers seemed to do a good enough job of keeping everyone abreast of national and local news, too, but what did a cab driver care about that? The best news—the juicy stuff of marital tussles, back-door wife-cheating, deer-jacking, booze-running and crafty felons' capers in evading the cops—that news came to him every day, courtesy of his backseat passengers. And now, here came pretty Catherine, huffing and puffing along in her mink coat. As far as he was concerned, the best news—what he shared with his family at the dinner table as a substitute for an unaffordable night out on the town—came from the best-dressed passengers, the ones who, paradoxically, tipped the least. And the women among them, bless them, just loved to talk about their troubles to a lowly, sympathetic, down-to-earth cab driver. Someone just like him.

* * *

The house lights had dimmed and the newsreel preceding the feature presentation at Tegus' Palace Theater that night, *Little Caesar*, starring Edward G. Robinson had just started when Steve Snyder whispered into Doris's ear that he wanted to go out and have a smoke. She nodded and squeezed his hand, whispering, "Hurry back," and then, Steve was up and out of his seat, finding his way along the hushed and darkened aisle toward the lobby as the movie flickered on. There, he found Paul, the usher, elbows on the counter of the ticket booth, talking with the woman inside it.

"Just the man I was looking for!" exclaimed Steve, an un-characteristically-broad smile flashing across his narrow face.

"Everything all right, Mister Snyder?" asked Paul as he turned toward Steve, a worried look appearing on his face. He'd been playing rummy with the woman on the other side of the booth's window, dealing cards through the cut-out part of the glass partition and now, at this interruption, he set his hand face-down on the counter so he could pay close attention to whatever it was Steve wanted. Steve Snyder, in Paul's estimation, was someone you probably didn't want to have on your hands as an unhappy customer.

"Oh, sure, Paul. I've just got a question for you, that's all. I need some advice. You know I'm an out-of-towner. Heck—let's face it; I'm just like a fish out of water in St. Jay!" He paused to chuckle and then put a hand on Paul's left shoulder. "Let's step outside for a minute and shoot the breeze," he suggested. "I could use some air—and a smoke." Under this persuasion, Paul went, half strong-armed, half walking, through the front door and then stood on the sidewalk, wondering what was going to happen next—and what Steve was going to ask him.

Eastern Avenue was slick with rainwater, and this glossy coating reflected the glare of strings of bright lights on the theater marquee that jutted out over the sidewalk. The chill breeze blowing in from the railroad yards brought with it the smell of coal smoke, and it stirred scatterings of litter that laid in darkened doorways along the thoroughfare. Just as Steve reached into the breast pocket of his suit, a large black sedan turned off Main Street and slowly approached, pulling close to the curb as it came near. Paul suddenly wondered if he should cut and run. But—rather than stopping, the big car instead accelerated and rushed by, splashing water from the gutter toward Paul and Steve, who dodged it by adroitly jumping backward just in time. "Gee, man in a hurry," commented Paul, somewhat relieved, jamming his chilled hands into the pockets of his pants. He'd watched enough gangster movies to know what a setup for a rub-out looked like. Or so he thought.

"Aren't we all?" asked Steve, turning to face Paul. "You know what they say: 'He who hesitates is last.'" He tugged a pack of Luckies free from his pocket. Paul smiled and nodded. Steve shook a cigarette loose and offered it to him. "Go ahead, kid. You're old enough. You know your age, and you know your job, right?"

Paul nodded. He reached out, plucked a cigarette free and planted it in his mouth. "Of course you do," commented Steve, taking one himself. He pulled a lighter from another pocket and flicked it; the flame glared briefly as Steve lit Paul's smoke, then his own. Steve's face momentarily glowed with the sinister appearance of a horror movie's villain. His cheekbones cast shadows so deep Paul could scarcely see the man's eyes when he snapped the lighter shut. It made a sound like a trap being sprung. "Ever think about having another job? One where you don't have to wear a monkey suit like that one?"

"Yeah, I guess so," mumbled Paul. The garish usher's uniform, with its multitude of buttons and a cap that looked like a bizarre aberration of a Turk's fez was something he wore as a badge of courage; it took all he could muster to wear it on nights when there was a movie some of his classmates would attend. They'd invariably poke fun at him for wearing it. "But there isn't much work around here. I figure when I graduate, I'll quit here and hire on down at the creamery; they're always looking for help." He dragged on his cigarette, then looked down at his feet as if idle time was swirling around them, weighting them down, keeping him there. In St. Jay's grasp forever.

"Listen, kid: Do you want to work harder, or do you want to work smarter?" Steve took one last drag on his Lucky, then tossed it into the gutter and watched it slowly float away. Then, he stared at Paul.

"Smarter, for sure. What are you getting at?"

"What I'm getting at, Paul, is you could do some work for me. I'm in business, big business. And it's all done on the QT —know what I mean?" He nodded, as if to draw Paul into his confidence. Paul's nose wrinkled, indicating interest; Steve, a natural-born observer of human nature and its usual failings, pressed on.

"Do you mean," asked Paul, who paused to cautiously look up and down avenue, "the booze racket?"

"It's no racket, Paul; it's business," Steve answered, matter-of-factly, "just like any other business. Everybody's into it, because everybody wants it. It's just that simple. People like me just take care of a basic need, that's all. We serve a purpose."

"Look, Steve, I don't have a car or anything. I don't want to get mixed up in trouble and wind up in jail." He tossed the spent cigarette away and shook his head.

"Kid, we all want to play the straight and narrow and do the right thing, don't we? But ask yourself something: Have you ever seen a Boy Scout driving a Cadillac?" Paul gave him a wan smile and shook his head.

Steve laughed. "Didn't think so. Look, you're not going to get in any trouble. All I want is a little information every week. You're not going to get shot or anything. There are rewards." He reached into his jacket and pulled out a roll of ten-dollar bills.

"Information? Like what?" asked Paul. He tipped his ornate cap back and rubbed his forehead.

"Like where I can buy hops right now. Lots of them. Beer business is good, and there's a setup going on I can't talk about. It's for a big brewery that'll need them to make beer. All totally hush-hush. I know there are folks around here who grow the hops we need. But they keep it all to themselves. They don't share the harvest. I just want to be put in touch with them, that's all." He peeled a ten off the roll and handed it to Paul. "And make them a proposition." Paul looked at the bill and Alexander Hamilton's stern-looking green face as though he'd been handed a bar of gold, and no wonder; ten bucks was just a few dollars shy of what his father earned in wages and meager tips each week as a taxi driver, after paying his cut to the cab's owners. "Can you do that?"

Paul's head was swimming. Swimming with ideas of ditching the monkey suit and buying a real suit. Maybe even a car. Maybe. "Yes, I can do that," he answered. "Hey, you know what? I've heard about some old guy up Lyndonville way who grows a big crop every year. My dad heard about it from two guys who are loggers and do odd jobs. They truck the stuff out now and then, after the harvest. They get drunk a lot and when they do, they like to talk."

"Good. Let's meet here next week, same day, same time. And if you've got what I'm after, there's another ten in it for you, Paul." He stuck out his hand, and Paul shook it. "And another one after that. It's gonna be just swell working with you, Paul, because I know I can trust you. Trust you to keep a secret. Now, I've got to get back inside, before my date thinks I've sneaked out on her. You know how furious dames can get if they think they've been dumped."

Chapter 20

Bad News

Bad news travels fast. Bad news also sells newspapers. These two things were first and foremost on the mind of the editor of the *Passumpsic Chronicle* as he clumsily hung up the telephone on his nightstand, after thanking the caller for rousting him from slumber. He fumbled for the lamp in the darkness, finally turned it on, yawned mightily and rolled out of bed. It was just past eleven on a starless, frigid December night. The cold of the floorboards made his bare feet ache until he tugged on his socks and put his slippers on. "Where on earth are you going?" his wife asked crossly.

"Hansen Larsen's farm, way out on Kingdom Road," he grunted, pulling off his nightshirt and then searching for his trousers and shoes. "Big fire. A really bad one. Sounds like the whole place went up."

"Well, just be careful. Don't do anything stupid." The editor, Ed Alvord, rolled his eyes. He'd covered all kinds of fires before for the paper that he and his wife owned. Accidents, homicides, suicides and more; anything that involved danger. He'd once—taking a calculated risk—jumped from a bridge onto a tethered boat floating below it in order to get a dramatic picture of an unfortunate man going down a river during the

Great Flood of '27. The forlorn-looking fellow had been sitting astride the roof of his washed-away house, desperately clutching onto its shingles. Ed won an award from a publishing group for that photo after it was picked up by syndicated papers; the unlucky homeowner hanging onto his house, hedging his bets he would find a happy landing spot, was never seen again. Everyone takes calculated risks when they think they have to. Sometimes they're right. Other times, they're dead wrong.

As a seasoned newspaper man, Ed was prepared to document anything that might happen at any moment. Much like a United States Marine who says he never goes anywhere without a knife and a flashlight, Ed never went anywhere without a camera and a reporter's notebook. Both the camera—loaded, of course—and the pad and pencil were on the seat of his trusty Dodge sedan out in the garage. Now fully clothed and wide-awake, Ed hot-footed down the stairs from the bedroom, grabbed the car keys and let himself out the kitchen door. It was, of course, unlocked. With Dutch's September appearance at Joe's Pond now forgotten, no one in the community had had good reason lately to lock their front or back doors in this sleepy town. But perhaps, after reading the news that would soon unfold in the pages of the next issue of the *Chronicle*, they would.

The Dodge sped off into the darkness, the editor spurring it along the bumpy, frozen dirt roads as fast as it would go. The sight that greeted him when he arrived the Larsen farm, as he had been told, was far from one of a fire that was a minor incident. The burnt-out husk of Hansen Larsen's old farmhouse was a blackened, collapsed shell, caught in the spotlights of the fire engines that surrounded it. The attached storehouse, shed and outhouse had suffered damage as well. Sheriff Johnson flagged the Dodge to a halt, then strode over, placed one foot authoritatively on the car's running board and aimed his flashlight into the car. "Well, I'll be! It's Ed the ed!"

he bellowed. His breath momentarily fogged the car's window, which the editor was in the process of rolling down. "What brings you out on such a fine evening?"

"Same as you, John. The early bird gets the worm."

John stared at him. "The worm? Are you saying it's your exclusive, or do you think there's foul play here? That some lousy worm started this fire?"

"Well, maybe," replied the editor, gazing at the wreck of the house. "Look at how evenly everything went up. I've seen fires that were set before." John turned to look at the remains of the house, then tugged thoughtfully at one corner of his mustache and nodded.

"We'll see what the fire chief says. There are trucks from other departments here, Hazen's Corners, too, so there's plenty of help to go poking through and see what's what. If there's anything suspicious, they'll find it and let me know." The editor stepped out of the Dodge, raised his camera and as he took a picture of the house, the flashbulb fired and froze the scene of destruction on film as if caught in the glare of an exploding skyrocket. Steam and foul black smoke reeking of burnt wood, tarpaper, furniture and untold possessions still poured from the house's broken windows and a huge hole in the roof. The flames had been vanquished, but toxic smoke still rose from the ruins and stung Ed's eyes.

Several firemen, all in water-slicked black rubber coats, boots and helmets now cleared away what was left of its porch and entered the house, looking like invasive beetles swarming a doomed tree. "It was too hot for them to get in there 'til now," observed John. "We don't know if Hansen's in there, but those boys will find out."

"Who called it in?" asked the editor, now scribbling notes on his pad.

"A neighbor, half a mile down the road. He's a night watch-man who was just leaving for his shift at the scale company.

He stopped to let a car go roaring by, with a big truck following right behind it. Then, he saw the glow over the treetops from the flames. If that hadn't happened, my guess is there'd be nothing left now but ashes and a cellar hole."

One of the firemen who'd gone inside the house now stepped. "Sheriff!" he hollered. "We've found someone." John and Ed walked briskly toward the open doorway and when they arrived at it, John grabbed Ed by the arm. "You can't go in there. Too dangerous," he advised. But Ed wasn't paying attention to him. Instead, he was inspecting the door. Its handle had been broken and the striker plate ripped from the door's frame.

Ed then looked at the fireman who was standing by, and asked him, "Did you boys break that door down?"

The fireman shook his head. He pulled off his grimy helmet and wiped his sooty brow with a blue bandanna. "Nope. It was like that when we got here. I was first out and my truck was the first one here."

"John, are you with me on this?" queried Ed, scowling and scratching notes on his pad. "Somebody must have broken in. You want suspicious? That's suspicious!"

John nodded soberly. "Yup. Now, Ed, you just stay here and cool your pipes. I'll let you know soon enough what we find in there." He switched on his flashlight and beckoned to the fireman, who donned his helmet and gingerly walked back into the house, with John right behind him. Ed hovered expectantly by the door, ignoring the cold. The wind that had picked up since his arrival only made it colder, but at least blew the hurtful smoke away from his eyes and nose.

Long minutes later, John's backside appeared in the doorway. "Stand back, everybody!" he warned. He backed up slowly, carrying something heavy, sharing the weight of whatever he was carrying with the fireman. As they emerged, Ed could see it was the dead, charred body of Hansen Larsen, sitting upright in a chair. He had been tied to it. Then, the sheriff and the fireman, stunned by their gruesome discovery, put the chair down on the frozen ground and stepped back, even as several other firemen gathered around. Ed realized that for once in his life, he was too horrified by what he saw to raise his camera and snap a picture.

Finally, someone spoke. It was the old fire chief from Hazen's Corners, who had joined the onlookers. "Can't say he died just of smoke inhalation just now, can you, sheriff?" he asked John smugly.

"Can't," John muttered. He stepped toward the body and looked at it closely, then poked one gloved finger at what was left of Hansen's flannel shirt. The fabric crumbled away, revealing several savage puncture wounds. "Won't. This man likely bled to death first. Look at the burned blood—pools of blood on his pants and on the chair."

"You've got another dead one in the barn, sheriff," advised the weary-looking chief. He jammed his hands into the pockets of his coat. "Don't think he died of smoke inhalation either. Fact is, I think he's been dead for quite a while before the fire. I've seen a lot of bodies myself in the war, over in France. But this one takes the cake, if you'll pardon my saying so."

The assemblage of firemen, plus the sheriff, his deputy and the editor trouped over to the barn, leaving Hansen, sitting bolt upright in his chair, his hands on the armrests as if just sitting expectantly down to supper, to fend for himself. "We kept a hose on the barn all along," explained the chief, "to keep it from going up. It had a lot of hay in it. Nothing else. Although it looks from tire tracks like there was a car in it that was driven away." John nodded in agreement as the group made its way into the dirt-floored barn. "The door was wide open when we got here. And so was this hole." He held aloft a large flashlight and pointed it toward an excavation in one stall, where a shovel lay on the ground.

The group drew closer, and finally John stepped forward, knelt at the edge of the hole, and peered down into it. The chief aimed his flashlight downward. Under a mass of dirt, crumbling white power and moldy decay he could just make out the wizened outline of a human hand. Puzzled, he turned to look up at Ed. "Lyme," said Ed laconically. "It's what you pour onto a body when you bury it, and you want to make it disappear fast."

"This is going to be one hell of a long night," John grumbled to himself as he stood up, and shook his head in disgust. He pulled a handkerchief from his pocket and covered his nose, pondering what to do next.

"Sheriff," commented Ed, after he snapped another picture and the flashbulb popped like fireworks, "I think yours is going to be a lot longer than mine."

* * *

Paul stood outside Tegus' Palace Theater, waiting for the last of the late-show moviegoers to empty out. One by one, the lights inside were being switched off and at last, the old man who ran the projector and whose job it was to close the place up walked unsteadily through the door. He swiveled around, turned the key in the lock, said goodnight to Paul and went then shuffling off down the sidewalk toward Railroad Street. Then, all was quiet until Steve, driving a new Ford V-8 sedan, pulled up to the curb. Paul stepped over to the car. It was shiny-new, yet wisps of hay were stuck to its windshield wipers and bumpers. Steve leaned far over and cranked down the passenger side window.

"Nice to see you, Paul," he said. "Good job. You gave me some good tips the other night.

So, here's a $20 bill for you." Paul, astonished, stepped forward, smiled, and reverently took it.

"Any time, Mister Snyder."

"See you, Paul." Steve cranked up the window, put the Ford in gear and motored down Eastern Avenue. He then hung a right, passing by the spot where one of LeClaire's other men had failed and crashed a new car. *What a sap*, Steve thought, remembering what he'd been told of it. Right now, things were going well for Steve, and all things were coming to him. Like the new Ford of LeClaire's he'd just reclaimed, and the Thompson gun lying under a blanket on the seat beside him, just within reach. Steve was becoming known in certain circles; in fact, respected by his peers. He was known as bad news for anyone who crossed him. Steve smiled at the thought and put his foot down; the Ford surged ahead and before he knew it, he was doing 60, hurtling off into the night to take care of other business. Like bad news, Steve liked to travel fast.

Chapter 21

Sunday Best:
December 18, 1932

It was Sunday morning. But even before the first church bells chimed in Lyndonville other bells—those of telephones in homes all over town—began to ring, one after one, as callers spread the news of the tragic fire at Hansen Larsen's. Snug in bed and sound asleep, Lila was rudely awakened by the insistent jangling of the telephone downstairs. Her father, Sven, already awake and brewing coffee in the kitchen, could be heard as he made his way to the hallway phone, picked up the receiver and answered. The long pause that came afterward, and then, the brief questions he asked: "Ya? What? When? How did it happen?" stirred her emotions. She listened intently now, suspecting full well that something bad was up. And when she finally heard her father say, "Oh, no. No. Oh, Lord, no. I am on my way," she was fully-alert. Inspired to run downstairs and discover what sort of catastrophe had occurred, she swung her feet out of bed. "Lila!" Sven bellowed from the kitchen, as he hung up the phone with a *thunk* that could be heard from Lila's bedroom, "Get up and get dressed! We have to go—now!"

Several miles farther south, on a side street in St. Johnsbury, another telephone rang, this one in the Ross family's household. Bud, who'd been reading his newspaper in the kitchen while Joey stoked the monstrous cookstove into action got up, ambled over to the wall-mounted phone and politely answered. It was Junior on the line, asking for Billy. "Joey," said Bud, turning toward him as he held the receiver, "go upstairs and get your brother. Junior wants to talk to him. Sounds like he's being called in to work. Go ahead; I'll watch the fire." Joey handed him the poker he'd been using and headed toward the hallway. He sprinted up the stairs, secretly delighted with being assigned the task of getting his big brother out of bed on a day when he was known to enjoy sleeping in, a pleasure he'd been denied as the youngest of two brothers. He stopped at the door to Billy's bedroom and knocked. There was no answer.

So, Joey pounded on the door. At last, there came a muffled groan from inside the bedroom, and at last Billy spoke. "What do you want? It's Sunday. Knock it off."

"It's Junior on the phone. He needs you to come in to work."

"Tell him to go to hell."

"It's important!" insisted Joey, fibbing; he had no idea what the call was about.

"I'm not working today. That's final," Billy grumbled. Joey twisted the door knob and pushed open the door. As soon as he did, Billy stretched out one hand from where he lay on his bed and tried to force it shut. "I told you, you little squirt, knock it off, now! he yelled. But Joey held fast.

"Boys!" called out Bud from the kitchen. His voice came booming through the house in a rare show of authority. "That's enough of that. Billy, come down here and talk to your boss; I'm not going to do it for you. My job is not to do your job."

At this, Billy threw back the covers and rolled slowly out of bed, groaning. He stood unsteadily, then staggered toward the open door as if in a daze, and grasped the doorknob. He almost knocked Joey over as his weight fell on the door. Then, he recovered his balance. "Rough night?" Joey asked knowingly.

"Stuff it, Joey," hissed Billy. Bleary-eyed, barefoot and still in his long-johns, he slowly made his way through the doorway as Joey stepped aside and then went downstairs, grasping the handrail every two or three steps as he went. "I am not—not, working on a Sunday," he declared as he entered the kitchen and headed toward the telephone. "I'm not doing it."

Bud, meanwhile, had built a roaring fire in the old cookstove. He pitched one last small chunk of maple into the stove and, satisfied with the results, closed the door, turned to face Billy, and offered his advice: "Times are tough, son, but you've gotta make hay while the sun shines."

"Hay's for horses, dad," groused Billy. He frowned. "What's Junior want me for today? He knows I've got plans. He even let me take the limo home last night."

"Removals, he says. Two people are dead after a fire up Lyndonville way. Sounds like it was homicide. The fire was set."

"Great. That means the cops and the county medical examiner will come and do autopsies. I'll be gone all day fooling around with this. Where did it happen?"

"Hansen Larsen's place," answered Bud. Joey, listening in from the upstairs landing, felt as though his heart skipped a beat when he heard this.

"Count yourself lucky you've got a job, son, and a boss who trusts you to let you use his fancy car to kite around in on a day off," Bud admonished dismissively. "My boss doesn't give me one." He turned his attention back to his newspaper and raised the barrier of its pages against Billy's well-anticipated invectives.

"That's just the point, dad; this was *supposed* to be my day off!" Billy spat back. He then picked up the phone, cleared his throat, and said "Good morning," to Junior as smoothly and calmly as though nothing had passed in the last few minutes to stoke his temper to hit the boiling point. It was Billy, the charming actor, at his best.

"Good morning, indeed, you dumb lug!" replied Junior sarcastically. "It's one hell of a morning. I've got a real mess on my hands. Someone torched Hansen Larsen's farmhouse last night, with him in it. He's dead. Or should we say, well-done. The sheriff tells me it was arson and there was foul play involved. And when the firemen went looking around the place, they found another stiff buried out in the barn, partially unearthed. You'll have to come up here, take the hearse and wait up there to do the removals once the medical examiner's done." Billy sighed in resignation, his best-laid plans for spending another day off and half an evening romping around a large, well-provisioned house with pretty Mary Lou now evaporating.

"Okay. I've got it," Billy snarled.

"And you know what this means," added Junior. The cops will be all over the place for the next few days, so mind your manners. Stop in at T.R.'s on the way up and tip him off the heat's going to be around for a while."

"Will do," replied Billy, after unclenching his teeth.

"And one more thing. Remember: Sven can be a wild man if something sets him off. Imagine how you'd feel if you just found out your brother had been murdered." There was no reply; Billy was smiling. He felt his dark mood begin to lift. "I just tried calling Sven, but there's no answer. He's probably on his way to his brother's place right now. Don't do anything to cross him when you get there. You know he can be a real animal if something sets him off."

"I know," said Billy, and as he hung up the phone, his composure now restored, he glanced at the foot of the stairs. Joey was standing there with a puzzled look on his face, wondering why Billy was grinning at him now.

* * *

It was mid-morning by the time Billy steered the long, black Packard hearse into the dooryard of Hansen Larsen's hardscrabble farm. The sun, low on the southeast horizon, was almost invisible behind a film of light gray overcast, and an evil, cold wind had kicked up out of the north after he'd left Junior's. And it was beginning to snow. He rolled down his window a bit and tossed his spent cigarette out; the wind carried it off like a whirling dervish into the woods beside the road, where it disappeared into the underbrush. He would have driven by Hansen Larsen's unobtrusive driveway, marked only by its zany but well-weathered 'No Trespassing' sign and battered old mailbox if not for the lack of leaves on the trees. This allowed him an excellent view of a dozen or more cars parked in a jumble outside the burned-out house, and as many people, some with badges pinned to their jackets, milling around.

Sheriff Johnson, exhausted from long hours spent on the job, could raise his hand no higher than his waist to motion Billy to stop. "Glad you're here, Billy," he said, leaning tiredly into the hearse through the open window. "I've got two bodies to get off my hands. One man died last night, just before the fire, I think; the other one killed—well, I just don't know how long ago." He shook his head. "Right now, *I'd* kill—for a cup of hot coffee."

"I know the feeling," said Billy. "I'd kill right now just to have a day off."

"You and me both, pal," said the sheriff, in sympathy.

"Where are they?"

"Bodies are under a tarp in the back of that pickup truck over there," said the sheriff, trying his best to stifle a yawn. He pointed toward a black Model A Ford truck sitting outside the barn. "I'll have to get the medical examiner over there before you get started, or move anything." Off he strode toward the truck, beckoning to a tall man in a gray fedora and overcoat standing near the ruined farmhouse to come along with him. Billy obligingly drove the hearse slowly through the crowd, turned, then backed it up toward the truck's tailgate and stopped a few feet away from it. That was when Sven Larsen made his rather dramatic appearance.

Sven's ancient truck came howling up the steep, bumpy driveway in low gear, jouncing along as fast as it would go, sounding like a dive bomber zeroing in on a target. Its huge tires easily bounced over several large rocks in its path and then, it skidded to a stop opposite the farmhouse. Sven hopped out of the cab and strode over toward Sheriff Johnson. The mood of the assembled crowd suddenly turned from one of pious respect for the dead to awesome respect for a man who stood well more than six feet tall, and looked as though he was capable of knocking out Joe Louis, even with one hand tied behind his back. "Where is he?" demanded Sven. "My brother; I want to see him!"

Both the sheriff and the man in the hat and overcoat waved Sven over to the pickup truck. They slowly raised the tarp. Sven clasped his hands together and lowered his head, as if in prayer. *Crap*, thought Billy. *Drama.* Drama wasted time, after all, and time was Billy's most precious commodity. He'd seen enough drama, and waited through it at funerals, services and burials while people cried, droned on and prayed. He lit another cigarette, then held it out the open window and let the smoke waft away. He looked over at Sven's geriatric-looking truck and noticed Lila sitting in the cab, staring back at him through a cracked windowpane. So, that was his kid brother's squeeze? Well, that was what he'd heard, anyway. There she was, alright, little Miss String Cheese. He waved at her, and the tall, skinny girl waved back, a somber expression on her face. Suddenly, Billy felt the pressure of someone's hand on the arm he'd been dangling out the open window. Startled, he dropped the cigarette. It was Ed Alvord, editor of the *Chronicle*, and it was obvious that Ed wanted to talk with him.

"What do you say, Billy?" asked Ed. "It's been a while. Been a while since the last one of these."

"The last one?"

"The last killing done with a blade in these parts. Just like that out-of-state dandy they pulled out of Joe's Pond a while back."

"Don't know anything about that," Billy remarked laconically.

"Well, for your information, it appears Mister Larsen here was tied to a chair by an intruder and might have been tortured for information. Needled to death with a blade, most likely to make him talk about something."

"That so?" asked Billy, matter-of-factly. He looked down and dug deep into a jacket pocket for his smokes, in order to act busy. He now felt for certain that Ed was digging for info to connect the dots from this troublesome mess to Dutch, and would then unearth Dutch's racket with T.R. Totally verboten: Never trouble trouble, 'til trouble troubles you.

"Yes, indeed. Tell you what: Another thing here is those two Rottweiler dogs Hansen Larsen had, particularly that vicious one, Hardy. Nobody on this road liked that dog and from what I hear of it, Hardy didn't like any of them, either—unless maybe he got off his leash and got a hankering to taste 'em."

"So?" Billy asked, lighting another smoke. He started to jiggle his right foot nervously, and looked in the rearview mirror, hoping that the medical examiner and the sheriff would get done with Sven and get on with it, but they were talking, huddled around the pickup.

"So, Billy, why would someone break into a house, kill a man with a blade but kill his two dogs inside with a Tommy gun, do you suppose?"

"Dunno. Hey, wait a minute! A Tommy gun? Nobody around here's got one. Are you sure?" For once, Billy's face showed some concern.

"Sure am," remarked Ed, scribbling in his ever-present notepad. It was more than of passing interest that the young man he was now questioning had just indicated he might know who in the area—and who did not—own a submachine gun. "Those dogs were chopped into hamburger by more than 20 bullets, all of them .45 caliber. That's a lot more than a handgun's clip holds."

"That so?" commented Billy. He glanced at the rearview mirror and saw that the sheriff was waving to him. "Gotta go, Ed," said Billy, smiling to him, quite relieved at getting off the hook.

"They need me; duty calls!"

"And do me a favor, Billy," piped up another voice. It was Lila's. She had gotten out of the truck and had walked over to stand beside Ed. Now, she looked at him sternly and said, "Tell your brother I want him to call me." Then, she turned on her heel and stalked off toward the barn.

Into her place briskly stepped the man in the fedora and gray overcoat. "I'm the medical examiner who'll be accompanying you today," he informed Billy, "for the removals." Billy nodded and smiled; good—things were moving along now. It would mean a short trip down to Junior's. But then, the rest of the story unfolded. "We'll be leaving for Burlington shortly," he announced. Billy's jaw dropped in astonishment. "The autopsies can't be performed here. I have to take these bodies to a forensic pathologist I consult with. Don't worry; you'll be put up overnight at the state's expense. I know it's a long trip, but we can't wait until tomorrow." Billy gnashed his teeth, held his breath, and stifled a mighty curse as he hopped out and prepared to load the hearse, and spend the rest of Sunday and part of Monday out of town.

* * *

The barn was—except of a large pile of hay spilling out of one of its open doors—empty. Lila wandered through it in a daze, remembering childhood visits to the farm; jumping into the hay, visiting with Aunt Agony and walking through the garden. But one thing was plain: the hops were gone. The entire crop, harvested in the late fall each year and put up in the barn until it was sold in early winter, had vanished. So had the new car she had seen the last time she had been here with Joey.

And now, it was Joey she wanted to talk with. Was the secret out? Had Joey talked to someone?

But—there was more than one secret out now, wasn't there, with the discovery of the body Lila suspected had been buried in the barn. Her Uncle Hansen had been a rascal—that, she knew. He was a big, tough old man who played rough with some bad people from time to time. But now, was her father marked for death as well as her uncle?

She looked over at the ruined farmhouse and what was left of its front porch, left in shambles by the firemen with their poking and prodding. There were the steps where she used to sit with Aunt Agony on sunny summer days and shell peas. She tried to put the acrid smell of the house fire out of her mind, and imagine venison stew bubbling away on her aunt's cookstove in the kitchen. She turned and looked out beyond the barn through an alleyway of bare maples to a spot where there had once been a vegetable garden and, later on, a bountiful green jungle of hop vines; today, there was lonely naked, frozen ground littered with poles and lengths of twine that lay scattered as far as the eye could see.

Out in the dooryard, cars were leaving; doors slammed shut and plumes of smoke emerging from the vehicles corkscrewed upward into the frosty morning air. One after another, the cars drove slowly down the stony, meandering driveway that let out onto to Kingdom Road and headed off to various directions. First, the shiny black hearse left; then, the sheriff's dark green Hudson and right behind it, Ed Alvord's baby-blue Dodge sedan. Finally, only Sven's rumpled-looking old truck was left, its engine grumbling away, idling away the minutes as if in in symbiotic company with the burned-out farmhouse that had seen better days, pondering its fate. And now, Sven, her father, was walking toward her, telling her it was time to go home. For the first time in her life, she saw tears in her father's eyes.

* * *

Ed Alvord yawned mightily as he turned the key in the lock of the door to the upstairs editorial office of the *Passumpsic Chronicle* and let himself in. He placed his camera on his desk, doffed his hat and then his coat, hooking them both on a brass coat rack. This was a workplace arrival ritual he performed every weekday morning, but today was Sunday, and it was going on 9:00 a.m., well past breakfast time. He heard his stomach rumble loudly as he pulled his notepad from his hip pocket and dropped it onto his desk. No matter; breakfast could wait. There was a story to write. He rolled up his sleeves, dropped into his chair, flipped through the pages of notes and thought for a moment. Then, he inserted a piece of paper into his typewriter and began to write copy for what would be the front-page story of the *Chronicle's* next issue:

> Sheriff Says Murder
> Lyndonville Farmer Dies in Covered-Up Crime
> The body of well-known local farmer Hansen Larsen was discovered during the investigation of a fire of suspicious origin that destroyed his Kingdom Road farmhouse late Saturday night. Firemen from as far away as St. Johnsbury and Hazen's Corners assisted Lyndonville's in fighting the blaze

that took several hours to subdue. The alarm was called in by an alert neighbor.

Inasmuch as a gangster's new Thompson submachine gun can be had for the princely sum of $225—almost half the cost of a new Ford automobile today—one can only wonder as to what vicious criminal enterprises from afar, flush with ill-gained cash, are now at work in the Northeast Kingdom. Such was the speculation when it was found that not only had Hansen Larsen been repeatedly stabbed, resulting in death prior to the blaze, but that his two watchdogs had been dispatched with some 20 bullets of .45 caliber. These, according to experts on the scene, presumably came from a Thompson gun, of the kind known to have been used in the Valentine's Day Massacre and referred to in police jargon these days as a "Chicago typewriter".

Ed stopped to read more of his notes, and to catch up with his thoughts again; they had been racing, going faster than he could type. Once he had everything in mind, he began to type once more:

The very nature of this crime brings to mind the gruesome discovery of the body of a New York man who had been stabbed to death in similar manner. His body had been weighted and dumped into Joe's Pond, and, much to the alarm of a group of Sunday school children, floated to the surface of its calm waters during a picnic they were enjoying on its shores this last late summer.

Ed stopped again and briefly thought about what Billy Ross had said concerning Thompson submachine guns. The kid obviously knew something about criminal goings-on he likely wouldn't divulge—unless someone started stabbing him. Probably something going on right under Sheriff Johnson's nose and his ample, push-broom mustache. Ed stopped pondering what Billy Ross might be mixed up in and began pounding keys on the typewriter again:

> It is the belief of local authorities that this out-of-state man was involved in the illegal liquor trade that bedevils our fine Green Mountain state, and that he ran afoul of another criminal element trying to take control of a cross-border smuggling scheme. It is clear that the booze racket has brought crime from afar to the doorsteps of our fine community, and that law enforcement needs to be put on notice to put an end to it.

Ed halted once more, this time to reflect on what he had just written. He nodded approvingly after he finished reading it. "Well, so much for the holier-than-thou stuff," he grumbled to himself, with some satisfaction. He rolled his chair back from the desk a bit, reached down and opened the lower right-hand drawer of his desk. After rummaging around a bit, he found the pint of smuggled Canadian whiskey he'd stashed there in case of emergency—or the need to have a sharpener when working late. Without offering a silent prayer of thanks—or apologies— to the booze racketeers, he unscrewed the cap and took a swig. He thought some more. There were lots of pieces to this puzzle that had to be solved, that of the suspicious fire and the two dead men out on Larsen's farm—most of them missing, it seemed. When he closed his eyes momentarily, all he could see was a distraught Sven Larsen. When he asked the big, sorrowful man what his thoughts were about Hansen's passing, Sven, thinking only of the funeral, had remarked: "I want him laid out in his Sunday best." But then, come to think of it, besides Sven, there was his little daughter, ignoring all else while running off and making a beeline to the barn. What had she been looking for?

Chapter 22

A Snowball's Chance
in Hell

It was dawn on a dreary December day and as St. Johnsbury residents awoke—stretching, then yawning—finally tumbling out of warm beds into frigid upstairs bedrooms, where they stood uneasily upon ice-cold floors, lights began to appear, one by one in the windows of homes up and down the quiet streets. It was Sunday the 18th, early on in the winter, but a major snowstorm and then a brutal cold front had blown in the night before. Hundreds of chimneys in the valley sent pillars of white smoke soaring up to the heavens, still an ominous, foreboding gray, as residents stoked their stoves, rubbed their hands together, and begrudgingly began their day. Heavy snow mantled the swaybacked roof of the building where the Ross family lived, out on the end of Passumpsic Street, and icicles left over from yesterday's all-too-brief afternoon thaw hung from its soffits like long, lethal daggers.

The Ross family's ancient Pontiac reposing in the front yard, a car that seldom saw use by its ever-frugal, penny-pinching owners, could have been mistaken for a winter carnival ice sculpture. The snow, in blanketing the town, buffered the harsh sounds of a steam locomotive already at work at this ungodly hour, switching cars down at the yards and coupling them together, the deliberate hammering of its exhaust sounding like slow, muffled drumbeats through the thin walls and frosty windowpanes of the Ross family's home.

And that drumbeat was what the men of the railroads marched to as the Depression wore on, wallets remained razor-thin, and bread lines of the unemployed grew longer each day, it seemed. The best and most coveted jobs were held by the senior men, men who worked seven days per week. In the downtown railroad yards, there were those who staffed the station with its clattering telegraph sets and busy waiting room, the roundhouse teeming with dark, grimy, panting locomotives, or who tended the coal tower, or worked out on the tracks in the frigid chill of winter or savage heat of mid-summer—they all worked in three eight-hour shifts, called tricks. But another trick, so to speak was when you worked in the yards as a brakeman, hanging onto boxcars as a train was switched, twisting brake wheels or giving signals to an engineer; the trick was that you not get caught and crushed to a pulp between the couplers of boxcars weighing 30 tons apiece that came crashing together—or not to slip and fall under the cars and their cold steel wheels that could neatly slice you in two like a ham shoulder being lopped apart on the butcher block at Sam Rivard's. You learned to stay alert and stay alive. If you worked, you worked 56 hours per week unless you begged a day off and lost your pay. And otherwise, you followed the drumbeat—the steady, day after day drumbeat like that on a slave galley—that of a railroad man's job in the '30s.

"You promised a week ago you'd go up to Hardwick with Joey and cut us a Christmas tree, Bud," said Joey's mother, shooting a glance that conveyed a look of mild annoyance across the kitchen at her husband, who sat comfortably in his chair awaiting breakfast. "Time's gettin' short," she added for emphasis. She wiped both hands her on her apron and then went back to wrestling with an assortment of cast iron pots and pans, jockeying them into proper positions on burners atop the monstrous stove in order to cook breakfast. Joey had brought in an armload of firewood from the shed upon arising and had, to his credit, gotten a roaring fire going in the stove in no time. On the back burner, brown liquid bubbled in the glass top of a battered old percolator, the one Bud had nicknamed "Old Faithful".

"I reckon we can do that today for sure, Beth," answered Bud, easily taking his cue that it was high time for action. He cleared his throat for emphasis, and looked at Joey, who was sitting next to him at the table. "I've been meaning to do that all week. Just hadn't had the chance to make arrangements 'til yesterday so someone on the spare board could cover for me and I could take care of his run. Old man "Wheels" Warner's the conductor on the mixed train to Swanton today, and we'll ride up the hill with him. He'll stop the train and let us off up near the forest. We'll cut us the nicest tree you've ever seen and we'll bring it back in time for dinner, riding back home on the way freight. Frank Flannigan's the engineer for the return trip, and he'll let us ride up front, in the cab. Might even let us sneak home a pail or two of coal, too, since I gave him a couple of perch after I went ice fishing last week, and he told me he'd look out for me." At this, Bud slapped Joey's knee and winked at him. Joey turned to his father and smiled to signify his approval of the plan for an adventurous day out on the railroad—and into a bit of the wilderness—with his dad. The man who was almost always away at work; the dad he scarcely knew.

"Your wheeling and dealing with those boys you work with on the railroad will get you fired if you don't look out," Beth grumbled disapprovingly as she dropped thick slices of bacon into a frying pan; the meat began to sizzle as the conversation in the kitchen took up a somewhat heated tone. "That railroad will be the death of you yet. All we need is for you to be let go by the company for being caught making one of your swap deals. Times are hard enough as it is. We could lose the house and have to go live in some Hooverville in a shanty. Do you know Alma, down at the lunch counter at the 5&10 store, J.J. Newberry's?"

Bud shook his head and stuck his hands into the pockets of his blue denim overalls. "Nope."

He shifted in his chair and eyed the coffee pot on the stove, preparing himself for what he guessed might be a short sermon regarding morals, a sermon that would be delivered prior to the breakfast plates being passed.

"She got fired a while ago for giving away coffee and a sandwich to a panhandler, some shiftless old hobo she felt sorry for who came drifting in from the train yards and sauntered into the store, looking for a handout. Nothing's free in this world, Bud. You should know that. And jobs are hard to come by. Lord knows I'd work if I could find any work!" She mashed the bacon down into the pan and frowned. "Get the breakfast plates and cups and saucers down, now, Joey, would you?" A loving smile suddenly creased her careworn face. She opened the icebox and brought out a bowl of eggs.

"Yes, mom," Joey answered dutifully, getting to his feet. He took two steps toward the wooden cabinet over the sink and slowly, carefully brought down the plates. These once-expensive pieces of china bore the names of their original owners: the railroads that passed through town. These plates had, through various turns of events, passed through the hands of railroad men and into the Ross kitchen. The plates, as well as cups and saucers, bore the names and insignias of the Boston & Maine, the Maine Central and the Canadian Pacific. These items were either chipped castaways or else purloined swap items that came from various railroads' dining cars. All except for one. One that was now in Joey's hands that had the name J.J. Newberry's spelled out in small, maroon-colored script in the glazing around its rim. "Mom," asked Joey, puzzled by the odd-appearing item, "what's this one? Where did this one come from? I don't remember it." Beth put down the spatula she'd been holding, stepped over and peered at the plate.

"Oh," she exclaimed. And then, "Oh, yes." She quickly turned away, cleared her throat, then shuffled back to the stove to resume cooking, making sure all the while that her back was to her husband, who had just picked up yesterday's newspaper. "I think I got that from Alma."

Bud stayed wisely behind his paper. He knew full well who the panhandler had been; it was an old fellow all the railroad men knew, a man they had nicknamed Dusty. Dusty was a homeless man who did odd jobs around town and lived beside the tracks in a tiny shack he'd made out of old packing crates, pieces of tin and cardboard. He scavenged coal and scrap wood wherever he could find it without stealing it, and used it to heat his little home. Dusty, Bud knew, didn't have a pot to piss in nor a window to toss it out of. And Dusty was a disabled veteran of the Great War, without family and without any friends, other than the railroad men who helped him from time to time, simply because the government would not, in its defeat of the Bonus Act for World War I veterans. Dusty was no hobo. He was too proud to be one. Bud, as a family man who knew how to keep the peace, had the good discretion to admit it any time he was wrong, and to keep his mouth shut when he damned well he knew he was right.

There was silence for a moment, then Bud put down his paper, turned to Joey and asked, "Where's Billy? Isn't he awake yet? Better go upstairs and roust that sleepy brother of yours. He has to work today, like it or not. If he's late, he won't be able to catch his ride up to Lyndonville on the morning milk truck." Joey nodded, put the topic of discussion down on the table among the other plates, and left the kitchen. He climbed the narrow, creaking set of stairs to the top landing and peeked cautiously around the corner and through the open door into his older brother Billy's dark bedroom. The sounds of muffled snoring emanated from beneath a blanket draped over the large lump that was Billy's figure. He had, in fact, at some point during the evening pulled the quilt and covers up over his head, thereby exposing the bottoms of his two bare feet. Joey hesitated momentarily before proceeding farther. His brother was older, taller—at five feet ten inches—and stronger than him; in fact, as strong as a grizzly bear from the time spent working at Coughlin's, and also helping out at T.R. Donovan's ice house now and then, loading trucks and roughhousing with his tough pals who worked there. He was also headstrong and could easily be provoked into a state of bluster that was laced with oaths and threats of fisticuffs if he didn't get his way. And now, it was high time for Joey, all of 17 years old, 130 pounds, and five feet, seven inches tall on a good day—as he liked to say—to "poke the bear".

Joey stepped over to the bed, grasped what he figured would likely be his brother's shoulder and shook it, saying, "Billy. Billy! Wake up, for Pete's sake! The only response was a groan and then a pig-like snort from underneath the covers. "You've got to get up! If you don't, you'll miss work. Mom will raise hell." He pulled back the blanket, and discovered Billy was sleeping on his back; his mouth was wide open. With each snore, Joey could smell something. It was booze, he knew; he had smelled that stuff before. Joey grabbed one of Billy's arms and shook it, then slapped his face; there was no reaction. Billy, who could have passed for a corpse, slept on, apparently still snug and warm in his red union suit. There was only one thing to do, short of dousing him with a pail of water, Joey reasoned. And water was not within reach—nor would it have been wise to use. Joey padded over in his stocking feet to the bedroom window. It was spiderwebbed with frost, and through it he could just make out the distant streetlights on Portland Street. There was, of course, freshly-fallen snow on the windowsill. Joey opened the window, slowly at first, then flung it up, letting in a blast of frigid air. He scooped up a handful of snow, returned to his brother's bedside and—not without some difficulty—stuffed a perfectly-rounded snowball down the front of Billy's union suit. He hightailed it for the kitchen as quickly as a sensible sort of man will when he "joins the birds" and jumps off a doomed, runaway train. The results were almost instantaneous, and were, of course, heard downstairs.

"Lord in heaven! What *is* your brother doing up there, Joey?" his mother asked him, at first looking at him and then raising her eyes to the ceiling, apparently fearing that it might collapse at any second and deposit Billy and his bed directly on the cook stove. "It sounds like he's got a bowling alley up there." Several loud crashing noises were heard, then, the sound of a window being slammed shut.

"Jeezum! Jeezum Crow!" boomed Billy's voice, loud and clear from his bedroom. "I'll get you! I'll get you for that!" He came thundering down the stairs and burst into the kitchen, still clad in his union suit, which now sported a large, dark stain down the front; water dripped from his bare feet onto the floor. Bleary-eyed though he was, he glared at Joey with the intensity of an institutionalized madman who has just seen the person who signed the commitment papers. Bud, who had never been known to be mad at anyone for so much as a day in his life, stoically maintained his composure amidst the rumpus.

Bud got up, helped himself to a cup of coffee and calmly sauntered back to his chair. There, he paused to look at Billy before sitting down. "Son, get yourself upstairs and get some clothes on, you red devil. Get ready for breakfast. Stop the foolishness," he admonished. He then turned his back to Billy, sat down and sipped his coffee as though nothing had happened.

Billy, fists clenched, spun around and stomped off to climb the staircase to his bedroom.

Joey suppressed the brief urge to laugh or to smile. Then, the moment passed. He had heard his brother come home late, very late last night, long after the time all other members of the Ross family usually retired: ten o'clock. Joey's guess was that Billy had been out entertaining himself at either the notorious Bucket of Blood or else at Grandy's Arcade over at the Wideawake Block. There, there was bowling, roller skating and other diversions. Both places hosted bands on Saturday nights on their dance floors, and it was rumored that if one wanted alcohol, it was there, too, for the asking, provided you were discrete (and, of course, could pay an exorbitant price). "If you want brandy, go see Grandy" was the saying some of the local high school kids from more well-to-do homes had. They were the few who claimed to be "in the know" about whatever fashionable (and illegal) things could be had in the days of hard times and Prohibition. All it took was a fair amount of risk and some money.

Joey's gaze drifted over to the cook stove, then up at the ceiling. Directly over the enormous stove were six small dimples in the ceiling. These dimples, each of which perfectly matched the size and circumference of burner plates on the stove, were the direct result of Billy conducting a scientific experiment a few years ago on a warm summer day. It was in fact a day when there was only a smoldering, left-over fire in the stove, his father was at work, and his mother was outside hanging laundry on the line. Billy was trying to determine what, exactly, would happen if an entire stick of jumbo-size firecrackers was lit, tossed into the stove and allowed to explode. Once he had observed the loud and rather spectacular results in which six cast-iron burner plates took off vertically like rockets to plow into the ceiling and the kitchen was blackened with soot, Billy made himself scarce. Joey, ever inquisitive, had then innocently come to the kitchen to see what had happened. And thus, Joey took the rap, as well as a tanning session of sorts administered by his father with his belt, out in the woodshed.

For Joey, for the most part, dealing with his older brother Billy was tough. Sometimes it worked and when it did, it was like being one of two peas in a pod. More and more often though, it seemed, it didn't work out, and then it was pretty much: you hit me, I hit you back, but twice as hard. For Billy, Joey was for the most part a minor annoyance. But a day would come when Billy found it very convenient to have a younger brother he could lean on.

* * *

The train easily chugged along at a moderate pace after leaving the St. Johnsbury station, but its locomotive began to labor as it hauled the heavy train up the hill west of town, first rattling over a bridge spanning the Passumpsic River and then tagging alongside it, following its snakelike course west, up the valley. It squeezed through a narrow spot where a highway bridge crossed the tracks, and then the locomotive pounded along with a new burst of energy, sending a great cloud of smoke skyward; cinders rained down and rattled against the windowpanes of the baggage car coupled close behind it and on the roof of the coach several cars farther back.

Soon, the train crested the steep grade, and after a brief stop at Danville, continued on. Bud told the engineer at the station stop at Hardwick he would signal him for a stop just a few miles out of town—and so, just after the train clanked through a small covered bridge and across a highway and slowed, Bud slid the baggage car's door open a bit and peered out. Sighting the objective of his journey in the distance—a stand of balsam fir trees on the north side of the tracks—he yanked on a signal cord. The engineer, upon hearing the *beep* of the signal in the cab, backed off the throttle and then gently applied the brakes.

The train ground to a halt with its last car—the coach—just clear of the crossing where the railroad tracks cut across the highway between Hardwick and Wolcott. The two-lane road, reduced by heavy snowfall to a narrow channel cleared infrequently by highway plows, had little traffic on it. What few vehicles that were traveling that frigid day were large trucks that were growling slowly along, tire chains flapping noisily about their rear wheels; the roads were ice-covered and slippery, hardly suitable for travel by auto. The brakeman, upon being ordered by the conductor to walk east down the tracks in order to flag down any following train and avert a collision, grumbled as he arose from his seat beside the warm coal stove, and rubbed his hands together. He grabbed his gloves and a red flag from a storage cabinet, walked through the car and disembarked. Muttering a few choice words at this interruption of his scheduled journey to Swanton, he trudged a few hundred feet beyond the train, stopped and took up his post, standing between the rails. There, he impatiently awaited the whistle signal from his train—one that would call him back to the warm interior of the car and a continuation of the journey. As he moped about and waited, he hoped and prayed he would not hear the whistle of another train fast approaching from the east, one that he would have to flag down in time for it to stop without colliding with the coach.

From their plush-covered green seats inside the car, the passengers chatted and speculated as to the cause of the unscheduled stop. Several of them inquisitively opened their frost-covered windows a crack and peered out briefly to see, but the cold air rushing in dampened their enthusiasm, and the windows quickly slid back down. "Here we go, late again, and yet another stop," groused one passenger. "Small wonder why they call the 'St. J & LC the Saint Jesus and Long Coming.'

There ain't a snowball's chance in hell we'll get to Swanton on time now."

"Maybe we hit a cow," suggested a woman wrapped up in a shawl who had brought her sewing along with her, as the needle in her lap flashed and zigged and zagged while she created what she hoped would someday be a treasured family heirloom. Now, perhaps, due to the delay, it might well be finished by the time she reached Swanton, she reasoned. "Wouldn't doubt it."

"*I* doubt it," answered a man seated across the aisle from her who had resigned himself to the vagaries of the St. J&LC. "Not this time of year, anyway." He put down his paper, pulled out his pocket watch, studied it briefly, and then returned the timepiece to his vest pocket. He shook his head and glanced at the woman, a frown on his face. "At the rate we're going, ma'am, you might have a whole quilt done by the time we get to Swanton. But I wouldn't be surprised to find the crew stopped so they could shoot a gosh-darned deer out of season."

Two rows behind the man sat a salesman and a parson, sharing a seat; the salesman studying a brochure for his company's new tractors and the out-of-state parson holding a Bible in his lap, staring out the window. Upon hearing the possible explanation for the untimely stop, the parson turned to his traveling companion and asked, "Good grief! Could that be true?"

"Oh, stopping to take a deer out of season? Could be," replied the salesman calmly, putting down the brochure. He had obviously placed his fate at the hands of the train crew and was content with this theory of their preference for venison versus getting to Swanton on time. "Happens all the time in these parts. We call it deer jacking. Not as much as in the old days, before the game wardens really got out there. But it happens. Mostly at night, though. What say we go out on the back platform so we can have a look-see for ourselves?"

"That sounds good," agreed the parson, putting down his Bible and reaching for his coat. "I could use some fresh air. It's so good to be out of the city."

"You'll find the country air is good for you," touted the tractor salesman, as if he were delivering a pitch on the benefits of living in Vermont's Northeast Kingdom. "Much better than what you're used to, back in Providence. You did say you're just up from Rhode Island, didn't you? Up here, you can smell the forest everywhere. Big trees, pines, fir and balsam, lots of them; mighty trees. A fine, invigorating, natural smell. The scent of the north woods. Vermont even ships out little balsam pillows down country, to folks who like the woodsy scent. Tourists buy 'em, too." That said, the two men arose and ambled out to the rear of the car. They let themselves out the door and into the open vestibule, where they stood and looked back toward the distant and rather unfortunate brakeman, who was dutifully holding a red flag and trying hard, stamping his feet, to ward off the onset of frostbite.

In the baggage car that sat roughly 500 feet farther west and at the head end of the train, right behind the locomotive that had been hauling it, Bud hauled the car's sliding door all the way open. Bud and Joey had strapped on their wooden snowshoes, and Bud had his shotgun slung over his right shoulder. "Got the bag for our tree, Joey?" he asked his son.

"Yes, dad," Joey answered. He was clutching a large, light brown burlap sack, a big smile on his face.

"Then, let's go!" hollered Bud, as he launched himself off the baggage car and plopped softly, snowshoes first, into a pile of snow beside the car; Joey jumped, too, and followed Bud as he clambered up the small crater that his impact had created in the snow, and shuffled off into a nearby stand of balsam firs; the webs of their snowshoes left broad, waffle-textured imprints in the snow. The bristly but finely-shaped tree tops, ranging from five to eight feet tall, poked up from the snow that hid what might have been another three or four feet beneath the white powder left by the recent snowstorm. "What do you think, Joey? Maybe that one?" He pointed toward a tree that was a perfect cone shape. The wind kicked up and blew away the steamy moisture of his breath as he spoke. Behind him came the steady, *one-two*, *one-two* cadence of the air pumps of the locomotive, pounding like the feet of a small child who has been told to stand still and is stamping the ground with impatience.

"That's the one!" affirmed Joey. "That's best tree I've ever seen!" Remembering what to do from the previous year's tree-hunting expedition, Joey shook the tree to free as much snow and ice from the branches as he could. Then, he kicked the fallen snow away from where it lay around the tree. He turned around and tromped off, circling back clumsily on his hand-me-down snowshoes behind his father, and covered his ears while Bud edged up to within inches of the tree. Bud pulled the shotgun down off his shoulder. He stooped, braced himself, pulled back both hammers of the shotgun and aimed at the tree's trunk, halfway up. He fired two slugs, one right after the other. The tree neatly snapped in two and the upper part, destined to decorate the Ross family's living room, toppled gently into the snow.

"Okay, let's bag it now and be quick, son," ordered Bud. "We can't hold the train up much longer." The two stuffed the tree into the big brown burlap sack and headed back to the train, Bud holding part of the sack over his shoulder and Joey supporting the rest of it as best he could.

Back on the rear platform of the combine, the salesman and the parson had both jumped at the sound of the shots being fired so close by. "What did I tell you?" remarked the salesman to his erstwhile companion as he gave him a knowing look. The parson stepped to one side of the platform and gazed forward at the head end of the train, just in time to see two distant figures heave a large, bulky-looking brown object into the baggage car and then clamber aboard.

"My goodness! So it's true! It's true after all!" exclaimed the man of the cloth, clearly astonished at seeing what he took to be a dead deer being loaded into the car. "I saw them put it in the baggage car!"

"Yes, indeed," attested the salesman, nodding his head sagely. "Happens all the time. Steak's expensive at the meat markets, and most folks around here aren't exactly rich. Some of these backwoods characters are real Robin Hoods." The locomotive's whistle sounded several times and the brakeman, heaving a sigh of relief at hearing this known signal, his breath registering briefly as a small puffy cloud in the chilly air, rolled up his flag and began to walk energetically toward the train, worried it might leave without him.

A horse-drawn wagon, its team clopping along the highway, was hauling a load of manure and soon drew near the railroad crossing and the train. The load was steaming-hot, fresh from a large dairy farm's barn, destined for a field nearby. The foul odor from the wagon, overwhelming in its intensity, suddenly wafted into the noses of the men standing on the coach's rear platform as the wagon bumped over the tracks and slowly rolled by.

"Oh, dear Lord," uttered the parson, wrinkling up his nose. Nearly gagging in disgust, and looking at both the salesman and the brakeman who had just clambered aboard, he asked, eyes wide with horror, "Please tell me, boys—I must know—is that *balsam* I smell?"

Chapter 23

Hand-me-down
Friday: December
23, 1932

The skies turned pitch black after sundown and the temperatures soon plummeted toward the zero mark. Yes, it was cold, Joey thought to himself—colder than a witch's heart —as he headed home. It was fast getting on toward supper time when he at last turned the corner onto Passumpsic Street and his neighborhood the night before Christmas Eve. It had been snowing heavily earlier that day, and while at work at Sam's he had often had to put on his heavy coat and gloves, go outside the storefront and shovel the sidewalk. Now, as he went along, thankful that the snow had stopped and the day was done, his thoughts turned toward Sunday; Christmas. Today had been just another school day, and his classmates complained about being cheated out of a three-day weekend because of the way the holiday fell on the calendar. All this would fall on deaf ears at home, for most of their fathers worked six days per week— Joey's, seven—to make ends meet.

Christmas, apart from the living room display of the tree he and his dad had harvested, now decorated with tinsel and heirloom ornaments, plus a perfunctory visit by his cranky old aunt and a turkey dinner following her arrival, wouldn't go too far to dispel the gloom he felt at this dreary time of year. The brutally cold north wind seemed to crawl down his neck like a cold finger and dampened whatever seasonal cheer the holiday lights downtown could impart. It made the colorful light bulbs sway wildly between lampposts where they were strung as if it was determined to rip them down. Christmas carols blared from speakers outside the J.J. Newberry's 5&10 as Joey passed by its doors where a blue-uniformed Salvation Army man stood, stamping his feet in a vain effort to warm them. His breath as he said hello to everyone came out in warm puffs of steam, though his face was chilled the mottled colors of salami. He was ringing a bell manically, as though he were a wind-up mechanical man. A red kettle beside him on the sidewalk yawned wide-open, awaiting donations.

Passers-by and shoppers, those few who were out and about, dropped whatever pennies and nickels they could spare into that big pot as they went by it, and met the man's gaze with a smile. If they were poor, as many of them were, they either didn't know it or else would never admit it. In a way, they were much like Joey's parents. The less fortunate people, they all knew, were the ones who were homeless and on the move in the cold that night, riding freight trains town-to-town in search of work and warmth, in search of handouts or soup kitchens, in search of something meaningful. They were the ones who had lost it all—their jobs, their families, their souls, in the rough and tumble-down days of the Great Depression.

Joey's thoughts turned to the New Year. What would he do for work, once school let out come June? All there was to living in St. Johnsbury, it seemed, was that if you wanted to work and earn a living (and were lucky enough to land a job) you had just four choices: you could work for the railroad, where there were some benefits—if you lived long enough to enjoy them. You could go to work down at one of the factories, tethered to a machine, where you'd have a job for life, but might wish you had a life after work. Then again, you could work insane, early morning hours at the creamery and sneak a bottle of milk home if you dared, but had to lug heavy 40-quart milk cans around. That would work until the day your back gave out and you then envied anyone who had a regular job on a freight train, or who worked normal hours down at the scale works. Or, you could get into the illegal booze business as a rumrunner and make a small fortune. Like Dutch, or "Cadillac Mac". And live large—as long as your luck lasted.

Joey halted just short of the driveway to the Ross homestead, startled by what he saw. There were two cars parked by the front door, ones he did not recognize. Perhaps his aunt Josie had come to visit early, he thought. But, neither of the cars were hers. Could it be that his big brother was in trouble? Was the sheriff here? If indeed he was, well...that would not surprise him. He walked forward again, and stopped just short of the front porch steps. Because could hear his mother's voice, and that she was crying. Joey peered through a window into the parlor.

Hat in hand, the superintendent of the railroad, Dave, was talking to Beth. "I'm sorry, Mrs. Ross. Sorry as a man can be. It was an accident. An accident plain and simple." Standing beside him, shoulders drooping under the weight of what news they'd had to bring to the Ross household were Andy, the railroad brakeman and Chuck, the locomotive engineer, both of them Bud's stalwart friends.

Joey's felt his heart skip a beat, then plummet to the bottoms of his feet when he heard Chuck say: "He was a good man, Bud. One of the best. It wasn't his fault; we think a grab iron broke when we were shoving two cars into the mill siding, and he fell off the one he was riding. It's all I can say, ma'am." Chuck's shoulders sagged as he covered his eyes with a grimy hand, then began wiping away tears. He knew he could not tell Beth the horror of what he had seen when he had found Bud, lying on his back under a 30-ton boxcar, the knife-sharp edge of a cold steel wheel resting on his chest. Bud's mouth had been open, the vapor from his last breath fast rising into the frosty air, almost as if he were trying to explain what had happened; what had gone wrong in the last few seconds of his life.

But, as it is so often said, dead men tell no tales.

Frozen in terror at first, Joey finally stirred and stepped backward, as if he could somehow reverse time. Then, he turned around, looking for some way out of the world that seemed to be spinning out of control. The Ross household had been this world, his home life; now, he couldn't bear to bring himself to enter it. There was one refuge left, however: the outhouse. He retreated to it, stepped in, slammed the door shut and sat there in silence.

So, it had finally happened. One of the things his mother, Beth, had always worried about: the death of Joey's father on the job. Joey could, without much imagining hear her voice, lambasting Bud: "That railroad will be the death of you!" In the darkness and erstwhile sanctity of the ramshackle outhouse, he placed his hands on his knees and tried to calm himself. As he did so, he felt the patches sewn there by Beth on his hand-me-down trousers, and gripped them hard as anger washed over him. And now, the words of an old adage came to him: "Use it up, wear it out; make it do, or do without." And that was how it went, Joey reasoned bitterly. The railroad had had its use of his father, whom he barely knew, except for the rare Sunday off, taken without pay. It had used him up; it had worn him out; it had made him do with what little he earned, to do without. And now, it seemed, as the end result, Joey would have to do without, too.

Chapter 24

Down on the Farm

"**Y**ou need to get on the phone and call that girl of yours, Ross, and get her off my back. I'm a funeral director, not your social director. She's called here five times this afternoon for you. Says you have to get up to her place pronto," Junior groused as he pulled down the funeral home's garage door. As it slammed shut, he turned and glared at Billy, still sitting behind the wheel of the hearse he'd just backed into the service bay. "The last call was just two minutes ago. It's a damned nuisance."

Billy shut off the ignition and slumped back in his seat, enjoying a sense of relief in having brought the hearse back to Junior's establishment unharmed. Snow and dirty brown slush dripped off the car's tires and fenders, trickling down into a drain in the floor, and all was quiet except for the ticking sound of the Packard's big engine as it began to cool. The drive over snow-blown Route 2 to Concord, the retrieval of the deceased, dealing with the dead man's distraught family and then the difficult return trip had taken up most of Billy's afternoon. And now, thought Billy, most of the evening would, if it was Catherine who'd been calling, be taken up by her. He'd been avoiding her for several weeks now, and Junior knew it. So did Joey, and just about everyone at T.R.'s. Junior eyeballed the spectacularly-defiled Packard hearse that was usually showroom-clean. "God, what a mess that car is," he complained. He spat on the floor in disgust.

Resisting the urge to tell Junior to go to hell, Billy held his temper. After all, Junior had insisted on handling Bud Ross's arrangements himself, and had the good sense to give Billy two days off for good measure. Junior could be charitable—when the spirit moved him—and when he wasn't drinking. That was when other sorts of spirits moved him in diverse, less-noble directions. The funeral service had been closed-casket; the viewing had been private.

Billy flung open the driver's door of the hearse, stepped out, stood, stretched and yawned. "Sorry, Junior," he said. "The roads were really bad. I had to put tire chains on to get up there—hillside farm. Then I had to wait on the doctor after I got there, and after that I had to wait for some relatives to say their goodbyes, dry their eyes and soil their hankies. Been a long day."

"C'mon Billy," snapped Junior. "Cut the crap. You think you're tired? I've got what's going to be an almost all-night date with this stiff. I never met the man and already he's making me hate him. Let's get him out of my car and onto the table. Then, you can call your honey and make your peace with her." He stepped toward the back of the car, and Billy followed him.

"So," inquired Billy casually," as he tagged along, "just to make sure, who's been looking for me?"

"Didn't exactly sound like her, but it was Mary-Lou what's-her-name, or so she said; you know—the one taking care of old Silas's place for her sister." Junior turned, and shot him a bemused and highly-dramatic look of innocence; overacting thusly in times of adversity was his escape route from immediately seeking the solace of the bottle. "What's the matter? Loved and left that one already?" Junior leered at Billy as he grasped the hearse's rear door handle and gave the door a tug. He was familiar with Billy's reputation as a womanizer, and somewhat envious of this handsome young man who, without much effort, seemed to have girls flocking after him wherever he went like a gaggle of squawking seagulls trailing along behind a deep-sea trawler.

The door swung open and Junior stood there a moment, peering into the depths of the Packard hearse at the figure lying on the gurney. The body was large, and the crisp white sheet covering it had formed a sort of peak in the middle—a place where it crested directly over the corpse's ample belly; it resembled a snowy Swiss mountaintop in miniature. Junior sighed. "Okay, Mr. Tuttle," Junior said, as if speaking to the deceased. "Let's get you out of here."

"What's the matter, boss?" asked Billy, at last sensing Junior's frustration.

"He's a big old boy, this one," grumbled Junior. "And he isn't going to be easy to handle. I'll have to call Sven over tonight to get everything done. Let's see if we can get him out and onto the table. How the hell did you get him in there?"

"It wasn't too bad," ventured Billy. "Some of his neighbors were there to help me, and—boy, did I ever thank them!" Junior grasped the end of the gurney and grunted as he bent, tugged and began to pull it from the hearse.

"You didn't have to shell out cash to them or promise them anything, right?" asked Junior, suspiciously. Junior always liked to keep things simple—and economical.

"No," Billy answered. Then he snickered. "A couple of them said they were glad to see the old bastard finally go!"

"I think I'll be, too," Junior grumped. Then, he smiled and looked at Billy. "Ready to help make old King Tuttle here ready for the afterlife?" Billy nodded. Junior pulled again, and Billy grasped the opposite end of the gurney as it finally emerged from the car; both men briefly staggered under the heavy weight of the body before the gurney's legs and casters dropped to the concrete floor and locked into place. Then, the two slowly wheeled the conveyance down the hallway and over to a nearby table made of stainless steel. In a series of coordinated grunts and tugs, they managed to drag the body over onto it. As they did, one of its arms flopped out of the sheet and—almost as if trying to defy gravity—very slowly descended toward the floor. Its hairy hand, all five fingers in a claw-like pose, looked as though it was reaching out for something it desired. Without any compunction, Junior deftly grasped the arm and quickly stuffed it back under the sheet.

"Full rigor hasn't set in yet," he announced dispassionately, before turning to Billy and asking him: "Hey—deadbeat, you'd better call that girl and get things straightened out with her. She's probably just had too much bourbon and bon-bons to-day, sitting on her ass up there on the hill with nothing to do except moon about you. One: I don't need her calling me here again tonight. Two: You've got that pickup in Canada to do for me soon. So, go wrap up your business and get it done tonight, okay?"

"Yeah, okay, okay," said Billy. "I'll call her right now." He trudged over to the telephone near a workbench cluttered with bottles of chemicals, tangles of syringes, clusters of surgical knives and clamps. He picked up the phone's receiver. Snow-melt dribbled off his rubber boots, leaving pools of water and shiny footprints on the floor. He jiggled the phone's hook re-peatedly until the operator came on the line and asked, in her squawking, caustic voice, for the number. Billy gave her the out-of-town exchange name and Mary Lou's number, the one for Silas's place.

He looked out the mortuary's lone window as he waited for the connection to be made. It came in a series of herky-jerky, scratchy-sounding clicks as the operator plugged jacks into her switchboard and made the connection. The sun, conspicuous by its absence for most of the snowy day emerged briefly, and valiantly shot bolts of sunlight through the clouds before burying itself behind the mountains. As Billy watched, a blood-red tinge lingered briefly on the clouds that lingered over the hilltops, the ones on the farm where Mary Lou lived—then, that, too, vanished. The phone rang and rang.

"Do you want me to keep trying?" asked the operator.

"No, thanks," replied Billy, and hung up. Conflicted now, he turned to Junior to see what he would say.

"Your ass is in the frying pan now, isn't it, Romeo?" jeered Junior, who had been listening. "You're in for some hot tongue and cold shoulder. But I suppose you've got to drive up there tonight to kiss up to her." Junior stared at Billy for a while before he spoke again, asking: "Don't you?" Not waiting for the answer, he stepped over to the workbench, his head down, brow furrowed in concentration. He had put on his white lab coat, and he began to paw through the clusters of bottles, searching for something. He looked for all the world like a mad scientist in a horror movie. He looked up suddenly, as if he'd just been shocked by some kind of electric current, and locked eyes with Billy. "And I'll bet you want to use the hearse, right?"

"Yeah, I was just about to ask."

"Against my better judgement: okay, but you're going to have to wash it down when you get back—and that had better be soon. Got that?" Junior warned. He frowned at Billy for added effect. Junior hadn't shaved today, had awoken late, and then taken a significant time to sober up during the sun's brief winter transit time over Lyndonville.

"Sure, Junior, no worries," said Billy, getting ready to open the garage door.

"One more thing, Ross," added Junior. He picked up a lethal-looking, sharp-edged surgical instrument from the table and waved it in the air menacingly for emphasis. "You need to get yourself a goddamn car!"

Yes, Billy thought, as he drove cautiously out of the funeral home's driveway, just to show a little respect for Junior, in case he was watching. Yes, he sure as hell needed to get himself a car. The problem was that between entertaining Mary Lou on nights out, with all of her demands, and just now coming off a bad losing streak in a number of poker games on whatever nights he didn't spend with her, the money had been trickling away faster than it had been coming in. Gone, mostly. He turned onto the street that led west toward Gilman Road and Wheelock and put on the gas; the long, heavy car responded by slithering sideways, headed for the guardrail posts; heavy though it was, the hearse could be a slippery bastard in the snow. Billy corrected the steering, let off the gas, straightened the car out and kept going. The snow wasn't really deep, but the roads were greasy underneath and a cause for caution, something he never had much use for unless he knew he was in really deep trouble. Deep trouble was when something went seriously wrong on a run up to Canada, or when making a local booze delivery and Junior was needed on the double to fix things with the authorities. And so, a call would go discretely out from Billy to Junior that included the code words—just in case anyone—like the telephone operator, was listening in: "Send extra flowers."

What the hell did Mary Lou want, anyway? Billy tried to think things through as he drove along. She knew damn well that this was his night out for poker, and that he'd also be busy with a job out of town the next couple of nights. Demands irritated Billy. Maybe—just maybe—something had gone wrong up there, though. The hired hands left the farm late in the afternoon each day, so perhaps something was amiss at the house or in the barn, something that had gone awry after they went home. Or maybe it was the case of trouble with the hired hands themselves. One of them being a smart-aleck, or "fresh" as Mary Lou would put it, with her ever-so-southern spin. But, well—Billy could be fresh, too. And he loved that. He would find out soon enough. Probably some silly thing, not really deep trouble. And Mary Lou could be charmingly silly. At least it wasn't Catherine chasing after him again and trying to pin him down to ask him whatever the big question was that she'd been stewing about. That was a relief. He could deal with that later—when he wanted to.

The big black car churned along through slush and briefly bucked like a startled horse as it pitched over a frost heave in the road. Soon enough, Billy knew, mud season would arrive and the dirt roads in the hills and valleys would be a horror of muck with the appetite of quicksand, just one of the reasons why some of the older folks put up their cars on blocks in their barns or garages for the winter in late November and didn't renew their registrations until April, when they put their autos back on the roads. Like traditional red union suits, Johnson jackets and woolen ear-flap hats, horses, sleighs and snowshoes were still in vogue in Vermont come wintertime, and winter apparently wasn't through with Vermont—yet. And while Billy wasn't through with Catherine—not quite yet, any-way—he was trying to figure out a way to make it all work out.

The sky—already a deep, navy-warship gray from the de-parture of the sun—grew darker still and snow began to fall once more. It came at first like confetti fluttering down on a parade, but then, the shower of snowflakes became more earnest in nature. Billy turned on the windshield wipers, and as the hearse slowed to take the turn onto Hubbard Hill Road, its wipers sped up, rapidly flipping back and forth, quickly flicking the snowflakes away. He slowed, looking for the turn-off to the farm and when he found it, turning slowly into the drive, he couldn't help but gaze up at the old house on the hill. While Silas had kept it "pretty neat", as the hands put it, it somehow looked different tonight. The big building, with its steeply-pitched roof, sharply-peaked dormers and bulging bay windows, plus the huge barn and its twin silos, all stood out as one gigantic entity in silhouette against the murky western sky. By day, as Billy knew it, Silas's farm was the postcard-perfect image of a rural Vermont homestead. Tonight, in the gloom of a gathering storm, its black signature on the steep hill was indistinguishable from that of a dark, ruined Highland castle. Not one light was showing on it.

Billy drew the car up at the back of the house, and after he steered it into the dooryard, the headlights painted the barn and barnyard a pale yellow. The barn doors were shut, as they should have been, and wisps of steam wafted from the manure pit nearby, a sure sign the hands had done their chores, mucking out stalls and doling out hay to the cows, and had then gone home. But why was the house dark? You could always tell when flatlanders were living in a Vermont house, Junior had once said: they'd leave the porch lights on 24-7. Mary Lou, with disregard for any cost, because it had nothing to do with her, usually had the house lit up like a carnival at night, although she only occupied one small part of it, the guest house.

The diminutive guest house had been built—tacked onto the back side of the home itself, really—as a summer kitchen, back in the old days when Silas was first feeling expansive and had hired a cook, who kept her quarters upstairs in it. Rather that stoke the monstrous cook stove to prepare meals in the kitchen of the main house during the hot months of the year and raise the temperature indoors, another junior version within the small summer kitchen was used, thus leaving the house cool. Now, with the cook long gone and Mary Lou its only occupant, the little guest house's outside door let out into the back barnyard and beyond it, several hundred acres of spruce and pine forestland.

Billy urged the hearse, slipping and sliding through the snow, around the corner so its headlights could play over the guest house; surprisingly, the door was open. Was the electric power—one of Silas's concessions to the 20th century—out? Perhaps that was why Mary Lou had called. But still—there was obviously heat inside; a wisp of smoke was coming from the chimney of the small structure. There was none spiraling from the tall chimneys of the house itself, of course, as there was no need to heat the whole building. At least Mary Lou, in her quaint daffiness, understood that. Maybe—just maybe—Billy reasoned she had left the door open after going out to see where the power lines might be down. Leaving the headlights on, he turned off the ignition, stepped out of the car and headed for the door.

"Mary Lou!" he bellowed, cupping his hands together to form a megaphone. But there was no answer. He stopped and stared down at the snow-covered ground. Sure, the door was open, but she must not have left the building, he reasoned; there were no footprints to be seen anywhere in the snow, although it looked like something had been dragged away from the door, out into the barnyard and off into the woods.

With a sense of urgency now, he sprang forward, ran to the doorway—and immediately tripped over something just inside. Billy fell like a log, headlong into the front hall. He landed on his stomach, skated forward briefly on the polished hardwood floor, and as he did something jagged gashed his forehead. As he went down his right arm had hit something—something large and heavy, and almost immediately whatever it was fell on him. Shards of broken glass and chinaware scattered all around him.

Billy swept his arms around in order to pick himself up, and felt needling pain in his fingers as unseen objects cut into them like tiny daggers. He dragged himself to his feet, stumbling over what had fallen on him, and looked back out the doorway. He strained his eyes, trying to discern what he had tripped over when he entered, and—failing that, fumbled for the light switch he knew was on the wall by the door frame.

As the lights came on, Billy looked down, straight down—and discovered lovely Mary Lou at his feet, staring up at him, her mouth wide open as if in wonderment. She was lying just inside the door, her body twisted sideways. Her white terrycloth robe—the one he'd bought her a just week ago on a shopping spree at the department store in St. Johnsbury—was soaked a deep raspberry red of blood. It had welled up from a multitude of punctures that showed where the robe's fabric had been torn and driven deeply into the wounds caused by whatever evil thing—and person—had made them. But Mary Lou was all done bleeding—done long ago that afternoon.

* * *

Junior, a frown on his grizzled face, rummaged through the clutter of bottles on the workshop bench and at last found the one he had been searching for, a one-gallon glass jug. It contained the specific chemical he needed to begin the night's anticipated mortuary work; in short, it was the handy sort of preservative he had come to appreciate for its restorative effects. He reached for it, the one containing an innocuous-appearing clear liquid, labeled: "Embalming Fluid. Caution: Contains formaldehyde, methanol and various disinfectants. For professional use only." Beneath those words, the paper wrapper bore a small skull and crossbones logo and the maker's name. The hollow-eyed death's head seemed to float, grinning, over several secondary precautionary warnings—among them, one to keep the chemical out of reach of small children. Although the jug was full, its label was well-worn, dulled with brown fingerprints—Junior's. He turned to gaze briefly at the corpse lying on the table, sighed, and then turned back to look at the jug. He picked it up and without hesitation removed the cork stopper, lifted the neck of the container to his lips and took a long, healthy swig—swallowed—and then set the bottle down heavily. He exhaled and smiled as the potion he had swallowed burned its way down to his gut, and then his breath was suddenly alive with the scent of pure juniper. It was brand-name British gin, the real McCoy, smuggled in straight across the border from Canada.

What the hell was Billy Ross up to on Silas's farm tonight? Junior ran the possibilities through his mind, then shook his head. That new girlfriend of his—Mary Lou—was an operator, as far as he was concerned. He'd seen her type before. Other girls had called here looking for Billy, too. So many, he could hardly tell them apart. He reasoned he would have to keep close tabs on Billy from now on. Junior pulled a tray containing an assortment of surgical instruments over closer to him, and then cleared a work space on the bench. He took another pull of gin, putting off the call he would have to make, to Sven, for the moment. *Christ; why didn't Ross buy the girl a diamond ring, a car and a boat, and get it all over with,* he wondered?

Junior sat down on a stool and thought for a bit to clear his head. The room swam in his vision. He took another swallow of gin to help it all settle into place. He had made a co-operative deal with T.R. to send Billy Ross up into Canada and bring back two things—one for him, one for T.R.—on one trip. First of all, T.R., the old fool, had bought himself (or so he said, anyway) a mail-order bride, a young lady of some professional capabilities in social circles who would have to be spirited out of her home town and brought back across the border without attracting attention of the authorities—or her current employer, to whom she was seriously indebted. Secondly, Junior had arranged the purchase in Canada of three cases of an extremely rare, well-aged French cognac worth a fortune in the U.S., which he had an eager, state-side buyer lined up for. If all went well, it would be a profitable trip for Junior and an armload of amour for T.R., provided that the old boy's heart could take the strain.

Now, Junior rationalized, as he drank a bit more and then exhaled, blowing away the fragrance of the booze he consumed the way a smoker fogs a room with each outgoing breath, that he was putting his life-breath of creativity into this little world of the dead—his funeral home. It made him—as he became a disciple of the bottle, so he thought—a magic man; he was soon ready to shrug off the fears of the living and to work his deeds with the departed in the dead of night. All good. He had shaken off the fear that haunted him whenever he worked with the dead once more. It was gin, top-shelf stuff, not the bath tub rotgut the kids talked about that he was drinking. It was high-class booze, pure and simple. Junior, in his wisdom, had labeled it as poisonous fluid simply to keep Sven from sampling it to death when he wasn't around, draining his liquor resources. His head buzzed like the wings of a busy bee about to go to work in his delirium of a hive and for a brief time, he was happy—very happy—until the phone on the wall jangled and enraged him with the distraction of its strident ringing. He hauled himself to his feet, knocking over his stool in the process, and trudged over to the telephone. He picked up with one hand, leaned against the wall with the other to steady himself, and at last answered the call. It was Billy on the line.

"Junior! Junior!" Billy hollered. Junior held the telephone away from his ear and grimaced.

"Who the hell did you *think* it was, Mr. Tuttle answering the phone?" he growled. "What's going on up there?"

"I've got trouble up here. Big trouble—you see," there was crackling on the line, but Junior could hear that Billy's voice was shaking. "I can't explain it, but I need you up here," Billy continued. "You'll see."

"What?" bellowed Junior, longing to get back to his business at hand, upset by the interruption.

The plan for the evening was to have Sven help wash the body of the unfortunate Mr. Tuttle, give it a shave and haircut in the process, prepare it for the trocar incision and infusion of fluids, and then set it aside pending the arrival of the deceased's burial clothes. These would preferably consist of a dress shirt, a necktie and a suit (if Tuttle in fact had ever owned one, which Junior doubted) all to be brought by and dropped off by his family. And now, it seemed the evening's best working hours would trickle away and go down the drain —much like the deceased's life blood eventually would, once certain incisions had been made.

"We have to do a removal, Junior. I can't do it. I just can't."

"Ross, you're not making any sense. Get your ass back down here," ordered Junior. He resisted the temptation to hang up the phone and then pound one of his fists against the wall in frustration.

And then Billy said, his voice almost cracking: "Send extra flowers." Then, with a loud *click*, the line went dead.

Chapter 25

Trouble is as
Trouble Does

Junior fumed and cursed under his breath as he cautiously drove along the snow-covered highway—the travel lanes all but invisible save for a few faint tire tracks to follow and the guardrail posts to steer clear of on either side of them—on his way to Silas's farm. He had borrowed Sven's beat-up old GMC truck after summoning the big oaf to the mortuary, asking him upon arrival to begin the preparatory work on the body. Then, Junior had driven off into the gloom of early evening to see what in the world Billy was doing up on the farm, and what sort of trouble he'd gotten into. Based upon prior experience, Junior had brought along two things he figured would be useful in getting out of any tight spot that might involve either the authorities getting too close, or else someone horning into his business: a roll of ten-dollar bills for one scenario and for another, his trusty Colt .45 automatic.

The rusty old pickup truck plodded along through the darkness; although it was weighted down for traction with big blocks of granite lodged in the bed, and had tires knobby enough to have belonged on a small tractor, Junior was reluctant to push it to its wobbly limits. This was despite the fact Sven told him that with its snowplow and four forward gears, the truck could go any place in foul weather that a mule could, and even faster. *A mule indeed, you big jackass*, thought Junior. More than likely, Sven's kind of dashing through the snow would be to some neighbor's backyard still for a fill-up of high-octane moonshine. Yes, indeed; that would do it for Sven's refreshment on a late-night drive, with a four-on-the-floor and a fifth under the seat on the way home. On a hunch, Junior felt around the floorboards under the seat, expecting to find a bottle but instead finding something soft and slimy, something that he hoped was nothing more than a greasy old rag. It was.

Junior took his eyes off the road for a second in order to look at and then toss the offending rag across the cab. Just as he looked up, almost blinded by the swirling snow and glare reflected from the headlights, the dark figure of a person appeared, flashing across the road in front of him like a streak. There was no time to react, and Junior breathed a sigh of relief a second later at not hearing a sudden *thump* and feeling the GMC briefly lurch over something. "Crazy damn fool!" he barked.

When at last Junior pulled into the driveway leading up to Silas's farmhouse, he was relieved—but also puzzled—to see only one vehicle parked outside, the hearse. Lights were on both outside and inside the house. So—what was the problem, he wondered? With the effects of the guzzled gin starting to wear off and his head beginning to clear now, Junior sat quietly for a few moments in the truck as its anemic engine grumbled away, collecting his thoughts. Perhaps, after all, this was a set-up; an ambush. He pulled the gun from his pocket, then reached out with his left hand, rolled down the window, and honked the horn several times. A figure, framed in the yellow light coming from the open door of the home's guest house appeared, then staggered out and beckoned to him.

Junior let out the clutch and steered the truck closer with his free hand, letting the headlights play over the person, and stopped. It was Billy. Billy lurched forward now, waving his arms like a madman, yelling something Junior couldn't hear over the noise of the truck, so Junior shut off the wheezing, clattering motor just as Billy arrived and grasped the door handle, the way a drunk reaches out and tries to save himself from collapsing when he can feel himself going down. "You've got to help me," he implored.

"To do what?" Junior snapped. "Who the hell is in there?"

"Mary Lou." Junior now saw there was blood trickling down Billy's forehead.

"She did this to you? What are you trying to pull? Who's in the house, and what's going on,

Ross? Don't try to con me!" Junior snarled. "You know better than to set me up!"

"You don't understand, Junior, so shut up and listen!" Billy blurted as he leaned in through the open window until his face was inches away from Junior's. "I'm the one being set up!"

Now, Junior could see tiny pieces of broken glass glittering on Billy's shoulders and that his necktie was loose, as if someone had yanked on it; there was dirt on his shirt collar, too. His hair looked as though a cyclone had coursed through it, and what appeared to be a large bruise was beginning to well up on his forehead. He appeared to be in a state of shock.

"You've been set up, eh? You look like you went a few rounds with Jack Dempsey. So, you're saying Mary Lou didn't do this? And—there's no one else in that house—right? So, it must be you did this to yourself, tonight, then? C'mon." Junior opened the door and with it, he pushed Billy backward and he staggered briefly, but then found his footing in the snow. "I want to see what's in there for myself." Still holding the gun with his right hand, Junior slid off the seat, stepped off the truck's running board and plopped into the snow. Keeping a wary eye on the windows of the house, and hugging the .45 close to his side, he trudged toward the open door of the guest house.

After regaining his composure somewhat, Billy followed him, and when they arrived at the doorway, Junior stopped in his tracks and stared at what was inside in disbelief. Junior had seen many dead bodies in his career but usually, with some notable exceptions, those were just the sort left behind by those who had passed away peacefully, or who at least *looked* peaceful when at last their end came. But here was the once-lovely belle Mary Lou lying dead on the dirty floor, twisted sideways like a broken doll tossed into a toy store's trash bin, eyes wide open, lifeless in her blood-soaked robe. She was surrounded by splintered shelves that had once held empty Mason jars and her sister's fancy cups and saucers on the wall in the entranceway. The broken boards lay on the floor amidst a scattering of shards of broken glass and china. White, sharp and cruel-looking, they sparkled like ice floes floating on the pools of her cold, coagulating blood. A trail of dirty footprints and trickles of water from melted snow led off from the hallway into the interior of the house—and then back again.

"This is a mess, Ross," grumbled Junior, as he turned to face Billy. "Your mess, not mine. What the hell do you expect me to do with it? This is bad, really bad." Junior sensed that he was on the verge of dipping his feet into something that would take him down—not snow, but quicksand.

"Look, Junior, this is what I found when I got here." Billy was shaking almost as badly as a dog that had gone for a swim and at last found its master to shed some collateral water on.

"What?" spat Junior. "A war scene? Looks to me like there was a battle royal here between you and your little lovely before I got here. And then someone went tramping into the house—God, look at those footprints!" He pointed the gun at them for emphasis. "But I suppose that wasn't you." He swiveled back toward Billy, with his gun pointed at him. "Was it?"

"It was me, but it wasn't like that," pleaded Billy. "There wasn't a light on in this place when I got here." He stepped closer and pointed at Mary Lou's body. "The guest house door was open and I went rushing in in the dark and tripped—over her." He looked momentarily as if he would be ill, but recovered his composure. "And I fell and went into the shelves; hit my head. And when I got up, I hit the lights and saw—saw what—saw her. Oh, my God!"

"So, what's with the footprints?" queried Junior.

"Mine. I went in to find out if someone was hiding in the house—whoever did this. Because after I turned on the lights in the guest house, I looked out back beforehand; there were no footprints in the snow. Anywhere. Just a narrow little trail where it looked like someone had dragged something small from the back steps out into the woods. I figured someone could be in the house. But nobody was."

"And then, of course, you called me," said Junior. "Thanks ever so much, Billy," he sneered. He sighed and then carefully opened his coat and stuffed the gun into the waistband of his trousers. Then, he stooped to take a better look at Mary Lou. He reached out to touch her neck, held two fingers on it briefly, then consulted his wristwatch to see what time it was. "No pulse; cold as a stone. I'd say she was likely dead a while before you got here, I'll grant you that much." He turned and looked up at Billy, who at first appeared to be the perfect picture of a nervous wreck, but then apparently pulled himself together enough to nod solemnly a second later, and then swallowed hard. Perhaps, Junior thought, the young man was trying to think of something to say in appreciation of his wry, undertaker's observation—one that might let him off the hook for murder.

"You haven't cried one bitty little tear for that gal tonight, have you, Billy?" Junior asked slyly, looking for a reaction. "That two-bit tramp."

"I loved her—don't say that!" Billy blurted, suddenly animated. "Don't say that about her!" And then Billy could hold his grief in no longer. He dropped to the floor, covered his face with his hands and sobbed.

Junior rose and stood a while in thought. Once the sobbing had ceased, he spoke. "Those wounds on her—those can't be from a knife," Junior mused, as if suddenly intrigued. "Those are consistent puncture marks, after all, not random slashes. She looks like she was stabbed with a spike—something round —almost like a piece of pipe with a pointed end. Did you see anything like that in the house when you walked through it tonight, turning the lights on?" Billy shook his head soberly. "And I hope, I really do—that you don't have a tire iron with a sharp end on it in the hearse, do you?"

Billy shook his head again. "No, just a four-way lug wrench."

"Thank God," said Junior. "Because you and I are going to be on the spot for this. So, we'd better get our story together and get it straight, because whoever did this covered their tracks really well—and because you've been seeing this girl for weeks. Now get up off your ass, get on your feet and listen. Remember: a girl called me tonight, several times, while you were over in Concord; she said her name was Mary Lou, and she wanted you to come up here as soon as you got into the shop this afternoon, right?" Billy nodded.

"And I told her you were out on a run and I'd give you the message?" Billy nodded again. "So, you came here as soon as you could, right?"

"That's right," affirmed Billy, brightening at the prospect of the story coming together.

"So why did you then call me, and not the sheriff?" Junior asked gruffly. Billy stared at him. "Oh, c'mon. This one's easy.

You fumbled and fell when you got to the door of the guest house and found the body. You panicked—you reached out to turn on the lights—and then somebody slugged you—knocked you out. You came to and panicked, and called me—and then you went through the house, turning on the lights, room-by-room—looking for the killer."

"Why would the sheriff believe me?" asked Billy.

"For one good reason," snapped Junior, "you don't have her blood all over you. And whatever you saw, whoever left here after he did what he did, his tracks—whatever you saw, that he might have used to cover them up—might still be visible by the time the sheriff gets off his duff and gets up here. Whoever did this to her would have been spattered with blood; one of those punctures was her carotid artery, after all. Another good reason: you were motivated to find the killer. You *did* love her, you said—right? Now, I'm going inside to find the telephone and call the sheriff." He stepped carefully over the body, then stopped to look down at it. Something was wrong, and in his gut, Junior knew it. If Mary Lou had, by his estimation, been stone-cold dead for perhaps an hour or more before Billy's arrival—who, in fact, had really been calling him at the mortuary just before Billy arrived there this afternoon?

After several seconds regarding the departed and mulling this over, Junior looked up at Billy, and spoke sharply to him. "I know you must feel bad, kid, but if it will make you feel better, I think she died quickly." And then, he added solemnly, "You could, too, in a few months, if you don't stick to your story tonight."

* * *

Sheriff John "Big John" Johnson stared at Mary Lou's corpse in disbelief. "She was a purty-lookin' young woman, I'd say, before all this happened," he lamented, in his homespun way, finally turning to look at Billy with sad eyes. "Your girlfriend?"

Billy bobbed his head up and down. The sheriff stroked his broad mustache absent-mindedly, almost as though he was brushing away toast crumbs. But he was thinking—thinking of finding a proverbial trail of bread crumbs for clues as he continued to question Billy.

He cocked his broad-brimmed hat—still speckled with snowflakes—back on his head as he took in the crime scene. In the intervening time between Junior's call to John and his arrival, Junior had utilized his professional skills and managed to clean Billy up a bit in order to make him look a tad more presentable—and believable. Behind his big, sad puppy-dog eyes, the sheriff was processing information and drawing a few conclusions that he'd keep under that big hat of his for now. John was well-liked within the realm of the Kingdom, and had the appearance most days of an amiable, oversize teddy bear of a fellow. But, in common with a lot of men his size—Sven included—he could be a formidable force to reckon with if crossed, or lied to.

"You say you don't remember much after you went in the doorway, right?"

"That's right," answered Billy. He was sitting in a straight-back chair just off the hallway, in the kitchen of Silas's farm house guest house. The fear of the electric chair was upon him, and he had his hands clasped on his knees in order to keep them from shaking.

"Yeah, that's when the lights went out."

"You told me the lights were out when you got here, Billy." The sheriff stared at him, puppy-dog eyes wide open, awaiting an answer that would be satisfactory. Or not.

"I mean, that's when *my* lights went out," Billy attested, flustered now. "Look, I told you: "I think I might have been knocked out by somebody—I just don't know! I came to on the floor!"

"Listen, John," implored Junior, stepping in between the two, "the kid's had a rough time; he was in shock when I got here. Ease up on him a bit, will you?"

"Okay," answered John, "but tell me one thing, Junior: what did Billy tell you had happened here when he called you on the telephone?" John's deputy, leaning casually against the wall and chewing gum in slow motion, mostly to keep himself awake as the minutes passed, was purely a bored spectator in this event.

"He told me: 'send extra flowers.' That's our code for trouble; send help. We have to be discrete in my business. I've drilled that code into his head. It's no wonder he used it. You boys have your code words too, in law enforcement. C'mon, John; the kid displayed some courage, considering what he found. He did was he was trained to do." Now done, Junior sat back in his chair, crossed his legs and relaxed, letting the message sink in. The sheriff turned back toward Billy, acting as he did so like a tag-team boxer who's been rebuffed by one of his opponents and was now seeking the second man he could most likely to plant a fist on as he stepped across the ring.

"Now Billy," began John, "you told me you saw a trail of some sorts leading from the door of the guest house out into the woods. Would you show that to me, please?" Billy meekly arose; the sheriff, his deputy and Junior followed, stepping carefully over the unfortunate Mary Lou. The four men huddled in the doorway and looked out into the back barnyard.

"It's there," said Billy, "or, it *was* there. See?" He pointed downward, just beyond where a multitude of boot prints converged at the doorstep. "It's kind of like a channel under the snow." All concerned peered at the barely-visible trail, fast-disappearing under the steady snowfall. "Someone else was here besides me."

John looked at him point-blank, and without expression, asked, "Is that so?"

"Listen, I didn't kill her! I didn't!" Billy blurted.

"I never said you did, son," said John. He could see that Billy's once-guileless façade had begun to show some cracks. Then, he turned his attention to the tracks. He stepped out into the dooryard, knelt, and studied them closely for a few moments before rising and re-joining the other men. "Those aren't footprints," declared John. "Not to me, anyway. Looks almost like something got hauled clean away into the woods by an animal." He stared off into the dark clusters of snow-mantled pines and spruce trees as far as what little light there was would take his gaze. "Can't say what exactly made it, or where it goes. Too late and dark to look tonight. But the snow's let up; we can chase that trail down tomorrow, first thing."

He spun around and headed back inside, pulling his hat down on his head as he did so, as if to indicate he was done thinking things over. He was. "Junior," he called over his shoulder, "I'm calling the county medical examiner tonight, the state's attorney and any doctor I can get a hold of. The body stays where it is. You know the law; you can't touch it. The M.E.'s a pain; ordinarily he wouldn't get his ass out of his office chair unless it was on fire, but I'll build one under it if I have to, to get him here tomorrow morning. My deputy will secure the site." The deputy suddenly stiffened and gawked at him, speechless, no doubt in horror at the thought of having to spend the night in a large, drafty old house—not with a pretty young woman, but instead, her cold corpse for a companion.

"And Billy Ross," announced John, fixing Billy with much narrowed puppy-dog eyes, "you're coming with me. I'm taking you in on suspicion of murder."

* * *

Junior headed back to the mortuary. What else was there to do? The old truck he was driving wobbled over the snowy roadway, the feeble glow from its headlights barely showing the way back to Lyndonville. This whole thing was trouble, plain and simple. He ran his mind over several concerns; the most pressing of all was his immediate need to replace Billy— after all, who could say how long Sheriff Johnson would have him locked up in the jam? Now it fell to Junior to get another trustworthy driver who could make the run up to Canada to bring back his valuable liquor and T.R.'s bride. That was the part that couldn't be put off. Too many careful, confidential arrangements had been made, and to take the plan apart now, at this late date, would have too many implications—some very costly.

He could feel a headache gaining force, pounding away at his forehead, and his mouth had gone dry, mostly from sucking in his breath every time the sheriff asked Billy yet one more leading question. Junior took his mind off his worries briefly; the thought of that disguised jug of gin, just waiting for him, inspired him to give the old truck a bit more gas and hasten the progress on the way to the mortuary. He was relieved when at last he pulled up beside the back door, killed the engine, and went inside. What he saw immediately unnerved him.

The recently-deceased Mr. Tuttle was naked, hands and feet smartly splayed out, lying on the stainless-steel table. Sven had made all of the necessary preparations—and more. To his horror, Junior saw that Sven had gone ahead and begun the embalming procedure—without him. And there—high aloft, upside-down and tethered to a bracket, almost bone-dry and with its last dregs just now draining into the body's arteries through a bubbling tube connected to its neck, was his embalming fluid jug that had once contained a gallon of his prized, smuggled-in, top-shelf British gin.

Chapter 26

Cold on the Trail

Sheriff Johnson stomped along, step-by-step through the fresh, powdery snow, keeping a wary eye on the faint trail that he was following. He was leaving behind a parallel one of large, webbed prints from his wooden snowshoes. It was early morning, and well below freezing. Not knowing where the trail would leave him or how long he'd be out in the woods, he'd taken the precaution of putting on heavy boots and an extra layer of clothing. As he'd suspected last night before leaving the site of the murder, the snow had indeed tapered off early in the evening and not completely covered the odd-looking trail he was now following, the trail that led from Silas's house into the woods. While it was a long shot, Johnson considered it possible that Billy had taken the murder weapon off into the woods, buried it, and clumsily tried to cover up his tracks leading back to Silas's farm. But the trail led on, and on, and on.

Johnson's young, eager-to-please deputy Sam had asked if he should come along, but the sheriff had just shaken his big head. He'd told the deputy to get some sleep, then to go over the farmhouse with a fine-tooth comb and lift fingerprints from the telephone, the glassware, the doorknobs and furniture. This time alone in the quiet woods, stomping along through the new snow with a clear blue sky overhead and bright sunlight spilling full-tilt over the eastern horizon, was a time for reflection as well as investigation. A red squirrel chattered and scolded him from an oak tree while beneath it, two gray squirrels porpoised through the fresh snow, then paused to dig for acorns. Johnson was digging, too, but he liked to do it alone.

The year 1932 had been an election year. With several unsolved crimes—among them the murder of the John Doe whose body had surfaced in Joe's Pond—and an unsolved burglary of the sheriff's storehouse of confiscated booze still on the books, the sheriff had had trouble in the polls, and a rough time come November elections. A former deputy of his who'd crossed him years ago, now a small-town cop, had run against him and lost, but the margin was uncomfortably close. You had to watch your step as a gun-toting lawman, the sheriff mused as he made his way through a stand of tall birch trees and began to climb a hillside. Being a straight-shooter and ducking oncoming bullets was one thing, but when it came to politics being mixed-up with law enforcement, you had to watch your back, as well.

The trail, now very faint, wound around the birches in a tight circle and led off uphill. When the sheriff gained the rise of land, he found that he was in the far end of the back yard of a large white house; close by it stood a small barn and a garage. It took a moment for him to realize where he was, because he had only seen these buildings from the perspective of the distant road until now: It was the Hollingsworth homestead, (or, as many of the townies called it, "the Hollingsworth estate"). The Hollingsworths had money, but were discrete and didn't flaunt it. The husband and wife probably could have afforded his-and-hers Cadillacs, but instead drove a middle-class, Series-90 Buick sedan and a practical little Oldsmobile coupe. The Hollingsworths, Johnson knew, were sensible enough (and well-off enough) to winter in Florida; the house and outbuildings appeared to be shuttered and buttoned-down for the winter.

And here, the trail went cold. There was no further sign of it; at this elevation, blowing snow had obliterated whatever had been left of it. It would have been inconceivable, the sheriff conjectured, why Billy would have come all this distance—well more than a mile—to discard a weapon and then return to the scene of the crime, especially in the condition he was in. The sheriff looked about, shook his head, shivered from the cold, and pondered the long walk back to Silas Scrivvins' place. Perhaps, he thought, it would be easier to remove his snowshoes and hike down the road to where he'd started at the farm. Then, he heard a car's horn honk. He looked out towards the road, and instantly recognized the car that had pulled over by the driveway's entrance: It was Ed Alvord's blue Dodge sedan, and Ed was behind the wheel, waving to him.

Sheriff Johnson headed toward the waiting car as quickly as he could, his short, bobcat-style snowshoes flopping their way through the powdery snow that covered the driveway. Ed was a good fellow, but the sheriff knew enough to keep his guard up when dealing with a newsman. As a lawman, Johnson could dodge bullets just as well as he could shoot them, but he knew he was better at asking questions than he was at dodging them. He was sensible enough to know that when it came to dealing with natural-born reporters, you had to watch your mouth. Just as he reached the car, Ed popped open the passenger side door. Johnson stooped, unbuckled his snowshoes, grasped them and then piled into the Dodge.

"First time I've ever seen a gumshoe on snowshoes!" Ed wisecracked. "I heard you were out here, playing detective."

"I guess there's a first time for everything, Ed!" remarked the sheriff. Ed put the car into gear and drove off, as Johnson pulled off his gloves and then stuck his chilled hands in front of the heater's outlet. It was toasty-warm inside the snappy-looking Dodge, and with good reason: Ed had optioned the car up as nicely as he could, with a deluxe heater and other things when he ordered it up in Newport at Natole Motor Sales. All things considered, Ed, as owner of the *Chronicle*, could have afforded a Chrysler. But, as a self-professed penny-pinching, cheap old Vermonter, he was sensible enough not to flaunt whatever wealth he'd been able to put by during the lean Depression years. After all, he knew the value of a dollar just as well as he knew the value of a good story. And now, he was out to get one.

"Find out anything about that trail?" asked Ed, keeping the speed down to about 30 to ensure he had maximum time to question Johnson, also because the road was slippery, even though the Dodge's rear tires had chains on.

"Not a thing, Ed. It just goes cold there. Too much blowing snow last night; it wiped out whatever might have been there."

"So—you've got a corpus delicti, but no weapon, no blood-stained dagger at the end of the rainbow, eh?" Ed took his eyes off the road for a moment and grinned at the weary-looking sheriff.

"Nope. That *would* indeed be a pot of gold at this point, Ed," groused Johnson, rubbing his hands together. "And—by the way—not a word about this." Johnson shot a glance at him. "Not now, anyway. I've got too many troubles and too little time on my hands to get this case put together."

"Have you tried to make that kid talk, sheriff?" asked Ed, not taking his eyes off the road this time. The glare of sunshine off the snowbanks lining the road was bothersome; Ed squinted and steered east as best he could, driving straight into the sunrise. "You guys have ways, right?"

"Not like what you might read about in those dime novels, Ed, or about what the big-city cops do. I don't beat prisoners with a rubber hose until they confess to something they might, or might not, have done. If I hand something over to the D.A., it has to be airtight, and it's got to be clean."

"Have you talked with Junior yet?"

"Not really. Just a few words last night, that's all. He's my next stop. "

"I did, and I've got a theory," continued Ed. "What say we pay him a visit, since we're going his way now? I'll circle back and drop you off where you left your car when we're done." He waited for the answer and let the Dodge loaf along at minimum speed.

"Well, I can't see as it'll do any harm, Ed," said Johnson, after pausing to think things through. "But, anything you hear is strictly off the record."

"And when you have a case to hand over to the D.A.?"

"Ed," answered the sheriff, now thawing out at long last and feeling some semblance of warmth in his bones, "you'll be the first one to know."

* * *

Junior was somewhat less than cordial upon finding Ed and Sheriff Johnson knocking at the door that led into his office, but he let them in nonetheless. Junior went on at length about the phone calls he'd received the previous night with the caller asking for Billy, and also about what he had seen both on his way to, and at, Silas Scrivvins' farm.

"You said you almost hit someone last night, someone crossing the road while you were on your way to the farm, and not too far away from it, didn't you?" queried Ed.

"Believe me, whoever it was is lucky, that's for sure," said Junior. "Like I said, someone just shot across the road in front of me. No time for me to swerve. So, what?" he asked, looking at Sheriff Johnson. "Am I up for manslaughter now? Look, I didn't hit that person, whoever it was."

"Didn't say you did, Junior," answered the sheriff coolly. "Fact is, nobody got killed out on that road last night; nobody got hit. All I'm wondering is this: Maybe that person saw, or knew something about, what went on up at Silas Scrivvins' farm. Where did this happen? And what did the person look like?"

"All I saw was a person in black. Just like a shadow. They just shot across the road. Just past the 40 mile-per-hour sign where the speed limit changes from 30. You ought to know that spot, I guess, from all your years chasing taillights in this county!" At this, Junior chuckled, leaned back in his office chair, propped his feet up on his desk and lit a cigarette, hoping that the two men would be satisfied with this and leave soon, so that he could plan his next move.

* * *

Ed and Sheriff Johnson clambered out of their cars and then stood side-by-side on the road, looking at the 40-mile-per-hour speed limit sign Junior had told them about. Ed had driven the sheriff up to Scrivvins' farm to retrieve his car, and now the two men pondered the event Junior had described to them. It didn't take them long to recognize the trail the sheriff had seen earlier, or what it was. Its two snake-like paths neatly bisected the road. One pair continued on downhill; the other led uphill—directly toward the Hollingsworth's house. "Skis," said Ed, calmly. "This was someone on skis." The sheriff just looked at him, dumbfounded.

"It's a new sport," explained Ed. "A Scandinavian thing, cross-country skiing."

"I believe I've heard of that somewhere," mumbled the sheriff, scratching his chin as he pondered the situation. "I thought it was a Norwegian thing."

"Well, you could say it *was*, John," remarked Ed. "The Norwegians won the skiing event at the first Winter Olympics

Games in France, a long eight years ago. Now, the kids over here are getting into it. It's the latest in winter sport." Sheriff Johnson tilted his broad-brimmed hat back on his head, then rested his hands on his hips and just stared at him.

"Oh, c'mon, John; it's a downhill thing: What goes up must come down," Ed continued. "Somebody was obviously up there at the Hollingsworth place, and they must have skied down through here, just last night, once they left Scrivvins' farm after someone dropped them off at the driveway. Just look where those tracks lead back uphill. I'll bet you'll find they go right into Scrivvins' dooryard, where everyone's tire-tracks trampled them—once you follow them. And—look—from here, they head down there." He then pointed toward a distant side street a quarter mile away where a row of shabby-looking tenement houses stood. Their once-pristine paint had faded away during long years of neglect, giving them the scruffy appearance of pairs of dirty old white socks that would probably never come clean, strung out together on a line on wash day. "What a great way to make a quick getaway and leave no identifying footprints. But whoever did it must have figured the snowfall would cover the tracks up. Seems like you might want to investigate, and find which house they lead to. Right now, I have to go; have to put tomorrow's paper together."

The sheriff nodded. Then waved his right hand at Ed, like a cop halting traffic. "Hold on a minute. So, maybe I've got a witness here? Or do you think Billy was telling the truth? That maybe someone on skis killed that girl, got away clean, and let him take the rap?"

"Maybe. Just maybe. Like you said a while ago, sheriff," answered Ed slyly, opening the door of his Dodge as he prepared to leave, "I guess there's a first time for everything."

Chapter 27

The Plan Comes Together

"So—now what?" As soon as he had asked Junior this question (and then shot a glance of supreme annoyance at him) T.R. Donovan poured himself a generously-sized glass of whiskey—the second of the evening—and then unceremoniously dumped a few chunks of ice from a nearby bucket into it. The glass tinkled merrily, making almost the same sound a pay phone does when coins are dropped into it to make a long-distance call. T.R. had some concerns about a long-distance trip he had been planning, one for something of his to be illegally brought across the border from Canada. Now, he was making a call of sorts—calling in Junior's promise to deliver the goods.

The two men were sitting at a table in the unkempt office attached to T.R.'s cavernous ice house, the place where the roughneck workers and hangers-on usually played cards, but it was late, well after working hours. T.R. had built a roaring-hot fire in the nearby wood stove in order to warm himself up to the occasion of talking business after the cold, afternoon quitting time of 5:00 p.m. "Don't rightly know," answered Junior, reaching for the bottle. He poured himself a drink and then settled back into his chair. "Depends on the what happens with Billy."

"No ice?" asked T.R., as if offended.

"Not now," replied Junior, sipping the whiskey, obviously savoring it. He held his glass up, looked at it, then at the bottle and its distinctive, trademarked label. "Canadian Club, eh? This is good stuff, but not *that* good. I don't believe that label's real."

"You shouldn't, Junior," wheezed T.R. as he began to laugh. "It's a local product. And I've got a guy down at the *Chronicle's* press room who prints those labels for me and sneaks them out the back door whenever I need a batch." He guffawed briefly at the disclosure of his dirty little secret, then pulled out a white handkerchief and honked his nose into it, sounding momentarily like a trumpeting bull elephant.

"So, who makes this stuff, T.R.? It's got a real kick to it."

"Some fellow up in East Burke who likes his secrecy. They tell me it's called 'chicken whiskey', and it's quite popular."

"Why?" asked Junior, obviously puzzled

"Because they say that after two glasses of it, you won't care where you lay." T.R. laughed heartily, holding onto his ample belly, and Junior grinned. "Now, that about the package?"

"You're worried about my package. I'm worried about mine, too."

"You have my sympathies, Junior," harrumphed T.R. "Now, look at my position, and let's see if I can get your stony little undertaker's heart to bleed a few drops for me tonight, since you're drinking my booze in my joint. I've got a fine young lady on the hook up in Canada, all bought and paid for, ready to come be my bride."

"My sympathies go out—to her," sneered Junior, as he sipped his drink. "You got a picture of this femme fatale who needs to be boosted across the border? And—more importantly—has she seen a picture of you?" Junior put his elbows on the table and leaned forward toward T.R., observing that the overly-large gentleman was beginning to get beet-red in the face with embarrassment, and leered at him.

"Right there, on the wall," replied T.R., pointing proudly at a small, gold-framed photograph of a black-haired, dark-eyed woman sporting a mischievous smile, as if the photograph was a trophy. Junior emitted a low whistle of surprise and wonderment at the sight of the woman in the photo, indeed a record catch, especially for a man of T.R.'s age.

"T.R., you've robbed a lot of people, but I've never known you to rob a cradle!" he remarked.

"And I'll bet you've never robbed a grave, Junior," retorted T.R. triumphantly, draining his glass and reaching out for the bottle. "Didn't have to; you do well enough with the live ones paying for the funerals."

Junior waited until T.R. had filled his glass and set the bottle down before he grumbled, "Pass it over."

T.R. shoved the bottle across the rough table. "Close enough?"

"Close enough." Junior opened the bottle and poured himself another drink. He leaned back in his chair and sipped the whiskey, enjoying it, regardless of its heritage.

"Thank you, Junior. Glad it worked for you. I heard you had a long reach in this community, but I knew it wasn't quite long enough."

"You know," mused Junior, "you've got quite the racket here with your day job. Your legit business is mostly water, if you know what I mean. Pure profit. How long do you think this dandy little cover of yours will last? After all, more than half the people in Saint Jay have refrigerators now. Times are changing."

"They are, old boy, they are," chuckled T.R. "But I think I've got another year left in the ice business; then, I'm done.

Prohibition might be done, too, after Roosevelt gets into the White House and Hoover's out on his keester. Put your money on a horse, I say, never on a horse's ass."

"So, T.R.," asked Junior, after clearing his throat, "why are my services required to send my boy—who is now in the jam, by the way—off to Canada to sneak your beloved-to-be across the boundary line into the good old U.S. of A.? Why not just put her ass on a day coach on the train? Then, you could sweep her off her feet at the station when she shows up, take her to the nearest church and tie the knot before she changes her mind."

"It's not that simple, Junior," answered T.R. "She's a working girl and needs to get out of the mess she's gotten herself into. Almost signed herself into slavery, as it were. She's up to her ears in debt and needs to get out of Canada. Her boss has her papers and there's not a chance she'll get across the line on the train without 'em." He nosed into his glass again like a hippo seeking water, and guzzled until the shards of ice tickled his nostrils and soaked his white mustache.

"Sounds risky. Sounds to me like you want me to send Billy charging in on a white horse to spring her. Only Billy's cooped up right now."

"Right, Junior. And you want those bottles of age-old French cognac brought across the line, don't you? The stuff you've got a buyer for down in the city. Big money, ain't it?"

"So—what?" asked Junior.

"That's what I asked you in the first place," grunted T.R. "So, you can't make the trip yourself?"

"I've got a business to run, T.R. Maybe yours isn't so crucial, with all the folks buying refrigerators now—plus the fact it's winter. I don't know the roads up that way, or the ways around customs. And—if I get caught—it'll be curtains for my business."

"Your business *is* about curtains, Junior," laughed T.R." He paused, thought, then held up a finger. "Say—doesn't your boy Billy have a younger brother?"

"He does; what of it?" Junior was feeling the effects of the booze now; he squinted at T.R. in an effort to bring the portly man into focus.

"Look, Junior, that kid drives for old man Rivard doing grocery deliveries. I hear he's pretty good with a car, plus, he'll be motivated to make some extra money. Why? His dad's dead now, and his brother's behind bars. Odds are he won't make bail, and I'll bet his mother's got past-due bills, to boot, and is probably damn near frantic. What's to lose?"

"My car, you dope, if he gets caught with booze and an illegal coming across the line," retorted Junior. "The Feds will confiscate it. I can't risk that."

"No risk, Junior. Look here: If the deal goes bad, you call the cops and report it as stolen. He takes the rap, you get the car back. It's that simple. Besides, he's not 21 yet; he'll get off with a slap on the wrist. Furthermore, who'd listen to him if he tries to spill the beans on you? He's a kid with a brother in deep, deep trouble. And, by the way, what do you think? Did Billy do it? Did he kill that girl?"

"I don't know," answered Junior, looking down at the table top as if he were studying it, and he was; there were countless initials and obscenities carved into it. He felt some relief at not seeing his name mentioned. "Right now, I don't."

"So, look," said T.R., weaving a bit in his chair as he grasped the armrests and then reared upward to speak with startling authority. "I know you and Billy have been friends. But dammit, Junior, this is where friendship ends. Each of us has himself to look out for."

"T.R., I think you're right. I'll go talk to Joey Ross and see if I can bring him around to make the trip. Who knows when Billy's going to get sprung, after all? Or, at all?"

"Now, at last, you're talking," remarked T.R. "I knew I'd bring you around to my way of thinking. Guess I've won you over." He leaned over the table, grasped the bottle, and divvied-up its contents between his glass and Junior's.

Junior held his glass up in order to toast T.R., who sat back now, placated for the moment. The old man looked bloated, glassy-eyed and toad-like as he lounged in his arm-chair, thoroughly-intoxicated but still mildly-attentive. "T.R.," announced Junior, swerving slightly, "here's to you, my friend tried and true. You're my kind of crook—after all, you've never held public office."

* * *

It was late in the morning the next day by the time Junior had shaken off his hangover and driven to the county sheriff's office. He had stopped along the way at a diner to dose him-self with an extra-large coffee, which seemed to have helped to clear away some of the cobwebs. Now, with the smartly-dressed deputy's permission, he walked through a doorway and into the area containing the holding cells. All were empty, save for Billy Ross's.

"Take as much time as you want," said the deputy, a smirk showing now on his youthful face. "He's not going anywhere soon. Just rap on the door when you're done and I'll let you back through." He turned on his heel and left the room, slam-ming a steel-cased door shut behind him. Then, from the other side came the ominous sound of his key turning the lock, securing the chilly, dimly-lit room.

"Junior! I wondered when you'd be able to get here. Can you get me out?" Billy exclaimed, gripping the bars of the cell.

Junior shook his head. "Not now. You've gotta be patient. You haven't been arraigned yet and until you are, no one can say what bail will be—*if* the judge allows it at all. Murder's a serious rap, Billy. Bail could be set as high as six grand.

Bootlegging's one thing—maybe $2,000. But you're in deep. It could be three times as much."

Billy released his grip on the bars of the cell, plopped onto his bunk, and dropped his head into his hands. Close beside the bunk were a toilet, a sink and a small wash stand. "I'm screwed," he said. Then, he looked up, hope in his eyes. "You could raise six grand, couldn't you, Junior?"

"Not the way things are right now, Billy. It's the slow season. But there is some hope, if we can work something out." Junior waited for Billy to bite on the bait. It didn't take long.

"Like what?" Billy stood once more and gripped the bars. "Work what out?"

"The job I told you about." Junior lowered his voice, and stepped closer to Billy, and began to whisper the rest of the answer. "Those cases of French cognac that are worth thousands—and the package T.R. has bought. If I can bring all that in, I'll bet I can throw your bail. But you have to help me make it happen now, and with another driver."

"Who?" asked Billy, all ears. But Junior could see that he was disgruntled.

"I can't tell you." Junior whispered, casting a glance over his shoulder to make sure the steel-case door was not ajar with the deputy's ear filling the gap. "If I did, they could try to pry that out of you in court if something goes south. I can't take that chance. I'm taking enough of a chance talking with you right now about this."

Billy nodded soberly. "So, what do you need from me?"

"Maps, Billy," answered Junior, pulling several blank sheets of paper from a pocket, and producing a pen. "Draw me the two best routes over the border and back from Sherbrooke, and another one that's a back door. And tell me where there's a safe house, maybe even a line house, right on the border."

"A back door?" Billy took the proffered papers and pen, and looked up at him, bewildered.

"Yes, a back door. Another way home, the long way home, in case everything goes dead wrong."

Billy, casting any concerns about Junior's dealings with the dead or any sense of wrong to the winds, put the sheaf of paper on his knees, and began to draw.

* * *

Joey Ross was stacking cans of soup on a shelf down at Sam Rivard's Cash Market when Junior walked through the front door late that afternoon. Sam greeted Junior by name, and then Junior walked past the checkout counter and through the store's narrow aisles until at last he found Joey. "Joey!" he blurted, working up a patronizing smile. "Good to see you! How are you?"

"Well, I'm no worse than yesterday, Junior," replied Joey laconically. There were circles under his eyes, and the lump he'd felt in his throat at Bud's funeral service wasn't gone, but it had changed into something else. It had hardened like flint as he'd felt anger and resentment well up up inside him before he'd swallowed it all. But it hadn't gone away; it sat in his gut now, cold as a stone.

He stuffed the cans onto the shelf one-by-one like a machine. The loss of his father had shaken him badly, but his best friend at school, Paul, had helped him get his mind back on studies, and his job, too, as menial as it was. Joey was the glue holding his family together—what was left of it, now that Billy was behind bars. But his hunch was he would soon have to quit school and go to work full-time to support the household. "Heard anything from my brother?" he asked.

"Matter of fact, yes, Joey," answered Junior smartly. "He's holding up pretty well. Tough kid. Hey, you know that; you're his brother. He says hello. And he also needs a favor."

Joey turned to face him, set the last can of soup down on the shelf, and wiped his hands on his apron. Then, he put his hands on his hips and stared at Junior in amazement. "Really? Me? A favor?"

"Yes, a favor. Joey, your brother's in big trouble. It could be months before he gets cleared of the crime everyone thinks he committed and gets out. Or even makes bail. It's all expensive. And now, I'm without his help. Everyone's got bills to pay. You, me, your mom. Billy's going to need money, too. He needs your help. And I hear you're pretty good with a car."

"Why?"

"He was going to run an errand for me next week, an errand up in Canada. Just over and back across the border. And now, of course, he can't do it. I can't, either; I've got a business to run. He wondered if you might be able to fill in for him. And I'll pay. Same as I would for him." Junior rocked back on his heels and clenched his hands like someone at a graveside committal service to end, waiting for an answer.

"If I were Billy, I'd ask how much," stated Joey. "So, now that I'm suddenly worth as much as Billy to you, I'm asking: How much?" Junior's face suddenly puckered up in surprise. Several seconds passed before he spoke.

"How about a hundred dollars?"

"For what, Junior? I could make a hundred dollars here, if I had a mind to it."

"Not in your lifetime, kid. Not at what Sam Rivard pays per hour. Now, let's talk about a deal." Junior paused to look up and down the aisle to make sure that no one was listening. "Let's talk turkey."

"Oh, so I'm driving a bunch of turkeys across the border? Or is it a stiff?" Joey made pretense of going back to stocking the shelf, but stopped. Billy liked to play him, but he was done with that. And to hell with Junior, if that was his plan, too, today.

"Neither, Joey." Junior stepped closer to Joey, grabbed him by the collar of his shirt, and pulled him closer. Joey could smell the liquor on Junior's breath. And now, he knew: this was going to be booze business. "Joey, you listen to me, and you listen good. This is real business, for real dollars. Because if it all works out, those dollars will get your big brother out of the jam. And it will pay you well for your time. Very well." He released the grip on Joey's collar, and Joey took a step backward. "Gonna listen now?" Joey nodded.

"So, what's the deal?"

"I'm glad you listen to reason, Joey. We both know times are tight, and we need to bring in all the money we can; winter's not over, not by a long shot. So here it is: You drive my car up to a place near Sherbrooke, a resort, and pick up a passenger. It's someone my pal T.R. Donovan's expecting. She has to leave the country on the QT, if you know what I mean. She's got herself in some trouble, and he's helping her out of the predicament she's in with her boss. You hand over the money that I'll give you to her boss, and scram—with the girl. Simple, right?" Joey nodded.

"So then, you two spend the night at a joint, at my expense on the way back, and leave an envelope I'll give you on the front seat before shut-eye time. When you get the car out of the barn the next morning, it'll be all set with *my* package— what I want— stowed aboard. And you bring my car, and my package and T.R.'s, too, back. No risk at all. Simple, isn't it?"

"Sounds simple. Run it through customs, right, when their office is open?"

"Oh, no, Joey, no. That's out of bounds."

"Why not?"

"Rules of the game, Joey. The law plays by their own rules. There are other ones a hell of a lot more enjoyable than theirs that can set you up for success. We just can't do it the law's way this time."

"We?"

"You and I. Your brother's out of the game now."

"Game? Look, Junior, I'm not sure if I'm game for this. I know what game really means. Game birds get shot. Everyone knows that." Joey turned away from Junior and started stocking the shelf again.

"Look, Joey, I'm making this offer not just for you, but for your brother. You've got a family here, Joey, and you're the man of the family, what with your brother in the clink. Think about it."

Junior was beginning to become annoyed.

"Then it's $400. Period," said Joey, going calmly about his business. He put his head down and tucked his smile deep under his open shirt collar where he knew it couldn't be seen. By God, if Billy could play Junior, then he could, he reasoned. He'd seen enough of Billy in action to know how to act the part.

Just then, Joey dropped a can of soup. It bounced off the floor, then landed and rolled over to rest beside Junior's feet. Junior picked it up and handed it up to Joey, resisting the urge to use it to smack his head and knock some sense into it. "That's an awful lot," Junior remarked, working up his best undertaker's smile. "I can't do that. How about $250?"

"Look, Junior," said Joey, acting as unconcerned as he could be, "I might be a dumb hick Vermonter, but I'm not gonna make a dumb deal."

"Then, $300? What do you say?" Junior was grinding his teeth now. He wanted to get moving.

Joey thought, long and hard. The sum was half the price of a new car. It would get him and his mother through the winter. Hamburger at Rivard's Cash Market went for ten cents per pound and a loaf of bread for seven cents. The mortgage payment for the Ross family's house was $18.00 per month. At last, after juggling the numbers and figuring that he'd waited long enough, he turned to Junior and said, "Okay, it's a deal. When do you need me?"

"Next Wednesday afternoon. I'll pick you up with the limo when you call me. I'll have maps ready for you, plus cash that'll cover everything on the trip. Your pay is half down, half when you return. You'll be back in time to work for Sam on Saturday morning; you'll never miss a beat!"

"I don't know if I'll ever miss anything about this town, Junior," said Joey disgustedly. He looked the undertaker in the eye. "What makes you think I'll come back, if I'm that good at sneaking across the border? Why would I bother to come back?"

"Because I think you're an honest kid, Joey. Besides, your family matters to you, doesn't it?" Joey nodded. Junior stuck out his hand, and Joey shook it. "Call me tomorrow, Joey," said Junior. Then, he left just a quickly as he'd come into the store. Sam sauntered down the aisle and noticed that Joey hadn't finished stocking the shelf yet.

"Been talking to Junior Coughlin, have you?" he asked Joey, who nodded. "Look out for him, kid," advised Sam, frowning and shaking his head. "He's one smooth operator."

"I know," said Joey.

Chapter 28

The 6:35 from White River

"Time, gentlemen; time!" shouted Sam Rivard from behind the store's counter, as if he were a barkeeper announcing closing time. In fact, it *was* closing time, 6:00 p.m. While it was warm and cozy inside the little supermarket, it was dark and cold outside, and the store's illuminated outdoor sign shed a pool of faint light on the icy sidewalk below as if it were a far-distant sun, trying in vain to warm an evenly-more remote, frigid planet.

Sam reached for the light switches and flicked them off and on to reinforce the message to any lingering shoppers: it was time to go home. Meanwhile, Joey made the rounds with a push broom, sweeping down the aisles. Finally, Sam rang up the last customer's purchase, bade him good night, and locked the front door. "All set, Joey?" Sam asked, looking around to see where the boy was, just as he appeared around a corner, and propped the broom up against the wall.

"Yes, Sam," he answered solemnly, dumping dirt from his dustpan into a nearby wastebasket. "All set." He untied his white apron and hung it up on a hook by the front door.

"Are you going to go down to the jail to see your brother tonight?" asked Sam. "He probably would like to have a visitor. As far as I know, he's all alone; Big John doesn't have any bootleggers, drunks or wife-beaters in the jam right now, so I'll bet he could use some company." Joey stared back at the jovial man in silence.

"Oh, heck Joey, I didn't mean it *that* way!" blurted Sam after enduring an awkward moment of silence. "You know what I mean. He's a good kid. They'll find out who really did it. Couldn't have been him. Heck of a thing, being in a cold, cramped-up cell all alone down there." He slugged Joey in the arm playfully. "Everybody likes Billy Ross."

"Of course they do," remarked Joey just as quickly as he thought: *Everybody but me.*

"Tell you what, I've got something for you to take to him. With my compliments. Here you go, Joey." Sam thrust a brown paper bag into Joey's hands. "There's a pack of smokes in there, a big ham and cheddar sandwich, today's *Chronicle* and an apple. Why? Because I don't know how well Sheriff Johnson feeds anyone who's cooped up in his jail, that's why." He beamed with pleasure at the idea of possibly becoming known as a good Samaritan, instead of simply being a gabby, grasping old grocer. *Change is good, after all,* thought Sam, mentally polishing his reputation like the bruised Mac apple he'd burnished with his apron before he dropped it into the bag.

Joey blinked, stared down at the bag he was holding, then looked up at Sam. "Sam, I'm going to have to take a couple of days off."

"Don't worry about it, Joey. I know you're going through tough times. Your family's been through hell. When?"

"This weekend, and maybe Monday, too. I'll let you know as soon as I can. I'm sorry, Sam." Joey stepped over to the store's tidy little office alcove, plucked his coat and hat off a hanger and put them on as he returned, stopping only to grasp the top of the paper bag that contained Sam's offerings. "I'd better go now." Sam nodded, and at this, Joey was out the door, his shoes crunching through a crust of ice on the sidewalk.

Where am I going, home? he wondered as he trudged along. He stopped, sucked the icy-cold air in deeply and then let his breath out in one, long sigh of steamy vapor. It lingered over his head like the balloon of a comic strip's character, but there were no words in it giving him any sense of direction. It vanished a second later in the chilly breeze. He turned on his heel and headed back toward the store. And then came the realization—he could be gone—gone from this town just as quickly as the mist of his breath had disappeared.

He could not, would not, go home. Not yet. The events of the past few days made his mind spin like the needle of a compass gone wild, but he kept steady on his feet as he plodded along. He passed by Sam's store, its lights now doused for the evening, and kept on going, headed downtown. He paused on a street corner, took another deep breath, and finally let it out slowly. Would he go to the courthouse? Did he really want to go to there to see Billy in jail, and listen to him cuss and swear? He looked up the dark street that led to "the Plain" where he knew the brick courthouse stood, strong and sturdy as a bank vault. Billy? He shook his head at the thought. Sheriff Johnson could keep him up there tonight. Joey stuffed the paper bag under one arm, jammed his hands into his pockets and started walking again.

A few cars ground slowly by on Railroad Street, splashing through shush and throwing it toward the curb, but Joey deftly sidestepped it without complaint whenever that happened. They were people headed home from work, presumably to warm, happy homes where, he groused bitterly, nothing of any significance ever happened, no one suffered any injustice, and life went blithely on. He slowed his pace and glanced upward as he passed by Nolin Brothers' Store to look at the huge clock overhanging the sidewalk: the time was 6:25.

He ambled on, passing by the J.J. Newberry's 5&10, then Moore & Johnson's store, and turned the corner where the New Avenue Hotel's tall brick turret and its witch's hat of a roof marked the southwest corner of the block. Lost in thought about his conversation with Junior, he came to finally, and found himself nearing the railroad station. His wallet bulged with the dollar bills scrupulously saved over the past several months as well as one very important item: his father's railroad pass, good for free passage on any railroad—to any place, at any time.

Joey had found out, sometime back around Labor Day, that Billy had been robbing his father's little piggybank of its quarters, nickels and dimes all along to feed his appetite for booze and pleasure, nibbling away at it like a rat that slyly takes just enough of the cheese every night not to be noticed. But he'd kept quiet, keeping this little secret as a weapon to use against his big brother the next time he needed it. Now, with his father's coveted family nest egg discovered to be nearly empty with no explanation, the sense of guilt at not telling his parents about the disappearance hung around Joey's neck like an anvil, while he could see that mounting debt hung around his mother Beth's neck like a noose. Not knowing which way the proverbial winds would blow, or in which direction the compass would point, Joey had found and pocketed his father's railroad pass—before Billy could return and get his hands on it once more.

The station was ablaze with lights, both inside the big brick building and outside, under the platform roofs. Beyond them, the light glimmered on silver ribbons of rail that led off into the pitch-black depths of the railroad yard, where cat's eye dots of red, green and amber glowed from lanterns. As Joey watched, a clear white beam of light appeared at the south end of the yards and began to grow larger—and closer. He realized that it was the 6:35 train from White River Junction pulling in.

Joey shuffled toward the station and stepped up onto one of the platforms, which had been scraped clear of snow and ice. Except for a man tugging a baggage wagon along toward the train's anticipated stopping point, the driver of an idling taxicab parked nearby and a man sitting behind the wheel of a Ford next to it, smoking, the platforms were deserted. Had it been summertime, the place would have been crowded with passengers, bustling with workers, and the benches full of old-timers leaning on their canes, gawking at all the comings and goings. They came here, too, to scratch and spit, to spin marvelous yarns and stupendous lies and to read the papers, scanning the obituaries, should one of their regulars be among the missing. Tonight, the benches were empty, but tomorrow's obituary column was full, the type already laid out in cold, lead slugs, lying supine in trays in the *Chronicle's* dank basement press room, ready to print by sunup. Time marches on, after all.

The train swept into the station and slowed beside the platform where Joey stood, the enormous black locomotive hauling it seeping steam and smoke as it rolled along. Flames flickered in its firebox and hot water trickled down from pipes beneath the cab. The grimy-looking fireman peered out his window, goggles pushed up over the brim of his denim cap, and raised a gloved hand to wave to Joey. The wheels of the locomotive slowed and it at last shuddered to a halt; a warmly-dressed conductor swung down from a passenger car and plunked a step-stool onto the platform. The very first passenger to alight from the train was someone Joey instantly recognized: it was Doris.

She was dressed, not in her waitress uniform and a cheap-looking jacket but high-heel shoes, a fur coat and an elegant-looking hat. A porter alighted from the train and brought her a small suitcase, just as the well-dressed man who'd been sitting in the Ford hopped out of his car, tossed away his cigarette and rushed over to embrace Doris. He grabbed the suitcase, handed the porter a tip, and headed back to the car, hand-in-hand with Doris. "Wait, Miss!" called out the porter. He'd returned from the coach lugging an awkward-looking canvas bag as long as he was tall that had two baggage claim tickets dangling from it. Doris turned to look at him to see what he wanted. "Your skis and poles!"

"They're checked through to Burlington," said Doris. "Thanks!" The porter waved to her in acknowledgement and placed the bag on a nearby baggage cart. Doris and the man who'd met her jumped into his car; then, it started and quickly drove out of sight.

Joey sat down on a bench, puzzled about what he had just seen. It was almost as though Doris was leading a double life, and had a boyfriend who looked a lot like Dutch, the dapper-looking but dangerous man he'd had a run-in with at T.R.'s ice house long months ago. He realized that he was still holding the bag Sam had given him. He pawed it open, pulled out the pack of cigarettes, and tossed it into a nearby trash can. Then, he did the same with the apple and the newspaper. He re-moved the sandwich, unwrapped it, and took a bite of it while he watched as mail sacks were tossed off the train and stacked in a jumble on a cart. It was then Joey realized that he was being watched, watched by the driver of the idling taxi. The man looked familiar, although Joey couldn't quite place the man's face. But the resemblance of the other man to Dutch, inarguably a dangerous character, kept bothering him. It was then that it hit him: the man with Doris tonight was Steve, her date the night Joey had ushered at the movie theater on Halloween.

Just then, a young couple hopped off the train and hailed the cab; the taxi's driver got out, walked around to the car's opposite side and opened the rear door. Joey sprang up and headed out of the station and its platforms. He had decisions to make, but they didn't all have to be made tonight. His mother, hopefully done with her moaning and crying for the day, would have gone to bed early. He took another bite of the ham and cheddar sandwich. Suddenly, the spinning of the needle of his compass didn't matter; it was enough, tonight, to be eating his big brother's lunch.

Chapter 29

Down the Drain

Ed Alvord rolled his chair back, put his feet up on his office desk and sighed. His desk sat bathed in light cast by a single bulb that dangled overhead, recessed in a shade shaped like a Chinese hat; all else was dark—the office, the windows, the entire building. It was all over—at least, for another day. The latest edition of the *Passumpsic Chronicle* had been put to bed, and both the upstairs office and the press room had fallen silent an hour or more ago. It was going on 7:00 p.m., he discovered, as he looked up from his paperwork to glance at the clock on the wall. He heard the melodic whistle of the night train coming in from White River Junction and St. Johnsbury, and then its other sounds as it chugged across the highway, slowed, and ground to a stop in the chill evening at the brick-walled station down the street. It was a timely reminder that it was getting late and well past time for him to go home. He yawned, finished the last of the glass of whiskey he'd poured himself, and poked at the pile of out-of-town newspapers cluttering his desk, toying with them.

As an inveterate newshound and sifter of information, he subscribed to several mainstream Vermont newspapers whose circulation, in his opinion, barely brushed the bounds of the

Northeast Kingdom. Among those he read each day were the *St. Albans Messenger*, the *Burlington Free Press* and the *Rutland Herald*. But otherwise, he would never know, back in little old Lyndonville, Ed reasoned, if a hometown boy made good abroad, or if a local farm girl married a tycoon and went on a lavish honeymoon wearing newly-cut diamonds, or if a bad boy who'd left town took up his evil trade again and got arrested in another place. His alertness—akin to that of a watchful spider spreading a wide-reaching web—was what kept him both on his toes, and in business.

But he almost missed it this time. As he stood, then gathered up the papers and prepared to toss them into his wastebasket, the college sports column in one of the Burlington papers, with bold print calling out: "Lyndonville's Hollingsworth Captain of New Ski Club Team" caught his eye. Ed yanked the page out of the paper and placed it on his desk. He then sat down, and poured another, but much smaller, glass of whiskey. And read.

"The college's new so-called Ladies' Ski Club, formed by girls who are winter sports enthusiasts, recently returned from a weekend spent skiing at a Canadian hotel near Saint-Sauveur in Quebec, where special arrangements have been made to facilitate the new sport of cross-country skiing. The group of students has petitioned the college to consider the formation of a college ski team, and have elected Catherine Hollingsworth, a native of Lyndonville, Vermont, to represent them as its captain.

Miss Hollingsworth says that she became enthusiastic about the sport while in France several years ago, in the company of her parents, Mr. and Mrs. James Hollingsworth while they were vacationing in the Alpine regions of that country, where the sport of skiing is better-known. The Hollingsworths are well-regarded for their philanthropy and their interests in banking and Vermont industries, notably mining concerns currently in operation in the Central Vermont region. The Hollingsworths are currently wintering in the Fort Myers, Florida area and are expected to return to their lovely hilltop home come spring-time."

Ed grasped the telephone and yanked it across the desk, pulling it closer to him. The cord knocked the pile of news-papers onto the floor, but Ed ignored this. He waited for what seemed an eternity for the operator to come on before giving her the command: "Get me Sheriff Johnson on his home line, quick." A few seconds later, the candlestick-styled tele-phone in the nicely-wallpapered hallway of the Johnsons' snug little home in St. Johnsbury began to ring. The low-ceilinged, brown-shingled house was a Sears Craftsman home, a master-piece that Sheriff John Johnson had built by himself while a young man; it had arrived in a boxcar, and he'd unloaded it, built it, stick-by-stick, paid for it on installment plans while a deputy, and now, he was enjoying one of its comforts; namely, its bathroom.

"Oh, I'm sorry; he's soaking in the tub," John's wife told Ed. "But I'm sure he'd like to talk with you, if it's as important as you say it is. I think the cord will reach." She traipsed down the hallway, rapped on the bathroom door, opened it, and thrust the telephone, much to her husband's surprise, into the bathroom.

"Who the devil is it, Dorothy?" mumbled the big man, after stirring the suds in the claw-foot bathtub, opening one sleepy eye and peering at her. The hot bathwater was up to his chin, and he was drowsy, almost asleep.

"Ed Alvord down at the *Chronicle*. Says it's an important call." She stood there, patiently holding the phone out as it were a tray of hors d'oeuvres being offered up at a party, not sure what her husband was going to say, and whether or not he was going to take it. But, one thing was for sure: the phone was getting heavier and heavier as the seconds passed.

"They're all important, aren't they, dear?" John grumbled good-naturedly.

"So's my roast, John. It's in the oven and I have to check it," she answered. John's right hand and forearm, wet and sudsy, rose up from the depths of the tub like the muscular arm of Neptune reaching for his trident in order to spear something he detested. He grasped the phone. Then, his wife was gone, thoughtfully leaving the door ajar in case some entertaining words might spill out of the bathroom and into her ears. Much like Ed, John's wife liked to keep her ears up and follow the news, too, even if it was only local in nature.

"Ed?"

"Yes, this is Ed. Say, John; are you sitting down?"

"Matter of fact, I am, old chum. I'm soaking my sorry old ass in a tub right now, after running all over hell's half acre and freezing it off asking questions today, thanks to you."

"Did that trail lead back up to the Hollingsworths' house?" asked Ed.

"Yes, it did. Like you said, it looks like all the vehicle traffic wiped out whatever marks or footprints might have been there, before the person left the scene."

"What about those houses, down where the trail ends? Did anyone in those houses see a skier?" asked Ed.

"Nobody saw anything. Typical."

"So, I have a skier for you. Maybe."

"Who?" Fully-alerted, John sat up in the tub; rivulets of bathwater ran down his back. He reached for a towel.

"The Hollingsworths' daughter, Catherine. She's a skier. College student up in Burlington. It's in today's Burlington papers." Ed settled back and waited for the response he was sure would come.

And it came.

"What's she got to do with this if she's in Burlington?"

"Well, John, do you know for a fact that she was in Burlington on the night of the murder?" There was dead silence on the other end of the line.

Then, finally, John replied: "Okay, Ed; I don't."

"Looks like you'll be burning the midnight oil tonight, sheriff," commented Ed.

"You burn my ass, Ed," stated John, as he reached over the side of the tub, set the phone down on the floor and arose. Then, he stooped, pulled the drain plug, and at last grasped the towel. He took a while, drying himself off a. bit, before he picked up the telephone again. "Still there?" he asked. Now, he was frowning. It took a lot to get Sheriff John Johnson worked up to a good thundercloud of a frown, but he was there now.

"Still here. Look, John; your career might be going down the drain if you don't solve this one."

John looked down at his feet, and the bathwater exiting the tub. It was forming a whirlpool, taking water, soap suds and all down to the sewer, just as his wife called to him that dinner was ready. "Thanks, Ed," he said, "I'll keep you posted. Call you tomorrow," before hanging up. He slowly stepped out of the tub and toweled off. He'd be damned if he'd face the public this naked, without facts to stand on, but he wouldn't cover up anything, either. The truth was out there, and he'd find it, hell or high water. Then, the smell of the roast in the oven wafted into the bathroom and dispelled any thoughts that were left over from the long day, or about what his next moves would have to be.

* * *

The next day dawned bright and cold, with bright-white clouds soaring high in the clear blue sky, although a record-breaking January thaw was in today's forecast. The sheriff, emboldened by the infusion of a big breakfast and several hot cups of coffee, finally emerged into the frigid backyard of his home and cranked his big Hudson patrol car into life, once he'd boosted its balky battery and squirted some ether into the carburetor. Shivering from the cold, he closed the car's hood, hopped inside, and then nudged the still-chattering car out onto the highway and headed north toward Lyndonville.

There was business to attend to today. First, the matter of the one door of a tenement house that hadn't opened to his knock yesterday. He was duty-bound to collect all the evidence he could, and to keep going until he had questioned every tenant about the mystery skier. Second, he wanted to pay a visit to Billy Ross's mother and chat with her a bit. As it was, Billy was in need of some fresh clothing, which his mother would, he assumed, provide. The boy was, of course, entitled to a speedy trial according to the law, but just how quickly it took place was a matter left up to him and the D.A. As a matter of fact, the arraignment hadn't even been scheduled yet, simply because the sheriff was still collecting evidence. Third, although it was probably not related to the case, he'd have to catch up with Catherine Hollingsworth, but he had to chase every lead and possibility down. And now, fourth—but most important of all—he had to determine what had become of the murder weapon. But time was running out, he well knew, for a successful arraignment. It was going to be a busy day.

On a whim, he decided to pull around behind the row of tenement houses when he arrived to check with the renter of the apartment, who had been absent yesterday. Perhaps, he thought, he could judge by lights showing in the windows, or other signs of activity, if anyone might be inside the apartment he was headed to. What he saw surprised him: On the back porch of what he surmised was apartment 1-C were two trash cans, a number of boxes, and a pair of skis and poles that had been propped up against the wall next to the apartment's back door. A well-kept, late-model Ford sedan was parked close by, standing out in marked contrast to the assortment of careworn Model T Fords and other jalopies near it.

The sheriff motored around to the front of the building, got out, walked briskly over to the front door marked 1-C and rapped on it with bare knuckles. He stood there and shivered in the cold a few seconds until the door swung open and a young woman wearing a gray waitress's uniform greeted him with stony silence and a blank stare. "Sheriff John Johnson, ma'am," said the lawman. I need to ask you a few questions."

"Oh, my. What about?" she asked coolly, glancing furtively over his shoulder for a split second.

"About something that happened up on the hill, night before last. I think someone who lives in this building may have seen something having to do with an altercation at Silas Scrivvins' place. They were out skiing just after sundown, and wound up near here. What's your name, ma'am?" The sheriff pulled a pen and notebook from his jacket, and noticed that the woman was staring, not at him but at his badge.

"Doris Martin, sheriff. And, for the record, I don't ski. Heck, I don't even ice skate!" She looked him in the eye this time, and smiled. "Can't keep my balance, and I hate the cold!"

"Don't think I asked you if you were out skiing the other night, but that answer'll do," grumbled the sheriff as he wrote down the woman's name.

Just as he did so, a man's voice sounded from the adjoining room. "Hey, honey! What's all the rumpus about out there, doll?" A second later, the man revealed himself as he shuffled into the front hallway, barefoot and disheveled, dressed only in rumpled trousers and an undershirt. His eyes were blood-shot, his hair a tangled mess. "What's up?" he demanded as he entered. And then, recovering quickly: "Oh, sorry, officer; didn't realize who you were." The sheriff observed that the thin-faced young man's eyes were now darting back and forth, alternately glancing at the window and then the door; it was not a good sign.

"As I said to the lady here, I'm looking for someone who was skiing by the Scrivvins place the other night and might have seen something strange going on. There was an incident up there I'm investigating."

"Well, I don't know what that place is, sir, and I'm no skier!" stated the man with a laugh. "Doris here is my cousin and I'm just down here from Newport for a few days to visit. Couldn't get here for the holidays, 'cause I had the flu. All better now!" He grinned like the Cheshire Cat, stuck out his right hand and the sheriff reactively reached out shook it. The young man's eyes were dark and watchful. And the palm of his hand was damp.

"Your name, sir?" asked the sheriff.

"Steven. Steven Martin, sir," came the reply.

"And what do you do, Steve?" asked the sheriff, taking note.

"Oh, why, I sell cars."

"Which kind?" asked John, pretending to be interested.

"Fords, sir. They're to ones to beat! I work up at Natole Motor Sales."

"Those new cars really are, Steven," said the sheriff, tucking away his notebook, with a wink and a nod. "I sure have chased enough of them! Even caught myself a few! Well, thank you, folks. Sorry to have bothered you." He tipped his broad-brimmed hat and was out the door within a minute after thusly bidding the couple goodbye, and promptly drove out of the dooryard. In less than another minute, he circled around, parked his patrol car behind a shed and peered out at the back of the tenement building. He was just in time to see Steve open the back door, furtively look all about, grab the skis and poles and then toss them far underneath the porch of the building. So now, it wasn't just that the skis and poles had been hidden for suspicious reasons, but that Steve's cover story didn't wash;

after all, as the sheriff well knew, Natole Motor Sales sold Plymouths, Dodges and Chryslers—not Fords.

* * *

About half an hour later, the sheriff's knuckles were rapping on yet another door, the one of the Ross household. Beth, ever antsy and worrisome, had heard the sound of the patrol car pulling up outside and quickly peeked out a window. "Oh Lord," she exclaimed at seeing Sheriff John Johnson, "it's the police!" She scurried to the door, dreading what the big lawman, now climbing out of his car, was going to tell her— or, to ask her, for that matter. Beth had been worrying about who might come bearing bad news about Billy, or else asking pressing questions about him, questions to which she had no answers. In her ongoing bereavement—first, suffering from the loss of her husband and now, having her oldest son incarcerated, taken away and under arrest for murder, she saw herself clearly. She was the central, tragic, victimized figure in a drama that kept on unfolding, with no end in sight. And as a seasoned dramatist, Beth played the part perfectly; she was already sobbing by the time she opened the front door.

The sheriff, becoming unsettled by Beth's appearance as the door swung open to reveal her troubled-looking face, doffed his hat. "Mrs. Ross, I'm sorry, sorry as a man can be," the big man humbly said. He shuffled his feet awkwardly on the slush-covered porch. "But there are a few things I think I need from you."

Beth swayed and placed one hand over her heart. Beth knew instantly what the sheriff wanted: he wanted to take her down to his office for questioning. The police had ways, Beth knew, to make you talk. Some people who had been arrested had been beaten with a rubber hose until they confessed or else gave up information, or even had their teeth knocked out, in order to make them talk. This was what was called, in the tabloids, "spilling the beans". After all, Beth read all the newspapers that told of these terrible things. Oh, no, wait; worse: The sheriff was looking for Joey, thinking Joey was in cahoots with the killer. The big man would take him away and beat him up, trying to implicate him in the murder. The murder Billy couldn't have committed; Billy, for all his faults, was still a good boy. This, Beth knew. Or perhaps, come to think of it, now, the sheriff had a search warrant and would ransack the house before taking both her and Joey away. She trembled with dread. "What do you need?" she asked at last, when she had caught her breath.

"Well, you see, ma'am," explained the sheriff, "Billy's in need of a shave and a shower, as well as a change of clothes. I thought you might be able to give me a spare shirt and a pair of pants or two the boy could have, if it wouldn't be too much trouble, Mrs. Ross."

"Well, well," stammered Beth, calming down considerably, "that's no trouble at all. I'll see what I can find for you. Won't you come in?" She smiled meekly and pulled the door open a bit wider. The sheriff stepped into the hallway and let the door swing shut behind him with a solid *thunk* as Beth scurried off upstairs. Snow melted off the lawman's boots and soaked the carpet as long minutes ticked by while he waited for her to return. Had he made a mistake in not searching the Ross house, he wondered? Probably not. Whatever weapon was used to kill Mary Lou had, by logic, to be somewhere at the scene, perhaps lying under the snow where it had been tossed, after the fact. Both he and his deputy had searched old Silas's place from top to bottom and back up again for any kind of bladed weapon or sharp tool that could be tied to the crime, but had found nothing. Footsteps sounded on the stairway as Beth descended.

"Here you are, sheriff," said Beth, handing him a pile of neatly-folded clothing. "That red flannel shirt on top is his favorite. It was hanging in the closet and I'm glad I found it right away. You can have all of this, and let me know if you need anything else." Then, she paused. Beth was as gray as a charged-up thundercloud that was ready to burst and let loose a downfall. "Is Billy okay?"

"As good as can be, ma'am," replied the sheriff, grasping the bundle of clothing. "And as I'm sure you can understand, I can't say anything else right now, under the circumstances. You're welcome to come and see Billy during visiting hours. Is that something you'd like to do?"

"I'm not sure if I can bring myself to see him there," Beth said, her voice shaking. "At least, not today."

"Oh, I almost forgot, Mrs. Ross. Do you happen to know someone named Doris Martin?"

"No, sheriff, but I've heard of her. She works as a waitress at the lunch counter, downtown at the 5&10. Billy used to be sweet on her, but then all that changed somehow. Matter of fact, Joey says he saw her just the other night, getting off the train from White River. Some sharp-looking fellow in a new Ford car picked her up and they drove off together."

Just beneath the brim of his hat, the sheriff's eyebrows rose momentarily in curiosity. "I'd like to talk to Joey, ma'am," he said. "Where is he right now?"

"He just left for school," answered Beth hesitantly, wiping her hands on her apron.

"Well, when he gets home, please tell the young man I'd like him to come down to my office at the courthouse. I have a few questions I'd like to ask him. I'm sorry to have put you to so much trouble, Mrs. Ross. Are you alright?"

But now the thundercloud had burst and Beth was behind her hankie, wiping away the tears and fearing the worst once more. The sheriff tipped his hat to her and let himself out, closing the door softly behind him. He opened the door of his car, hopped in and dumped the clothing onto the passenger seat. He started the car and had driven no more than a couple of blocks when the pile of clothing tumbled over. And he noticed something—a white piece of paper—that was now sticking out of the pocket of the red shirt. He pulled the car over to the curb, set the parking brake and grabbed the paper. It was a letter, written on the stylish-looking stationery of one Catherine Hollingsworth during late November. As he withdrew it, the envelope that had contained it fell out. It was addressed to Billy Ross. The sheriff began to read the letter.

"Billy: I think you well know why I am writing to you, after seeing you with that cheap, awful woman when I came home, treating her as if she were the toast of the town. I can only suspect that you've been the victim of some foul, evil scheme she has cooked up to make you hers. I am begging you to write me as soon as you can and tell me if there has been some mistake, and that you are not in love with her, and will come back to me. But otherwise, I will assume the worst—and I will make her pay the price. Ten times the amount of hurt losing you cost me. Do not wait for me to return at Christmas time; my parents have decided to close up the house and winter in Florida. Again, do not wait to reply. Catherine."

The sheriff tucked the letter and its envelope into the pocket of his shirt, let off the car's parking brake, swung the car out onto the road and gunned the engine. Now there was a really good reason why talking with Catherine Hollingsworth should become the top priority of the day. Arriving back at the courthouse and his office, he parked the patrol car and strode inside. His deputy was at the duty desk, reading a magazine, his feet propped up on one of its open drawers. The deputy's feet came crashing down to the floor as soon as the sheriff came blustering through the door and gave him an order: "I have some phone calls to make. I want you to round up some volunteers and go up to Silas Scrivvins' place. Work the whole outside area over with rakes and shovels. See if you can find a tossed weapon." The rattled deputy, who'd almost been dozing, was still pulling on his jacket when Sheriff Johnson tossed him the patrol car keys. "Take the car," he barked. "I'll likely be here the rest of the day."

No sooner was the dutiful deputy out the door when the sheriff got on the phone and asked to be put through to Ed Alvord at the *Chronicle*. And when Ed finally answered, the sheriff posed questions: "Ed, you have a society column in that paper of yours. Tell me how I can get in touch with Catherine Hollingsworth at the university in Burlington, and how I can reach her parents down in Florida. Quick." A broad smile grew under the sheriff's mustache as he took a question, and then answered. "What's in it for you? Well, Ed, it's first dibs when I finally put all the pieces of this puzzle together and have a story to tell."

Chapter 30

Shifting Gears

That same afternoon, the temperature rose spectacularly, to everyone's delight, but the uncommonly warm, bright day seemed to drag on as Joey sat in study hall. January thaw, the highly-anticipated annual reprieve from the frigid throes of winter was suddenly upon the Northeast Kingdom, and it had come early. To some believers, it was almost as though an optimistic weatherman had been proven right in his December prediction that spring was "right around the corner" after all. The dramatic weather change was thrust upon the cold land as quickly as a blizzard would have been by nature itself, but now, this was instead a warm, welcome breath. The old-timers, nature-lovers numbering none among them, were not lulled into complacency by what they knew to be a false truce. None of them trusted this respite from the all-too-frequent nudges of Old Man Winter's cold shoulder to linger; they knew far better. The thaw would be brief in its tenure but blessed, none-theless, by those who basked in it and reveled in its temporary warmth. It was most apparent when the sun—conspicuous by its absence for days—had reappeared like some long-lost friend sailing high above, shining brightly and fiercely, melting snow with a vengeance. And, also when warm winds that accompanied it blew into town with a sigh that seemed, even if it was only in the lower 40s outdoors, magical—even tropical.

It was when snowplows and men laboring with shovels could at last break through tall drifts of snow that had piled up and made passage on secondary roads impossible for days, when farmers who'd not spoken to their neighbors for a week or more could finally make their way out of their dooryards, travelling on still-frozen roads to visit them, or to gather supplies in stores. These were the few but treasured days of relief before winter resumed with renewed vigor, well before the horror of springtime mud season arrived, a time when dirt byways and back roads would turn to gelatinous muck. Passage over them would be all but impossible, and men would curse Mother Nature for her perverse and unreliable complexion (thereby blaming this mythical woman of no Biblical repute whatsoever for their foiled travel plans, and letting Eve off the hook as the biggest tempter of all time).

It was the perfect time for Junior to make his move.

As he sat in the classroom, Joey could see, whenever he looked up from his book in study hall, snowmelt dripping rapidly down from the eaves outside the big windows. It was as if the whole, frosty-white world outside was melting. From behind him, he heard the quiet rustle of paper on the move and then felt a nudge against his left elbow; a note had been passed forward to him. Joey casually looked up from his reading to glance at the teacher, Mr. Stinson.

It would have been honorable, had Mr. Stinson been as well-regarded by the students as he was by the principal, to have him at the helm of this vast and usually-unruly, hard-to-control study hall. But Mr. Stinson was not without his faults. First, he was a horror when provoked by some misdeed, much like an old watchdog that enjoyed barking to no end when rudely awakened. Second, it was rumored that Mr. Stinson, said to be a veteran of the Great War and one suffering from horrific combat wounds, had a steel plate in his head and an artificial leg—although it was not known as to which leg it really was—and exactly where on his head the steel plate was located. Various energetic and playful students had tried—through the years—to determine if (and if so, where) this plate actually existed. They often tried when Mr. Stinson fell asleep at his desk in study hall. They would stealthily approach him, make-shift fishing rods in hand with magnets attached to the ends of the lines, warning off all others not to giggle or express the slightest emotion as they dangled the magnets over his head. Then, too, some of the students took turns lighting matches stuck into Stinson's shoes; he outfoxed them every time, just as he did the hopeful fishermen. Stinson heard them just at the last moment at every turn; he'd awaken and rise from his chair, rampant and belligerent, defeating their attempts once more but never able to catch them or identify them for the same reason he never actually served in the military: he had tunnel vision.

Keeping a wary eye on old Mr. Stinson—attired in a sensationally-outdated, moth-eaten suit, baggy white shirt and a clumsily-knotted bow tie—who had drifted off to sleep not long after the bell had rung, Joey slyly palmed the note and opened it, taking great care to make as little noise as possible. "Cops are looking for you. Sheriff at your mom's today, Paul," read the note. Keeping the note and his pen up, concealed closely behind his history book, just in case, Joey penned a reply on the little piece of paper: "How do you know?" He folded, then palmed the note in his left hand and wiggled it behind him; an unseen hand grasped it and spirited it away; in a few minutes, it was back again with a reply from Paul: "Friend of mine saw it and thought you should know."

It was the perfect time for Joey to make a move.

He paused to think for a moment. The sheriff could be onto him, and what he'd agreed to do for Junior—or not. The sheriff could be playing him against his brother—or not. Joey could leave and make some changes, or he could stay and pretend nothing was going to change. He was finally facing himself, and what he had to do. And when he was done thinking, Joey stood up, turned, and faced the study hall class. He put a finger to his lips, asking for total silence. Grinning as he did so, he tossed his pen into a corner of the room next to Mr. Stinson's desk, turned and darted to the classroom door on the other side of the classroom. By the time the pen had clattered to its noisy stop on the floor and Mr. Stinson had awakened, bellowing like a bull to know what was going on as the students roared with laughter, Joey was already out the door and halfway down the corridor. Little was he to know that Paul would be hot on his tracks, just as soon as the laughter in the classroom had subsided and Mr. Stinson dozed off again, not realizing as he drifted off to sleep that not only one, but two of the students in his charge were now absent.

* * *

The pay phone on the wall just inside the St. Johnsbury J.J. Newberry's store jingled merrily as Joey dropped a coin into it and it worked its way down through the black-and-chrome telephone's innards, bouncing off unseen internal bells like a freewheeling pinball in a game of chance. Joey was taking a chance—a chance that Junior would answer. Joey waited— nearly breathless after running all the way down to Railroad Street to make this call—and listened expectantly for the operator to pick up. He had to cover his free ear, as the sounds of parakeets chirping in the five-and-dime store's pet section, cash register bells ringing next to him, and the clashing sound of dishes being scraped clear of food and dumped into the sink at the nearby lunch counter interfered mightily. These sounds also interfered with waitress Doris Martin's ability to listen in on the conversation as she stood nearby, doing a painstakingly-thorough job of wiping down the counter, checking salt and pepper shakers along the way to make sure they were full, and the ashtrays empty. After a series of clicks, buzzes and a brief burst of static, Junior got on the line and answered. Doris checked the ashtrays again, as Joey spoke.

"Junior, it's me, Joey. I'm ready to go."

"Great, Joey. How soon can you leave?"

"Right now." He glanced around the store, and did not see that anyone was listening. However, Doris, completely out of his sight, had ducked down beneath the counter, making pretense of stacking dishes.

"Excellent," replied Junior. "Because we don't have much time to get to work." He paused to take a pull on the flask of gin he happened to have handy. That was excellent, too, he thought, after he put it down. "I've been meaning to call you. Where are you right now?"

"Newberry's, in St. Jay." Had Joey turned around just then, he would have seen Paul sitting on the bumper of a green Studebaker parked outside, watching him through the store's large, plate-glass windows. It was almost noon. The sun was beating down fiercely now, and Railroad Street was glistening in its light, slippery and wet with runoff from melting snow and ice.

"Alright," answered Junior. "I'll be down with the limo as soon as I can be there. Be outside. You're sure you're in on this?"

Joey took a breath before answering: "I'm in."

"Okay, Joey. And you know, as much as I appreciate this, it's really something that will do your brother a world of good. You above all need to know that. He needs to get out of the jug and the mess he's got himself into. It's not just for me, Joey, it's for Billy." There was an audible *click* as Junior hung up, a corresponding *clunk* in the five-and-dime store when Joey did the same, and a *thunk* as Doris slipped upon hearing this as her fingers, slippery with a bit of soapy-dishwater, dropped a thick stack of dishes on a shelf underneath the lunch counter.

It was just after 1:00 p.m. when Junior arrived. He drove southbound past the 5&10, abruptly pulled a rather dramatic U-turn in the middle of the street, and then nudged the big black Packard limousine over to the curb where Joey was standing. Junior reached over and popped the passenger side door open. "Get in, kid," barked Junior. "We've got a deal now, and we need to get moving."

No sooner had Joey hopped in than Junior gunned the car's massive engine, threw it into gear and the Packard surged forward. Junior turned to grin at him. "This car's got a lot of horsepower, Joey. I don't buy cheap. See? This car's got 384 cubic-inch straight-eight under the hood. She's a Custom-8, almost top-of-the-line." Joey observed that Junior had crooked teeth, a crooked smile and—much like former President Calvin Coolidge—Junior had the sort of narrow, wizened-looking face and pointed nose that made folks conjecture that he might have been "weaned on a pickle".

Junior finally shifted into high gear, and then let the Packard loaf along at 35 or so, its engine mumbling in protest of not being unleashed to maximum potential as it puttered along up Memorial Drive toward Lyndonville. "Trust is important, Joey," stated Junior, steering the big car around a sharp corner. He gave Joey a sharp look. "I hear that you can handle a car."

"I've done that a lot for Sam with his delivery van," stated Joey. "Dad let me drive the old Pontiac, too."

"There's a big difference between a tin lizzie like your dad's —plus old Sam's jalopy, son that'll have its fenders fly off at 40 —and a real car like this one that'll do 85 and more in a hurry," groused Junior. "And for what it's worth, Sam Rivard's little business and his jalopy aren't worth a pisshole in a snowbank compared to my business and my cars. Now, I want to see if I can trust you." The big Packard had been cruising along the road adjacent to the Passumpsic, where conches of ice along the river's banks glittered in the sunshine in contrast to its dark, swirling waters. Junior pulled the car over and stopped at a spot just beyond St. Johnsbury Center and its tiny post office, where the view of the valley to the west was clear. To the east was a small cemetery perched on a hill. The grayish tombstones of the dead protruded from the glistening white snow like tree stumps in a long-forgotten, logged-off forest. Over in the south east corner of the cemetery stood what appeared to be a small white garage.

"Now, let's see what you can do with a car." Junior opened his door, hopped out, and beckoned to Joey to slide over and take the wheel. Once Junior was seated on the passenger side, he gave Joey the command: "Let's go to Lyndonville. Fast." Grasping the huge steering wheel with his left hand, Joey nudged the floor shifter into first with his right hand, gently let out the clutch, and the massive car began to move, making little if any noise. He quickly found that looking down the car's long black hood and trying to line the radiator cap up with the side of the road was almost like sighting down the barrel of a long rifle. "Step on it!" Junior snapped. Joey did, and car fishtailed promptly sideways. Junior snickered. "You've got to get used to her, kid," he observed. "She's a heavy old gal, but she can be a slippery bitch until you get her rolling. Once you do, you'll be fine."

Junior was more than a tad uneasy at letting the kid drive the limo, but wanted to test the boy's mettle. If he was going to run an important errand, then he had to prove his worth. "Let's see you downshift to stop the car, without using the brakes," he ordered. Joey backed off the gas, double clutched, and shifted effortlessly out of high gear into the next lowest; the car slowed ponderously; then, Joey took another, another, and another, until the Packard finally rolled to a gentle stop.

"How'd you know my car had a four speed, son?" asked a surprised Junior.

"I've read about 'em," replied Joey, grinning from ear to ear. He was beginning to enjoy the experience of driving an expensive luxury car, even though he considered its owner to be a shifty, almost ghoulish character.

"Okay, kid. Now, step on it. Let's scram." After swiveling in his seat, looking to make sure that no other cars were ahead of, or behind his car, he twisted back in his seat to look at Joey, and casually asked, "Oh, by the way: Do you know how to do the bootlegger's turn?" Joey nodded, and smiled. "Okay, then. Show me." Although he doubted the kid could pull it off successfully, Junior grasped the armrest anyway. The kid was starting to look cocky; maybe he really *did* know, after all. He didn't have long to wait long to find out.

Joey backed off the gas, braked slightly, then cranked the steering wheel hard to the left. As the Packard started to drift and turn, he yanked on the parking brake; the long, heavy car made a ponderous U-turn in the middle of Route 5, somewhat like an ocean liner being turned around and berthed by tugboats—but much faster. Junior asked him to turn around once more and with that, the Packard continued on to Lyndonville. Satisfied, Junior crossed his arms, sat back in his comfortable seat and thought about things as Joey familiarized himself even further with the handling of the powerful, two-ton automobile. As usual, Junior was thinking about things that would mean something beneficial for Junior.

For one thing, Junior reasoned, the kid seemed eager to please, and motivated. That would have to figure, what with Joey's father cold and stiff as a board, his brother Billy moping around in jail, and their grieving, overwrought mother to support in the meantime. The kid worked for old Sam Rivard, a renowned cheapskate and penny-pincher. Joey would no doubt spring at the chance to earn more dough, given the chance, if Junior gave him one. Maybe even quit school and work full time. And Billy? What about Billy? Billy was starting to look like trouble. Had he, or had he not killed that girl, after all? Junior still couldn't fathom an answer that he could trust, and trust was important. Billy might beat the rap after all, but that might not matter.

Having the stigma of dealing with the dead as an undertaker was one thing; dealing with the stigma of employing an accused murderer, no matter if he got off the hook, was another. And Junior was, above all else, a wily businessman and a shrewd card player. He did know one important thing in the game of life: if you got dealt a bum card, you ditched it before it burned you; you then picked up another card and took a chance on it. He suddenly came out of his reverie and realized his Packard was hurtling along at better than 60, just as it burst through a patch of snow on the road and never wavered. The kid must have had a lot of fun driving old man Rivard's truck as though it was a race car, Junior reasoned. Astonished, he glanced at Joey; the broad-shouldered kid, all of 17-going-on-18 with an unruly shock of brown hair had a firm grip on the big steering wheel and he was smiling, as if he were just as thrilled as if riding a roller coaster's first car. "You're doing fine, kid," advised Junior as he nodded in approval and grinned at him, "just fine."

Several minutes and as many miles later, Joey at last slowed the car as he approached Lyndonville and the rooftops of the railroad's freight house and passenger station hove into view. The Packard bobbed gently as it crossed the railroad tracks and entered the downtown area. "We need to gas up the car," Junior announced, telling Joey to pull in at the Corner Garage that stood at the junction of Depot Street and Broad Street. Joey deftly cut across traffic and pulled the car to a stop under the portico carved out under the corner of the big brick building, where two gas pumps were and a uniformed attendant stood waiting beside them, almost as if he'd been expecting the Packard's arrival. In fact, the young man had been idling away, girl-watching as women shoppers and high school girls, just out of class, strolled by the garage; one of them was Lila. She spotted Joey almost immediately and came running over to the car.

"Joey, where have you been?" she asked as she dropped her school books, sprang up onto the Packard's running board, and flung an arm through the open window and then around his neck. "I really wanted to see you. I asked Billy to tell you to call me. But you never did. Oh, c'mon Joey, tell me what you're up to!" In her exuberance, she jumped up and down, making the big car rock gently like a large boat encountering a swell at its mooring. The attendant filling the gas tank chuckled while he chewed gum, ogled the girl and enjoyed the little drama playing out. Lila's classmates were enjoying it, too, where they had gathered close by, gawking, giggling and elbowing one another.

Junior would have none of it. "Get off my car, miss," he growled, "or I'll have your old man tan your scrawny little hide when you get home, until you won't walk right." This only made the gathered audience shriek with laughter, especially when Lila turned her backside to Joey and Junior and wriggled it in defiance.

"Go right ahead, Junior," she replied sassily. "Don't waste my daddy's time; do it yourself! If you can!"

Junior was ready to respond, but the gas tank had at last been filled, and the attendant intervened: "That'll be $3.50," he said, sidestepping around Lila. "Check the oil?"

"Never mind," said Junior, passing the cash over to Joey. He gave it to the attendant, who headed off into the garage to ring up the sale. "Let's go, Joey. We've got all kinds of stuff to go over before you leave."

"Where are you going?" Lila blurted, looking concerned. She withdrew her hand and clutched the door of the Packard, as if she intended to keep it from leaving town.

"I can't tell you Lila. I just can't," said Joey. "But I'll call you, just as soon as I get back."

"He'll call you, Lila," Junior fumed. "He says he'll call you. Now—for the last time—get off my car!" Dejected, she dropped off the running board, picked up her books and stood back, pouting and displaying an upturned nose, as Joey started the Packard. And then drove off toward Junior Coughlin's establishment to prepare for the evening trip to Canada.

"Silly stuff, Joey," remarked Junior, as he settled back in his seat. "You don't need her hanging around your neck when you've got a job to do, any more than you need your momma's apron string hanging around your neck. Speaking of your mom, what the hell did you tell her about your trip north of the border?"

"Nothing," answered Joey. The day was moving along, as if it was going faster than the Packard could.

Junior allowed himself a smile of smug satisfaction; *good*, he thought. *Best to keep everything quiet.* The biggest mill around, so to speak—other than Ide's big feed plant in Saint Jay—was the local rumor mill. Its members' tongues wagged like tails of hungry dogs under a dinner table looking for a juicy handout when there was news of comings and goings overheard on a party line. Some of those folks, unfortunately, were teetotalers and Women's Temperance League members, unsympathetic to the bootlegger's cause. Sometimes, the law would listen in, too.

"Don't worry, kid; I'll think up something to tell her. I'll tell her, and I'll handle it for you."

"Thanks," answered Joey. "I'd be grateful for that."

"It's the least I could do, kid." Junior smiled and gave Joey a conspiratorial slug in the shoulder. Junior would, after going over maps and instructions later on this afternoon with Joey, forget all about that promise. Handling a bottle of gin, and taking a rather repetitious series of slugs from it once Joey had left for Canada, held much more of an immediate promise for gratification. Junior, it was rumored, had a nasty reputation of doing the least he could do for those who did the most they could do for him. And, even worse, most of those rumors were true.

Chapter 31

The Shuffle Play

Just as Joey Ross was getting instructions on how to sneak into Canada on his mission for Junior, Sheriff John Johnson was getting some instructions via telephone from the State's Attorney. They were blunt, to the point, and loud—loud enough that the sheriff had to hold the earpiece of the phone away from his ear to avoid having it scorched. "Johnson, you'd damn well better fish or cut bait in this Ross case," the attorney bellowed. "The press is driving me nuts and so is the public; Billy Ross is a popular kid in St. Johnsbury, and they think he's getting a bum rap. You can't hold him forever without coming up with either a murder weapon or a witness."

"But," began the sheriff.

"No buts, Johnson. I'm giving you 24 hours to give me solid evidence for a case I can prosecute, or you're going to have to cut Billy Ross loose and go face the music. And the deceased's sister and her relatives, as well. Let's just hope they don't hire a high-priced Burlington lawyer to go after you for false arrest and negligence."

"Anything else?" the sheriff asked tolerantly, although especially peeved by this point.

"Yes. Somehow, lack of due diligence comes to mind." There was a loud *click* as the attorney hung up his phone with the force of an irritated judge swiftly bringing down a gavel.

The sheriff sighed, hung up, and rubbed his furrowed brow in frustration. He had solved tougher cases before but now, besides being saddled with the chore of solving Mary Lou's murder, he was being henpecked by those seeking answers as to who had set the fatal fire at the Larsen farm and when the perpetrator would be called to account for it. He kicked his office chair back a bit, stretched out, and put his feet up on his desk. To hell with paperwork. He leaned back and observed the ceiling fan overhead, its paddles describing lazy circles as it spread some vestige of warmth around the office. The last feeble rays of late afternoon sunlight filtered through the windows and quickly began to fade. It was time to noodle things, and—come to think of it—he realized he hadn't heard back from Ed Alvord as to whether or not he'd been able to get contact information on Catherine Hollingsworth.

He sat up, pulled himself over to the desk, yanked the phone close to him and called the *Passumpsic Chronicle*. Ed's wife answered, and in due course got her husband on the line. "How the hell are you, Ed?" the sheriff inquired.

"Busy," Ed blustered, sounding especially grumpy. "You should know that; it's another press day."

"Sorry, Ed, but I wondered if you'd gotten anything on Catherine Hollingsworth."

"I have, as a matter of fact. I found out where her parents are vacationing in Florida, and spoke with them earlier. They were good enough to give me the number for the sorority house Catherine belongs to at the university."

"Ed, remind me I should deputize you sometime," the sheriff remarked appreciatively.

"You should, John. That and a badge would get me into a lot of places without asking, and out of a lot of jams I might get myself into, without having to call you for a get out of jail free card." Both men chuckled.

John glanced at his wristwatch, realizing that it was well after school hours and that Joey Ross hadn't stopped by as requested. "Ed, look, I have to go over to the Ross place for a few minutes, Can you swing by here in about half an hour with whatever other info you dug up on Hollingsworth?"

"Sure can," came the reply. And then: "Just make sure the coffee's on, and it's not the swamp water your deputy makes."

* * *

It was going on dark when Sheriff Johnson nosed his patrol car into the Ross family's driveway, where the old Pontiac sat like some forgotten relic of the past. The headlights of his car played across it, and then the porch of the forlorn-looking old house in time to catch Beth in the act of opening the front door. She was already crying and wringing her hands as she emerged. "Ma'am," uttered the tall sheriff as he emerged from the car, "Whatever is the matter?"

"It's Joey, isn't it?" she sobbed.

"Mrs. Ross, I just came by to see if he's here; he never stopped by my office this afternoon. He's done nothing wrong I'm aware of."

"Well, sheriff, I couldn't tell him to because he didn't come home tonight after school," answered Beth.

"The last time you saw Joey—did he say anything odd?" The sheriff pushed his broad-brimmed hat back on his head.

"Well, yes: he couldn't imagine why Doris Martin told the baggage man she had skis checked through to Burlington, when he saw her getting off the train from White River the other night. Skis?"

"What night was that, ma'am?"

"Two nights after that poor young woman died, up on Silas Scrivvins' farm."

It took a few seconds for Sheriff Johnson to process the information and store it away. His brown, puppy-dog eyes were wide open now and his big ears up, all tuned in to what the distraught woman on the sagging porch of the old house was saying. "That's all, Mrs. Ross?"

"Well, only that he was surprised to see she was all dressed up in fancy clothes and a fur coat, the way he'd never seen her look before, and her boyfriend, Steve, picked her up and drove off with her in a brand-new Ford car." The sheriff wrote down a few things, then pocketed his pen and notebook. "You will find my son, won't you?" implored Beth.

"Mrs. Ross, listen: Your son isn't a missing person—yet," he said. "I'd advise you to give it some time. He may have stayed late in school. He may be out late with friends. For all I know, I may find him waiting for me when I get back to my office. Good night, Mrs. Ross." He tipped his hat and was gone. Beth stood on the porch, watching the taillights of his car receding into the darkness, hoping for Joey's return, until she could stand the cold of waiting outside no longer. She went inside, heaved herself onto a couch in the quiet of the living room and cried herself to sleep.

Sheriff Johnson, in a high state of anticipation, drove rapidly back to his office. Now, he was anticipating more trouble, and possibly chasing down potentially false leads. Upon entering, he found that Ed Alvord had arrived. Ed and the deputy had cleared off his large oak desk and were playing pinochle on it. "Glad you showed up, John," remarked Ed laconically as he played a card with a look of resignation on his face and looked at the grinning deputy seated across from him. "His coffee's not worth a damn, but he's beating the pants off me."

"All set for me to head home now, John?" asked the deputy. The sheriff nodded. "And, 15 minutes extra duty time?" He pointed to the clock on the wall.

"All good if you'd like me to run you in for illegal gambling while on the clock," answered John.

"Didn't think so!" answered the young man, who stood, hauled on his coat, put on his hat and headed out the door. "May the best man win!" he hollered over his shoulder, as the sheriff took his place at the desk.

The sheriff elbowed the card game aside and pulled the telephone toward him. "Got that number, Ed?" he asked. Ed pulled a piece of notepaper from the pocket of his shirt and handed it to the sheriff, who scrutinized it briefly, then put in a long-distance call to the university's sorority house. Within a minute, a breathless, co-operative and very giddy-sounding Catherine Hollingsworth was on the line.

Yes, she knew Billy Ross. She and Billy had been "a number" for a while but had had a falling out. No, she didn't know Mary Lou Lamar, but she had seen her around town. Yes, she had read about the murder. No, she knew nothing about it except what she'd read in the newspapers. Yes, she'd met Doris Martin at Newberry's the last time she was in town. And, yes—that was the last time, after Thanksgiving. Yes, she skied, but no— she'd been nowhere near Lyndonville on the night Mary Lou had met her demise. Catherine stated she had been staying and cross-country skiing at the White Cupboard Inn in Wood- stock on that weekend, a place where there had been some talk of constructing a ski area. She agreed to sign a deposition to that effect. And that was that. The sheriff hung up the phone, a look of defeat on his face.

"What the hell is it, John?" asked Ed. He had picked up the cards and was now playing solitaire.

"Perfect alibi. She was away skiing in Woodstock."

"Was she? Was she, John?" Ed leaned across the table. "How about some good old-fashioned fact-checking here, before you flush your career down the toilet and say goodbye?" Ed grinned at him like a shark. "Call up that inn and let's get the skinny on her. *If* that really was her."

A minute later, the sheriff was on the phone, calling the inn, with Ed on the deputy's extension.

When the innkeeper answered, the sheriff identified himself and shot a barrage of questions at him. Without hesitation, the man verified that Catherine Hollingsworth had indeed signed the guest register, that her luggage was tagged with her name, and that her skis were, as well. And, there was a baggage claim tag on them.

"Can you describe Miss Hollingsworth, please?" asked the sheriff.

"Sure can," answered the innkeeper. "Brunette, maybe 5' 6", green eyes. "Had a fancy suitcase, big fur coat, and had skis and poles, a real outfit; all the latest, I'd say."

"Anything stick out, seem odd to you?"

"Well sir, she complained about dishes and silverware being dirty at the dinner table. Said she knew how to do better than that. Didn't go over too well with my staff, I can tell you that. And those skis she brought, well—she never used them, the whole time she was here."

"Really?" asked the sheriff, leaning closer to the phone. He knew by this time, of course, that Catherine Hollingsworth had blue eyes and blonde hair. He had seen enough pictures of her in the society pages of the *Passumpsic Chronicle.*

"Yup. And, you know, there's good skiing on a pasture near here, too. Lots of local kids go and ski there, and we've had people come here to stay and go over there to ski. There's been talk of putting up a rope-tow lift here, like they have up in Canada, but nothing yet. Maybe next year. We have plenty of snow. So maybe she just wasn't in the mood." The sheriff thanked him and hung up the phone. And then Ed hung up his. John and Ed exchanged glances. Ed collected the cards, stacked them into a deck and then cut them.

"Somebody's playing us," said Ed, as he looked up and dealt, "and I think it's two somebodies."

Chapter 32

The Line House

"You look pretty sharp in that outfit, Ross," observed Junior, stepping back to take a look at the boy. "Really good. Professional. You should work a funeral or two for me, once we get back into the busy season." Junior had outfitted Joey with the formal black chauffeur's jacket and cap usually worn by Billy whenever the occasion—usually an expensive funeral—called for it. The sleeves were a tad too long but the uniform—plus the addition of chrome-plated letterboards clipped inside the rear windowsills of the Packard, spelling out the name of Coughlin's Funeral Service—completed the picture of a young driver on an earnest mission to retrieve a grieving woman in Canada and bring her across the border into Vermont, just in time to be at her dear brother's funeral service. At least, that's the picture Junior wanted the authorities to see and believe, if Joey was unlucky enough to run afoul of any of them.

Night was falling and the lights were on already, glowing warmly and helping to dispel some of the chill of Junior's mortuary where the Packard sat waiting, while Joey poured over the map Junior had given him. His jacket pocket bulged with envelopes containing cash for the forthcoming trip, plus his advance. "You'd best get going, Joey," remarked Junior. "You've got 60 or so miles to go and you sure as hell won't make it all tonight. The roads are in bad shape."

"Where to, then?"

"There's a line house up near Beebe where you can hang your hat for the night and get some shut-eye. And get a fresh start tomorrow. Anyway, it's also where you'll stop off to pick up my cargo when you come back." Joey nodded. "Remember, the dough in one of those envelopes I gave you, the one marked Francine; that's for your expenses on your way up and for when you pick up your passenger in Quebec at the address I gave you. The other one that's marked Gaston, that's what you give the guy at the barn at the line house on the way back, when he puts the car inside for servicing. When you leave, everything'll be set—for my part of the bargain."

"What's the place called?" asked Joey uneasily.

Junior stuck out a finger and pointed at an X marked on the map. "It's just called Royale's. It sits right on the border on the back road you see on the map. It's a local joint. You brother's slept over there sometimes, when he's on a job. Gaston Royale's the owner."

"What's a line house?" asked Joey, shifting around, feeling a bit uncomfortable in the oversize uniform.

"Hey, kid, it's a tavern, one that sits right on the line between Canada and the good old, thirsty-dry U.S.A. The bar sits right on the line; the boundary line's even painted across the floor to mark it, and if Johnny-Law from our side comes a-bustin' in to make a pinch, why, all the booze and the happy folk retreat to the north side of the line, where liquor is legal and they can thumb their noses at him and drink up. Simple, eh?" he chuckled and looked down at his watch. "Ready to go?" he asked.

"But not through customs?" Joey was cautious, feeling Junior out.

"We can't do that, Joey. There isn't time for that, and all the formalities. You have to go through unnoticed and bring back a young lady who's lost her husband—and not too long ago—before anyone's the wiser. She's in bad circumstances; up to her ears in debt and needs to get out of Canada. And, there are bad people who have eyes on her. T.R. Donovan's agreed to help her out, gentleman that he is, because her boss is a cruel person, and holds her working papers and her passport. T.R. tells me she has relatives back here in the states that he knows, and she can settle into a nice life once she's safely across and all's said and done. It's a rescue mission. But—it all depends on you."

"Me?" Joey shuffled his feet. He stuck his hands into his pockets and felt the envelopes with wads of cash—Junior's—with one hand; the keys to the Packard with the other. He felt uncertainty rising upward from his feet, but downplayed the urge to quit the game Junior was playing.

"Yes, you. Look, Joey, this isn't for me—it's for your brother. And for that poor young lady. I'm the one taking all the risks here, going out on the limb for T.R. with my car and my reputation. And when you deliver, whatever could possibly be in it for me with what else you're bringing back goes to springing your brother and getting him a proper lawyer. See, T.R. is, after all, a generous man!" He smiled, as he usually did whenever he told a monstrous lie, and slapped Joey on the shoulder. "Now, buck up and hit the road."

Joey consulted the makeshift map again. "Will it be a long stopover at that line house—Royale's—on the way back?" he asked.

"Yes. The travelling's slow and the going's rough up that way, from what I've heard, so the boys up there will put the car into the barn, load it and check it over so you'll be all set to come back as quick as you can. The main thing is: don't be late. It's all been set up. Just don't ask too many questions and don't get too curious. It could confuse things; I've made all the arrangements."

In fact, Junior really had, except for leaving out one important detail: He neglected to tell Joey everything about the load —other than the young lady— to be carried on the return trip. The important one.

* * *

The big headlights of the long black Packard did little to cut through the gloom. A scrim of fog descended after sunset, smothering the state highway and the barren fields alongside it. Joey kept the speed down to 30 as he cautiously felt his way along beyond the crook in the road in the town of Burke. The cheerful-looking porch lights of the corner store that had seemed to welcome him as he entered the little town, and then swung around the curve close by it, now receded into tiny dots in the rearview mirror and vanished.

Farther on, the way grew even darker and the road, black and slick with snowmelt, ever narrower. And just over the crest of a hill, without warning a deer—a huge buck with an equally large rack of antlers, darted out of the fog-shrouded roadside and improbably came to a halt in the middle of the road, staring deadpan into the car's headlights in aimless curiosity. There was no time to stop, only to stand on the brakes and swerve to the left. The Packard spun out of control on the slippery road. It turned completely around and burrowed rear-end first into a low-lying snowbank. And then it began to settle, tipping ever-so-gently until a sickening *clunk* provided an audible indication that the car's bumper had contacted the wooden posts and wire cable of the guardrails.

As if vindicated by this turn of events that had interrupted its nocturnal stroll, the deer snorted, turned and gingerly leapt over the guardrails with the grace of a ballerina. It swiftly disappeared into the night. The Packard, meanwhile, had stalled and despite Joey's efforts, it refused to start. He hopped out, flashlight in hand, to survey the damage.

To his relief, as he played the beam of the flashlight around, he found that nothing had been broken, dinged or dented, but both rear wheels of the big car had slid just over the shoulder of the road and were now buried axle-deep in snow. By some miracle, the Packard had—thus far, at least—avoided breaking through the guardrails and plunging into what appeared to be a deep ravine. There was only one thing to do: dig.

Joey fought his way through the heavy, mushy snow, opened the car's trunk, rummaged around and at last found a small shovel. He went to work with the speed of a demented man now, clearing snow away from the wheels and then, the underneath of the car, shovel-full by shovel-full. And just as the last of the snow was cleared, the Packard crept backward another inch, as if displaying its ever-growing affinity for whatever lay at the bottom of the dark gully below. The guardrail wires were taught now; they creaked as they began to take up the strain of the weight of the heavy automobile, tenuously holding it back from the abyss. Joey dropped the shovel, ran to the driver's side of the car and hopped in. To his relief, the big, straight-eight engine started immediately this time. He put the car into gear and let out the clutch, but the rear wheels spun, useless to propel the car out of its predicament. The Packard had taken many widows and widowers off on trips to bid farewell to their loved ones' burials. Now, it seemed that the car was determined to head off to its own eternal resting place. But Joey knew that if that happened, Junior wouldn't just grieve or simply bid it farewell; Junior would get even.

Chains. There just had to be tire chains in the trunk, Joey reasoned. He hadn't seen them when he got the shovel, but maybe he hadn't noticed them, in his hurry. Putting them on the rear tires would be the only hope of getting the car out and getting back on the road. Soon. He turned the ignition off, opened the door and stepped out once again. He had left the car's headlights on, but it still seemed as though the fog—never mind the darkness of a damp, chilly, moonless night—was still closing in on him. Somewhere off in the deep woods beyond the stranded car an owl hooted. Joey shivered, stuck his hands in his pockets briefly for warmth, and felt the envelopes of cash Junior had given him. Money talks—that, he knew. But he also knew it doesn't have much say in whether someone can survive for hours on end when stranded on top of a mountain in near-freezing temperatures. Alone.

He was about to trudge back to the car's trunk when he heard it—the unmistakable sound of a vehicle coming on the highway, laboring along up the hill. Flashlight in hand, he turned in the direction the sound was coming from, intending to flag down the car. Getting help, or a tow, would get him out of his predicament; Joey knew there were precious little other means of human assistance in this woebegone spot. On his way here, he had stopped seeing the glow of lamps or kerosene lanterns in the occasional remote farmhouse or lonely little cabin long miles ago. A glow appeared in the bank of fog to the south, then the glow became two spots of light. The growl of a large engine grew louder, as did the rhythmic clanking of tire chains. At last, the bulky form of a large truck of ancient origin broke through a sea of gray fog like some apparition, as if it were the *Flying Dutchman* making one of its fabled appearances.

Joey stepped into the middle of the highway, waved his flashlight, and the vehicle groaned to a stop, turning just enough toward the Packard to illuminate it. The steam spouting from the truck's radiator cap and smoke issuing from its exhaust only made this fog-shrouded night-time meeting more eerie. "Junior!" bellowed someone in the truck. "That you?"

"No it ain't, you fool," came another voice from inside the truck's cab. "That's Joey Ross, with his brother's Sunday-go-to-meetin' uniform on!"

"Yeah, it's me," answered Joey, just as someone hopped out of the truck and approached. It was Seth. "Boy, am I glad to see you!"

Seth stared thoughtfully at the Packard, perched precariously on the edge of the road. After half a minute of rumination, he spat a wad of tobacco onto the highway and observed: "Well, Joey, you're in some trouble, now, ain't you?" Joey nodded. Seth turned to stare at him now. "What on earth are you doin' up this way with Junior's big fancy car, anyhow?" he queried.

"Driving up to Barton." Joey shuffled his feet. From what he knew of Seth and Tom, they were both notorious gossips. About some things. Of course, Joey had to pass through Barton; he'd leave the rest of the itinerary out. Better left unsaid.

"Oh, I see; fillin' in for your brother." Seth scratched his chin in thought. "Got yourself in a minor mess here. What happened?"

"Deer ran out in front of me. I couldn't stop in time." A door on the truck opened with a squeal of rusty hinges, then slammed shut, and Tom came ambling over.

"I see. What's up there in Barton?" Seth asked inquisitively.

"Booze? Women?" asked Tom, chuckling. "Betcha it's both!"

"Must be," offered Seth. "Ain't much else to do up Barton way right now, unless you want to sit in an ice shanty out on Crystal Lake, jiggin' for fish and all of a sudden wishin' you were at home, curled up with a bottle, a fine young lady and a nice, hot woodstove. So, where's the action?"

"Look, fellas, there's no action. I have to pick someone up. A passenger, that's all. And there'll be hell to pay if I'm not back on time. Can you pull me out?"

"Seems to me there should be some consideration for such a worthy deed, seein' as how Junior is a businessman and whatnot," commented Tom. "We'd starve without a little extra income on the side in the winter—you know, when we're not goin' in the hole come spring, burying all of Junior's stiffs."

"Five bucks would cover it, Joey," advised Seth, nodding sagely. "He's good for it, and you know it. Fork over a fiver—a Lincoln—and we'll yank Junior's big old bus right out of where she lies in a jiffy, and you'll be back on the road in no time."

"Sure is cold out here, ain't it?" remarked Tom nonchalantly. "Cold and pitch black."

"Blacker'n a whore's heart," observed Seth solemnly, looking about as if in wonder of the desolation of this eerie spot, just as the owl hooted once more.

Joey rummaged through the pockets of his black jacket, at last finding several loose dollar bills he'd had the good sense to put there while at Junior's. He counted out five singles and handed them to Seth. "I knew you'd see the sense in it, Joey," Seth said, apparently satisfied. "Junior can make it right with you when you get back." He turned and headed back to the idling truck, clambered aboard, then swing it around and backed it up as close as he could to the stricken Packard. Tom dragged a long chain out of the truck's cab, then busied himself by hooking one end of it to the rear of the truck and the other end to the Packard 's front bumper.

"Okay!" yelled Tom. The truck rumbled slowly forward a foot or so, then, its wheels spun and its tire chains flailed when the tow chain became taut. It stayed so until Joey thought that either it would break or the car's bumper would come flying off, but the Packard didn't budge. Tom looked at Joey with a look of supreme annoyance. "You sure you left it neutral?" he grumbled. Joey nodded. "Better get in the car and give it the gas when I say so," he said. Joey got behind the wheel and started the car. He didn't have long to wait. "Give it to 'er!" he roared. Joey let out the clutch and punched the gas just as the truck surged forward and then stopped; the Packard popped out of its resting place. It flew toward the truck as nicely as a cork leaving a freshly-opened bottle of champagne, soaring toward a restaurant's wall. The car stopped inches short of colliding with Tom and Seth's idling, smoking relic.

The tow chain rattled as Tom unhooked it while Joey sat as still as a dazed rabbit, gazing at the back of the old truck. It had high sideboards, and they were splayed outward from the weight of some kind of heavy load within. A trickle of foamy liquid was dribbling out of the crack between the twin doors and splattering onto the snow. Joey suddenly realized what it was. "Beer! Is that what you guys are hauling, Tom?" he asked, leaning out the window. By this time, Tom had removed the heavy tow chain, slung it over his shoulder like a soldier's belt of machine gun bullets, and was headed back to the vehicle's cab to stow it away. Instead, he turned around and stepped slowly over to Joey's open window. He paused reflectively, then struck a match on the fender of the Packard and lit a cigar he'd had clenched in his teeth all the while.

"Now, Joey, in your circumstances, you should know that what goes on in the woods, stays in the woods. Right?" he asked. The match was still lit; in its flare-like glare, Joey could see that Tom was puffing on his cigar now, and had the beginnings of a wry smile spreading across his pockmarked, unshaven face.

"Yeah, I can understand that, for sure," he vouched, fidgeting in his seat. It was high time to go. Anxious to leave for his announced destination of Barton, but actually one much farther north, he slipped the car into gear and held one foot on the brake. Tom tossed away the match and thumped the roof of the Packard twice with his right hand, as if he were swatting the rump of a dallying horse to make it gallop away.

"Bon voyage, mon ami!" shouted Seth from where he sat in the truck, startling Joey with this sudden change to French, of which he had some knowledge. *"Et un bon retour!"* Having used up his extent of the language, Seth sat back behind

the truck's wheel and chuckled. Joey let out the clutch and the Packard, still sleek and shiny, slipped away into the foggy night, unsullied by its dalliance with the guardrails. The surprised expression on Joey's face as he drove off apparently did not go unnoticed by Seth, who had wished him a good trip—ostensibly to Quebec—and a happy return. The border-crossing implication was obvious to Joey: Seth suspected. *No, hell,* Joey thought as he sped along: *Seth knows.*

* * *

Long miles later, the Packard was rolling along merrily; the ornery stretch of twisting, tortuous mountain roadway was behind its taillights now and the fog had, in part, lifted enough to permit Joey to work the Packard up to a fair speed. Over to the right, it appeared as though the landscape had disappeared; there was nothing to be seen but a black void. Then, when lights appeared in the distance and the beams of the car's headlights were reflected from the steel ribbons of railroad track coming close alongside, Joey realized he was abreast of Crystal Lake, and approaching Barton. When he finally pulled into town, he stopped at a tiny filling station. The Packard seemed to have a fondness for gasoline, and Junior had told him besides to keep the tank, "Never less than two-thirds full" to ward off a freeze-up in cold weather. "Best not to take a chance," he'd advised.

The old, gray-haired attendant took his sweet time, first pulling on his coat, then putting on his cap, then finally ambling out of the station as reluctantly as an old draft horse that doesn't want to leave a warm stable. He halted by the driver's side door of the Packard, swiped the cuff of one sleeve against his nose and then asked the perfunctory, "Fill 'er up?" Joey nodded, and the man shuffled to the back of the car and pumped the gas. When he had finished, he returned and asked if he should check the oil. Joey shook his head. "If I were you, son," the elderly gent cautioned, "I'd be on guard, driving out on the highway this late like you are, alone. Been too much trouble around these parts. Hijackers. I guess it ain't enough that them bootleggers are back on the move, too, what with the thaw, and the law's after them tonight. That'll be a dollar seventy-five, son."

A few minutes afterward, Joey spurred the car into motion again, and after another half hour he had put both Barton's tidy downtown and the twinkling night lights of Orleans far behind and below him, the car scudding across patches of ice and drifted snow lying along the high plains that arose north of town. He navigated the twists of Pleasant Street, 3rd Street and then Main, the state highway, as he passed through Newport's quiet downtown, dodging potholes and places where streetlights were out. He headed northward, stopping now and then to consult the map Junior had given him. Close to midnight, after losing his way several times but recovering after consulting the map and retracing his errant steps, he succeeded in finding Royale's. It was on a secluded, single-lane dirt road that was, quite thankfully, still frozen and not a morass of mud. Despite the late hour, the place was ablaze with lights and the parking lot was crowded to overflowing with cars—most of them with Vermont license plates. When he pulled into the dooryard, stopped, and rolled down his window in order to find his way further, he was immediately reckoned with. "Who are you and where are you from?" called out a disembodied voice. The two rather loud clicks that followed indicated that a weapon was being cocked and readied for action.

"Ross. Coughlin's car, northbound," Joey called out, as he'd been instructed to. Joey blinked as a flashlight came on and was shoved at him, aimed at his eyes. Then, a heavy hand descended on the handle of Joey's door, and yanked it open.

"Where's the other guy?" asked the owner of the flashlight. "Don't you try to con me; you're not Ross. I've seen this car before, but not you." Joey could see the business end of the barrel of the handgun that was pointed at him as its owner beamed the flashlight all over the inside of the car, in order to satisfy himself that Joey was alone.

"The other guy's in jail; he's Billy. I'm Joey, Joe Ross, his brother." And, so—there it was for him, acknowledged and accepted at last. It was the link between Billy and Junior, and the booze racket, finally being revealed to Joey—as he sat uneasily behind the wheel of the idling Packard and asked the man: "Are you Gaston?"

"Gaston's inside, like he always is, the old goat. Gimme the keys," commanded the man holding the flashlight. The gun was withdrawn and then its owner, impossible to see because of the glare of the flashlight, stuck out his free hand, palm up. As Joey turned the ignition off, he realized that he'd been clutching the Packard's big steering wheel for the last tense minute with something akin to a death grip. Once released, his hands shook slightly as he handed over the car keys. The gruff, unseen man gave him another key in exchange. "Turn in your room key tomorrow and we'll get your car out of the barn and bring it around for you. This is how it works, in case you don't know. Now, get your ass out of the car. Don't worry about the car or the law; the barn's just across the line, in Canada. I'll take it from here." With a sigh of relief that one stage of the journey was over, Joey slid off the seat and ambled off wearily toward the lights blazing in the windows of the line house, what appeared to be a large, two-story frame building.

There was no sense in knocking on the rough, splintered door of the place that so obviously served as a tavern; the music booming from a radio within, and the hoots and hollers of drinkers and dancers reveling to its jazzy noise would have drowned out the sound—likely even that of someone being shot out in the parking lot. Joey cautiously shoved the door open. Immediately, a dozen rough-looking men at the bar wearing dirty denim and tattered sweaters or Mackinaw jackets swiveled around on their stools. They craned their necks to see who was entering. They scowled through their beards at him, then, one-by-one, they turned back around in order to pay attention to their drinks, and resume their closely-guarded conversations with each other.

The dance floor—if it could be called that—had a black line painted down its center, delineating the international boundary line, just as Junior had said. And several couples, better dressed than the denizens of the bar, whirled dizzily—and, in some cases, woozily—about to the latest music piped in from WDEV on a large Philco floor-model radio. Other couples sat drinking and smoking idly at tables, and began to holler comments as they spied Joey: "Hey, fella!" hollered one young man, holding his glass of whiskey aloft, "Where's the funeral?" His girlfriend, a pretty thing in a fancy pink dress seated across from him laughed hysterically, so hard that she lost her grip on her martini and knocked it over. A tidal wave of gin flooded the table and its waterfall on the opposite side quickly drenched the trousers of her date.

All became silent in crowded room a second or two later when the song on the radio came to its end. The martini's olive, free of its obligations, rolled merrily across the table, dropped off the edge and hit the floor with an audible *plop!* All eyes in the line house were focused on the couple now. "Get up," the young man said to his girl sternly. He was furious. "You know the rules in this joint."

"Honey," she beseeched, "I didn't mean to…"

"You have to walk the line. All of it. In good time. Or else, you're shut off."

In an instant it was as if Royale's line house, a dark, lowly den of iniquity of drinkers and customs-dodgers of some repute had suddenly become a high school auditorium with a sports game in progress; it was now filled with sideline cheers and chants of: "Walk the line! Walk the line! Walk the line!" Anyone so unlucky as to have an empty glass or mug pounded it on their table to add a drumbeat to the message. The young lady rose rather shakily and unsteadily. Tearfully, she made her way over to the far western end of the building as her boyfriend glared at her for embarrassing him as Joey stood, mesmerized, at the eastern end. The radio blared anew and now, Bing Crosby's hit, "Please" was on the air. The young woman began to tiptoe unsteadily along the black line painted on the floor, one foot after another, arms flailing clumsily along the way each time she lost and regained her sense of balance.

"Ten!" someone called out, beginning the countdown. Then, "Nine! Eight! Seven! Six!" as more voices joined the chorus. The woman tried to hurry now to cover the distance across the dance floor in the required amount of time, and wobbled badly now and then, recovering at the last possible moment each time from keeling over. "Five!" Joey watched her as she approached, growing closer with the passage of each second, just like the deer in his headlights had. The pretty woman in pink, much like the deer he'd encountered earlier tonight, he realized, was heading for a head-on collision with him. Unlike the deer, though, she was quite drunk. And she was smiling a lopsided smile at him.

"Four!" came the chant. "Three! Two!" By now, everyone but the sturdy folk hunkered down at the bar were on their feet, joining in on the fun that bordered on ritual humiliation. The woman, fluttering like some woebegone bird in distress, and running on the last of the gin fumes in her tank, finally ran out of gas. She tripped and headed for the floor as her eyes rolled up into her head and she passed out. Joey jumped, reached out and caught her just in time. She was as limp as a child's worn-out doll. But she was someone else's toy. Her boyfriend, gin-soaked trousers and all, left his table and staggered over to loudly threaten Joey with bodily harm. At this sound, an extremely annoyed Gaston Royal emerged in less-than-sober wonderment from the kitchen, like some great, gray wolf that had been awakened and provoked into leaving its lair.

After demanding to know what the hell was going on and without receiving any plausible answer, Gaston took a swig of rum from the glass in his hand in order to calm himself down. The hoots and hollers from members of the revelers-turned-audience, who had been hoping for a less-than-chivalrous ending to the line-walking ritual of Royale's, indicated a general disapproval of Joey's behavior and their jeers seemed to demand action. Gaston persevered and investigated to the best of his abilities, considering his condition, after reluctantly setting his rum down on the bar.

"Give her to me, chump!" hollered the irate young man to Joey as Gaston approached, lumbering along. Both of Gaston's fists were clenched, not a good sign. Meanwhile, some attentive person had turned the radio off in order to better follow this impromptu entertainment without distraction; now, an audible murmur arose from the couples on the dance floor and those at the tables. A fight this near to closing time would be an epic event, one promising bloodshed on the order of warring pit bulls; already, money was out on the bar top as grizzled, sneering men placed their bets.

"You can have her, pal," Joey answered. He turned and handed the limp body of the girl in pink to her boyfriend, who took her in his arms and glared back at him. "I didn't make a play for her."

"The hell you didn't, and besides," complained the other man crisply, nose up and chest out, "this house has rules. You broke the rules. You can get the hell out." He turned away and trudged off towards the door with Joey's catch of the day, swaying slightly as he went. The woman's heels left small black marks on the dance floor as he dragged his listless trophy along, bit by bit and prepared to leave, discretion being the better part of valor. Accordingly, groans of disappointment came from the ringside tables. Now, Joey was keenly aware that old Gaston was lurching very close to Joey, and now looming large. So close—face-to-face—that Joey could smell the rum on his breath.

"Whoever you are, young fella, I don't think you belong here," Gaston growled menacingly, poking Joey several times in the chest for emphasis. In doing so, Gaston used his left forefinger to hammer this point home while he kept his right hand clenched; Gaston tended to swing with that one. "*T'as pas d'affaire a faire ca*; what you did, you are not allowed to do. Understand? You break my rules, you go, now, eh? This is my joint."

"Look, Junior Coughlin sent me," explained Joey, in desperation. "Northbound," he whispered, offering the code word for his prearranged trip.

"Bullshit, I tell you," scoffed Gaston dismissively, pouting and shrugging his shoulders for emphasis, until he fairly resembled a gargoyle perched on a cathedral's parapet. "That fella there and his pretty young lady, my customer, you almost pick a fight with him; he don't like you. You break the rules of my place. I don't like you, either."

"I'm Joe, Joey Ross, Billy's brother." He withdrew the room key from his pocket, and briefly dangled it in front of the big, barrel-chested old man., whose bloodshot eyes immediately grew wide.

"Billy?" Gaston asked in astonishment as his eyebrows shot up, quite taken aback. "You are his young brother, eh? *Bon chagrin!* Good grief!" He grasped both shoulders of Joey's black suit coat and shook them playfully; this action incited a few cheers from the people at the tables, hopeful that they might at least see a minor dust-up before the night was over, now that they'd been denied ringside seats at a dance floor brawl. "So, you are the youngest of the family, no? Unless," and at this he leered at Joey and leaned even closer to him, "your Mama, she has another bun in the oven, no?"

"No, I'm his young, and only, brother," Joey answered. "So, you do know him?"

"Oh, yes; him I know, and his boss, too. That Junior, the cheap American. He told me there would be a trip, and what he wants, but not about you as the driver. *Tres bien!* So, tell me now, why are you here, and not Billy?"

"Simple. He's in jail."

"*Oh, non c'est mauvais.* That is too bad."

"And," added Joey, "if I can pull this run off, it will get him out. I hope."

"Come with me, son," mumbled Gaston, grabbing Joey by the arm. He steered him off past the bar and its curious, scruffy-looking crew toward the kitchen door. When they had finally passed through into the sanctity of the quiet area of the cook's domain, where the loudest sound was that of water dripping from the leaky tap into the expansive sink and its armada of dirty dishes, Gaston let go of him as quickly as a tugboat's skipper cuts his line to a sinking barge. "You are here tonight, right? And then you come back through tomorrow, no?" Joey nodded. "Then, then—that is when I need the money. And you get your stuff." He winked and rubbed his right thumb and several fingers together to complete the picture of a demand for payment.

"Tonight, you go sleep upstairs," continued Gaston. "Do you want a drink?" Joey shook his head. "A girl? *La putain?* I can get them; I'm not too old to know how, you see!" He snickered like a schoolboy telling a well-worn dirty joke.

"No, thank you. I just need to go to bed, if you don't mind too much," Joey answered, bringing out his room key. Gaston looked at it with apparent curiosity.

"*C'est pas sit ante pire.* That one, it is not so bad," he advised. "Right up those stairs." He pointed toward a set of stairs in the far corner. "That is the back way. No one will see you."

Joey twisted the key in the lock of room 22 and pushed the door open. The creaking sound it made was almost drowned out by a sudden burst of laughter from the bar room downstairs. He fumbled in the dark, at last finding a light switch, and twisted it on. Then, he pushed the door closed. The accommodations were spartan: A dresser, a desk bearing untold numbers of dark circles from drinks that had been placed upon it in times past, a battered side chair, and a swaybacked bed. Without bothering to turn out the light or lock the door, Joey heaved himself onto the bed the way a castaway on the high seas might have, abandoning his waterlogged raft and collapsing, exhausted, on the shore of an appealing tropical island. Soon, he was fast asleep.

Downstairs, Gaston Royale emerged from the kitchen anew wearing a clean apron, another rum in hand, and tended to the bar, swaying on his feet. "Attention!" he bellowed to his assembled audience of drinkers and carousers, most of whom were from the United States side of the border. "*Dernier appel!* Last call!" And suddenly, Gaston Royale was *their* island of tropical paradise in the dead-dry sea of Prohibition.

Chapter 33

Long Distance Calling

"The things I have to do for friends!" Ed grumbled to himself as he angle-parked his Dodge outside the front entrance of the J.J. Newberry store. It was just after morning opening time, and Ed was able to get a parking spot close enough to the window by the lunch counter so that he could easily look inside and see who was there. Yes, there she was: Doris was behind the counter, working with another woman and a kid who might be a dishwasher. Ed stuffed his reporter's notepad into his pocket, grabbed his camera and heaved himself out of the car.

Ed yanked open the store's front door, stepped inside and sauntered through the aisles to the back office, where he found the manager at his desk, immersed in paperwork. Ed leaned through the open doorway, rapped gently on the doorframe, and the young man, momentarily startled, looked up.

"Why, hello, Ed! Nice to see you, but I don't have an ad for you this week, sorry," he said politely before returning his attention to a pile of invoices.

"It's not about an ad, Pete. I've got some space for the "Around Town" roundup next edition and I thought it would be nice to get a group picture of your lunch counter crew and cashiers. They're mighty popular folks."

"Wow, Ed; that sounds great!" the plump manager exclaimed, taking off his reading glasses and setting them down. "Any publicity is welcome—unless it's about a shoplifter, a slip-and-fall customer or something like that! Let me walk you over there, and I'll set it up in a jiffy." He rose to his feet and went waddling off to the counter with Ed following close behind, camera at the ready.

Within five minutes, the manager gathered the store's two cashiers, the dishwasher, Doris and another waitress together behind the lunch counter, explained everything, and with Ed's coaching, had everyone (including himself) properly posed for the shot. Everyone smiled, the camera's shutter snapped as the flashbulb popped, and then Ed passed around his notepad, asking everyone to write down their names. Once it had been returned, he jotted down a number beside each name, indicating the person's location in the photo, from left to right.

Within the next 20 minutes, Ed thanked everyone and drove off to his office, whereupon he took the camera down to the the *Passumpsic Chronicle's* basement darkroom. A scant two hours later, after emerging, he was at Sheriff John Johnson's desk, handing him both the notepad and a crisp, 8X10 print of the image taken at Newberry's. "Nice work, Ed," remarked John, gazing at the photo. The deputy, standing behind John and peering over his shoulder, got a good look at it too before it was handed to him. "Okay," said John, turning to him now. "Beeline it down to Woodstock and see if that innkeeper can spot his 'Miss Catherine Hollingsworth' in that photo. Mark it up and get a deposition, too. And don't forget: Bring me the page from the inn's register the day 'Miss Catherine

Hollingsworth' signed in. Now get going." But the deputy still stood there holding photo in his hand, staring at John.

"Oh, all right," groused John as he fished in his pocket for his keys. "You can take the patrol car."

* * *

Back at the J.J. Newberry's store, Doris poured herself a cup of coffee, then looked at her wristwatch. That watch, a tiny, yet flashy Elgin white gold watch, was the envy of every woman who worked at the department store. When asked why she had it, something only a high-end city jewelry store sold, Doris would answer: "So no one would think it was something I stole from here!"

When the smart retort invariably came: "So, where *did* you steal it?" Doris would only laugh, and say that the only thing she'd stolen was some other girl's boyfriend, one who had expensive tastes. While Steve had become an accomplished criminal, Doris had become an accomplished storyteller.

The store's pay phone rang. Doris quickly put down her coffee and ran to it. "Long distance for a Miss Doris Martin," announced the operator, once Doris picked up and answered.

"This is Doris Martin."

"Hold, please; I'll connect you." Then came a series of clicks and finally, through the sizzle of line static and bad connections, the faint voice of Steve Snyder.

"Any more news on that Ross kid?" he asked.

"Nothing more," answered Doris, looking around carefully to make sure no one was listening in. "The last Paul saw of him, he left town with Junior in the limo. By the time Paul got up to Lyndonville, Junior's place was closed and the car was gone."

"Was anyone there?"

"Yeah, Junior. Down in the mortuary, drinking. The kids at the garage say the two of them stopped earlier at the Corner

Garage and filled the tank. They thought they were headed north to make a run—must be just the kid is."

"How about that! Old Junior's had quite the booze racket going on, right under my nose, right in my territory, all to himself. So now, with Billy on ice, he sends a teenage kid out to be his wheelman." There was a long pause, then: "I'll find him."

Chapter 34

The Double Deal

It was going on toward late morning by the time the sun had finally risen—sluggishly, as if it was begrudgingly dragging itself up—high enough over the tall treetops for its light to filter through the film of dirt on the window of room 22 of the line house. As these feeble rays of sunlight made their way through the grimy portal and slightly warmed the room, its occupant, Joey, finally stirred. He looked at his wristwatch, and discovered that it had stopped running during the night. Ignoring the grumbling of his empty stomach, he rolled off the bed. He stood, stretched and yawned, then staggered, half-awake to the window to have a look outside. Despite the dust and dirt on the windowpanes, he could see there were no cars in the parking lot. The rowdy drinkers, floozy dancers and denizens of the bar downstairs had all apparently scurried home during the wee morning hours in a vanishing act worthy of a master magician's handiwork. In a panic, he wondered what time it was. After all, he had to vanish, too.

Joey let himself out of the musty-smelling room, tramped down the stairs and made his way through the still-cluttered kitchen into the dance hall that also served as a dining room. It smelled of stale beer and cigarette smoke, and a scrawny-looking cat that had been gnawing on some leftover piece of food lying underneath a table scampered away as Joey entered and called out, "Gaston!" There was no reply, and the only sound to be heard was the dripping of water—as regular as the ticking of a metronome—from the tap in the kitchen sink. Until footsteps sounded and floorboards creaked, far off behind him.

"Gaston's gone," a hollow-sounding voice called out from the dark pantry beyond the kitchen. Joey spun around in time to see its owner, a thin, worried-looking fellow, emerging from it. The gray-haired man was wearing grubby-looking pants and a tattered flannel shirt, and was in the process of putting on an apron as he clumped along toward Joey, an unlit cigarette dangling from his lips. "I am just the dishwasher, Jean-Claude. Gaston, he does not get up 'til past noon. He likes his rum, likes to drink all night 'till there is no more. So, he is gone; gone—you know?" The man smiled a smug, knowing smile as he watched Joey's reaction to this revelation. The man struck a match, lit his cigarette, then leaned against the doorway. He looked like a tumbledown scarecrow propped up against a barn. He then inhaled deeply, savoring the smoke before asking, "*Peux-tu me dire quelque chose?*" He then smacked his forehead, as if chastising himself. "Oh, sorry, *mon ami!* I forget to use the English! And I drink the rum, too. Can you please tell me something?"

"Sure," replied Joey.

"Are you here on some business?"

"Some," answered Joey cautiously.

"Not pleasure, then eh? I see you are alone." The dishwasher grinned at him, exposing teeth yellowed by nicotine and long years of enjoying its effects.

"So, you are northbound, then. Do you leave tonight?" The dishwasher puffed on his smoke, then casually flicked ashes onto the floor as he awaited an answer.

"No, right now."

"What?" The man looked startled. "No one drives except at night for the business. Too risky during the day."

"But I have to go," replied Joey. The little dishwasher shook his head. He tossed his cigarette butt onto the floor, stomped on it and crushed it out with the verve of a man trying to consign a downed wasp's nest into oblivion.

"You think so? Okay, you go ahead, young fellow. I will not try to stop you! *Bonne chance!*" The man rolled up the flayed sleeves of his old shirt and sauntered off into the depths of the kitchen, his nose in the air, presumably on his way to perform some actual work. Joey headed for the door of the line house, jerked it open, and stepped outside into the gathering sunshine. Sunlight warmed his face, and a soft, gentle breeze greeted him as he walked toward the barn to claim his car, gasping his room key in his right hand.

The blessed, well-anticipated January thaw was still upon the land, but as almost everyone on both sides of the north-south border well knew, in a fatalistic sort of way, it would be a brief one, much like a cease-fire in some kind of a long, drawn-out winter war that broke out every year. Ever-capricious Mother Nature, in cahoots with old Man Winter, would go hand-in-hand with the old curmudgeon in her efforts to try to fool the folks of the North Country into a false sense of security; that the war was over and that spring was close at hand. Yes, those who lived along the border could deal with this sort of perennial disappointment. Considering not only that but also the vagaries of the ongoing Depression as they struggled, almost hand-to-mouth to survive from season-to-season—they were quite used to it.

As he neared the barn, Joey called out: "Hello! Anybody here?" But there was no answer.

Upon reaching the door, he grasped its rusty handle and slid the door open. To his horror, he saw that the barn was—

empty. The Packard—and whatever other cars had been stored there the previous night—was gone. Joey felt his heart pounding now, plummeting straight down toward the bottoms of his feet, like a runaway, out-of-control elevator plunging toward doom at the bottom of a long, deep shaft of despair. In a panic, he ran back to the line house and into the kitchen.

"What's the matter, sonny?" asked the dishwasher, now up to his elbows in soap suds as he scrubbed dishes in the sink, rinsed them and then set them aside, one by one in a drying rack. He had the radio in the dining room on now, and it crackled with static as the voice of an announcer reading the news came in from the distant United States. The newsman seemed excited to report, citing facts in rapid-fire fashion, that in New Jersey a Coast Guard cutter had fired 49 one-pound shells and its machine guns at a rum boat, and had captured a booze cargo of some $25,000 in value after seizing it. "Hear that, sonny?" exclaimed the man at the sink, over the clashing of colliding dishes. "Their problem is: they got caught. Not smart enough, I'd venture. But, 25 grand? Who the hell says booze don't pay, if you can make it to the finish line?"

"I just want my car, that's all," said Joey angrily. "Look, I'm just at the starting line. What the hell is going on around here?"

"More than you can know right now, lad. Just give it some time. It'll all work out. It always does when someone comes snoopin' around and we have to get careful-like."

"What aren't you telling me?" Joey resisted the urge to grasp the little man and shake the answer out of him.

"Some fellow came around last night asking if anyone had seen that big Packard—the one you drove in with. Nobody knew him, so our boys sneaked your rig out of the barn and drove it around while Gaston kept him busy and he scouted all over for it. Finally, he was satisfied it wasn't here, and he left. Looked like an important man, he did, so we obliged him. Had a brand-new car, a Ford, so we figured he was an undercover G-man. Or, more likely, a gangster."

Now, in addition to the rumbling of his belly becoming more apparent and upsetting him, Joey felt beads of perspiration rolling down his back. "Was he?"

"We don't know. All we know is that we didn't like him." At this vague and sardonic comment, the dishwasher shrugged, and paused to light another cigarette. "Your car will be back; do not worry. We have gone through such little things like this before." Joey looked at him incredulously. Then, his stomach rumbled loudly enough for the dishwasher to plainly hear it and ask, "Want something to eat?" Joey nodded. "Then, you go there." The dishwasher pointed to a huge wooden icebox sitting beside the big, cast-iron cook stove. "Ham, roast beef, salad anything you want, except the booze. And when you are done," he suggested, with a wink, "maybe you can dry some dishes, eh?"

* * *

Joey's impromptu feast was just a distant memory by the time he heard the sound of cars approaching the line house. He had been whiling away the time by listening to the radio and stapling together paper menus to help old Jean-Claude, now that the dishes were done. He absent-mindedly stuffed the stapler into his left jacket pocket, jumped up from the chair he'd been sitting on in the dining room, making it clatter to the floor, and ran to a window. Two vehicles were pulling into the dooryard. One was a beat-up old farm truck loaded with hay; the other was Junior's Packard. Both vehicles were splattered with slush and mud, and the truck was limping along with one of its tires nearly flat. Joey quickly jammed on his chauffeur's hat and headed for the door. He'd barely gotten outside, expecting the truck and the car to stop, when instead they kept on going down the drive. They paused at the barn just long enough for the passenger in the truck to hop out and slide open the door, and the old truck and the Packard were driven inside. The passenger, a gruff-looking fellow, looked about apprehensively as he leaned against the door and pushed it in his effort to close it. "Wait!" hollered Joey, as he sprinted toward the barn. Foolishly, he was in too much of a headlong rush to realize what the fellow was doing now, instead of closing the barn door.

As he came to a halt Joey found himself looking into the barrel of the rather ugly-looking automatic pistol. The man was pointing it at him and bellowing, "*Hey, vous arrêt!* Stop, you!" Two seconds later, as Joey caught his breath and the man menacingly pulled back the slide of the .45 a shout came from the front door of the line house. It was the dishwasher. Joey turned around in time to see him wave his arms—and then for Gaston to emerge from the building, staggering slightly and blinking like a rudely-awakened bat suddenly exposed to sunlight, and shove the dishwasher aside. Gaston was clad only in his long underwear—a red union suit—and a pair of slippers.

"Jean-Claude! *Ranger l'arme!* Put that gun away!" hollered the dishwasher. "He's Junior's man! *Américain!*" Shaken, Joey turned back and watched as the man with the gun sneered, stuck his nose up as if in disdain of this order, and pocketed his weapon.

"So, you want your car, eh?" the gunman asked Joey. "Then follow me. We will be glad to have you and that car gone." He turned his back on Joey and disappeared into the depths of the barn; Joey followed him. The man joined his companions, two others who were grunting as they pulled wooden crates out from where they'd been concealed beneath the hay piled on the back of the old farm truck. He hefted one of the crates from the truck's bed, and reverently sat it down in front of Joey. "That's one of the three cases Junior sent you for, in case he didn't tell you. Recognize it?" The side of the oak crate holding twelve elegantly-style bottles was stamped with words all in French. Joey shook his head. "Didn't think you would. That's Grand Champagne Cognac, Louis XIII, Rare Cask. The most expensive brandy in the world—far as I know."

"You got some money for me, kid?" came a voice from behind Joey. It was Gaston, his face and hair gray as a ghost's, lurching along toward him with an outstretched hand. He blinked anew as his bleary eyes grew accustomed to the dark and the cobwebs of intoxication slowly cleared away. "You know the deal, *mon ami.*"

Joey swallowed hard before he spoke, but when he did, it was with authority. "The deal was for me to pick this up on my way back south, not my way north."

"Yeah, for sure it was, but you brought bad news along with you, that fellow who came here looking for you last night. He is following you and I want no part of him. I think he is some slick gangster who's got your number. I don't want him to get mine. You pay and you leave now. That's my deal."

"Junior told me you said you'll put me up when I come back through. Is that off, too?

"*Tres bien!* Good for you; good guess! So, I talk out of both sides of my mouth, I know. But, Junior, he does that too. So, now, the money, *s'il vous plait.*" The men unloading the truck had stopped to watch Joey and Gaston, and exchanged nervous glances as Joey slowly reached for the right-hand pocket of his jacket.

"I have it Gaston, but I want to see the rest of the brandy, the other two cases," huffed Joey, summoning up as much bluster as he could. "I have it right here in my pocket; you show me the stuff." Gaston waved drunkenly to his men, who hauled the two requested cases from the truck, carefully set them on the floor and then stepped back from them. Joey walked over and inspected the shipment; the bottles were full and the seals on them were intact. He nodded his approval and dug into his right pocket for the envelope of cash Junior had given him, the one marked with Gaston's name, as Gaston's men slowly reached into their pockets for their guns.

Using only his right thumb and forefinger, Joey gingerly plucked out the envelope, keeping his eyes on the men. He handed the envelope to Gaston, who stuck it under his purplish nose, opened it and riffled through the big bills like an excited rabbit sniffing a head of lettuce. "Is it all there?" asked Joey. Gaston nodded. "Then let's get it loaded." Gaston waved to his men; each one grabbed a case of the brandy and headed toward the rear of the Packard. It was then that Joey discovered the bullet holes in the back of the car. "Where did those come from?" he asked disgustedly, pointing at it the damage. "Junior'll have a fit."

The men guffawed. "It's not so bad," said one, sneering at him. He stuck a forefinger into one of the holes, wiggled the finger around in the cavity and then grinned at him. "*C'est un petit*. It's just a little one! We've seen worse!"

"What did you do guys with this car last night?" demanded Joey.

"Just what we had to, that's all," said the man, withdrawing his finger and frowning. "You should be happy; we got that gangster off your tail. So what if we pull a job now and then on the side, eh?"

"Just load the car, and I'll be out of here," sighed Joey. "Get the booze in the trunk."

Gaston stepped in front of Joey, came close to him and spoke to him in low tones. "Maybe you should go. I think you should go—in the trunk," he said, with an evil smile. "I want my troubles to go away." As Gaston turned around to face his men and give the next command, Joey reacted; he pulled the stapler from his left jacket pocket and jammed it into Gaston's back. With his right hand, he grasped the neck of the startled old man's union suit and steered him around to a point where the men, in the gloom and poor lighting that filtered in through the doorway, could easily believe that he was holding a gun on Gaston.

"Drop your guns and load my car," commanded Joey.

"Do what he says, boys," grumbled Gaston in disgust. "I guess this is how it ends. As long as he leaves, one way or another, I'll be happy—even if it's his way, dammit."

"You drive, Gaston," said Joey, again shoving the make-believe gun into Gaston's back as the men glowered at him, laid down their guns and then placed the cases of brandy into the wooden trunk on the Packard's luggage rack.

* * *

The sun was going down, and so was the temperature by the time the Packard had gone about five miles up a particularly desolate stretch of road, and Joey ordered the double-dealing Gaston to stop and get out. "You would leave an old man out here to freeze?" complained Gaston, now shivering from the cold, playing for sympathy. "In his underwear?"

"Your boys should be along in a few minutes, once they pump up the flat tire on their truck," Joey answered as he slid over to take the wheel. He tossed the stapler out and it fell at Gaston's feet. "You're wearing red, so you should be easy to spot."

"You little bastard!" sneered Gaston, his teeth chattering, as he saw what Joey had tossed to him, and stared at it in disbelief. He hopped up and down in an effort to warm himself.

"*Bonne chance*," offered Joey, blowing him a kiss and shifting the Packard into gear.

"You wish me good luck?"

"Yes," answered Joey, as he started to roll up his window, and began to pull away. "But then again, I do talk out of both sides of my mouth."

Joey glanced at Gaston's figure in the rearview mirror now and then as he drove away, heading north, until it was just a tiny dot. It seemed to glow briefly before it disappeared, like a tiny, red angry fire, burning itself away to nothingness in the rays of the setting sun.

Chapter 35

The Pickup

The road north out of the border town and away from the wretched line house was a horror. The feeling of relief Joey had felt at seeing Gaston disappear from view in the rearview mirror was soon replaced by one of apprehension as the sky began to grow darker with each passing minute. Stars began to sparkle overhead, a distraction Joey avoided, concentrating on the driving; it seemed the road was growing rougher with every mile. Then, too, Junior had warned him about the hijackers who sometimes preyed on vehicles not travelling in convoys at night in these remote parts. The thought that he had had the presence of mind to stop and lock Junior's precious cargo in the trunk after leaving Gaston to fend for himself was little consolation. But then Joey came to his senses, realizing that any hijackers would be on the lookout for a car travelling south to Vermont, not north away from it. He gripped the steering wheel tighter and tighter each time the car slithered around a curve or began to slide out of control and he corrected quickly, almost instinctively, steering the heavy car back on course.

Even though the recent thaw had melted a good deal of snow, the way was still narrow—sometimes wide enough for only one car to pass through where drifts had piled up during recent heavy storms and the plows had struggled to buck through them. In places where there were valleys sheltered from daylight by deep woods of pines and evergreens, thick layers of slick ice still coated the highway and glimmered in the headlights. Every now and then the one of the big Packard's wheels would hammer into a deep pothole and shake the car badly enough to make Joey bring it to almost a complete halt. Speed was out of the question, and it was well after dark when at last he could see the lights of the resort he was headed for twinkling in the distance.

He momentarily took one hand off the wheel and patted his jacket, making sure one last time that the envelope was still in his pocket. The envelope stuffed with cash, the one marked with a woman's name: Francine. "That place where you're going, kid," Junior had explained before he set out, leering at him wolfishly, "is the rumrunner's Riviera. Only you're going to see it in the off season. So, all bets are off on you finding a deck chair, a babe and a swimming pool. You're to make the pickups and bring back the two packages, T.R.'s and mine, pronto; *tout de suite*, as they say up there. Got it?" Joey momentarily remembered nodding in assent that afternoon, then snapped his attention back to watching the road ahead and looking for the driveway Junior had told him to turn into. He soon found it. Its entrance was a gateway flanked by two tall concrete pillars surmounted by what looked like enormous crowns; the wrought-iron gates hanging from the pillars stood open, unguarded.

As he drove through the open gateway, the moon revealed itself, as if sliding out from behind a small cluster of clouds to the east. The huge, fortress-like shape of the Chateau du Roi, fairly bristling with turrets and battlements, was hauntingly illuminated, appearing like an evil witch's castle in a fairy-tale book. Joey whistled softly in amazement at the size of the grand, rather medieval-looking building made of massive blocks of granite. "It ain't the Frontenac, kid," Joey remembered Junior telling him, "but it's quite a ritzy place. Don't trust a valet and let him get his paws on my car, whatever you do. Drive around back, park it yourself, and go to the door marked 'Gentlemen Only'."

Thus, ignoring a valet who was frantically waving a flashlight's beam at him from the building's front portico, Joey steered the Packard around the hulking chateau to a rear entrance and parking lot, where perhaps two dozen or more cars were parked. Joey switched off the ignition and the big car fell silent for the first time in several long hours. Heaving a sigh of relief, he opened the door and stepped out into the chill night-time air. He'd taken several steps toward the entrance when he stopped and came to his senses; valet or no valet, the Packard had been spirited away once already. He'd be damned it if would happen again. He retraced his steps to the car, unlatched the hood, and then the distributor cap. He removed the rotor, placed it in his jacket pocket, replaced the cap and gently closed the hood after looking around to make sure no one had seen him. There; with its ignition system disabled, the Packard would be going nowhere tonight, even if some skillful thief tried to hot-wire it.

It felt good for Joey to stretch his legs and stride across the parking lot to the doorway. He let himself inside once he had climbed up the steep set of stairs. The immense door made of oak gradually closed behind him with a final *clunk* that resonated in the hallway and almost made him jump while he was staring about. The walls of the dimly-lit place were white, and stretched upward a dozen feet or more to meet an arched ceiling. The stuffed heads of game animals—moose, deer, elk and even wolves——were hung in various places on the walls. Over the door bearing the bilingual sign, "*Messieurs Seulement*" and, "Gentlemen Only" hung another trophy—an enormous stuffed lake sturgeon, a fish likely pulled from the waters of Lake

Memphremagog in the absence of any game warden's presence. He placed his right hand on the ornate brass knob and tried in vain to twist it, but it was locked. He rapped on the door. He didn't have long to wait before he heard the sound of footsteps coming from someone approaching from the other side.

As he waited, Joey hoped that the business of collecting this, the second "package" would likely be taken care of quickly, once he handed the money over to the proper person. Then came the rattling sound of the door being unlocked, and it swung open. Before him stood a short, balding, impudent-looking little man clad in a dark purple uniform. The man's bulbous nose, perched over a pencil-line mustache, nearly matched the color of his uniform. "Chauffeur?" asked the little man, looking Joey up and down and pouting.

"Yes, chauffeur; I'm a driver."

"Then you cannot be here. You stay with the other drivers, in your room over the garage, the place where they put your boss's car." He started to pull the door closed.

"Wait, you don't understand," pleaded Joey. "I'm here to pick someone up." At this, the man's eyebrows shot up.

"You, you are here," the man snorted in surprise, "to pick someone up?"

"Well, I'm here to see someone named Francine," replied Joey, frowning at this challenge.

"Francine? Who gave you that name?"

"My boss. He sent me here."

"Oh, so—I see now," said the little man with a chuckle. "While the cat's away, the mouse will play, eh? So, he sends you here to have some fun while he has dinner and enjoys the show. Does he pay you well?"

Joey nodded, trying to dodge the man's questions as best he could without committing too much information. "Well," said the man, nodding back at Joey and winking, "I hope so too.

You can come with me, young man." At this, he held out his right hand.

Joey stopped himself at the last second from reactively reaching out and shaking hands with the man in the uniform. He realized that the man was asking for a tip. He reached into his pants pocket and fumbled for change, coming up at last with a half-dollar and two quarters. He placed them in the man's palm. The little man looked down at his hand as if Joey had deposited bird droppings on it. Then he looked up at Joey and smiled a thin, sardonic smile. It flashed as briefly underneath the mustache as a lightning strike. Then, after pocketing the change, he cleared his throat and spoke, his face all wrinkled, as though he had just tasted something sour: "I take it you are from Vermont, no?"

* * *

The man led Joey down a corridor and into a large, high-ceilinged room. Without so much as a word, he turned on his heels and left. As Joey stood there, puzzled about what to do next, he marveled at the enormous Persian rug that covered the entire floor as he felt his shoes sinking down slightly into its plush depths. Ornately-woven tapestries depicting the exploits of Canada's fabled French discoverers and adventurous fur-traders of the 1600s covered much of the wall space; warm lights glowed in a chandelier strung high overhead, and a grand staircase spiraled upward out of sight from where a large, mahogany desk and a gilded chair, looking like some sort of throne, reposed in one corner of the room. But he was not alone.

A young woman's voice called out from the shadows behind him and the sound momentarily startled him: "Hey girls; look what the cat dragged in!" Joey spun around to find her and two more women staring at him with the intense curiosity of several cats suddenly having a loose, wayward canary delivered to their alleyway. The women exchanged glances while an awkward silence fell over the room. It made Joey remember the time he'd accompanied his father into an auto dealership showroom in Saint Jay where several salesmen were lounging about, and it seemed no one wanted to be the first to outdo the other, pounce on a prospect, and sell a car.

"Damned cat!" commented a second woman. She was wearing a gold silk dressing gown and matching slippers, and had been reading a magazine, which she tossed onto a nearby table. "Brought us small fry. Maybe we'd better throw him back, eh?" she added. She rolled her eyes at her companions, then turned to flash Joey a coy-looking smile. "Welcome to the Chateau." She looked Joey up and down, taking in the sight of the somber-looking, rumpled black unform he was wearing. Say, kid, where's the funeral?"

All three women burst into laughter, and although Joey could feel the blood of embarrassment rushing to his face, seemingly setting it on fire, he kept quiet. "C'mon ladies," said the first woman. She lit a cigarette, waved out her match with a flourish and blew a smoke ring into the air. It drifted up toward the chandelier and slowly dissipated. "He's a chauffeur, a working man. Isn't that right, pal?" she asked, turning toward joey and batting her eyelashes at him. "I do *so* like men in uniform!"

Just as Joey nodded, the third woman spoke as she raised herself up from where she'd been reclining on a chaise lounge and sat facing him. She stretched, yawned and looked at him crossly. She was wearing a lavender negligee and nothing else. "What are you doing here, anyway, young fellow?" she asked suspiciously. She gathered up her long, red hair into a bunch and tossed it quickly over one of her bare shoulders, where it flailed back and forth as the woman briefly shook her head, as if to settle a few remaining strands. The motion reminded Joey of the way a horse flicks its tail to wave away a bothersome fly, but it both bewitched and excited him. "Well?"

"Look, I'm here to see someone named Francine," stammered Joey.

No sooner were the words out of his mouth than a fourth woman spoke. Her gruff voice, coming from the staircase was loud and emphatic as she slowly descended, step by step to make her dramatic entrance into the room. "Anyone wanting to see someone here will have to see *me* first. I am Madame LeClaire. This is my house. And who, pray tell, are you to ask for one of my girls by name? I have not seen you before."

"Joey Ross, ma'am. Sorry; I don't mean to cause any trouble. The man I work for sent me here and told me to ask for her. I'm from Vermont." He realized he was still wearing the chauffeur's hat, and removed it in a show of respect. "I think a good friend of his knows her, too." At this, there were giggles from the three women, but not the one who'd been descending the stairs, who now stood just a few feet away, hands on her hips. She was tall, plump and matronly-looking, with a head of finely-combed grey hair. She was smoking a pungent-smelling cigarillo, a small cigar, in an ivory holder that was stained with red lipstick. Save for her rumpled purple nightgown and the smoke, she could have passed for a parishioner at any small-town church attending a Sunday service.

"And what do you bring with you, *mon ami*, besides this referral?" she asked haughtily.

"This," answered Joey, pulling the envelope marked with the name Francine from his jacket pocket. Holding it close to his chest but with the name on it plainly visible to Madame LeClaire, he withdrew several 10-dollar bills. "I'm here to pick her up." At this, Madame LeClaire lost her composure, coughed until Joey thought she would swallow the holder and the petite cigar whole, then guffawed with laughter.

"Oh, my! So, this is the way your boss told you how to pick up a girl, eh? Oh, *tres bien!* And a generous one, too!" She took a drag on her cigarillo, and then moved closer to Joey. "One I would like to get to know!" She slowly exhaled, blowing smoke at Joey, and winked at him. But the smoke could not overcome the scent of stale perfume or obscure the sight of her caked-on mascara. She took the bills and unceremoniously stuffed them down the front of her gown, then grasped Joey by the hand and began to lead him toward the staircase, with all the aplomb of a tow truck operator hauling away a small car found abandoned alongside a busy highway.

Immediately there were calls of protest from the disappointed women, like discouraged alley cats who were seeing their precious canary suddenly fly away.

"*Bonne chance!*" hollered the first.

"Next time come see me!" implored the second one in the gold dressing gown, as she picked up her magazine and began reading.

"*Cheri!*" called the redhead lamentingly. "For what you are paying, you could have had all three of us! More bang for the buck!"

* * *

Madame LeClaire huffed and puffed as she climbed the stairs, occasionally grasping the handrail alongside them as Joey followed along behind her. When they reached the second floor, she rapped on the first door to the right of the landing. Joey looked down the corridor and saw that there were several other doors; some of them had various types of men's hats hanging on the doorknobs.

After a few seconds had passed and there was still no answer, Madame LeClaire gently opened the door a crack and called out, "Francine? There's a young gentleman caller here to see you, American. I will send him in." Now, she opened the door wider and practically shoved Joey inside after taking his chauffeur's hat from him. Finding himself at a loss for words, Joey turned to face her. "Now, you remember this," she warned him, waving her right forefinger in front of his face. "You have 15 minutes. More than that is extra. You want more play, you have to pay." With this admonition delivered, she closed the door.

Joey panicked briefly; the room seemed empty. Had he been played? Fleeced? Moreover, it seemed Junior had sold him a bill of goods about going to Canada to save an unfortunate working girl from drudgery, and spiriting her across the border to welcoming arms. There seemed to be a lot of welcoming arms right within the chateau—most of them available for a price. Junior obviously wasn't truthful, nor completely trust-worthy. *It's always about money, isn't it?* Joey reasoned. And now, something came to him. Something old Sam Rivard had grumbled to him one day, when he was waxing philosophical about his falling out with an old friend: "Joey, a man has just two friends in his lifetime—his checkbook and his dollar bill."

"*Cheri?* I will be right with you!" came a woman's cheerful-sounding voice from behind a set of dressing-room screens. A pair of black silk stockings and garters had been draped over them, but suddenly disappeared with an audible *snap!* as they were yanked away by the person on the other side.

Just who are my friends? Joey wondered as he looked about the lavishly-appointed room, with its enormous, plush-looking four-poster bed as its centerpiece. And then, it came to him: his friends at the moment were the 300 American dollars promised him for taking the risks he was taking now. They were the reason for him finding himself in the spot he was in now—on his own, in a foreign country, with a dwindling supply of cash in his pockets and with time running out for him to run the little "errand" for Junior.

"Hello?" The voice called out again from the other side of the screen, snapping Joey out of his reverie. Then, a young woman peeked out from around one end of the screen. She was perhaps 25 or so, Joey thought, with dark eyes, black hair, and a rather mischievous expression on her face. The expression seemed to melt away in a few seconds. "You are so young," she said, almost scornfully. "And the Madame, she brings you to me?"

"Listen," said Joey, "she may have walked me up the stairs to your door, but I've been sent here by someone else." He cleared his throat. "Are you Francine?"

"Of course!" Now, you answer me. Who sent you here, and why, if you do not come here for yourself?"

"By someone who is paying me to take you to Vermont."

She stepped out from behind the screen, dressed in a black nightgown. "You? And someone you do not name. Who has sent you?" She frowned at him.

"Junior Coughlin. For his friend T.R., T.R. Donovan, that is. Do you know him?" At this, the woman in black held a forefinger to her lips, invoking silence. She glared at him, then tiptoed past him to the door—after briefly shoving him aside—where she stopped and put an ear to it. Apparently not hearing anyone moving outside in the corridor, she gently opened the door, and peeked outside, then closed it softly. She turned around just as Joey also did.

"How do I know for sure?" she asked. Joey reached into his pocket and withdrew the envelope Junior had given him for this part of the trip. She smiled when she saw her name written on it. "That is his writing! That is his!" she exclaimed, clapping her hands together in delight.

"Where is he?" she whispered. The mischievous look was on her face again, and now Joey recognized her; the dark-haired beauty in the gold framed photograph that hung on the wall in T.R.'s ice house, the photograph he'd seen long ago when he'd ridden his bike there to find his brother. "He did not, by some chance, come with you tonight, did he?" She smiled at him.

"No, he's not here with me; he's back home Vermont," Joey answered.

"We must leave—now," she said in hushed tones. "There is no time to waste. T.R. did not tell me what time you would be here in his letter, so I already have my suitcase packed." Francine stepped softly over to the big bed, knelt, and pulled out a brown leather suitcase from underneath it. "See?" she asked, looking over her shoulder at Joey. "Now, while I get dressed, go to the door and listen. Let me know if you hear anyone coming."

"Okay. Then I should probably get my hat now, while I'm waiting." Joey made a start for the door, but Francine leaped to her feet and stopped him.

"*Non, Cheri!* Don't you get it?" she hissed. "We cannot leave that way, and we cannot have Madame LeClaire know that we have left, that you, and I, are gone once we leave. Forget your hat!" She giggled at him. "This is like a paid parking lot, you know? And your time is not up yet!" She dove behind the screen and began to hurriedly get dressed. In a bit more than a minute, while Joey stood there feeling increasingly anxious, she emerged, clad in a black dress and boots, and tugged on a fashionable, warm-looking raccoon fur coat. "Now, *mon sauveur*, we will leave."

"How, exactly?" asked Joey, perplexed, glancing at his wristwatch. Time was fast running out; a full seven minutes had passed since he had entered Francine's room.

"The window, *la fenetre*, silly boy!" replied Francine as she stuck her dainty nose up, prodded her hair into place and then slipped a jaunty-looking black cloche hat over it. She peeked out at him impishly from beneath its brim. "We will use the fire escape. I have had this plan all along. So, T.R., he told you nothing about this, or what to do? Please do go and open the window now—quietly!"

The way down the rickety iron stairs that clung to the rugged stone walls of the chateau creaked and groaned under the weight of Francine, Joey and the suitcase Joey was tugging along, descending slowly, tentatively, one stair tread at a time, once they had passed through the window. Joey had had the presence of mind to close it, doing so without making a sound but now, his worry was that of being spotted. Thus far, no one could be seen below in the parking lot. He could see the massive chrome grille of the Packard close by, reflecting the moonlight. After what seemed like an eternity, he and Francine finally reached the ground, and headed toward the car.

Upon reaching the Packard, Joey told Francine to place her suitcase on the back seat. "The trunk is full," he explained. "Now, there's one thing left for me to do," he added, as he stepped to front of the car and gently opened the hood without making any undue noise. Francine, puzzled, stood there quietly and watched. Joey unclipped the distributor cap, then reached in his jacket pocket for the rotor. It was gone. He felt around frantically for it, but could not find it.

"What is wrong?" Francine hissed, trying to keep her voice down. "What on earth are you doing? Whatever it is, you'd better do it, *tout suite!*"

Finally, Joey found the rotor. It had fallen down into the lining of his jacket through a hole in the pocket. He had just grasped it and triumphantly put it into its place, snapping the distributor cap back on afterward, when someone opened the back door of the chateau, saw him and shouted: "Hey! *Qu'est ce que tu crois faire?"*

"What does he want?" Joey asked Francine nervously, slamming the hood shut and jumping toward the driver's side door of the car. "Better get in!"

"He wants to know what the hell you are doing, what do you think?" Francine answered dismissively, scurrying around to the other side of the Packard, and jumping in, just as Joey got behind the wheel. "He probably thinks you are stealing this car." Joey yanked the car keys from his pocket, jammed them into the ignition lock, turned it, and hit the starter. The Packard's massive engine grumbled into life. "Well, are you?" she inquired, peering at him, half-impressed, half-worried. Joey rammed the shifter into first, let out the clutch, and the car roared off down the driveway, headed for the front gates. Joey just turned to her and smiled. He could have a little fun, too, he thought.

Inside the rear foyer of the Chateau du Roi, the worried little doorman, the one who had called out to Joey, scurried inside and cranked the telephone by his desk. He excitedly told the operator to put him in touch with the local constable so that he could report the apparent theft of a large black Packard with Vermont plates. Just as the doorman was getting off the line with the constable, an angry-looking Madame LeClaire appeared before him and began pounding a fist on his desk, demanding to know what he knew about a boy in a chauffeur's uniform. The one who had just absconded with an employee who owed the madame several hundred dollars, and had left behind only the boy's hat. "Tell the boys to get the Pierce-Arrow ready for me," ordered the madame, "and my driver. And then find out where Snyder is, and what the hell he is doing."

Out in the black Packard that was speeding through the night, heading south, Francine pulled a small silver flask from beneath her fur coat and took a swig of liquor. "Want some?" she asked Joey, who was intent on following the signs pointing the way to Vermont. He shook his head. "Hey, I am sorry, now. I did not ask you your name; what is it?"

"It might have been mud if I got caught back there, even if I wasn't really stealing this car. But right now, it's Joe, but everyone calls me Joey. Joey Ross. That's me."

Chapter 36

The Road to Hell

The road to hell, as it's often said, is paved with good intentions. It was Joey's good intention—that of earning enough money to post bail for his brother—that had wound up putting him behind the wheel of Junior's car, and smack in the middle of what was fast becoming a dicey situation. To be sure, Joey thought as he drove along, he had proved his mettle in outfoxing old double-dealing Gaston, and in making good an escape from the Chateau du Rois with Francine. The cases of booze—worth a small fortune, he guessed—were secure in the Packard's trunk. He was, so far, holding up his end of the bargain, he thought smugly. Then, another thought popped into his mind: *Would Junior hold up his end?*

Francine stirred; she'd apparently drifted off to sleep before the car reached the worst, bumpy stretch of what passed for the main highway. Joey took his eyes off the road momentarily to glance at her. She blinked, looked at him, and in the faint glow of the dashboard lights he caught her smiling at him. All the eyeliner and heavy makeup she wore made her seem like a glamorous movie star, captured in the dim glow of lights in some ritzy cabaret in a Hollywood film noir. But, of course, as Joey had quickly realized, she was a hooker. Right now, in between customers (or, as they say in the taxi business, off duty at the moment).

"Where are we?" she mumbled, leaning over toward Joey. Her breath smelled of cigarettes and whiskey. Her clothing smelled of bed. In this, what would prove to be last few months of Prohibition, whiskey—and other libations—were still fancy, expensive and sometimes hard to procure. Just like her.

"Somewhere south of Georgeville," replied Joey. In actuality, he wasn't sure. In between glances at the map Junior had given him and what few road signs he encountered, he at least figured that he was headed due south. But he was soon unnerved by the sight of a large body of water glazed with ice that lay to his left, glimpsed in breaks between swaths of tall, dark pine trees. Lake Memphremagog, which he had kept in sight—or thought he had—for a while upon leaving the chateau, had been on his right, not the left. He held his breath for a few seconds, then sighed and suppressed the urge to panic at the sudden thought that somehow, despite his care, he'd gotten turned around and was headed back north. He shook his head to clear it from the frightful idea, and from the drowsiness that he felt setting in after so many hours behind the wheel. He had the girl, he had the booze, and he hadn't lost the car. So far, so good.

He stole another glance at Francine. Here he was, about to deliver a pretty, fashionable girl to an old codger—a real sugar daddy if ever there was one. Chances were good that she'd clear off after spending a couple of nights with him and a good chunk of his cash. And Junior? What would Junior do after getting his booze and his car back and paying Joey, if he did indeed come across with the dough? Why, of course, he'd get Billy back in the bargain. Exit Joey. So, what was in it for Joey, after all? Gratitude from Billy? Probably not. After all, Billy was for Billy.

Come to think of it, Joey reasoned sourly, maybe he should just keep on going. Turn his back on Billy, Junior, the whole mess. Right now, he was Francine's champion. He could explain about T.R. being such an old geezer, and she'd understand. She'd stick with him. The booze in the trunk? Well, he and Francine could live off that money from selling it, once they got out of the Northeast Kingdom. They could live high on the hog. Junior? Who cared about him? Junior was just a crook, and deep down, everyone in Lyndonville knew it, after all. Billy? He was just Junior's lackey. Come to think of it, maybe Billy had killed that little tramp Mary Lou after all. Let him rot in jail. Then, reality set in. It came up like a powerful backhand slap and smacked Joey right between the eyes. He took his foot off the gas a moment, and the car drifted slightly toward the centerline. He'd been thinking just like he knew how his brother did; only of himself.

"Whoops!" shrieked Francine giddily as she lost her balance, toppled over against Joey's right shoulder, pushing him against his door and giggled, "I think I am, how you say, a bit implicated!" She grabbed his right arm even as he yanked the steering wheel to the right and brought the Packard back on course, like a desperate helmsman steering a ship away from a rocky coastline. The car fishtailed on a patch of ice, then settled down and resumed its course. Francine now clung to his shoulder; he could feel her warm breath tickling the back of his neck before she asked, "Want a sip?" She let go in order to pull the flask from inside her fur coat, and dangled it in front of him for emphasis. He shook his head, and smiled.

Just down the road, two X-shaped, white railroad crossing signs reflected the glare of the big car's headlights. A few seconds later, the Packard bounced over the rails and rough-hewn planks of the crossing itself. "*Chemin de fer!*" announced the girl, giggling tipsily. She was definitely waking up now. And true to her Quebec heritage, she pattered on in French a bit more to add a bit of spice to the late-night conversation as the car swiftly passed a small roadside sign, lettered in French and English, that advised anyone traversing the international boundary line at this remote, unguarded spot to immediately report to the U.S. Customs House, *"U.S. Douanes et Immigration"* nearby. As woozy as she was, Francine had spotted it first. *"Nous venons de traverser la frontier!"* she exclaimed excitedly. "We just crossed the border!" She shifted her feet off onto the floor, and then bounced up and down on the seat briefly like a little schoolgirl who'd just guessed the correct answer to a tough question. "I am so glad. My English is more good now, no?"

"Tres bien," muttered Joey, peering through the windshield. It had just begun to snow. Not a bad thing and not unexpected in the Northeast Kingdom, but worrisome, as the roads were slippery enough as it was. Nor was Francine's French, interspersed with some broken English, something unexpected; just about everyone in Joey's high school class could *"parle Francaise"* a bit with folks from Quebec, if and when the occasion called for it. But, thank God for having made it back across the border; wherever Joey was now, at least it was someplace in Vermont.

"Attention!" blurted Francine. She jumped forward, put her hands on the dashboard and stared out the through the flurry of snowflakes at the road ahead with great apprehension. "Look!" Someone far down the road was waving a red light. *"Faites attention! Je n'aime pas ca du tout!* I don't like this one bit!" Joey let his foot up on the accelerator pedal and let the Packard slow a bit until he could clearly see exactly what was ahead—an accident? Soon, he could see that a large Buick sedan was pulled over alongside the road and one side of its hood was up. Three men stood beside the apparently disabled vehicle, one of them swinging a red lantern back and forth, the other two waving their arms, motioning Joey to stop. Perplexed, and perhaps losing his senses momentarily, Joey braked and shifted into a lower gear. Just as he did, one of the two men

not holding the lantern sprinted toward the passenger side of the Packard.

"Hijackers!" yelled Francine. "Floor it! *Aller!*" Panicked now, Joey put his foot down and the Packard accelerated—but slowly. Hijackers! How could he have forgotten Junior's warning about them, and been so stupid? The man leaped, aiming to hop on the car's running board the way a savvy hobo catches a ride on a moving freight train. Just as he did, Francine opened her door and shoved it forward with all her might. There came a loud *crack!* as the hijacker's body connected with the edge of the door. She slammed it shut just as Joey stole a glance at his rearview mirror. To his horror, he saw the dark figure of another man chasing him, silhouetted in the other car's headlights, running close behind the car and quickly closing the gap. In a split second, the man took a flying leap for the rear bumper—and missed. And a few seconds later—even more worrisome—the headlights of the supposedly-disabled Buick were began moving toward him. Quickly.

Francine twisted around on her seat and peered out the back window of the car just as Joey turned to steal a glance at her. Her face looked pale and drawn with apprehension in the glare of the headlights of the pursuing car. But in a split second, she laughed and her demeanor changed.

"I'll bet you can lose him real easy with this big car, eh?" she giggled. Then, she playfully poked Joey in the ribs, and he swerved involuntarily. When he reached out his right arm to push her away, she retreated, curling up against the door. She laughed, kicked her shoes off and stretched her legs out on the seat until her toes were up against Joey's right thigh, wiggling against it. "There," she said. "Is that not now much better?"

"Look, I'll lose him if I can get on a better stretch of road," Joey said. "Nothing to it." But the other car soon pulled up closer, dogging him, then began to weave left and right, its driver trying his best to pass Joey and cut him off. Then, through the swirling snowflakes, an intersection with a paved road appeared. Rather than braking, Joey cut the wheel and poured on the gas. The big Packard skated sideways on the slick pavement briefly before Joey corrected and kept on going; the other car's headlights narrowed to two pinpoints in the rearview mirror. The car's big straight-eight engine rumbled as if in triumph as Joey put his foot down, and at last, a smile worked its way across his face.

"Hey," mumbled Francine boozily, after taking a dainty, lady-like swig from her flask and giving Joey a look that bordered on affection. "We're purrin' now, ain't we?"

"Yes, we sure are," allowed Joey. He relaxed a bit, turned and gave her a wan smile. "Thanks, by the way, for showing that bum the door back there." But Francine, had turned to look at something else, her heavily-shadowed eyes wide in horror.

"*Oh, chemin de fer! Attention!* Railroad! Look out for the train, *Cheri!*"

In his rapturous enjoyment of Francine's company, Joey had let his guard down once more and not noticed he'd been approaching yet another rural railroad crossing. Nor had he seen that one of the Canadian Pacific's nightly freight trains to Newport was about to cross his path, but the engineer of its locomotive had obviously seen the Packard, travelling on what appeared to him to be a suicide mission. The speeding locomotive's whistle sounded a last, imperious warning, startling Joey. Badly shaken, he tromped on the gas, mashing the pedal to the floor. He and Francine barely made it across the tracks, almost invisible under new-fallen snow, before the massive train of half-a-hundred freight cars slammed by—leaving the hijackers in the pursuing sedan to stand on the brakes and wait, long past the time the Packard's taillights had vanished from their view down the dark road.

* * *

Several miles to the north, Steve Snyder pushed his Ford along southward as quickly as he dared as the snowfall increased and the going became troublesome. The tire tracks in the road looked a bit fresher now, and just as he reached the U.S.-Canada border on the deserted back road, he encountered what he recognized as one of LeClaire's bootlegging crews pulled over just past a railroad crossing, endeavoring to change a flat tire on their Buick. Steve eased the Ford over, stopped and cranked down the passenger-side window part way. One of the three men trudged over, carrying both a flashlight and a red lantern with him. "So, Steve" grunted the man, "you're after that kid with the big Packard too, eh?"

Steve nodded his assent. "You won't have to go far to catch up with him, I'll bet," ventured the man. "He's been on the run since he left the chateau, as far as we can figure; he's got to stop for gas somewhere. Soon, real soon."

"What's the matter with *him*?" asked Steve, pointing at one of the men who was sitting on the running board of the Buick, moaning and clutching his right shoulder. Did he get shot? Does that kid on the run have a piece?"

"No, he tried to jump onto the kid's car and take the wheel. That little bitch riding shotgun opened her door and nailed him with it; gave him a broken arm, she did."

"Clever girl," commented Steve wryly, smirking as he shoved the Ford into gear. "Lucky for you she didn't put all three of you in the hospital. I'll give your regards to LeClaire when I call in." He let out the clutch, stepped on the gas and the Ford sped off into the night, slithering sideways momentarily in the wet snow.

* * *

Joey's sense of relief at losing his pursuers, and stumbling across an unguarded way into Vermont soon vanished and his stomach fairly churned when he took a look at the car's gas gauge; its needle, far from indicating a full, 25-gallon tank, was tickling the zero mark. Through some miracle he had, as far as could see, found his way down the west side of Lake Memphremagog, meandering through a maze of back roads on sheer luck and dead reckoning; no thanks to Billy's crudely-drawn map. Now, the familiar lights of Newport glowed in the distance. "We've got to find gas, soon," he remarked. His brow wrinkled in concern, he looked over at Francine, but the girl was fast asleep. Soon, he was threading his way through a series of downhill curves, past the twin spires of St. Mary's Catholic Church. And, as he had suspected, no filling stations in town were open. Joey bit his lip and drove on, hoping to perhaps find something open farther on, toward Derby.

He turned the corner by the railroad station, then swung a right and headed east on Main Street up the hill. He whistled softly at the sight that greeted him a minute later: two illumi-nated Shell gas pumps, standing tall like night-time sentries on duty outside Warrens Hopkins Motors, a converted house that, besides being a filling station, also had a tourist home in its upstairs chambers. The lights blinked out a scant second before Joey pulled in beside the pumps. "Sorry, fellah, we're closed," came a voice from an open door in the house, which soon slammed shut.

As tired as he was, Joey sprang out of the Packard and rushed to the door, yanking it open before the attendant could lock it.

"Look, pal," Joey implored. Gesturing toward the Packard, whose funeral home emblems were clearly visible inside the rear windows. Francine was visible also, sound asleep, propped up against her door pillar. "Do you really want a widow to be late for her husband's funeral tomorrow?" It was pure bluff, but it worked.

"Oh, all right, fellah," grunted the attendant, pulling on a pair of gloves. "You win. What'll it be?"

"Fill 'er up," said Joey. He got back into the car, and Francine awoke. She peered out the. window and saw the sign on the building, 'Tourist Home—Welcome!'

She sidled up to him on the seat and whispered, "Can we stay here tonight? I am so sleepy. But—still, I could show you a good time!" She beamed at him, but then her eyes strayed to Joey's hands as he leafed through several dollar bills, preparing to pay for the gas.

"I think," mumbled Joey drowsily, yawning and stretching back in his seat, "you already have tonight!" He sighed, struggling to keep his eyes open. The next thing he knew, Francine was prodding him awake, and the attendant was rapping on the Packard's window; Joey had drifted off to sleep.

"What do you think now, dear sleepy-head, *mon ami endormi*, about staying here tonight?" Francine inquired, snuggling up close to him, and kissing him on the cheek. "You are my hero."

She beamed at him in adoration. "I am no longer LeClaire's puppet."

* * *

Although the room was tiny and cold Joey's bed, although small, was soft and comfortable. It was a welcome respite from the rough, bumpy and exhausting drive south from Canada, and from the hell of being pursued overland during a nighttime snow squall. While the snow had tapered off when the Packard was being put into the garage long hours ago, gusts of wind rattled the windowpanes now, and Joey stirred in his sleep. As he did, a floorboard in the room creaked like a rusty hinge, and Joey awoke. As stealthily as a cat stalking an unsuspecting mouse, Francine had let herself into his room. Now, she lifted the heavy quilt and covers slightly, and quickly slipped into bed beside him.

Joey bolted in alarm at this midnight intrusion, flailed at the covers and was about to shout something when Francine quickly covered his mouth and subdued him. "Shoosh, *Cheri*! It's only me," she whispered. Thus, reassured that he was not being attacked by one of LeClaire's thugs, he laid back, and her hand took advantage of this truce to slip down to rest on his bare chest. She pulled herself closer, and then nibbled playfully on one of his earlobes for a moment. He felt the warmth of her breath in his ear as she added, "You remember what I said? About a good time?" Fully awakened now, his heart pounding, Joey nodded. Francine giggled. Then, she told him softly, and in no uncertain terms, "I am here. You will see; I may be *un pute*, a whore, but you are true to me, and I am true to my word."

Chapter 37

Just the Ticket

Despite the hardships of long-distance winter travel, Sheriff John Johnson's deputy had done due diligence in collecting both the deposition from the Woodstock innkeeper and his inn's register page that bore Catherine Hollingsworth's allegedly-forged signature. Both items now lay on a desk between John and the judge he was visiting at the justice's snug little home office. As well, John had presented as further evidence the photo Ed had taken at J.J. Newberry's; the innkeeper had drawn a circle around the image of Doris Martin on the photo, and had named her in the deposition as the woman who'd registered as Catherine Hollingsworth. "Yes, your honor," affirmed John. "In conclusion, I believe the skis and poles I observed at the subject's apartment building were very likely used in commission of Mary Lou Lamar's murder."

"Very well then," said the judge. "I see no reason not to issue a search warrant in this matter. I think you have established substantial probable cause." He cleared his throat and with a well-practiced motion, swept up four pieces of his official stationery interspersed with carbons, rolled them into an Underwood typewriter, and began pecking away at the keys, talking to himself occasionally as he went along, composing the warrant: "...the premises and all parts therein...and for all vehicles parked at or near the premises which can be associated with this location...and for the person known as Doris Martin, believed to reside at the above address. There!" The judge slowly pulled the papers from his typewriter, inked his fountain pen, and signed them. After blotting his signatures, he crimped these documents with his seal of office, and handed the original plus one of the carbon copies to John.

John was pleased; he'd gotten everything he had asked the judge for, including the provision to search for and to seize any railroad tickets or similar matter. "Thank you, especially for doing this on such short notice," said John, tucking the search warrant into his breast pocket as he rose to his feet. "And so early." That consideration was offered because elderly justice was still dressed in his bathrobe and bedroom slippers. "Going to do a little ice fishing today? I hear the ice is still good and thick up on Joe's Pond, and we've got a good freeze coming soon."

"No, not today," answered the judge, cracking his knuckles and then sighing. "Too much paperwork. You?"

"Nope," replied John, planting his hat firmly and squarely on his big head. There was a smile of satisfaction appearing now just beneath his bushy mustache. "Today, I'm hunting!"

* * *

Once again, the sheriff found himself standing at the door to apartment 1-C of the drab-looking Lyndonville tenement house. There had been no answer to his knock, so he pounded on the rough wooden door this time, hard enough to shake the home's windowpanes. This time, he'd brought along some help. Earlier this morning, he had deputized and brought along an old acquaintance, Ben Harrison, an off-duty Highway Patrol officer, who was now standing right behind him. As a precaution, John's regular deputy was guarding the building's back doors and poking around a bit. Presently, there came the sound of a bolt being drawn back and the door creaked open a crack. A sleepy-looking Doris Martin peeked out at him like a mouse whose nest has just been uncovered in broad daylight. "You again. What do you want?" she mumbled drowsily.

"I want to know if you are Doris Martin," answered John.

"Yes, and you already know that," she groused.

"Then consider yourself served with this search warrant, Miss Martin," he responded, thrusting the warrant through the opening at her. She reached out, grasped it and then stared at it in disbelief. "It will tell you exactly what I want. Now, if you would please, ma'am, open the door for us." There came a rattling sound as Doris unfastened a security chain, and then the door swung open. John and Ben then stepped into the apartment.

The window shades were all drawn and only one light, a small floor lamp, illuminated the cluttered, tiny living room. Doris stood near it, still staring at the search warrant. "You could close the door, sheriff," she snapped over her shoulder. "This joint is cold enough as it is!" The door had no sooner been closed when she spoke again, obviously quite aggravated. "Skis? You want skis? I told you the last time you were here that I don't ski!"

"I know that," responded John coolly, stepping over to face her. "You told me you don't ice skate, either. So, tell me why you took a train ride down to Woodstock a few days ago to stay at an inn where there's skiing nearby, and took along a pair of skis and poles."

Doris stuck her jaw out defiantly and crossed her arms. "I did no such thing," she stated. And then, after a contemplative pause and displaying a snarky-looking grin, "What if I did?"

"I think you know you did, ma'am," answered John.

"You're lying to get me to take a fall. You don't have a witness that saw me get on or off any train."

"Oh, yes I do," replied John, hitching up his gun belt.

"Who?"

"Joey Ross."

"Joey Ross? Oh, come now, sheriff, that's really rich," snorted Doris, rolling her eyes. "Billy Ross's brother. Billy's just trying to beat his rap. Billy hates me, and now his kid brother's in on the deal. You're being played for a sucker, Sheriff Johnson. A sucker."

"Furthermore," continued John, "we talked with the inn-keeper. He remembers you and identified you as a guest registering under the name Catherine Hollingsworth during the time in question. We have the signature, and we can prove it's your handwriting."

"What time in question?" spat back Doris. The grin was gone now.

"The time that Mary Lou Lamar was murdered at the Scrivvins Farm." John let this sink in. It was still sinking in a few seconds later when there came a knock on the door; Ben opened it. Standing outside was the deputy, holding the pair of skis and poles he'd discovered, stashed underneath the back porch. "I'll take those," said John, stepping over to the door. He grabbed them and leaned them against the wall, thanked the deputy, motioned him to step around the corner of the porch, and closed the door. He turned to face Doris. "Care to explain who these belong to? Where they came from?"

"They're not mine," snipped Doris. "Never seen 'em before."

"Are you sure about that?" countered John. "Because the last time I was here, they were out on your back porch. Right after I left your apartment, I watched that fellow staying with you rush out back in a big hot hurry, and conceal them underneath the porch. Either he didn't want you to see them, or he didn't want me to see them. Which is it, ma'am?"

"Listen, I don't have time for all this," Doris snarled, brushing back her disheveled hair. "I have to go to work."

"So do we, ma'am. So, I think it's best if you come down to the station with us now so we can ask more questions, about why you were standing in for Catherine Hollingsworth, and get some answers. I'll be happy to give your regrets to the manager at J.J. Newberry's," grumbled John.

"What? Am I under arrest?" Doris asked.

"No, I'm placing you under protective custody for the time being. This is an ongoing murder investigation, and the killer is still at large. I believe you have information that may pose a risk to your life. By the way," added John, "is that your fur coat lying on the couch?" Doris nodded.

"Please pick it up and turn out the pockets."

As Doris did so, a cascade of gum wrappers, loose change, a matchbook and other items descended on the couch. Among these items was one half of what looked like a hole-punched index card, with the words "Passenger's Duplicate Baggage Claim" printed on it and a serial number, plus, in fancy, cursive writing: "White River Jct./Burlington, VT". John picked it up and examined it. There was dead silence until he looked up at Doris and spoke. "Ma'am, you'd better get dressed so you can come with us. You can use the bathroom. In case you have any ideas about leaving early without us, I should mention my deputy is stationed right outside the window. He won't be offended if you close the curtains."

* * *

Doris Martin sat down on the tiny stool within the cramped confines of the telephone booth in the courthouse foyer, got settled, and pulled the bifold doors closed, affording her some modicum of privacy. She then dropped a nickel into the phone and waited for the operator to connect her with the pool hall where Paul, her go-between with Steve, was known to hang out after school. Sheriff Johnson, hands on his hips, stood a discrete distance away from the telephone booth, waiting for

Doris to make her call. The phone rang several times before someone with a gruff voice answered and hollered for Paul to come to the phone.

Doris was chewing on one of her fingernails by the time Paul answered. "I need you to get word to Steve when he calls," she demanded. "The sheriff's got me in the jam. He knows. Says Joey Ross saw me getting off the train."

"And?" asked Paul, casually.

"Tell him to take care of it. Fast. And to get me out of here."

"Okay," answered Paul. He pushed down the cradle with one finger to disconnect the call, then released it, yet held onto the phone a bit longer, pretending to talk tough for the benefit of any kids standing around who might hear and be suitably impressed. He looked around, and caught a few interested eyes. "Yeah, I'll take care of it, doll. No worries," he said before putting the phone down. Yes, he'd certainly talk with Steve, alright, and Steve would take care of Joey. Having someone snuffed for the greater good? Paul reasoned that just taking a minor role in that would be a real stepping stone in his career. Exciting, too. Paul strutted out of the pool hall, imagining that he was wearing a new pin-striped suit, a diamond pinkie ring and a fedora. And that he was well on his way to becoming a real-life gangster, rather than simply being a lackey for one.

Chapter 38

Hot on the Trail:
January 7, 1933

"You can go now. You've been released," the sheriff's first deputy, Sam had announced as he unlocked the cell door, opened it wide and stood back to let the freed prisoner pass by. Suppressing the urge to say something smart, Billy Ross gathered up what few belongings he had, put on his coat, and strode out of the jail cell, stopping briefly only to make a call from the pay phone in the building's foyer. From the vantage point of his office window, Sheriff Johnson and recently-sworn-in second deputy Ben Harrison had watched as Billy stalked out the door, down the walkway and into the street. "He sure as hell looks mad," Sheriff Johnson remarked.

"He sure was, just as soon as he finished his phone call," added Sam as he entered the room, obviously having overheard the sheriff. Sam's habit of constantly eavesdropping could be either a curse or a blessing; a moment later, the sheriff decided not to chastise him for doing it. A long day later, he would be chastising himself for not digging a bit deeper.

"Who was he talking with?" asked the sheriff.

"Junior Coughlin."

* * *

The next morning, Sheriff Johnson and Ben stood side-by-side in the office, looking out the window again. A high-pressure weather front had blown in during the night, and now the wind was swooping down from the northwest, devastatingly cold. "Looks like our thaw is over," remarked the sheriff; Ben nodded.

"Looks like the case against Billy Ross is over, too," Ben added, frowning.

"Listen, Ben; we *had* to let him go. The State's Attorney was just about jumping down my throat about this yesterday. With only circumstantial evidence tying Ross to the murder, the clock's run out on holding him."

"Well, John, it's starting to look like the clock will run out on getting any further with Doris Martin, too, without Joey Ross's testimony. He seems to have disappeared like a magician's rabbit without any hope of us bringing him out of the hat." Just then, the telephone jingled. Sheriff Johnson held up a finger, then stepped to his desk and answered. Startled by what he was hearing, he grasped a pen and paper, and began scribbling while he listened to what else the caller had to say.

Ben fidgeted with the loose change in the pocket of his jacket while he waited for the call to end. He looked down at the badge that had been pinned onto the jacket, long hours ago when the sheriff had deputized him. He didn't like the recent turn of events, much less the disappearance of Joey Ross. It did not bode well for that clean-cut teenager he'd met last year.

His thoughts turned to the events of the last Fourth of July in St. Johnsbury when Joey Ross had helped him pull a bootlegger from a crashed Cadillac on Railroad Street. The kid had some pluck, that was for sure. He was a straight-shooter, in complete contrast to his older brother Billy, who obviously had a disdain for the police, the truth, and any authority.

There was a loud *clunk!* as the sheriff hung up the phone. "Good news!" he exclaimed. "We're in luck!" He shot an amused look at Ben. "What have you been fiddling with in your pocket there, Ben? A rabbit's foot?"

"So, what do we have?" inquired Ben, pulling his right hand from his pocket, revealing only a few pennies and some pocket lint.

"That was one of the boys in the lab up in Burlington, where I sent the skis and poles we seized at Martin's. Turns out there were small blood stains on the leather straps of the ski poles, some elsewhere. Very little, but enough to give them something to go on."

"And?"

"The blood is a match to the recently-deceased Mary Lou Lamar's blood type."

"Which drags in recently-implicated Doris Martin even further."

"And Catherine Hollingsworth, also, if I'm not mistaken," added the sheriff. "The picture's becoming pretty clear to me. And that picture is: Mary Lou must have been stabbed to death with one of those ski poles."

At this, Ben's jaw dropped in astonishment. "John, really? A ski pole murder?"

"Add it all up, Ben, and it makes sense. Everyone I've talked to about this case has told me the same thing: Billy Ross ditched Catherine for Mary Lou. Dumped her in a heartbeat. Murder by gunfire, poison, arson, that's one thing. Murder committed with a bladed weapon, that's hands-on, personal. No matter whether it's done with a knife or not, that implies rage. And, I'd say this case has jealous rage painted all over it, and a big effort by Doris and the man who says he's her cousin—if in fact he really is—to cover up what happened at the Scrivvins farm that night. Premeditated murder—and a getaway on skies."

Before Ben could say anything, the phone rang again. The sheriff yanked the receiver from its hook and answered; within seconds, he slammed it down. "Joey Ross was just sighted on Memorial Drive north of town, driving a black sedan!" he bellowed. "C'mon, Ben; we've got to get going and bring that boy in!" He charged over to the coat rack in the corner, grabbed his hat and jammed it on his head . "Let's go!"

"Should we split up?" asked Ben, as he buttoned up his jacket, and touched the grip of the Smith & Wesson .44 Special hanging on his hip, just for luck.

"Yes. Take my deputy's car."

"Is he coming with us?" asked Ben.

"Not on this jaunt," answered the sheriff, tugging on his jacket. "He can stay here and mind the store.

"Aren't you forgetting something?" asked Ben, pointing down at the .44 in his own holster.

"Oh, yeah," grumbled the sheriff, as he spun around and yanked a bullet-studded gun belt and its revolver off the coat rack, and proceeded to strap it on. "Want to grab a coffee to take with you?"

"Not the stuff your deputy makes," answered Ben, chuckling as he said this. "That dishwater of his isn't worth a damn, and besides, I've heard your prisoners complain about it all the time."

"So much," countered the tall, muscular sheriff as he barged through the office doorway, "for repeat offenders. That's *their* punishment."

* * *

At that particular moment, Joey Ross was sitting in the driver's seat of the Packard as it idled outside T.R.'s residence next door to the ice house. Upon being told that his bride had been delivered, albeit late, the grand old man himself had shuffled to the front door to receive his perfumed bundle of joy from Canada. Francine, all hugs and kisses, was clinging to his neck like a squid displaying affection for a big fish in a small tidal pool. Apart from feeling a certain sense of deprivation, remembering the previous evening's amorous encounter under the bedsheets, Joey observed that the new couple certainly looked happy. How long this happiness would last, he figured, was anyone's guess.

Joey put the Packard into gear, let out the clutch and waved goodbye. "Wait!" hollered T.R., just as the car started to roll. "I almost forgot to tell you! There's good news! Your brother was released yesterday!" Joey hit the brakes. It took him a moment to recover.

"No kidding."

"No kidding, son!" shouted T.R. energetically, squeezing Francine's slender waist. "I heard it from my boys this morning. The sheriff let him go, and he went home. Billy's a free man." Startled, Joey let off the brakes and as the Packard glided out of the driveway, he could feel his stomach churning. It was bad enough Joey was overdue by the agreed-upon 24 hours, but now Junior had his flunky back. Would he pay Joey as promised, or would he be as devious to deal with as Gaston? In short, would Junior try to double-cross him?

Joey wanted to take a peek at Francine in the rearview mirror as he left, but decided against it. It would have been too much like watching Gaston disappear in the gathering twilight, leaving him to his fate on the cold highway. Now, he had left Francine to her fate, too. But, after all, every person he'd encountered, it seemed during the past day or so had a game of their own to play. And Joey's game with Junior wasn't over—yet.

Rather than head north to Junior's, Joey decided to drive down to St. Johnsbury. He needed time to think. For one thing, he needed to eat. Perhaps the little restaurant near the railroad station could serve up a good breakfast, he thought. He certainly did not want to go home—at least, not yet, and be forced to deal with Billy. Or his mother, Beth, for that matter. God bless her; she might go into hysterics and faint dead away upon seeing him finally come home, and heaven only knew what lies Billy had told her about him while he was gone. More than anything else now, he knew he wanted to see Lila. But what, above all else, could he tell her about his travels with Francine, without omitting the all-important truth about what had happened last night?

Although he had driven up and down the highway, Memorial Drive many times—and ridden his bicycle on it as well—everything now seemed foreign to him. The farther he drove, the more the feeling grew stronger. He was sure of it: something had changed while he'd been gone. The answer came to him quickly.

It was him.

With a loud *crack!* a bullet zipped through the rear window and out the passenger side of the windshield, shattering it. A dove-grey Ford sedan that had been shadowing him, sight unseen, pulled up alongside and forced Joey's car to the shoulder, just as a long, black Pierce Arrow limo cut him off and blocked any escape. The Ford's right window was down and its driver, Steve Snyder, all business, was aiming a revolver at Joey. "Don't make any dumb moves, kid," he snapped. "I don't like to waste bullets, so there won't be another warning shot!"

A burly-looking man in an overcoat and stylish fedora jumped from the Pierce-Arrow and sprinted toward the Packard. He jumped onto its passenger-side running board and yanked open the door. "Where's the girl?" he barked.

"Not here," answered Joey."

"Yeah, I can see that, punk," said the man, a gold tooth flashing in his sharklike mouth as he got into the Packard, clambered across the seat and landed a left backhand on Joey's right cheek. The blow sent him reeling. "Pretty obvious, ain't it? So, one more time, tell."

"I dropped her off at Junior's," stammered Joey, lying as convincingly as he could under the circumstances. "Just a few minutes ago." Perhaps, he thought, the only way to save both Francine and himself would be to take a chance and double-cross his suspected double-crosser, Junior, before he made his play. Then, in the confusion, he would try to make his escape.

"Is that a fact?" This time, the man's right hand slapped Joey's face.

"I swear," Joey answered. He felt the warmth of blood trickling down from his nose. He looked nervously at the man's right hand, expecting another blow, and noticed a strange, circular scar on the back of it.

"Okay, kid. So, what've you got in the trunk?"

"Nothing," answered Joey.

"Show me. Because I think you lie like a rug, kid," grumbled the man, producing an automatic pistol and shoving it into Joey's ribs so hard he thought its barrel would go through him before a bullet did. "Like a lot of scum who've lied to the boss and wound up face-down, chowing on the office rug before they got what they deserved."

"For what it's worth, we bury them face-down, too," chimed in Steve. "Now, get out and unlock the trunk." Joey complied and walked around to the back of the Packard, hoping above all that some passers-by would come to his aid. But it was early, there was snow on the road and there was no traffic. Close beside the highway was the ice-encrusted, slow-moving Passumpsic River; across the way to the east was a small cemetery, one he knew that Billy had made many trips to with Junior's hearse.

Joey fumbled nervously in his pocket for the key. "Bring your hand out real slow, kid," cautioned Steve, now standing behind him, "so I can see it." Joey opened the trunk lid, revealing the wooden cases of precious cargo. Steve whistled in awe. "Look at that, will you!" he crowed, as the other man joined him in peering into the Packard's trunk. "Grand Champagne Cognac; top-shelf brandy, rare, high-class stuff! Looks like we can cut some recent losses on this trip! The boss will be pleased. Get those into the boss's car."

After the liquor had been stowed in the Pierce Arrow, Steve's accomplice returned. "What now, Steve?" he asked.

"We ditch the Packard," ordered Steve, all the while covering Joey with a gun. "Got a place in mind?"

"Simple! Right across the street," replied the thug, pointing a finger eastward. "See that little white building there in the cemetery? It's a hearse shed, where they used to keep the old horse-drawn hearse. But there ain't no horse-drawn hearses any more. That shed's been empty for years. No one will find the kid's car anytime soon; I guarantee it."

Within the next minute Junior's Packard, bullet holes and all, was driven into the shed as Joey was pushed into Steve's Ford and told to take the wheel. "You're gonna drive, kid, and no funny stuff," ordered Steve from the passenger's side. "Take us up to Junior's. I always suspected he was in on the booze racket. He carried it on right under my nose. I learned a lot about you and Billy—Junior, too—from your pal Paul."

Joey flinched. "What's the matter? Hit a nerve there, did I?" snickered Steve at seeing Joey's reaction. "Yeah, Paul and I work really well together. Incidentally, Joey, I hope you appreciate— by driving one of them—what a fine car Henry Ford's got in his new V-8. Too bad it's probably going to be your last ride."

* * *

With the Pierce Arrow trailing behind, Joey drove the Ford north toward Lyndonville, his right foot trembling on the gas pedal. He watched wistfully as he observed Sheriff John Johnson's Hudson patrol car approaching, wishing he could flag it down and get himself out of his predicament; it flashed by, headed south at high speed. "There he goes, Johnny-Law in a hurry. Probably lookin' for you driving that Packard, kid!" Steve observed, smirking in satisfaction as he looked down, placed a fresh round into his gun, and then spun its cylinder.

Dreading the journey's end, Joey pulled the Ford up to the curb beside Coughlin's Furniture and Funeral Service in Lyndonville. "Drive out back, where the service entrance is," commanded Steve. Joey steered around the corner, stopped just outside the garage door and rear entrance of Junior's and turned off the engine. "I'll take those," said Steve, yanking the keys from the Ford's ignition. He hopped out of the car and walked around to the driver's side. "Now, get out," he ordered, jerking the door open. "Remember; I'll have my gun right at your back." Steve started to prod him forward, the gun now concealed in Steve's jacket pocket. "Let's go in and see what Junior's got to say." Joey glanced inside the Ford, where he caught sight of a Thompson submachine gun lying on the back seat. "In case you've got any ideas of grabbing that piece, forget it," advised Steve. "That gun's out of ammo, or else I'd use it."

As he headed for the door, Joey turned slightly to look at the Pierce Arrow in time to see the driver, the gold-toothed man, open a rear door. Out stepped a stout, disgruntled-looking woman he recognized as Madame LeClaire, smoking yet another of her evil-smelling cigarillos. The driver brandished a gun, knocked off its safety, and stuffed it into the waistband of his pants. LeClaire pointed to the building's entrance door. "Open it—now! *Tout de suite!*" she growled.

Joey's right hand shook as he grasped and turned the doorknob, nudged the door open and stepped inside with Steve, LeClaire and her big, ape-like driver following close behind. Familiar sights, smells and sounds from his last visit greeted him anew: the hearse, its rear door open, dripping water on the floor, perhaps from a recent "first call" pick-up on snowy streets; the smell of disinfectant, alcohol and formaldehyde; the sound of some kind of pump whirring away in an adjoining room. A corpse, covered by a white sheet, lay on a table under a lamp in the center of the dimly-lit work area. Otherwise, the room was empty. "Chat him up!" prompted Steve, nudging Joey's back with the gun.

"Junior! It's me, Joey," he shouted. "I'm back!"

A backroom door popped open and Junior Coughlin appeared, carrying a tray of what looked like rolls of gauze and surgical tools. He stopped and stared at the group of people standing beside the hearse. "What the hell is this?" he blustered, setting the tray down on a table. Then, he focused on Joey. "Ross, why are you bringing these people in here? Who the hell are they? And where the hell have you been?"

"Look, Junior, I can explain," began Joey.

"Let *me* explain," wheezed Madame LeClaire, after taking a drag on her cigarillo. Lame and unsteady on her feet, she lurched a few feet forward toward Junior and then stopped, teetering unsteadily. "You have one of my people, one of my working girls here," she blustered, waving a finger at him. "I want her back. Now." She puffed on her cigarillo, then blew smoke at him as if she were a storybook dragon threatening a knight with incineration.

"Oh, really?" smirked Junior. "Might that be the one under the sheet?" He pointed at the dead body reposing on the table. "That's the only dame I have here. Now stop talking nonsense and get out."

"Now, you listen to me," began Madame LeClaire. "My name is LeClaire. You—and your errand boy here–have kidnapped one of my staff. Do you know who I am?"

"You mean, *Mrs.* LeClaire, the queen of Quebec's leading ladies-of-the-evening? As in Bernard LeClaire, the famous beer king of Canada? Rumrunner mob boss?" sneered Junior. "I don't believe it."

"He has been dead for more than a year," she answered. "So, now, they call me the 'Bootleg Queen,' and I run the show. Much bigger than your two-car show. Yes, he is dead." She paused, dragged on her smelly cigarillo, then withdrew it and wagged a finger at Junior as she warned him: "You could be, too. Sooner than you think."

"Hey, I'm Junior Coughlin and this is my joint, and my town," blustered Junior, standing his ground. "I don't care what your racket is. Ross, where the devil have you been, and where's my stuff?"

"They've got it, Junior," answered Joey. "They've got your booze. I couldn't stop them. They want Francine. I delivered her, just the way you told me to."

"Francine? You did?" asked Junior, bewildered. Joey nodded.

"So, you even know her name! That is her; that is my girl you have," chimed in LeClaire. "Don't play dumb." She pulled a small Colt pocket pistol from within her coat and aimed it at Junior. "That's enough stalling. You bring her out, and hand her over—now!"

"Oh, my!" giggled Junior, mocking her and her tiny, pearl-handled weapon. "A pea shooter! Now, *that's* gonna sting!"

"Where's that Swedish meatball, that big dope who works for you? I don't see him. Face it, pal, you're here alone," taunted Steve. "You're in a real jam. Turn the girl over; then, you'll get your kid back and we'll leave."

"You know who we're talking about, pal," growled LeClaire's driver, advancing toward Junior. "Stop playing games." Just as he pulled the gun from his waistband and deftly racked it, Junior grabbed a scalpel from the tray and hurled it like a dart. It hit the big, surly man in the throat and as he clutched at it with his free hand his weapon fired. But the shot went wild. Junior ducked under the table and a split second later emerged a dozen feet away. He took a shot at the struggling driver with the Colt .45 he must have thoughtfully stashed away in case of just such an invasion, and missed.

Steve yanked his revolver from his jacket, cocked it, and pushed Joey in front of him now, using him as a shield, yelling, "Drop your gun, Junior, or the kid gets it!" And then big Sven Larsen, bellowing like a bull, burst into the room like a wild man, firing a 10-gauge Winchester shotgun from his hip. Joey wrenched himself free as Steve let him go and fired back while LeClaire let go with three quick shots, and Junior returned fire, shot for shot. Joey dove for cover under the hearse and crawled out the door as bullets and shotgun slugs flew back and forth like angry hornets.

* * *

According to neighbors who heard the gunfire and reported it to the sheriff's office, the shoot-out at Coughlin's lasted barely a minute, but sounded like a fireworks factory exploding. The newspapers were in a frenzy to get their people to the scene, but Sheriff John Johnson denied their reporters and photographers access when they arrived by the carload. As Ed Alvord reported in that week's edition of the *Chronicle*, "...the scene of the shoot-out, which is still under investigation, with five left dead, will go down in history as a blood bath second in notoriety only to the infamous Valentine's Day Massacre of 1929. Prohibition and the rumrunning gang violence it has given rise to is the scourge of the Northeast Kingdom."

When Sheriff Johnson and Ben Harrison had arrived at Coughlin's that day to answer the emergency calls, they had encountered a badly-shaken Joey Ross sitting on the running board of a car outside the mortuary. "Don't go in there," Joey had said, head in his hands, tears running down his face. "Just don't." After calling out several times for anyone in Coughlin's to show themselves and come out, the sheriff and his deputized helper slowly advanced into the mortuary, weapons drawn. But no one, as they soon found out, could possibly have heard the calls to surrender. Sheriff Johnson, taking care not to miss any detail worthy of note, stepped over to the mortuary's table. He gingerly reached out, grasped one corner of the white sheet covering the corpse, and tugged it down slightly.

Beth Ross's eyes were wide open, as if staring hopefully into the afterlife, a place far beyond the low ceiling overhead and the drab, tiresome house downtown where she had toiled for years, struggled to pay the rent, had suffered the loss of her husband and raised two children, all the while taking in laundry to earn extra money.

"I didn't get the message in time enough to tell you," Sam, the deputy told him later on, when he arrived back at his office. "She had a heart attack. Had herself quite a start when Billy showed up at her door, but when he told her Joey had taken over his job and gone off to Canada to pick up a prostitute, I guess that's what did it." For once, Billy had told the unadorned truth.

The truth had set Beth free.

The sheriff would go home that night without telling Joey that his mother was dead; try as he might, he couldn't bring himself to. He had felt his heart sinking to the bottoms of his feet in despair when he wrapped up the crime scene. A long soak in a hot tub, and a tall glass of confiscated whiskey that evening would do nothing to erase the memory of the carnage he had seen. It was one he feared he would take to his grave. He asked Ben to tell Joey. Ben knew the boy; Ben would know how.

* * *

Several hours later, once the sheriff's investigation was wrapped up, Ben and Joey sat side-by-side in a little barrel-roofed diner in Lyndonville, a popular eating place that sat close beside the highway. Ben had brought Joey there after getting his long-awaited, sworn testimony about Doris Martin's arrival on the 6:35 down on paper, notarized, and off to the State's Attorney's office. And then, he broke the news about his mother's death. At first, Ben worried that the boy was going into shock, but then he seemed to recover. Sort of.

A heavy vehicle rumbled by, likely one of many log trucks headed for the mills, making their last run of the day. As it did so, it backfired, sounding like a rifle shot with a loud *pop!* that almost jolted Joey off his stool. "Relax, son," advised Ben, putting a hand on the boy's shoulder to calm him and attempt some levity. "That was only some old piece of junk sounding off. I can tell that from my patrol days. Hell, son; there isn't a truck in this town that's got a muffler on it!" But the humor fell on deaf ears.

The sun was going down, briefly setting the cloudy sky ablaze in vivid hues of orange. Joey watched it as it sank like a burning ship, slipping slowly under the wavy silhouette of the dark purple mountains, and at last disappeared. "Look, don't blame yourself. It's not your fault, what's happened." advised Ben. "None of it is." Joey, dark circles under his eyes, stared back at him.

"I don't know what's right any more, Ben," Joey said. He looked down, trying to escape any thought of where he had been—what he had done—what he had seen the past few days. And the horror of the massacre at Junior's. But his reflection, seen in the bowl of hot soup on the counter before him seemed to be staring back, demanding judgement and condemnation. What had he done? He'd run out on his mother, cheated on his girlfriend, done the bidding of a crook. He had lied and led five people to their deaths. And, finally there had come the blow of his mother's untimely passing.

"Listen, Joey," Ben began. "You testified this afternoon about what you saw at the railroad station, about Doris Martin getting off the 6:35 train. That testimony's gone a long way in a short time. Martin has confessed to posing as Catherine Hollingsworth the night of Mary Lou Lamar's murder, and being her accomplice in the homicide. That ploy gave Hollingsworth an alibi for being in Woodstock while she sneaked into Lyndonville, courtesy of Martin's boyfriend, Steve Snyder. She stabbed Lamar to death with a ski pole, then made her downhill getaway on skis she'd bought just for the occasion and brought along from college. She'd set your brother up to take the fall by calling Junior's and leaving messages for him to come to the farm as soon as he could. There's plenty of motive: both of those women hate Billy. The Burlington police expect to arrest Hollingsworth shortly. You've helped close a murder case. You brother's innocent; you've cleared your family's name."

Joey looked up from the bowl of soup and turned to stare at Ben. "What about *mine*?"

Ben grabbed one of Joey's arms to snap him out of his gloom. "Listen, Joey; your name is good. And I know what you tried to do is good. You can't blame yourself for what happened today."

"So, you're going to tell me something like, every dark cloud has a silver lining? I don't believe it." Joey picked up his spoon and stirred the soup, briefly dissolving the watery-looking image of him himself that seemed to float on the top, like some kind of scum. He had never felt lower than this in his entire life. Lower than a whale's belly.

"Here it is, boys; dig in!" chirped a waitress as she bellied up to the counter and set down two steaming-hot platters of steak, potatoes and green beans. "Get you fellows anything else?"

"No thank you, ma'am," answered Ben, smiling at her. The waitress turned her attention to Joey.

"My goodness, hon; I do say, you look as though you've seen a ghost!" observed the waitress.

Joey managed a wan smile. "No, ma'am. Just having a rough spell today, that's all." The waitress, her curiosity satisfied, smiled at him and sauntered off.

"Eat up, kid," offered Ben, "courtesy of the sheriff's office. But, look, Joey; don't think too hard about that dark cloud stuff. See 'em, those clouds?" He spun around and pointed out the window to the west, where a bank of gloomy-looking clouds were gathering in a graphite sky. "There they are, if you want to see them. They'll go away, later on. You have to understand them: they'll gather 'round you like cows—if you let 'em. You might as well call them. They'll come; oh, sure, they will. My advice to you is: forget 'em. Be grateful for what you've got."

Joey, who had picked up his own fork, almost dropped it at in astonishment. He had lost his father and his mother. He doubted he would ever speak to his brother Billy again. His sweetheart, Lila, had been orphaned with the death of her father, Sven. Joey didn't know if he would ever see her again. And he, Joey, would be going home to an all-too-quiet house tonight, one haunted by his memories.

"What do I have, Ben, what?" asked Joey, as he turned to look at Ben. He could feel the anguish rising, overpowering everything he saw and felt. It was turning into anger.

"You have what the five people who died in this town today don't have."

"What is it, Ben? I want to know! I want to know what I have, right now!" Joey fought back tears, and the sudden impulse to bring one of his fists down onto the counter in frustration.

"Tomorrow."

Chapter 39

Back to the Kingdom: October 14, 1985

Long years afterward in the autumn of 1985, with thousands of those tomorrows now behind him, Joey Ross, now cheerful and full of optimism, strolled along Broad Street in Lyndonville. After having breakfast at the busy little diner, the very place where he'd met with Ben so long ago in 1933, he'd driven the Olds into town. He'd ambled about the grassy park with its memorial and little ice cream stand, the place where the brick railroad station had once stood, then up the road to have a look at St. Catherine's church. Yes, praise be— the old landmark was still there! He slowly ascended the steps that led up to it, craned his neck until it ached and gazed up at the building's tall steeple, then turned and stood for a moment by the dew-covered park bench—far too wet to sit on at this early hour—and looked away toward the west. The weather had been clearing off nicely since his rude awakening in the motel room at quarter past six, and the rooftops and chimneys of the buildings in town were golden now with early morning sunlight as they warmed to the new day at hand.

He carefully descended the steep concrete stairway and made his way back to the car the long way 'round, passing by the towering, shingle-style building, with its imposing turret and expansive porch, that had once housed Junior Coughlin's store and mortuary. It was a gentrified country inn now, and its neatly-paved parking lot was jammed full of expensive-looking out-of-state cars; a "no vacancy" notice had thoughtfully been hung underneath the inn's sign to save the desk clerk the nuisance of having to shoo away any well-heeled visitors and disappoint them. It was, after all, Columbus Day Weekend, and leaf peepers from down country were out in full force—cameras, maps and credit cards in hand—looking for posh places to stay and spend money in.

There would likely be no one at all he would encounter today from his time, 50-odd years ago, Joey reasoned. T.R., old man Rivard, Sheriff John Johnson—they would all be gone. He waited for a break in traffic before crossing the street and heading for the park, where the gala event hosted by the NEK Historical Society was to take place. It was early yet; the event was advertised to kick off at 9:00 a.m. So, he reasoned, there was no need to step up his pace or use the car. He walked on.

He meandered past two cast-iron statues of lions that flanked a bank's entranceway and turned the corner onto Depot Street, loafing along past the spot across the street where Sven Larsen, sweetheart Lila's doting father, temperamental and strong as a bull, had routed the loitering hooligans, the gangsters and wheelmen from down country more than half a century ago. He slowed to look into the window of a video rental shop; seeming to look back at him—startling him momentarily—were life-size cardboard cut-out figures of Marty McFly and googly-eyed Doc Brown, main characters of the recently-released movie *Back to the Future.* "Available on VHS this December" promised a poster in the window. Behind them another cut-out, an ad agency's rendition of the time-traveling DeLorean stood, the sleek silver car depicted as emerging from a cloud of smoke.

Time travel. The idea stopped him dead in his tracks. Rooted to the spot, he stared at the display, almost in a daze, running his mind over his long journey from Florida and his arrival here. Was that what he was attempting to do today—to go back in time? The answer rose up from his well of memories that replied: "No." Two young boys walked swiftly past him and snickered at the sight of the old, gray-haired man, apparently transfixed by what he saw in the shop window, his mouth hanging open, his hands stuffed into the pockets of his blue blazer. Hadn't the old fool ever seen a video rental place before, they wondered? Maybe he was from the last century, they thought.

Well, he was—almost.

He looked at his watch, then stepped along once more, now prodding himself to pick up the pace a bit. Passing the brick fortress of the Cobleigh Public Library on his left, he crossed Main Street and headed toward the park, where a small white bandstand stood primly in its center. He could see that a small crowd had gathered around it already. The leaves of the trees were hues of gold, brown, red and orange; some had fallen already, and Joey's feet stirred through drifts of them from where they lay like weathered strands of a well-worn carpet as he trudged across the lawn of the park.

A blue-and-gray WCAX news wagon was at the curb nearby —as was the car. The Packard. The big old auto, much worse for the wear since the last time he had seen it more than 50 years ago, was secured to a flatbed trailer cordoned off with yellow crime scene tape. Next to it was a police cruiser, its lights flashing and the officer assigned to it sitting inside, placidly sipping coffee and eyeing passing cars suspiciously.

The cop lazily set the cup down on the car's dashboard, and the cup jiggled in time to the powerful motor's seeming impatience at being idled, a perfect picture of inaction. In front of the Packard was a small tent sign emblazoned with the red/black DARE emblem and the boldly-lettered words: "Learn why crime does not pay."

Joey arrived at the bandstand just as several reporters were beginning to interview a rather stout woman dressed in a puffer, sweatpants and pink-laced sneakers. She appeared to be in her late 50s or early 60s, and had tossed away her cigarette only when the reporters shoved their microphones in her face and prompted her. "I was there when one of those bootleggers came into Saint Jay, back in '32," she said, nodding her head as if to corroborate her own story. "I was just five or so years old—and my mamma called to me from across the street —it was the Fourth of July and we'd just got done watchin' the parade, and this car comes screamin' down the street and I ran over to her, just in front of it and almost got killed. She drug me away cryin'." She stopped to catch her breath. The newsmen exchanged glances, as if to say: 'So?'

"He just missed me. His bumper ripped my dress, that's how close it was! And then he cut the corner too fast and crashed. Oh, it was horrible, I'll tell you. He had booze in that car alright, but they didn't get it. And then, the car caught on fire."

"I remember that," said Joey, speaking up to the reporters. And then he looked at the woman, and spoke to her: "I was there. I *saw* you." But the news mavens ignored him; they had their prima donna and were going to indulge her as long as she sang a tune—pretty or not. Then, they would go back to their offices, boil down her notes and do a shake and bake story based on it, their pictures and a few words from onlookers, just beating their looming deadlines, and then go home for martini time. "I drove one of those cars," Joey muttered, as he pointed at the trailered, forlorn-looking Packard. "That one."

The woman's head lifted slightly, and then she seemed to be staring right through him—as if she'd heard a disembodied voice—before she looked down, and rummaged in her pockets for her pack of cigarettes and lighter. What was he after all, he wondered, a ghost?

"Excuse me; did I hear you right?" came a voice. It belonged to a volunteer from the historical society. The young man, notepad and pen in hand, stepped closer and smiled engagingly, preparing to knock down any possible defensive barriers. "We're always happy to hear from those who've gone before us and can shed some light on area history. Now—do you mean to say that you, sir, drove that Packard?"

"I did, for two nights. Many, many years ago," answered Joey. He turned to look at the once-magnificent car, now a rusty ruin resting forlornly on its flat tires. For a moment, Joey imagined the Packard emerging from some smoky time tunnel from the past, its radiator's chrome gleaming just as good as new, and his brother Billy and boss man Junior Coughlin standing beside it, stylish fedora hats on their heads, cocked at a jaunty angle. The image flickered in his mind momentarily like an old movie clip; then it vanished and was lost to time when the volunteer spoke again. And then the present rolled forward once more.

"Then you'll have to talk with some folks who've gathered here to remember those days," spouted the young man enthusiastically, not wasting a moment. He grasped Joey's arm and steered him over to a park bench where three women were seated, talking among themselves, their backs to him and Joey. "The father of one of these ladies worked for a mortician, someone called Junior Coughlin, who was the last registered owner of that Packard," gushed the volunteer. "He was a big man, a Swedish émigré, an interesting fellow. His daughter came here all the way from Maine for this event!" Joey felt his well-worn heart skip a beat. "Here; I'll introduce you." The young fellow bent over slightly behind the tall, slender woman with long gray hair who was seated in the middle of the bench. "Excuse me, please," he said politely.

The woman did not respond. *Hard of hearing, perhaps,* thought the young man. He gently tapped her shoulder to gain her attention, and then Joey moved close to her while he waved the young man away as discreetly as he could, softly saying to him, "Don't bother. I know her." He stooped, leaning far forward, and then he spoke directly into her ear: "There's one person here that I really don't know yet."

Joey gently placed his right hand on her shoulder. Startled, Lila spun around to look at him. It was a second before she recognized him—the longest second in his lifetime. As he waited for her to speak, it seemed to him as though the world had come to a standstill, like a scene in a movie strangely and inexplicably frozen. Lila gasped in surprise, briefly covered her mouth with one hand and then withdrew it, revealing an impish smile. Her eyes still sparkled with the energy of the giddy teenager she had been years ago, Joey thought, as he gazed at her in amazement. Powered by wheels of chance spinning away through dark stretches of time, the pair had improbably been reunited at a park bench, on this sunny October morning in the Northeast Kingdom. But, unlike any dictates of an odometer spinning forward or backward in Doc Brown's DeLorean— or that of the old Packard—it didn't matter for Joey, or for Lila, what year it really was any more.

"Who?" Lila asked, feigning innocence, reaching out to touch Joey's hand, and the future, as autumn leaves silently fell to the ground around them, and the world moved on once more.

"You."

Philip R. Jordan is a native Vermonter and hobbyist photographer. As a young man, he worked at various times as a freelance photographer, decorative painter, antique picker, store manager and tractor mechanic following college. He then entered into a three-decade career as a salesman traveling throughout New England, and afterward spent more than another decade with *Vermont Magazine*, retiring as its editor-in-chief and publisher in 2019. He has written books on transportation subjects, such as *Rutland in Color* (Morning Sun Books, 2003), has been a columnist for *This Old Truck* magazine, and been a contributor to *Old Cars Weekly*. His first novel, A*s Crooked as They Come (chicanery, comedy and disorganized crime in yesterday's Boston underworld)* was published in 2021 by Onion River Press. He most recently contributed content to Volume IV of the *Vermont Almanac*. He lives in a quirky old one-room schoolhouse in Sunderland, Vermont together with his wife, Edie, and just can't seem to stop writing and taking pictures.